Red thru Black

Secrets of the Keepers

✝

GD Thompson, Sr.

✝

authorHOUSE®

AuthorHouse™
1663 Liberty Drive
Bloomington, IN 47403
www.authorhouse.com
Phone: 1 (800) 839-8640

Published by AuthorHouse 04/30/2015

ISBN: 978-1-4969-6930-9 (sc)
ISBN: 978-1-4969-6929-3 (e)

Library of Congress Control Number: 2015902398

Print information available on the last page.

Any people depicted in stock imagery provided by Thinkstock are models, and such images are being used for illustrative purposes only. Certain stock imagery © Thinkstock.

This book is printed on acid-free paper.

A Dedication Long Overdue

The true value and worth of a mom can be defined by the successes of her children while she is not around. That says a lot about you, Mom. This is for my Mother, Veronica M. Wentzel, whom I lost when I was six, and took her secrets with her. Thanks to my mother's French roots, it has given me much upon which to reflect. Mom, for those few short years that I got with you, has put me where I am right now. I only wish you were here to share in my success that you helped create. You see, Mom, I am not where I am at because you died. I am here now because you lived with me those six years, and you live within me since you have been gone. I finally see that. I love and miss you…always. Lastly, Mom, you are my inspiration for the Red Thru Black Series. And now, that secret is out! This one is for you…

In death, as in life…forever!
Your Son, G D Thompson, Sr.

Dedication ll

This book wouldn't be complete if I didn't mention my little brother, Markwood, after whom my son Mark is named. Markwood was unborn when my mother passed away. He lived inside her when she died. He was born at the hospital from the dead body of my mother. He lived for twenty-four hours after being born caesarean. So to you Markwood, I miss you bro. He would be thirty six years old on July 27, 2015.

Markwood was such a special case because he lived in my mother when she had died. The doctors who birthed him thought he was such a miracle that they wanted his body for study. Unfortunately, I know they wouldn't understand him and no amount of study would have enlightened them into how he was capable of living in a corpse. But I knew all about my brother, perhaps not so young or maybe I did, but I definitely understood him later on. Markwood was like me, he was a keeper of the secrets too, and that was his power to exist and be born from the body of my mother. However, had he lived, he might have been put under the scrutiny of the unknowing doctors as to how he would have survived. Knowing what I know of society today, it doesn't deserve the power my brother held because for its' darkness, it would have picked him apart because it misunderstands much, and appreciates greatness much less. My mother alone wanted me stillborn, and she really didn't know the kind of thing I would come to be on this planet. There's no understanding there in wanting me dead. How much love and understanding might I gotten from her in life later on? I know how I exist today, knowing what I know, and Markwood would have been a grander thing than I, and I am misunderstood most of the time too, but I realize now why. With love comes understanding. So, if I am not getting a lot of understanding, then I am not loved. And, that is the point. And, I cannot hold on to selfishness and hate the fact that the one person in my whole family, whom might have understood me had died. No, I have to appreciate that fact that I knew there was a consciousness out there with the ability to live in the body of my mother, waiting to be born. And perhaps that is the point. See, I am special to have been the brother of Markwood, a consciousness better than I, and I have lived 42 years on this planet. I was able to continue to exist, but I wasn't born like my brother, I know I wouldn't have survived had my mother died with me. And, I guess that is my power. I exist knowing that potentially, for how my mother was raped and wanted me stillborn, I am an abomination. For how old he was, Markwood was the true hero. So, thanks Markwood, for being a light for me to appreciate my time on this planet because you showed me how much this planet and consciousness or the people on it, is worth to you. You helped me to see that life is still worth living even though I am an abomination. Even though our mother lost sight of me too for how I was born to her. You helped me to reach for the stars and never lose sight of myself no matter what. So to my brother, the grandest Keeper, modestly put of course, I love you Markwood, my brother in life, as in death. You see Markwood, love isn't measured in time, it's measured by heart, and I had you to love, as my brother if for twenty four hours, and then the rest of my time on this planet from your memory. I loved you to the end.

You're part of the reason I had to write. I had to at least come to tell your story. My story bro isn't as good as yours is though. I was just the abomination. You were the child prodigy that should have died. Oh, wait a minute, bro, according to our mother, me for her hatred and you for the fact that she was dead, we both should have died, and in both cases, she didn't have the conscious power to kill us. I always knew we could have related eventually had you lived. Oh but it gets better, when someone treats you, as though they hate you, to them wouldn't you feel dead? And, to both of us she was dead, but I am glad you didn't get to know how that feels, bro. I am glad you didn't get to experience how it really feels existing on this planet, as the abomination, that potentially, you and I would have been. Instead, I am glad it was only me. I am not quite sure if I could endure how that might have made you feel. You may have endured, but I am glad you were spared. Simply put, I love you bro, as I said, in life as in death. Oh and by the way, I am not the strongest because I went it alone.

GD Thompson, Sr.

A modest word from the Author...

If I seriously thought that you and I were nothing more than human, then I would just stop being, doing, dreaming, and living, and go walk the beach for the rest of my time on this ball of a planet. I had the opportunity of that choice to do that very thing, but I know that this is not the case. I understood the power behind what I know to exist deeper in my roots, as a consciousness behind the sentient thing I am. I know that we are so much more than human. We stopped short of understanding things wholly by choosing a term with which to call ourselves just because the males of this planet took precedence. Hence the word hu-man, which nullifies the fact that we are just humans. Deep down in every one of us is this knowledge too, that we are more than mere humans. And, it is upon this premise too that you continue to exist. There is a reason why we're seemingly stuck here on this planet. There is a reason behind birth and death and understanding what those things truly are. There is so much more to everything than most of us glimpse, that it is really worth not giving up, relying upon the supposed human premise to exist.

I was seventeen years old when I glimpsed my higher self and my potential, but it was for another seven years that I doubted it. It was then that I decided that I had to be more than human for everything I knew and saw and how I felt. In closing, it is a bit selfish and self-centered to think we are the only things that exist anywhere in the Universe or that there is just one Universe in which everything exists. Just look at a self-centered individual and you can see how many sentient beings upon this planet think there is nothing anywhere in the universe, but that which is human or of themselves. Understanding these things is a good way to defeat fear because there is a path for each and every one of us when it is supposed that we should seemingly die from our loved ones for nothingness. If that were the case, then why fight the inevitable...if everything we have ever done is pointless, but that is the point. Deep down, it is not pointless because we are more than human, to extents that our supposed sense of humanity stems from a deeper sense of ourselves long lost. Each and every sentient being upon one planet will exist again on another, if not the same one in a cycle. It is a guarantee. I live by that every day. It's why I write…it's where my love for my children stem in the lengths it exists. Even my wife and I relate in a long sense of our respective heritages, which has spanned many planets and Universes. Our creation of the word Universe stems from what we know of the many Universes that once existed to all of us. A Universe is but one Verse in the grand scheme of things, as in the many verses of literature. If we all can raise our awareness of these facts, perhaps we can all begin to understand our true individual and respective heritages.

See, my point is seemingly this. I was born to a woman who had an affair outside her marriage. She kept it so secret, but she was quite possibly the result of a tell tale heart because she became so guilty for it. However, my point is this for the sake of things. I was born into something I shouldn't have been a part of to extents that my mother wanted me stillborn. So, I am here to tell you that it is for what I know that drives me every day. It is what I know of each and every one of you that I have come to love and cherish every one of you. You see, it is this diminishing immortal sense in consciousness that is why there is such striving to go forward, but it is also why we sleep or get tired enough that we do seemingly die for a moment in our beds to be awakened in the next moment. But enough about that and me, this is all about every one of us.

Foreword

This is a work of fiction, but if you want to make it more than it is, that's fine with me. Personally, I like the way Kahlip looks at life and things for how it enables him to be. He has got to be, in the World of Red thru Black, my favorite character, even though, deep down he is not a true hero. His perspective and point of view, though perhaps eccentric and unusual helps him to stay out of the darkness that perpetuates depression and all those mental states of lower cognition. Enough said...enjoy!

...GD Thompson, Sr.

On the little factual side...

It is a fact that at one point in this planet's history, humans weren't considered humans...

It is also fact that at one point in this planet's history that those beings or pre-humans didn't eat or consume anything...

It is a fact that at one point those sentient things or pre-humans that would eventually look at themselves, as humans, didn't sleep...

If we, as sentient beings long ago didn't eat, and didn't sleep, and we weren't humans, then dare I say we were immortals that have lost something to become what we have to date!

Lastly, this was where the desire to find the fountain of youth, when sadly, our potential for immortality and youth is long gone...without ever the possibility of regaining it.

†

The Order of Chapters
Prelude
Part I

†

†

The Order of Chapters
Part II

†

✝

The Order of Chapters
Part III

✝

†

The Order of Chapters
Part IV

†

"To be Plaenellian to end all battles for control over perspective and point of view on Ayeraal or Earth in all manners of alien or human consciousness, which by definition…is the same. For aliens do not know of humans, and if you understand that, then you too, have been born to other planets and you understand the Secrets of the Keepers."

…Kahlip
Elder and third son of
Osodon and Oosiah

✝

Prelude

It was thought that Penny Horn just seemingly stopped being Penny Horn or that she had come to terms with herself and what she was doing. It was thought that she had reconciled with her heritage. However, in the dawn of the morning at the death of Kaerrie, Penny was still keen on who she was. The death of Kaerrie, their Plaenellian daughter, was a brave and bold new move on the part of Osodon and Oosiah. However, it wasn't known the lengths at which they would have gone, but the worst was always anticipated, especially by Kahlip. Kahlip didn't wholly know he was living with the enemy…or did he?

The worst part of wrath was the seemingly apparent way it worked. However, if there was a smart sensibility about how it was carried out, wrath could look innocent, and never did it always show itself for what it was. This was why Penny Horn would prove to be the formidable foe for every battlefield, even when the battle lines hadn't been drawn. The Plaenellians didn't realize they were still dealing with Penny Horn because they didn't understand that Mickey Dawn and Darion Knight had been working together. They would soon come to realize it however, sooner than later. Eventually, they would come to know of the deadly trio of Penny Horn or what would be known as the Greater Triad. There were three girls born to John and Joanna Horn, and their story had been hidden, as well, as their third little bundle of joy, who Lilly and John actually kept with them. Penny horn wasn't one girl, but three girls with the same name. And, together with their parents, those three little girls were created to oppose the Plaenellians who sought to undo the Influence of Osodon and Oosiah. And, Oosiah led the Triad or what was known, as the G.A.I.T. What many didn't know or understand that Osodon wasn't the real threat to the Universes. The worst enemy was the threat of the women scorned. And, Oosiah had been that woman scorned. And, this is why Mickey told Lehmich that Darion needed to work as planned.

See, in the beginning, for the wrath of Penny Horn to be affective, Mickey Dawn received secret communications about what Lily and John Horn were doing to bring about the rise of Penny Horn. Secretly, Mickey was part of the rise of Penny Horn. He was even told that it was Johanna and John, Lily's name was kept out of and changed in the communications to protect her, as it was seen that Lehmich was a potential threat. Darion, the other twin, and Mickey Ellis were long time friends...long time. In other words, Mickey Ellis was Osodon for his time, and John Horn might as well have been Darion Knight, but Darion was an Elder for an alien race that had sided with Osodon and Oosiah in the beginning of the universes to aid them in bringing about the changes in the Universes that they wanted. However, Kahlip had come to get in the way.

And, so...The wrath of Penny Horn Continues...silently!

Kahlip knew to be mindful. The war with Penny Horn wasn't over, but he'd learned much. That was why Karen had to leave the states. Karen also needed a deeper lesson embedded in her deeper roots in France. But she had to leave on what was supposed to be a whim or what seemed like a mere vacation. In secret, Kahlip had made several communications to Karen unbeknownst to Julius. Kahlip was fighting for his granddaughter, again, unbeknownst to Julius because there was a deep secret behind both of them of which they weren't aware. However, Mickey had warned Julius about Lehmich out of that whole keep your enemies close and friends' closer thing. Kahlip anticipated that, but he did what he could. And, Karen and Julius left for France. Kahlip, first, confided in Karen that he discovered something that pointed to something bigger in the battle with Penny Horn, but he couldn't disclose what. And, so went the defenses against the wrath of Penny Horn...

Kahlip held the phone tightly, as he listened. Kahnelle had called him moments ago. Then, Kahlip heard it. He heard Kahnelle say it. Penny had left him. Kahnelle admitted it sadly. Kahlip eventually spoke up. "She didn't say where she was going?" Kahnelle thoughtfully spoke up. "No…up and left…without word…or anything." Kahlip thoughtfully sat holding the phone. So, where did she go? Kahlip spoke up. "You know her past, Kahnelle. It poses a problem that she would just leave like that." Kahnelle spoke up. "Yes…Kahlip…the worst is that she had twin sisters." Kahlip knew what that meant. He spoke up quickly. "Kahnelle, that means there are three." Suddenly, he thought to speak, but held his tongue. Kahnelle spoke up. "Kahlip…you'll tell me if you see her, right?" Kahlip thought about what he said. He spoke up. "Yes…of course, Kahnelle." In that moment, Kahnelle thought about something. Then, Kahlip spoke again. "So, are you still on for France? You know I'd go myself, but I am trying to regroup with the grandkids. I am still trying to find them." Kahnelle spoke up. "Yes, Kahlip, I am still on. I am leaving tomorrow in the latter morning." Kahlip thoughtfully spoke. "Good…just get back here, as soon as you can." With those final words, they each hung up. Kahlip thoughtfully put his phone aside.

Kahlip reflected, possessing 'The Killian' Dawn. There were many Universes made to house the many forms of consciousness that were forged, much like the others. However, there was another form of consciousness that was said to serve all others. However, that form of consciousness became perverted. It questioned itself. Well, the answer to that is the premise of this tale. And, whether or not, that form of consciousness was strong enough to beat the odds and its doubt. There was a secret within the premise of this serving form of consciousness, and someone recognizing it enough, hoping it could counteract its premise of doubt within that consciousness...and the dark premise of the tale at hand. And, unlike all simple stories, it might have included one town or one city. However, this is not a simple story. This one begins on a planet, once called Ayeraal that existed in a much higher state, and ends on the same planet, as it began to slow down in its spin around the sun.

Kahlip thought of a while back, when he had his girls, for which they didn't know him as their father. Kahlip reflected on the distant past, seemingly so long lost to the days gone by. He thought of his three strong, young, and beautiful girls he passed off to their mother. He recalled what he said when he left them. "There are those who will read the books, those who will write the books, and there are those who will live the books. But you have to remember one thing. Your life is only as interesting, as you make it look. And, other's books are only as real, as you want them to be. So, you can be aliens or humans, Dawn Keepers or Dark Treaders, but remember one thing, girls. Be right and good with each other and to the other aliens of this place…everything else will fall where it should."

It was a month before Mickey Ellis spent his last days upon Ayeraal. Kahlip showed up at Heroes Hollow to talk to him. All the while, Kahlip felt something for the trees that forged the canopy overhead, but he threw that wonderment in the back of his mind for Mickey, and his purpose there. Kahlip had lost many years battling the effects of the Rifts between Universes, and he wanted to meet with Mickey one last time. Kahlip parked and walked down Heroes Hollow to take the motor effect from his entrance. As he walked, he couldn't help but think about the damage that had been done to consciousness on Ayeraal by way of the many Seyions that had been born to her. It fueled Kahlip's fire and, desires to have it out with the supposed great Almichen or Mickey Dawn. As much, as Mickey wanted it that way, Kahlip knew him, as just Mickey Ellis, the child molester. So, he finished the walk down the long driveway through Heroes Hollow. He anticipated Mickey and what he'd heard of his condition. Deep down, Kahlip couldn't help but think about Lisa and what happened to her, which is why Kahlip left. But he couldn't help but wonder why, in the end; Lisa finally gave in to the boy from long ago that had been torturing her with his Seyion sexual perversion.

Kahlip walked up the steps to the porch and then solemnly came to stopping at the front door, long before he finally knocked. He hesitated at first. But what made facing Mickey easier, was in knowing that Mickey was long past being capable of perverting the youth any longer, not that the damage hadn't already been done. Kahlip heard from Lisa that Mickey wasn't doing that any longer, but to her, he couldn't. She didn't admit that Mickey had touched his daughters.

So, he knocked and lowly at first. There wasn't an answer until his third knock. The door slowly slid open, and eventually, Mickey showed himself. He was so old at that point, but that was the effect of Ayeraal upon Seyions, as much for their child molesting habits. Mickey smiled with his aged face. He spoke quietly. "Lehmich…what a surprise." Kahlip didn't stir. He merely stared at Mickey. Mickey's once wide smile sharply dropped off his face. Mickey felt something in Kahlip he hadn't previously recognized. He then, stood staring at the man at his door. He hesitated to ask him in, but he didn't fully understand why. Kahlip waited to be given the invite. Mickey spoke again. "Won't you come in?" Kahlip with a straight face and lacking emotion, nodded, as he moved himself over the threshold into the house. Mickey felt the cold chill of Lehmich's body move past him. Suddenly, he didn't know the man he just let into his house. He watched Lehmich move into the living room, as he cautiously closed the door. He pondered Lehmich's icy presence. Mickey felt a nervousness that he hadn't ever before experienced in Lehmich's presence.

Kahlip sat upon the sofa with a heavy drop. He sat looking, as Mickey came to sit at the recliner. He leaned forward with his elbows on his knees, and his hands folded. Kahlip sat easier at that point. Mickey stared at Lehmich who sat coldly still. Mickey spoke up. "So, to what do I owe this pleasure?" Lehmich didn't answer at first. There were many dark things he could have said in that moment, but he held his tongue. He stared hard into Mickey. He guessed the first thing he should do is properly introduce his true self to Mickey. Mickey eyed him curiously.

Lehmich spoke up. "First Mickey, you should know something about me." Mickey looked at him when he said that. He was intrigued. Mickey spoke up quietly. "What's that, friend?" Kahlip looked into his lap thoughtfully and then up at Mickey. He spoke confidently. "Mick, I am Kahlip." Mickey spoke up quickly with his aged voice. "Well, I mistook you for someone else. I let you in erroneously." Kahlip quickly spoke up. "No…Mick…it was you that always called me Lehmich because you thought you could put everyone into your plan. Well, that is no longer the case. And, I am here to tell you that your time on this planet is over…you got a month Mickey." Mickey stared at the man he thought he knew once. Mickey threw a quick word at the man on his couch. "What?" Kahlip looked thoughtfully at the old Seyion. "That's right Mickey. I am here to let you know that we finally put things into action, and that will cost you time after the next month." Mickey looked at the man when he said that. Mickey spoke up. "I don't understand…" Kahlip interrupted him. "You Seyions think you know everything. You're so loyal to Osodon and Oosiah that you think you are invincible. Well, Almichen, I am here to tell you that we Plaenellians had just signed your ticket home. You will not be allowed to stay here any longer. You have, friend… only a month." Kahlip thoughtfully stopped speaking. He eyed Mickey and spoke once more. "And, how we did this, Almichen, is another Keeper secret." Kahlip stopped speaking and looked at him. Mickey was shocked, as he heard those words. Mickey spoke with anger. "What are you talking about, and who do you think you are…friend? Do you not know who I am?" Kahlip listened, as Mickey spoke. He considered something, and whom he knew Mickey to be his whole life. "Mickey, I spent too much time with you, not to fully understand who you are." Kahlip stopped speaking. He thought about something. "Mickey, if you don't understand…you are what is considered an escaped child molester. You escaped responsibility. You took advantage of the alien consciousness on this planet that didn't know enough to be aware of you…and, I hear you did this with my daughters, thanks to your sister who wasn't strong enough against you."

Mickey felt angry in that moment. He glared at the man on his couch. "I don't have to take this…I am the great Almichen, the boss Dawn Keeper!" Kahlip looked at Mickey when he said that. He noticed Mickey's aged angry expression. His wrinkles had angry wrinkles. Kahlip quickly spoke up. "Not to me, not on this planet, Buddy! Here you're just another Dark Treader playing mind games." Kahlip stood when he said that. He spoke with finality before he walked out. "Take heed, Seyion, you have a month. And, as far as my daughters are concerned, I will eventually be there for them, so don't worry even if your sister couldn't be. And, I still have my granddaughter to which to tend. And, something else, Mickey, don't feel too proud for what you have done to her or Amos for that matter. That's right, Mickey, I know about Amos, but you forsook your own son, but really, all you did was murdered your own brother. You will never be permitted a spot on Ayeraal again. You think you have escaped responsibility and consequence with what you have done. Think about that when the Seyion Universe is on the brink of destruction, and you have nowhere to go. You won't be capable of escaping true consequence." As Kahlip walked away, he thought about something. He considered something he had to say to Mickey. He turned and looked at Mickey. He spoke with frustration and anger. "The worse part, Mickey, you attempted to destroy your fellow Seyions. You tried to use the good name of Dawn Keeper to do it, and you turned your fellow Seyions into Dark Treaders." Kahlip thought about one last thing. He looked at Mickey with such disdain. "Mickey…we Dawn Keepers weren't supposed to become legend. You don't really understand what it means to keep the dawn do you?" Kahlip thought about something, as Mickey sat in his chair, staring at him with this dumbfounded look on his face. "Your first mistake was creating the illusions of beckoning the sun. The planet will spin without you. How fast it spins depends on the amount of darkness in consciousness connected to it. You have no idea about how to enlighten the spirit of anyone that doesn't suit you." Kahlip stopped speaking thoughtfully. He looked at Mickey with one last thought. He spoke up. "Mickey, if you were me, I'd be dead by now, and you would have claimed I was a Dark Treader. That's not what keeping the dawn is about. It's about love, Mickey, which you do not possess. You know... that which I am showing you now! It is taking a lot of love for you from me to be in this moment with you. And, it's that which you have to think upon, Mickey."

For the first time in his life, Mickey couldn't speak. He looked at the man near the door with a blank look. With those words, Kahlip was done and went to the door, opened it, and left. He didn't look back, as much, as Mickey watched him walk away. For the first time, Mickey had something with which to consider. Suddenly, though, he considered being loyal to the Master Seyion. And, for the first time he considered what he had become. And, perhaps he should have questioned his loyalty to the Master Seyion.

Outside the door, Kahlip took a moment. He stood thoughtfully, feeling emotions he hadn't let himself feel in a long time. He thought about what he said to Mickey. And, Mickey had done just what he claimed he did. In what he did, Mickey didn't realize one very important fact about Dawn Keepers. Dawn Keepers do not have enemies. Dawn Keepers do not fight for the darkness it takes to do such things. Then, the truest philosophy of his Plaenellian heritage came to mind. It was a simple statement about hoping for a brighter future is giving one's children brighter days. Mickey Ellis didn't understand that and thus, didn't understand the hatred he had, which didn't forge any real truth behind him being a Dawn Keeper. The point was, and Mickey didn't understand this, but Dawn Keeping wasn't about keeping the sun rising the next day or making sure it would. Dawn Keeping was about making sure the people that did awake the next day wanted to and with the love in their hearts to take on a potentially dark day. Mickey didn't understand that Dawn Keeping was about bringing light to that which is dark, and looking at others with such a dark viewpoint, was the hindrance Ayeraal has been dealing with since the induction of alien consciousness upon her or the destruction of the immortals.

Kahlip went through the memory of his last moments with Mickey, as he and Kaera finished cleaning up outside. Much later, as the night wound down, and their guests had long since gone home, Kahlip and Kaerrie sat in front of the fireplace, embracing each other. Kahlip thought about something in that moment. He withdrew from her grasp gently. He peered at her thoughtfully, loving and warmly, but suddenly the look turned to concern. Kaerrie noticed. She inquired, as to the change in his face. He looked at Kaera warmly in the eye, but there was something else there in his eyes Kaerrie saw. She listened intently, as he began to speak. "Kaera, it's about where we come from." Kaerrie eyed him thoughtfully. "Home?" Kahlip eyed her thoughtfully and considered something before he spoke. "No, Kaera, mom, and dad." Kaerrie eyed him attentively. She considered what he said. Kahlip spoke again. "Kaera…it's about what really happened. It's about God…and the Master Seyion, and, lastly…our mom and Dad, Osodon and Oosiah." Kaerrie deliberated over what he said. She silently proposed her own ideas about mom and dad. As she looked at Kahlip thoughtfully, she began to glimpse a part, perhaps, to what he alluded. She looked at him with finality and spoke. "Explain." Kahlip relaxed where he sat. His back arched and he rested himself on his arms. His knees were bent. "Kaera, the Master Seyion?" Kaerrie eyed him when he said that. She spoke up. "I don't understand." Kahlip then resituated himself, sitting completely forward. He sat with his legs crossed and spoke. "Kaera, it's what I found in the book…it's the information I have been missing." He stopped speaking thoughtfully. He looked at her for another way to explain his notions and what he saw. Kaerrie continued to look at him. "Kaera…there is no way the Master Seyion could have incarnated. Kaera…the Master Seyion is Osodon and Oosiah…our mother and father." Kaerrie first appeared confused. She stared at him curiously and with a longing to understand. She spoke up. "Wait…what?" Kahlip smiled and spoke. "You heard me correctly." She continued to look at him. It was all she could do. "Kaera…I found something in 'The Killian Dawn' that told me everything I needed to know."

He stopped speaking and eyed her to let what he was saying to her, sink in. After a brief silent interlude, he spoke again. "Kaera, the constructor of the Universes is too big to join our little party." Kaerrie eyed him when he said that. Suddenly, Kaerrie felt something, as she sat there with Kahlip, but it wasn't for him.

Suddenly, Kaerrie felt, as though she and Kahlip shouldn't be together. There was something missing between them. She didn't fully understand what that meant, but she knew somehow, deep down that, their relationship was not founded upon the truth behind their connection, or that they were each other's half. She looked into his eyes, attempting to feel something more for Kahlip, but it wasn't working.

As Kahlip sat there with Kaera, he couldn't help but appreciate her for what she was, but somehow, there was just something missing between them. He felt that, but could not explain it. Suddenly, Kahlip thought about his faith in Kahnelle over Kaera. He considered how his introduction to Kaera happened…in a hospital with Kahnelle's certainty about who she is. Kahlip was growing less certain. Secretly, so was Kaerrie. Neither one knew of the other's heartfelt pain, which only proved what they both glimpsed. Their hearts had not found their homes yet. However, that did beg the question of what Kahnelle was doing in introducing them.

What they had been talking about suddenly disappeared into the background for what their hearts were going through. In that moment, Kahlip realized a sullen truth. Being human meant having to fall in love because that one person that seemed to be the perfect match seemed too much like a dream. Besides that, Kahlip realized that he did have a job to do besides the human one he had. He knew Kaera or whoever she truly was had hers, as well. Sadly, he finally realized that Kaerrie wasn't in any way, a way to reference Kaera. Sadly, Kaerrie was not Kaera. And Kahnelle had it wrong, and a plan, which Kahlip needed to find out. However, all that had to be put on the back burner for what he needed to do. In that moment, Kaerrie felt something that she needed to address with Kahlip. She didn't feel right about being called Kaera, which isn't who she is, and she especially didn't like being confused for someone else. She spoke up quickly. "Kahlip, from now on, could you just call me Penny? That would be easier. And, better for the both of us." Kahlip nodded. He looked at Penny, and his heart broke a little more. Suddenly, Kaera was far away again.

The next day was his day off from the motel. Kahlip did still possess 'The Killian Dawn'. And, he had planned to investigate it further. However, he needed to do it in secret. With what this plan was that Kahnelle had him mixed up in, Kahnelle couldn't know that Kahlip was aware. Kahnelle definitely could not know that he still had the book.

Karen turned to Julius, as they awoke to another day in their new home in Paris. She considered something. She spoke up quietly. "Julius, is this going to work?" Julius was distracted with his thoughts enough to hear her. She nudged him softly. "Julius?" He turned to her warmly and smiled. He reached over and pecked her lips. He too, spoke quietly. "Of course, dear." He looked back up at the ceiling. He considered something. He spoke. "The only thing I ponder is Kahlip." Karen thought about what he said. She spoke up. "You think he knows about us." He turned to her. "Yes. I do." His eyes remained on her. She laid there thoughtfully beside him. She looked at him equally. "But what can he do?" As Julius laid there beside her, where he wanted to be, he thought about what she said. He spoke. "Well, there actually is a lot he could do. They are our offspring." Julius stopped speaking and considered something. "Well, Kahlip is, and Kaera and there is Kahnelle, but he is working with us. There is Kaerrie, Penny's sister." Julius stopped speaking and thought about what he said. Karen eyed him. She spoke up. "But what can be done?"

Julius didn't have a complete answer for her. He sat thoughtfully. He looked over at her, and then, back at the ceiling. He spoke up. "I know I said he could a lot, but to what specifically, I am not sure." Karen looked at him when he said that. She began to doubt what they did long ago. She looked intently at Julius and spoke. "Do you regret it, Julius?" Julius smiled and turned to her. He spoke. "Regret what?" Karen looked at him thoughtfully. "Regret what we're doing, dear." Julius then looked back up at the ceiling. "Karen, we wouldn't be where we are right now if we had not done what we did." Karen thought about what he said. He was right. The only way they were capable of getting to earth was to forge a change in some of the Universes. Karen considered something else. "But is this where we want to be?"

Julius thought about what she said. It took a good few seconds for him to answer her. "Without a doubt, dear. Without a doubt!" Karen was not so sure. She thought about what was going on. She considered how selfish she felt. Julius considered what she might have been feeling. "Karen, they were ours to use. We are the King and Queen of the Universes. The Creator charged us with that duty." Karen instantly thought about what he said about the Creator. "Yes, but Julius, bottling up the Creator like that?" Julius thought about something and spoke up. "Karen, we used our knowledge and fulfilled our duties. If that caused grief to the Creator, then so be it." He stopped speaking thoughtfully. He looked at her. He spoke again. "Karen, you think we did what we did unconsciously? No! We worked well within the perimeters of the Creation. And, our offspring are of no consequence." Karen thought about what he said. She spoke up. "If that were true, then how could Kahlip do anything about it? You know deep down he wants to fix the Universes, which would undo what we did. He would have to restore the Creator in doing that." Julius smiled thoughtfully. He turned to her and spoke. "Dear, you worry too much. Just enjoy yourself for once." Karen too, then looked up at the ceiling. She was thoughtful that perhaps Julius was right. The two of them finished out the next hour snuggling in bed. Then, it was time for their afternoon out.

However, for what Kahlip did do, Julius did not understand something. At least Kahlip pondered his lack of knowledge. In destroying the Amulet of the Keepers, he closed the door for consciousness of the Seyion Universe to be born outside of that Universe and for knowing what they were doing. Thoughts of leaving the Seyion Universe were then, destroyed, and, death or what the Seyions had never known in death would be become a reality. However, the concept of Dawn Keeping had been destroyed when that happened. Then, Kahlip learned something in that. There were subtle hints about what was really going on, and what the Keepers really were. Kahlip had a thought from that about the Dawn Keepers, and the Dark Treaders, as well. Suddenly, he realized to a degree, Dawn Keepers and Dark Treaders were the hopefuls of Osodon and Oosiah. Kahlip thought about that, which meant that Osodon and Oosiah forged the two groups to maintain what they had done. Too, he realized that something had to be said for the Creator. Kahlip thought about that. What happened to the Creator, that Osodon and Oosiah would have so much control? Kahlip thought about that. Kahlip understood something about creating. Low maintenance for what was created was the goal because it was easier to build self-sustaining objects that might take away from the energy for other things that could be done. He realized that was part of his knowledge, which empowered him, upon any planet to which he was born. Suddenly, he realized the condition of the body was evidence of a consciousness that wasn't prepared to be established upon earth. From that, he saw what science supposedly diagnosed. The mentally and physically impaired weren't filled with problems and illness. They were consciousness from a lesser complicated planet where body constructs were more simple. On a more complex planet in a more complex Universe, they would not be capable of maintaining a presence, as in a consciousness more skilled on a more complex planet system.

Kahlip thought about what his parents, Osodon and Oosiah had done. They were the ones that forged the breaks in the Universes that permitted such consciousness to be born on another planet to which they were not suited. That was why it was equally important to be what he is, as a Plaenellian. Kahlip thought about that, but he glimpsed a bigger purpose. Suddenly, he glimpsed a unification of Plaenellians. Then, he found something within the book of Killian. It further hinted something about its author, and the Keepers. He pondered the knowledge in anyone else. He thought quickly about Tina she was the first Plaenellian he had officially met on the street. Kahnelle was the exception because, as Kahlip was slowly realizing. Kahnelle was working under some guise with whom, he had not figured out. And, that potentially hinted to the fact that Kahnelle's other half was, as well. Suddenly, Kahlip thought about how Julius and Karen claimed they would work with them in destroying the Amulets and the books. There was something else Kahlip found within 'The Killian Dawn' that forced him to understand the true nature of the Dawn Keepers and Dark Treaders that was kind of shocking. It was information that would turn the nature of the understanding of even humans upside down. Kahlip applied what he knew to his understanding of the mentally handicapped that really, have no concept or sense of their humanity. In that knowledge of what existed behind the supposedly mentally handicapped, went the understanding for the potential the rest of consciousness from the other Universes had if the mentally impaired individuals could coexist, as such things. What a profound thought. Kahlip considered that. Socially, mentally handicapped individuals were a potential teacher for the rest of alien consciousness.

Kahlip only brimmed knowing what 'The Killian Dawn' held. There were things in it that Kahlip hadn't been wholly conscious to for too long, as well, there were things in it that he thought he had to learn. But there were other reasons why he had it, that he didn't mind not knowing because it didn't matter, he possessed it...or did it possess him? There were secrets he had to discover, there were things he had to uncover..., and probably the worst thing he had to come to terms with was the possibility that there was no solution to Ayeraal or Earth's problems, contrary to what he wanted to believe. And, never did he forget Secrealle or Secreas or even Sacrealle for what and who they were, but therein lay the truth behind them, as well, what Almichen or Osodon didn't know. It's what he would come to find out that even Oosiah doesn't know. There was a secret behind Secrealle, Secreas, and Sacrealle that no one understood, but Kahlip would...finally. That truth in them was that they could never die. If they could...there would never, be protection from one form of alien consciousness that is born to Ayeraal and completely taking over, making the planet, another form of their home world. The battles to do this have been happening for myriads of years. It was what defined wars to date. It was why there were spies in other countries. It was seemingly how one man or woman can betray his or her country, which no one understood. And, that was the curse of the Keepers because they knew what lie at the heart of humanity, its differences, and it's supposed misunderstandings. Underlying daily life, which no one fully understood was that the human race wasn't merely trying to survive…alien consciousness was just trying to find a root somewhere to finally come to rest, as in the golden days of yesteryear. Sadly, that was part of what Osodon and Oosiah had done. That was immortality…that was being one with one's planet. And, that was what Osodon and Oosiah didn't want to have happen any longer. Through that, Kahlip sought to understand why, and when he thought he found that answer, he realized he hadn't and went off to seek it again and again. However, there came a point where he thought to stop wondering why his parents destroyed the Universes, as they had, but only because he thought there was no answer. Until he thought he found another hint concerning it. This was what perplexed him about the solution to the Universal destruction, which was more frustrating than the answer for his parents' behavior, and what was more important to discover. And it finally began with learning the truth behind Secrealle and Sacrealle, and Secreas equally, which is what made them the enemy of Osodon and Oosiah.

And, there was one profound truth that Kahlip had hidden from himself for too long. It was why he came to possess the book. It was why he so loved the Universes that he gave of his efforts, as he did. It was what he had to lose if he didn't do that…

PART I

PART I

The Chapter for Secrealle

Kahlip knew his joy when he looked at little Lorande for the first time with her lovely and wonderful baldhead and short chubby figure. He saw the pleasure of being a father instantly. He looked at Lisa, then at Lorande again and again, feeling the joyous wonder of what he and Lisa had done. It didn't matter that Kahlip already had Karen, a second for her mother. Lorande was his and Lisa's special project and bundle of joy. Instantly though, Kahlip saw another child, in looking at Lorande, her name would be Frances, and he knew it, but she would be so much more. For the moment however, Lisa saw only Lorande, as she held her lightly and warmly tucked in that little pink blanket. Equally, Kahlip had to do the same, but he was still hopeful.

For Lisa, in looking between Lorande and her amazing father, Lisa felt love as if she had never before felt it, but she knew Kahlip wasn't any seemingly normal male thing. There was definitely something more to Kahlip than met the eye. Kahlip too, was a savior of sorts, but not to think too highly of him, she reconciled that any male thing that could come between her and Mick was a savior. The sad thing was that Mick was her brother. It wasn't easy to forget what Mick had done to her for what she pondered was his mental instability. Whether driven by lust or insanity, Mick had things going on in his mind that Lisa could never figure out. Kahlip had mentioned one time, and he said it so lovingly concerning Mick, but Mick was an alien form of consciousness, and that Lisa shouldn't look too hard on him for why. Lisa didn't fully understand Kahlip when he said that, but she took it to mean that there was a lot of love in Kahlip to be so filled with understanding. It still didn't make sense to Lisa. Ironically, in some ways she had listened to Kahlip, she did look at him with a kinder eye, which is why she would eventually forgive him, in a sense, and try to have the sister to brother relationship with him, that she thought she was supposed to have. For the moment however, she was in a hospital bed, holding her beloved Lorande, with her daughter's father enduring that same adoration for Lorande she possessed.

In one moment, looking at Kahlip, Lisa saw something in him that was timeless. Kahlip had this way at looking at life that was abnormal, but wonderfully unnatural or what she thought at least. That was part of what enchanted her about him. That was the thing about Kahlip; he wasn't charming. He was enchanting. And, Lisa had been enchanted. A side effect of this enchantment was that Lisa had found protection through him. Lisa was instantly rekindled with the notions she had about destroying her brother, the way she felt destroyed, but Kahlip stepped in. Kahlip told her that he could help her with Mick, that he would stop the molestation. He claimed that she would heal from Mick's effects. And, that was what Kahlip had done. Eventually, Lisa had come to forget what had happened to her because she had a knight in shining armor in Kahlip. Kahlip looked at her like the beautiful female creature she was. When they were together, she almost was able to forget that she was molested. She felt like nothing was ever lost in her for what Mick had done. Kahlip had healed her or at least that was how it seemed.

Kahlip endured the moment with Lisa, as she lied there in the hospital bed. He couldn't help but think of the thing she had going with Darion, which hurt Kahlip. And, what Lisa didn't recognize was that she wasn't wholly healed by him, and that was what Mick had done to her. What she didn't realize is that Mick and Darion or his twin at least were actually teamed up against her, and made Kahlip's job that much harder. However, that was what frustrated Kahlip that much more. Kahlip, as Plaenellian, as he was, was capable of treating Lisa, as if he was in love with her to such extents that there was no mistaking that, which he thought was between them. However, for what Mick had done, Lisa forsook that which was real love, and what that could feel like. Lisa had come to rationalize that what she had with Darion was seemingly normal. However, that was the power inherent in

Seyion consciousness, and proved who Darion and Mick actually were, and to each other. It was where the molestation stemmed. If molestation was a battle plan, then Mick was the first wave in the effect, and Darion was the second. Lisa couldn't see this, but Kahlip did all too well. However, that was the point. The first wave on any battlefield is supposed to have the most profound effect, then, the second wave comes in with less force to complete the mission for the field of battle. That was Darion. And, Kahlip was supposed to be the effect against the first wave or to make the second's job harder than it would have been without him. This meant that Lisa thought Darion loved her the way Kahlip did. It was one thing Kahlip knew Lisa wouldn't feel from him, and that was what he felt for her. Darion didn't love Lisa, as she should have been loved. And, when Kahlip figured out that Lisa really wasn't expecting Darion to really love her, His heart broke silently, and he stopped wanting a life with her. In the end, he rationalized that he had done his job with Lisa, protected her from Mick, and then was supposed to move on. That was what Lisa told him in not so many words. One thing Kahlip couldn't do was give up on Lorande and Frances, or little Karen either. But why was really important. Too, in the end, Kahlip glimpsed that Lisa and he couldn't wholly relate, which was what their relational issues actually were. In the end, Kahlip rationalized too, that Darion, the good brother, had promised to keep the bad one away for the protection of Karen, but he found out that hadn't worked the way he wanted it too. And, at that point, Lisa still had no idea that Darion had an equal twin, but not as good as he was or, as loving to Lisa, as the other twin. However, Lisa was so involved with Darion by this point, that she had accepted the vast personality changes in Darion, and lived with it, as evil, as he could come across at times. And, that was the truest effect of the first wave of the battle plan in Mick. He made Darion look not so bad, even when the good one didn't wholly have his heart in the relationship either.

Now, in all this that Kahlip knew was the value in his daughter for reasons other than just the fact that she was born to him. Lorande was a special child, which even she didn't know and understand all through her youthful life. However, Kahlip knew that about her, as did Mick eventually, but Darion didn't. Mick had only come to know when it was his second to last month before death. He and Lehmich, or who he thought was the man, were deep, in a conversation, on the beach behind the house at Heroes Hollow, when Kahlip disclosed it to him. At that point, however, Kahlip still needed to keep things between them on the same level. So, he tried very hard to keep his true identity hidden for he might have destroyed the image of him in Mick's mind, and blown his cover. However, too, in that purpose for their sitting on the beach, and casually chatting, existed Kahlip's deep desire to destroy Mick's self-appreciation and pride in him, for thinking that he had won in destroying Secrealle. That desire stemmed from the fact that Mick and who he thought Lehmich was had their battles between them daily. Mick thought he had a subservient male treat to do his bidding; all the while Mick had been played, and he didn't know it.

Kahlip took a moment and considered the battles with Mick he had over just the whole Lisa thing, as he sat there in the hospital room the night before Lorande was born. What a battle it was! Never before was such a blatant reminder present for Kahlip in the contrasts of alien consciousness than the one in Mick over the possession of the youth. Seyions were the worst for it, as Kahlip had found out over the years. And, Mick was, as bad as it was. They didn't even have to be his children; it was the possession of the youth in general. Deeply ingrained in Seyion consciousness was this feeling as if the youth provided a proper path to the desired result in the future birth. This meant that in the youth; laid a prerequisite for a birth of some other Seyion they needed born. Then, they would in turn influence that new child with their way of seeing the world with little to no resistance because the nature of the child would be shrouded in secrecy. This happened all too much in the beginning of consciousness on Ayeraal in the beginning. Kahlip thought about that in his granddaughter, Karen, who he still had to deal with and Mickey's effect in her. Sadly, he had come to realize that Karen was actually Kahlip and Karen's granddaughter, but Mickey and Karen the daughter's, daughter. Kahlip considered something else, as he waited that night for Lisa to get back from a sonogram. He thought about the fact that for religious dictate, and what really lie at the heart of the Aubrahteerians, they were not capable of child molestation. This was one of the effects of the battles inherent in the disgust for each other, the Seyions and the religious Aubrahteerians. The Aubrahteerians born to Seyions would have their parents put in mental institutions for their crazy beliefs or understandings of their Seyion heritage, and the Seyions born to Aubrahteerian parents would perpetrate molestation in an attempt to undo their influence upon Ayeraal or earth. This is what happened in the cases of molestation by the clergy. Whether or not it actually served its implied purposes, the overall reputation of the church and religion had been affected. Kahlip had talked to a preacher a while back who was battling with his son who didn't see his religious views, and they had many confrontations about that. Kahlip couldn't down his anxieties over his son's rebellion, but the preacher would have never understood that his son just might have been of a Seyion heritage or worse yet, just that of an alien nature. However, that was how it went in most cases. It was why science and psychology or psychiatry was needed to bring light to the plight of various consciousnesses for the very strange world they came to exist upon in Ayeraal.

So, Kahlip now had Lorande with Karen too, and to his befitting, appropriate knowledge, he would eventually have another…unbeknownst to an unwitting Lisa. And therein laid Lorande and her purpose.

And, to an unwitting Mick, Secrealle was still well protected. Little did he know, but that was what Lehmich delighted in, which Mick would come to hate, unknowing that his counterpart, Lehmich was behind it. So, Kahlip and Mick sat chatting about what he had done. Lehmich looked Mick in the eyes and spoke squarely. "Mick…you killed neither Secreas, nor Secrealle emotionally in doing in your brother. You know that, right?" Mick was much older by this time. He looked at Lehmich with a curious gait before he spoke. "What?" Mick didn't understand. Lehmich almost felt like he had to repeat himself, but Mick spoke again. "You mean what by that?" Lehmich looked at Mick with confidence. "You don't understand how it worked, Mick. You're old now, but you cannot change this fact now that you may know." Mick stared at him, anticipating what was to come. Lehmich spoke up. "Mick…you didn't realize the whole Secrealle thing was an encoding." Mick was thoughtfully curious. He stared at Lehmich. First, for knowing that enough to say it. Next, for the truth behind it. Mick felt slightly angered. "So, what does that mean, Lehmmy?" Lehmich stared at him, at first. "That means that Secrealle isn't a person that you can kill, Mick. It's not a person." Mick stared at him equally angered, as the previous moment. "WHAT?" Lehmich looked at Mick thoughtfully. He felt his frustration, and secretly and silently, Lehmich was truly enjoying the moment. "Mick, the word Secrealle is more or less an objective. The objective being what the word actually means. As in Secrealle, there are actually two letters missing to fully understand what Secrealle is. Those letters are a 'T' and an 'E', properly placed, identify who and what Secrealle is. Break the word in two between the second e and the a. You have 'secre' and 'alle'. Now, put the 'T' at the end of 'secre' and you have secret. The next word, 'alle', put an 'E' at the end, and you have the word, 'allee'. Hence, Secrealle is the Secret Allee. Heroes Hollow is the Secret Allee, as the Allee is French for Allee of Trees. Note the entrance to Heroes Hollow is aligned with the tree canopy and the vines. Heroes Hollow was made Heroes Hollow to shroud the Allee of Trees, which is why the statues of the supposed heroes were added to it. As Heroes Hollow, it hid the true Nature of The Allee of Trees. You thought you were destroying the person Secrealle with a plan, but the real plan was to protect Heroes Hollow, which has been done." Mick looked at Lehmich with frustration. He spoke. "So, you're telling me

that anyone can be Secrealle because the person is the mission."
Lehmich thought about what he said. He spoke. "Now, you see
it. That's right. It's like there is a division protecting the Secret
Allee." Mick thoughtfully eyed Lehmich. "So, what I thought
about Secrealle was wrong…what we all thought was wrong!"
Lehmich thoughtfully eyed Mick. He commented mentally. "That
what you thought was wrong. I knew better, but didn't tell you."
Mick sat thoughtfully shocked. Lehmich was secretly gloating,
but with a certain measure of reserve. He secretly liked that
Mick didn't know, and he had to be the one to tell him. Suddenly,
Lehmich thought about something in that moment. He spoke up.
"Mick, what we're talking about defines the French and Spanish
wars in St. Augustine back in the fifteen hundreds, when the
French named a river with an inlet, which would be renamed by
the Spanish, but the point is that the French were in this region for
similar purposes…its protection. However, it wasn't necessarily
the French for knowing this need for its protection, but notice
how the word Secrealle has French flair to it, as does Sacrealle
and even perhaps Secreas. Think about it, Mick, Sidolmo, and
the French heritage behind it." Mick thoughtfully listened but
for another second more, in his anger, which was reaching deep
down inside him; his stomach felt sick. Lehmich thought about
something else. He spoke up. "Mick…" But Mick interrupted
him. "No more…Lehmmy…no more. I cannot take anymore. I
have failed…almost." As he said that, an aged Mick stood from
the beach, but Lehmich thought about what he said. He pondered
what he meant. Almost! What did that mean? Lehmich watched
Mick walk away. Lehmich finished his sit by the beach. He was
enjoying the moment on a thought. He hoped what he did, worked
in telling Mick about the secret behind Secrealle. Lehmich was
trying to flush out those members of Mick's secret stash of people
he used to do the things only a Seyion mind would only dream.
However, Lehmich considered what he was really after…Mick's
Reapers. And, unbeknownst to, Mickey Dawn or Almichen or
whatever he chose to call himself; Lehmich knew what most
didn't. Mickey Dawn and a host of others were reaping people

through a chemical compound, engineered to give the appearance of a dead, graying form with eyes sunken in. This was done with a purpose of creating a panic with a new form of disease to spread fear, while the true reapers worked in secret. Lehmich had finally discovered how they were seemingly doing it under radar through what would seem like normal illness to a doctor, and it was never traceable, as in a heart attack. However, this seeking of the Reapers and protecting others from them, forced Kahlip to want to find a solution to the Universal problems. He wanted to right them, which would take care of the Reaper problem, and Osodon and Oosiah reaping consciousness for their successful restructuring of the various Universes and Planets for the new various forms of consciousness, which would come to exist upon them.

The Chapter of Sacrealle

It was a few short months before their beloved Frances was created. Then, in proper time, Lisa and Kahlip found themselves back at the same hospital, having Frances delivered. Kahlip's dream had come to fruition when he looked at Frances. She was smaller than Lorande, and had a bit more hair when she was born, but what mattered was when Kahlip looked in her eyes when she first opened them. She grabbed onto his first finger and he lost it. They instantly made a connection. Lisa held her equally warm in her pink hospital blanket, and as close. She looked at her with the same loving gait, as Lorande and Frances stole their hearts. Kahlip and Lisa started talking about how close she and Lorande might be when they get older. Kahlip thought they were going to be the best of sisters. Then, Kahlip thought about where the family was actually headed. Kahlip had been in and out of Lorande's life since she was born. And, he knew that was going to be the same with Frances. But he never questioned his sanity for getting into that situation where Lisa wouldn't want him around, as a father for his daughters. Although Kahlip did have something in mind for himself in contrast to his girls, Lisa woke him up to her thoughts about it.

It was shortly after they brought Frances home when Lisa and Kahlip had the talk. Darion was there and he had taken the others out back to play in the yard. He even took little Frances in her carrier. Kahlip and Lisa were on the front porch. Kahlip found out in that moment that Darion couldn't have kids, which was when Kahlip found out that Lisa was using him, as a baby port for what Darion couldn't provide. Lisa was creating her family for her and Darion. Kahlip was just the sperm bank. Lisa confided in him that he could be the uncle to her daughters, but that wasn't good enough for Kahlip They exchanged a few harsh words, but in the end, Kahlip had to give in to Lisa. He didn't want to, but he had no choice. He also found out that he wasn't on the birth certificate either, as he had been on Karen's, which had been kept from Mickey in contrast to Karen who would later change her name to Kira. Karen and Kahlip had little Karen, not Kira, and Kahlip. That was how he was able to stay in control of little Karen's future, and how he chose Darion and Lisa to take care of Karen. Darion at that point hadn't proved to be unfit until his brother began taking more of a position in his life or making more appearances in place of Darion. However, that happened much later when all Kahlip's girls were much older. What Kahlip didn't realize was that in choosing Lisa and Darion to watch over Karen, as their daughter, for his supposed job, was the reason Lisa rationalized that Kahlip wouldn't be the man she should take, as a husband and father to her girls, which included, now Karen, as well. She didn't tell Kahlip that, but she didn't have to. Kahlip figured it out. And, he realized that he had done what he had done to himself in contrast to Lisa. He made himself look unfit for the position of family man, husband, and father because he let his supposed job get in the way. And, that was when Kahlip became the uncle. Eventually to be Uncle Lehmmy.

However, Kahlip had a plan and with his supposed job, his girls were still his girls and he had watched over them their entire lives. He watched all three of them take their first steps. He watched them grow and prosper through the various food stages because he knew one thing that Lisa didn't. Lisa may have been there for them growing up, as if she raised them, but Kahlip had their hearts and vice versa. Lisa didn't love them, as much, as she should have. She didn't put into them the time and the effort and love Kahlip did from afar. He knew one day that her plan would fall through for the life she thought she had. Besides that, Kahlip knew whom his girls were, of which Lisa didn't know and had no idea. He knew they needed him or would eventually. Kahlip always asked himself what was the value of a father if he gives up his girls and ignores the fact that they are his. What was the value of a father that was more father than he needed to be?

Kahlip knew he had more love for his girls than Darion and Lisa put together, but they were level headed enough to be capable of harboring his girls until he could be with them, as their father. However, that day was so far away, and he knew it.

So, for what he knew of his girls, Kahlip became just the uncle that saw his girls to a point, then when the job took him far away, the girls had almost lost him, but only because he hadn't been in the foreground of their lives, but more in the background. At this time, Lisa thought that Kahlip had left their lives because he stopped coming around. She didn't realize he needed to stay in the background, and she couldn't be aware that he was present. In everything that had happened between them, the most frustrating thing about the connection he and Lisa made was the fact that Lisa used him, as a shield against her brother, then she used him, as a sperm bank. And, there were times where he thought it might have been different for her and him, if he had made a stake in her, as perhaps he should have done. Actually, he thought he did, but he realized that Lisa was just using him, as a shield against Mickey. As he thought about it, Kahlip realized he did the things he did for his supposed job because Lisa wasn't letting him in more than she did. Lisa, he eventually figured out, protected herself from him, as well, and to a certain degree, but it was Darion who eventually got through the entire door to her heart, but Kahlip couldn't understand why. In the end, Kahlip dealt with his heart in that situation. And, he rationalized that whatever happened, did so for the best. That didn't mean his heart didn't ache, but it did help him to get in touch with his Plaenellian heritage. And, for Kahlip, that became the proverbial curse of him for the Keeper he was.

Part of the curse meant Kahlip would be a bit cavalier with his heart, which was probably motivated by his French roots or the language of love. However, never once did he ever forget that his true heart lie with his girls and knowing them, as he did, meant knowing that each one of them had a specific duty to which their hearts led them. And, Frances was a Sacrealle type of a beautiful creature. He wrote all three of them in a journal, he had been keeping since they were born. Frances would be, he knew, a protector of the Sacred Allee, which is from where Sacrealle stems. Sacrealle was the culmination of two words, sacred and allee, dropping the d and an ending e left the name, Sacrealle.

Now it is some that think most Plaenellians came from the French bloodline, or worse that the Plaenellians started the French heritage. However, it's just that coincidentally there were a lot of Plaenellians born to them. Had it been wholly a Plaenellian tool, the French would have never had a king, nor would they have employed a Rosicrucian and an Aubrahteerian, as an advisor. Unfortunately, the various consciousnesses were born at random to the various heritages that became the nationalities they did. Kahlip, at that time had shared more with the French Bloodline than any other part of his heritage. It was how he knew the things he did, and it was why Augustine was so important for what the French were attempting to do in the fifteen hundreds. It was important enough for Mickey that he seeks out his path, and makes a claim in Augustine, as he had lived mostly in the mid eastern United States for much of his young life.

The point was that the Secrealles and the Sacrealles and the Secreas' were created under French Domain, that didn't mean that the French were those who started the various protection acts of the Plaenellians, but certain ones were enacted by Plaenellians of some French heritages. And, that meant the great and wonderful mentor for these concepts began with a Frenchmen, and confidant to the Plaenellians of yesteryear, named Astallees, whom Kahlip also hinted to in his journals.

So with Lisa having made up her heart, Kahlip was left abroad to find sporadic love with a cavalier heart, but it was his job that enabled him to find himself in the embrace of many women since Lisa denounced him. Through this time, Mickey and Kahlip, otherwise known to Mickey as Lehmich. Had gotten closer, but because Lehmich had to keep an eye on him. Lisa had found out that he and Mick were hanging out, and that was when her heart became more and more closed off from Kahlip, but really, Kahlip had discarded in his heart, any chance of having a life with Lisa.

So what she did to him didn't hurt. However, she hurt him where she could. There was a time when Lisa wouldn't let Kahlip around to see his girls, even as Uncle Lehmmy. And, unlike what Mick would tell in any story, Mick was, in a sense what got his girls to Florida, but only because he could get Lisa there. Actually, the way he told the story was that he saved Frances, Lorande and Karen by having Lehmich pick them up, but what really happened was that Mick found a soft spot for Lehmich because he finally understood that Lisa's girls were Lehmich's. So, Mick actually enticed Lisa to move down to Florida so Lehmich could be with his girls. However, Kahlip would find out that Mick had other plans. That was when he had to leave, in part for his job, but Kahlip at that point was still only going to be Uncle Lehmmy, and he didn't want that. So, he continued to watch them from afar. And, that was probably his biggest mistake because that was where Mick's betrayal of Lehmich actually began, and why Kahlip and Mick had become true enemies, which was ironic because Lisa and Mick were supposedly repairing their relationship, as brother and sister, when at one point Kahlip was a shield for Lisa against Mick. In and through all that, Kahlip realized then that he had a strong heart and a lot of love, which he did attribute to his French roots.

So, the betrayal began with Lehmich watching it all from the distances, but he could do nothing about it. He watched his daughter's lives fall apart with Mick at the center of his plot. Then, suddenly, Kahlip's daughters were having kids with no known boy to each of them that could be held responsible. Lisa had become a drunk by this time, and Kahlip trusted her with them at one point. And, that was when he knew what was going on. Mick for his Seyion heritage was mating with his daughters, using his girls against Lehmich for what Mick then knew. In a sense, it almost looked like Mick was getting back at Lehmich for Karen, Kira's daughter, but that was contrary to how he told the story. And, in all that, Kahlip finally realized that was how the Seyions infiltrated the Aubrahteerian influence and perverted it for what Mick was doing.

Many of the Seyion race had learned early on that their influence upon Ayeraal wasn't that strong, which is what Kahlip had surmised about Mick. In this knowledge, the Seyions figured out that they needed to piggyback the greater influence for the times, which is how certain religions became what they were, as in those that feel it is all right to have more than one wife, and it didn't matter how young she was. Even back in the early nineteen hundreds, parents were marrying off their young girls. Sadly, this is how the Seyion way of life had continued because girls that young were giving birth to just about any consciousness in the Universes that needed a home. Sadly, it was the Seyions that needed a new home the most for their dying Universe. This is in part, the reason for such a population explosion on Ayeraal or Earth. Each existing planet was taking on more and more consciousness from planets that were dying for what Osodon and Oosiah were doing. This gave rise to the need for protection of the birthing channels or the way consciousness was transferred between planets. And, that was where Astallees of the mid fourteen to fifteen hundreds, became so important.

The Chapter & Loving Memory of Astallees

Kahlip recalled Astallees from long ago easily. How could he not? Astallees and Kahlip were parts of the Plaenellians that forged the understanding of things for their day with the French Flair, but it was the knowledge of Astallees on Ayeraal that was more prevalent. Astallees, it could be said was a philosopher and anthropologist for his time. Anthropology made sense for Plaenellians throughout history, and it made sense because of what they knew. It could be said that Anthropology was a Plaenellian discipline, of which Astallees was a master.

Astallees was made a teacher by the time he was twenty years old for his relative nature to his community, but he kept his true nature aside, and aided the French community in becoming what it was to date. However, Astallees would never make a name for himself because he knew too much to get too high upon the social ladder to be remembered throughout history. However, those who knew his worth would never forget. It's like in life through the years there is always that one that sticks in one's memory. For Kahlip and his Plaenellian heritage, Astallees was that one, but that was the point about Plaenellians. Part of their curse was being capable of a longer memory, which went beyond what science thinks is the brain's power for memory. However, that didn't say anything less about science. Science did its job, but for those who knew or kept the Secrets, knew how to keep science in perspective. Kahlip actually valued the Rosicrucians for what they could do. They were important, and they helped out in a time when they were needed. And, Kahlip knew that there was a certain level of courage in the Rosicrucians they didn't necessarily get credit for, but for their time, in the influence of the Aubrahteerians, it took courage to exist, as a Rosicrucian or what they would become, as Scientists on Ayeraal or Earth. Kahlip had a special place in his heart for the scientists for what they went through in battling with the Aubrahteerians in the beginning. And, it wasn't mere coincidence that the vampire stories became the stuff of monsters and science fiction for it was the scientists that understood Vlad the impaler above any Aubrahteerian in that time. Even Astallees told the gruesome tales of the Rosicrucians and their beginnings on Ayeraal. Astallees recalled how they fought hard to become the scientists they became up to the fifteen hundreds. It was a lesson that Astallees used to teach in secret to those who held the secrets back in the day. And, as he wrote of the Rosicrucians in his journal through the eyes of Astallees, Kahlip teared up for what they went through. It hurt that such a peaceful race for their home world of Aubrahteery that they could become such a violent race on Ayeraal, and take out this violence upon the Rosicrucians who were actually and, only trying to help. It was a strange new place with various alien races on one planet and the Plaenellians valued the assistance, which is how the Rosicrucians got to Ayeraal to begin with; Kahlip understood that first and foremost. It wasn't mere coincidence that religion seemed to become the prominent influence first before the Rosicrucians rose up, as painstaking, as that was for them.

However, Astallees was good for more than just his philosophical or anthropological side. Astallees was also part of the early astrological society in the French Quarter in France at the time, which became what it was in the States in Orleans much later. Actually, Astallees, along with other star minds of the day, noted the stars and their relativity to certain latitude and longitudinal coordinates on the planet. It was this star tracking that led to the deeper understanding in Plaenellians of how to identify births from certain Universes, as the rifts in the Universes showed up in their star configurations nightly. This would later become the protection grid or what Astallees and his colleagues would generate, as early star charts. However, his colleagues weren't necessarily Plaenellian, so behind the design of the star charts was what only Plaenellians would understand about it. They weren't just an observation of what was out there, but the secrets within Keepers gave way to an understanding of the stars, as they could be applied to the paths between certain planets. That was really the value of the Rosicrucians for their science mind, as it related to the stars. Astallees actually acted in part, as an ambassador between the Rosicrucian Astrologists and the social community. This was where Astallees' connection to the French Community had value because Astrology was seen as devil's work for most French Aubrahteerians, whose backing was religious in nature, as France did have a king who had Aubrahteerian advisors. Astallees took the blow out of science for most Aubrahteerians. And, likewise in Astallees laid the truth behind the man, which was never a man nor woman, but a calling. Astallees was the name given to the Plaenellian who could take the responsibility. Therein laid the true nature behind "Allee", which began with understanding the path in birth to any planet. Then, because consciousness became formed on the land of the planet, the stars were relational to the coordinates of the planet itself. So the word Astallees, when complete meant A STar AllEE Signature or A star Allee Sign, which are the two sets of stars in a path that consciousness uses to get to a planet to be born, as in the Allee or rows of trees for the direction of that consciousness along the path on the ground. The concept of the sidewalk and the road were all based on this concept of the Allee with a difference. The Allee of trees had rows of visible trees guiding one down the road. In a sidewalk, or road, the guiding points outside of the walk or road are not seen. It's one's knowledge that upon a road or sidewalk, it is smart to stay between the edges of each.

Astallees and the Truth in the Round

From this understanding of the stars, was how those who kept the secrets knew the roundness of each planet. The point was that star patterns in a nighttime sky didn't stay the same as the night progressed. To those watching the stars at night would see a star map open up to them. This indicated that for the dark hours, only certain star paths would be seen, when the daylight hit, the stars couldn't be seen. So, it became understood that the planet was round because the stars just seemingly disappear when the light rise up. This was where the questions about planet flatness began for those Aubrahteerians or those in consciousness that existed on the planets in the times of the immortals or those who visited other planets by walking through what seemed like revolving doors. Of course, it would seem the world is flat, but that was long before the Universes were changed by Osodon and Oosiah. Long ago, the planets worked so well within each other that planet visitation was a matter of walking from one room to the next. This knowledge of the planet and its roundness is what existed in the desire to build the first ship. However, it wasn't the French that would come to brave such a mission, but it was Astallees, as part of the mind group that would motivate the others to do it. It was known that those who were brave enough for such a task had Plaenellian heritage behind them. However, Astallees wasn't the only Plaenellian mind in this effort. For the desire to take this brave journey to reach those who could, it had to go through the vast European Plaenellian heritages equally. Then, suddenly, every nation had a notion of shipbuilding. This was how and why sailors sailed on the stars, and eventually according to plots or coordinates. However, French Astallees was concerned with the progress of the European future where in the earliest beginnings when less land was present, boats were made to go between landmasses of Asia and Europe that were further apart. In the earliest beginning from what Osodon and Oosiah had done had slowed the planets equally, which meant that the elements of the planets at their high state or form were becoming less or separating because they were slowing down. So, shipbuilding actually had been a formed art because islanders needed to move between the landmasses that were growing year after year, more and more. In this beginning, these boats didn't have to be big because the islands they wanted to go between weren't too far apart. However, as populations grew on the islands, and the landmasses became connected because the planet was drying out, the oceans became smaller and smaller. Eventually the landmasses in the continents that could show from this drying effect lost sight of the other regions of the planet or other landmasses that couldn't be seen for the water existing around the continent. It was in these times that the early sentient beings on the planet were the remnants of the Anthrocyte heritage. And, sadly, it was in the slow death of the Anthrocyte heritage that defined the various alien consciousnesses left on the planet when Osodon and Oosiah did what they did, destroyed the doors and paths between Universes and planets, and caused those alien races to be trapped on Ayeraal or Earth. This defines what the various races and nationalities actually are, as one in contrast to another. It is also, why there is variations in skin tones, and dialects and belief structures for these various nuances.

Astallees and the notions of God

Sadly, evident in each planet exists, the notions of a certain deity or deities that reside over a certain social order. However, understanding them is easier to do upon the premise of the Astallees Notion. Astallees helped throughout the ages with understanding the various Gods there were because of what was known, first and foremost through Astallees. Sadly, these notions of Deities points again to the Osodon and Oosiah effect in the Universes, which is not wholly or widely know, but to the Keepers of the Secrets. Astallees, in a sense was the information and perspective gather, as the many other things Astallees could be. And with this, went what deities actually were and why two various notions of a deity could vary, having the same essential purpose over a social order. It is easy to understand why a God would be created because Osodon and Oosiah for their separation from the rest of the Universal social Orders wanted to be recognized for who and what they were. However, in no way were Osodon and Oosiah God. Osodon and Oosiah upon coming to exist, existed with limits to where and what they could do, but unfortunately it didn't take them long to figure out how to change that. And that is where the God concept stems, from the two individuals that wanted to mean more to the various alien races, which is evident in what they did after escaping the proverbial castle, so to say. However, the various Gods became what they did for the alien races for how Osodon and Oosiah had to gain influence over the race of the planet. However, before Osodon and Oosiah did what they did, the various races didn't have a deity concept with which to adore and worship. There was a reason, and this reason was the simple peace between the races and each other. Everything in all the Universes operated and functioned well until Osodon and Oosiah acted from their jealous and selfish desires. And, how each race existed per each planet was how and what each God or deity would become upon Ayeraal for what they were coerced into understanding per their planet. This is kind of the whole plot behind being created, as in what some parents tell their children about where they come from that it is important to honor they mother and father when in actuality, simple love worked miracles. However, that was the nature of the effects of various alien races being born to others than their own on an even stranger planet than their own. This has been the plight of every planet in every Universe for every alien consciousness. Sadly, this sense of worship defined the value of being a God, and why it led back to Osodon and Oosiah for what they weren't to the various alien races long ago. It was how invisible it felt to be them, which motivated them to do what they did, and that made sense.

The last thing Kahlip wrote in his journal was a simple entry. It stated this.

"It doesn't matter if Astallees was right or wrong, but one thing is certain, the certainty of action to saving the planets and the Universes is of the utmost in contrast to being right or wrong. Astallees' value defined making sense and setting the perspective over what was going on. And, lastly, it is easier to endure something when it is understood. Astallees understood perhaps way too much, that he didn't even enjoy being. I know for myself, it is hard to exist and feel good about myself when I am a consequence for what my parents had done. Astallees knew that and felt it too. I know it."

The Chapter in the Sacred Allee

There were many nights and days for Kahlip on the back porch, just taking time to contemplate things. This was one of those days. He sat comfortably on the elongated and slatted lawn chair facing the east with the sun at his back.

Long ago, tracking the births through star charts was a means to understanding someone born to a specific region. However, doing this lumped everyone born to that date or time to specific personality, leaving no room for anything of a variation. And, sadly, two of the most varying personalities could have been born to the same specific dates. The point was that dates to which one was born held really no validity for it didn't explain the various personality differences there could be, as in a child turned murderer, as an adult. However, it also became widely known that the various races weren't born to specific regions solely, and that the planet in its rotation affected the birth of a specific race. This meant that no alien consciousness moving from planet to planet had a known destination concerning the alien race on the planet they would be born to. This is what explained the varying personalities born to a specific race and the various nuances within them. It also defined what the star understanding of birth tried to do. However, it became a less then useful tool, as time progressed because the various personality differences were too nuanced to track per birth date. And, there was really less and less insight to personality because the alien races were coming at random to each Planet in the various Universes. But, to some, the information was a clue and what science had almost become in the best guess scenario, which still didn't say anything less of it.

From this perception of the star birth charts was where protection of the Sacred Allee stemmed. However, it wasn't necessarily protection of the Sacred Allee and the stars, but those born through the Sacred Allee. Throughout history, understanding the stars and the birthing configurations or the paths through the stars used, made it important to regulate the understanding of the use of the stars. In other words, the abuse of the knowledge could be detrimental for it was the Plaenellians that named their star path the Sacred Allee, and only they knew what that was or where it was and when it was applicable to identify someone born through it.

When Frances had been born, Kahlip felt something through her, which wasn't prevalent with Karen or Lorande. He studied the feeling in secret, unbeknownst to Lisa, but it was such a profound feeling that it was hard to keep to himself, but he knew he must. Besides that, Lisa probably wouldn't understand even if he tried to explain it. That didn't say anything less of Lisa, but it did indicate who Lisa was in the scheme of things. That was perhaps her and Kahlip's relational issues. The value of a good, strong relationship is the strength and relativity between the two in said relationship. However, as Kahlip had come to seeing, his relativity with Lisa revolved more around Mick, than what was really between them, but Kahlip had learned one thing in being Plaenellian. He needed to see the higher view of every relationship he potentially would enter into. And, sadly, that didn't leave him with Lisa at his side.

Penelope sat enduring lunch alone…again. However, she thought about herself in contrast to her mother, if she could get her to start calling her Kaera for her Plaenellian heritage she would be doing good, then, she wouldn't have to hear Penny any longer. She thoughtfully sat and ate and thought about her true heritage. She thought about that with every bite, and how some of it went down easiest with thoughts of her truest heritage, in contrast to the one her mother had tried to give her in Penelope, or Penny, as she liked to call her. It was a half hour past, when she first arrived. By now, her thoughts were entertaining notions of Kahlip, and how for how strong or present in her mind they were, he was with her. That was one thing she had going for her in the loneliness. When she was alone, she wasn't because there was no one to distract her from being in her memory with Kahlip. She needed those moments. She had come to appreciate the solitude just because it meant she was closer to Kahlip. She didn't mind being single because it meant she was that much closer to the one that was truly hers. And, Penelope had actually succumbed to the reality that she just might be alone the rest of her life. She thought about how she might have entertained a Plaenellian purpose with a man, but she only contemplated that. She couldn't be serious about it. It would have had to have been a matter of life and death for her to sacrifice her solitude and distract her from being with Kahlip, even though she knew her job was a distraction from Kahlip, and their distance between them, as he had a job to do, she was sure.

By then end of the hour, she was just rummaging through her plate with the remnants of her food. There was bits of salad, and the chicken grille, which was her favorite. As she thoughtfully played with the food, she considered what the planet had become. In the midst of that, thoughts of the Sacred Allee came to mind. She reflected on a last time she and Kahlip were together. She recalled how they talked about the eventual importance of defending the Sacred Allee as well, as the Secret Allee. She thought about what that meant for the North. As she thought about that, she thought about how that was why the Union began in the North and defined the sense of desired unity between the north and the south. Looking for reasons for the war was easy, but deep down she knew. The south was pro-Osodon and Oosiah, which had been a growing state of things since the first settlers came to the New World. Kaera reflected on her history classes in high school and college. She considered how she liked reading the many things written, which shrouded the truth behind the Osodon and Oosiah effect in Ayeraal. She thought about how the understanding behind what was written was sometimes done for effect, but the sad thing was that much of what was written was erroneous anyway. It was a back pedal to cover up, shroud the truth, not necessarily in that order and not necessarily consciously.

Much of the story telling happened because most do not really know the truth, and that means that what seems like news is taken out of context for what was really happening. Suddenly, she considered something. Kaera had a light bulb go off overhead and she just turned and stared through the café window on seventh. It was her favorite place to have lunch when she had an hour near the office. In that moment with the proverbial light bulb, Kaera thought about the story telling that happened in the news, and she realized that it wasn't necessarily a bunch of crap, but what most minds could understand and accept. She had heard many comments on or about the news clips, but they all resembled the same thing. In the end, there was the assumption that it was just meager storytelling. But the truth behind it existed. Something had to be said in light of what was happening, even if the truth couldn't be. Then, suddenly, Kaera really understood her worth, for what she heard about really anything at all. And, for its time and through the history of the alien races upon Ayeraal or Earth, she knew that it was important to push on, with or without Kahlip because there was always the hope that the next day she would see him again. As for her worth, no supposed human thinking creature would be capable of perceiving the road to getting the Universes back on track, which had to be done eventually, while the supposed humans slept well at night thinking they were safe in their homes, and moving about with their daily lives. And this happened while the battle with Osodon and Oosiah happened right before their eyes and under their noses.

Two years back, Kaera had become a mentor in her cities neighborhood community center, and she was a big sister at the why, and she had partaken in a program with the local orphanage that sought to have a big brother and big sister type program for the kids in foster care. Kaera ran on the premise that those who have the youth have the future. And, what she attempted to do with the children was just a simple thing, mentoring the youths that don't have parents to guide them. However, Kaera knew she got into it because something had to be said for making an effect with the kids. There was what Kaera was doing on the surface, being a Good Samaritan to other's kids. Then, there was what Kaera knew she was doing in protecting the future through affecting the youth in a loving way, changing the future in some way until the Universes could be returned to what they once were. Two of the kids she reached out to, she knew were special, like she was, and had a hard time dealing with being Plaenellian.

In her down time, she spent much time and many nights running through her mind, the solution and answer to the problems between the Universes. She kept running the moment the damage to the doors between Universes and Planets had been done. She kept replaying the moment in her mind, over and over, and what could overturn what had been done. Unfortunately, for Kaera and any other Plaenellian, they wouldn't have the true experience in mind, but the knowledge for what had been which was different. Plaenellians weren't there to see the destruction to the doors happen. Had they, they might have been capable of working faster to retrieve the solution. However, for Kaera and any Elder Plaenellian offspring, it took learning and processing the past each time they were born, to realize why they were born currently, and to which planet they were born. So, she imagined at that moment, that if he was not in the same moment, that recently Kahlip had pondered the solution, as well.

The Chapter of Secreas

The love story that is Secreas and Secrealle is of the greatest tales to be told. It was why both Kira and Amos had slips of paper that had the name Secreas on them. Then Karen before she became Kira, Karen and Kahlip did have a child together, but something in Kahlip told him that Karen wasn't his love, and would never be. Unfortunately, she was Secrealle to Secreas, which defined who they really were. It was for this reason that Kahlip and many others believed Mickey killed Amos because of his relationship with Karen before she became Kira, then after her and Mickey had gotten together. The point was Amos was a threat to Mickey through Kira. Mickey didn't want any challenges to his influence over who he thought Kira was, and when he murdered Amos, as Secreas, it killed Kira, but she was strong not to show it. That was part of the Plaenellian curse, which existed strongly within Kira. Long before Amos took Kahlip and his love's daughter to Florida, Amos, and Karen shared a romance to last them a lifetime in such a short time for what they both knew had to be done. And, that had been the banter between the two of them the whole time. Kahlip would tell Amos that he was lucky to have found his love, but then Amos would argue back that their time wasn't long enough to be together. Then, Kahlip would say that, at least he had her for as short a time it was. He would argue that he didn't get to have his other half for what he had to do, and that was the insight into Karen, as Kira because Kira was her Plaenellian name.

Amos did have some anger and frustration because his other half was touched by Kahlip, but that was also the curse in Plaenellians, whose minds surpassed that of mere alien races to see the reasons for things, as they happed per planets. The curse was in knowing what each other were doing with each other, knowing that what did happen did so for a reason. The point was to be able to understand that, which Amos did. He didn't like the fact that his best Plaenellian friend mated with his other half, but he knew he couldn't be the one to bring the next Sacrealle to Ayeraal, which Kahlip could. So, it was Amos that got to be the truer uncle, than Kahlip to little Karen. And, it was in Karen who her mother was that Amos found his attraction for her daughter. Karen was such a delight, as Amos thought of her when she was much younger. Then when he had to pick her up and get her to Florida, they bonded a bit more than he should have for he knew what he was to lose if things with Mickey went as bad as he thought, but there again was the truest measure of the Curse of the Dawn Keepers. And, unlike what Mickey thought, he would never truly know what that meant. He wasn't in any way reflected in the curse and it wasn't in him to possess the curse. He didn't possess it! The curse of the Dawn Keepers happened all around him in anyone that came up against him. However, Kira would know the curse most of all, whom in the end got the worst, form of it through Mickey much later after Amos had been murdered. Shortly after the last battle, when Amos had been killed, it was hard to live with Mickey, but Kira endured that every day. Sadly, she would come to know the price for her deception of Mickey, and the curse of being Plaenellian.

Three months before Mickey died; Kahlip came to him because he needed to confront Mickey for what he had done. He also wanted the pleasure of detailing for Mickey how he had been deceived for so long because Mickey had done something to him that he hadn't been capable of forgiving him for. So, every chance he got to take a little stab at Mickey for who he knew he truly was; Kahlip took it.

So, he knocked on Mickey's door one more time, at a time when he knew Mickey would be alone. Mickey answered the door apparently reluctantly, as Kahlip knocked four or five times. Mickey wasn't that slow in his old age, and he just knew that Mickey wasn't sleeping not to hear it. Kahlip and Mickey went way back so Kahlip should have been well aware of his habits. And, he didn't answer a call, even a knock on a door easily.

Mickey ran at his own pace for who he was. But he did eventually answer the door to find Kahlip standing patiently. Mickey spoke up, as he saw who it was. "Lehmich…my dear friend. How are you? Come in!" Kahlip smiled curtly, as he didn't take too well to Mickey's greeting of him because it was so fake, and Kahlip knew it. But, as always, he didn't cause a stir if he didn't need to. He just entered as Mickey suggested. He spoke, as he walked by Mickey. "Mick…we need to talk." Mickey looked at Lehmich with concern for his mannerisms, and shut the door. Lehmich spoke again. "I would like the ocean in the back ground. Can we talk on the back porch?" Mickey smiled and endured the heaviness of the moment. It did feel odd in the company of Lehmich. He spoke up. "Sure." Lehmich headed for the kitchen door to the back porch. Mickey followed. Something about the moment was different, and Mick didn't know if he was going to like where the moments were leading. Lehmich, of course, went through the door first. Mickey continued to follow him through the moment, and shut the door almost silently, as he noticed Lehmich went to sit on one of the porch chairs. He then sat reluctantly. He eyed Lehmich intently, anticipating what Lehmich wanted to say. Lehmich, in turn, looked at him with what seemed a heavy heart. Lehmich spoke with hesitation, but with secret excitement. "Mickey, Secreas isn't dead." Mick looked at his friend with questions. One of which was what was he talking about. Mick spoke up. "What?" Mick then looked at his friend with a confused gait. Mick didn't like what he was hearing. However, what he thought he had done was what he needed to do in contrast to who he thought Secreas was. Mick knew it was Amos that he killed. Amos was Secreas, and he thought he knew it. Lehmich looked at Mick another moment before he spoke. "Mick…Secreas isn't the man, and never the woman. Secreas is a directive." Mick looked at Lehmich when he said that. He questioned his ears. He spoke. "Am I hearing you correctly? Did you say that Amos wasn't Secreas?" Lehmich looked at Mick for saying that. He enjoyed putting Mick through the moment. "I don't know what you thought you were achieving, but Secreas isn't dead. Secreas is a directive, as I said. But Secreas is also a concept of what has to be done. The word Secreas is the makeup of two words, Secret and East. The two t's and one of the e's are dropped, and you have Secr eas or secret east. Also in this, the concept of Secreas is immortal, and can never die. So, this means that one more or another grouping of individuals that can take responsibility, did take responsibility when Amos was killed. So, your intent to do what was done wasn't achieved if you sought to destroy Secreas. If you sought to destroy Amos for the sake of killing the man, then you succeeded, but not in destroying Secreas the immortal creature or concept." Mick looked at Lehmich thoughtfully, as he explained. When he was done speaking, Mick turned to look beyond the porch to the deep ocean miles. He couldn't believe what he was hearing. Thoughtfully, he turned back to Lehmich. He spoke. "And, how do you know this?" Now Lehmich wanted to tell him that he knew the truth behind him, as Osodon, playing at being Mick, but he didn't want to enlighten him to who he is. He wanted to tell him he knew that Mick had tried to copycat a Dawn Keepers premise by doing what he did, and even in destroying Secreas, but he didn't. He did, however, answer Mick's question. He spoke up quickly. "I had to do the research, Mick. I have been doing a lot of that lately." Lehmich looked at Mick when he said that. Mick didn't like that look however. Mick, in turn had to inquire, as to what extent he researched because there were things Mick didn't want Lehmich to know. He spoke up. "Research on what." Lehmich looked at Mick casually, and intently to answer his question with a hint of elusiveness. Lehmich spoke. "Mick, we both know the value of knowledge. And, what is what and where it could be found. And, sometimes the truth is less evident or present. So, I find what I can and make the best out of it. It isn't necessarily what I intend on finding either. Too, there are times when I find things that I wasn't necessarily looking for." Mick eyed him when he said that. What he said made sense. Lehmich spoke again quickly. "I find things and I share them, as I find things. That's really the way it works. So, I wasn't looking to find what I found out about Secreas, but I wanted to share it with you." Mick could appreciate what Lehmich had to share with him. What he now knew was valuable. What Mick didn't know was that Lehmich was sharing with him things that he wouldn't be capable of using later on. Mick was being informed of the mistakes he would make, and without saying so, Lehmich was hinting that he wouldn't be in a position to make them again. Mick didn't realize that Lehmich was only telling him those things, too, to let him know, without saying so, that he was a fool to think he could use Dawn Keeper knowledge against Dawn Keepers. Lehmich didn't say that though. That was in the elusiveness Lehmich tried to speak in.

Mick considered something, as the two of them sat. Mick thought about Kira, and how things went after he killed Amos. There was a hint of a change in Kira. Mick thought about how she didn't seem the same afterwards, which he knew she didn't think he did notice. Mick took a shrewd eye in Lehmich's direction. Suddenly, he thought about Lehmich knowing where Kira went. He thought about what Lehmich knew, pondering if it was detrimental to Mick's potential and immediate future. Mick rationalized that Lehmich couldn't have known where Kira went. There was just no way. However, he did think about his kids and where Kira went, the other grandkids were sure to follow, outside of Karen. She was his special one, and nothing about Karen spoke of unworthiness. Karen was as special, as she could be. Mick smiled on that thought about her, as he took a gaze out into great beyond his rear porch. Lehmich noticed his smile, but didn't care to be dragged into what lay behind that. He could only imagine, knowing Mick, as he did. And before he told Mick he had to leave, he made a mental note about having to return see Mick again.

The Chapter of Secrets & the Allee of Trees

It wasn't too long after Kahlip saw Mick that he became curious about what happened to Kira. Really, it was that he researched to try and find her, as well in that, he was rekindled with what he felt about his other grandkids, which Kahlip was upset about that Mick threw them away seemingly, so easily, but kept Karen close, too close for Kahlip to reach her. It was why Kahnelle had gone to France to act on Kahlip's behalf. Then, there was Kaerrie, who had become an unstable aspect of his life, which actually hinted to something about her. Kahlip got a glimpse of something in her that he didn't want to recognize, but he had to.

It was the other aspect of dealing with Osodon, for which end he couldn't wait. The fortunate thing was that Kahlip knew where his daughters were and what they'd been doing, and attempting to keep up with the three of them wasn't at all easy, but he did it, as any good father would. However, he knew there was a higher purpose in it, which is what made him look like an outstanding father, then eventually what he knew he would earn, as the best grandpa in the world. He had only to seek out his grandchildren. This was a mere part of the secrets of the Allee of trees, which really is protecting the birth rites. Planting a seed is putting or setting value to the ground, as equally, as planting a seed in mating. This was another value to shrouding the secret allee with the concept of Heroes Hollow. And, that was another secret of the Keepers. Heroes Hollow implied that it was an honoring of the heroes that gave their lives to the families of Augustine. It was about heritage and what the heroes had done, but that was the point about family and heritage and life. Kahlip, as well, as any Plaenellian understood this.

This was part of the value in finding a solution to the breaks in the Universes, as well because there were so many various alien races being born to just about any other various heritage or alien race, that the familial heroes weren't heroes any more. And, this sense of familial ties is severed because the future generations aren't coming from the same place. And, this state of things has been tearing up all the planets in all the Universes with Sentient beings upon or in them. That was an inherent quality to all Plaenellians because where they were so connected to those who they were born, they suffered for the various races of their familial heritage. That was the point behind Plaenellians. As parents, they were setting the standard for being able to connect with their children for this difference in the alien race of their offspring. The Aubrahteerians were the worse for perverting this concept. If their child became too alien to their way of life they were probably seen as heretics of some sort, in which case, they would sever the familial tie, and potentially kill their offspring. Now, this is of course because of the Aubrahteerian dogma. However, that is only an extension of what they were as an alien race for their planet in their Universe.

Their dogma worked for what they were, as Aubrahteerians on the home worlds, but not in a situation where they were birthing individuals that didn't feel, as they did. For this, was why it was sometimes very volatile and detrimental to the offspring to be born to Aubrahteerian families or parents' of religious dogma. Throughout history, it was a common practice to destroy one's children because they didn't partake in the familial religion or beliefs. Even the homeless populations across Ayeraal were the result of the lacking in connection of offspring to the familial heritage. And, to extents or to some degree the past for Ayeraal is beginning to overlap the present. What this means is that in the beginning, there wasn't a man woman or child that wasn't homeless per se'. History is repeating itself to extents that the homeless population is becoming alien, in a sense, to the way of life of even humans. Back in the day, it was common to die because it was the nature of things. That was until the Rosicrucians were born and began to see another way to change the result in the equation of life. However, it was this need to survive as a segregate race on one, seemingly all-encompassing planet that really defined the life. However, underlying it was the distinct feeling that one would just die out because of the nature of declining consciousness. And, that was what was detrimental to Ayeraal for its addition of the Aubrahteerians to it. Life wasn't about fearing not having a life, but being a part of something bigger than one's self. Everything was important, which the Aubrahteerians didn't see which defined much of the perspective behind life on Ayeraal. For many alien races, planting a seed meant that the growth from that seed would produce favorable offspring with little variation from the parents, as in an oak that is planted which produces only another oak. However, this is the truth and proof behind the potential difference behind the future offspring of sentient beings. A seed of a plant produces the same result because it is coming from the same place when it is planted. However, this is the difference in sentient beings where the varying results stem from the fact that the offspring aren't coming from the same place. This is the creation concept inherent in all sentient beings that they sometimes wish to ignore, which points to the fact that at one point, certain measures of consciousness were prone to specific planets. However, this creation concept stems from the Aubrahteerians who had a majority of the influence over the planet in the beginning. Rosicrucians have been dealing hard with this fact since they first began coming to Ayeraal. Part of the proof lie in where the concept of the planet and the plant come from. It isn't coincidence that those two words begin with the word plan, which leads to a concept of creation. A plan-et is a set in the design. A plan-t is also a set in the design, but something added to produce a certain effect in a given area. Hence, the Aubrahteerians forged the concept of the known creation so well ingrained into the perspective of the humanity, that even scientists or the Rosicrucians have to use words created and forged by the Aubrahteerians. However, this points to a sense that there is something of a design behind the Universe. Ironically, the only thing really versed back in the beginning was something of a biblical set. This means that even the Universe was built upon the notion that only one verse was something small in the grand scheme of many verses. It doesn't take one verse to make up a book, but many verses. Hence, the universes lead to an understanding that Universe is a culmination of the Universes that make up the book of creation. With this in knowledge. There was a garden planted with all the planets as seeds of the Universes, which produced a certain measure of consciousness. And, for what transpires per each planet, is what can be seen, as happening on Ayeraal, as it dries up or dries out. Essentially, this means that Osodon and Oosiah had their plan, which was to change the proverbial nature of the Garden. The Allee of Trees, on a bigger scale refers to the planets set in the Universes, which produced an overall effect with everything, as it was designed. And, that was a Plaenellian secret. In a sense, this meant that Osodon and Oosiah had put all the Universes through an enormous alien interracial crossbreeding, which destroyed the original design, instead of maintaining everything, as it was designed. This also meant that each planet, where once thrived alien races on a continuum, the product would change. Hence, the mass confusion for consciousness having to become human. So to set consciousness at ease, while Plaenellians worked to reset the Universes. Certain races were employed to settle certain issues on each planet. However, this only provided bigger problems, further straining the Plaenellian effort of returning the Universes back to what they once were. Sadly, this was all done because of what the nature of the Allee of Planets actually, were supposed to be.

The French, in concept alone, understood the nature of the ladder, the steps in a path, which is really, what the Allee was meant to depict. Inset within the concept of the Allee of Trees was the knowledge behind what the trees actually were, as a ladder upwards, with a bunch of the same trees planted in a row. A ladder with rungs takes one onwards and upwards. The rows of trees in an allee indicate that there is a directive forward between the rows of trees, and en eventual destination. This allee of trees on a smaller scale is just two rows of trees. However, the bigger concept revolves around the Allee of planets pointing in a specific direction. And, this is something not prone to the French Heritage, and what defines Plaenellians born to each and every nationality. And, it was this sense of Allee that Osodon and Oosiah sought to destroy, but why was really important. Due to the true nature of the intent behind planets that existed, providence over destination existed with consciousness to achieve. This meant that consciousness could come to exist on a planet or reside within the creative consciousness eternally, and return back again. In a sense, the nature of human vacation was the premise upon which this nature of the flow of consciousness could endure. This meant that consciousness could stay planetary, visit other planets, or eventually go to the creative consciousness to reside for a period or what is thought on Ayeraal, as a vacation. See, it was work to exist upon a planet, but less like hard work, but a higher sense of work, which felt good to endure. This was the plight of Osodon and Oosiah. They worked, supposedly all the time. And to stop this from happening, they destroyed the Alle of Planets through the nature of this all encompassing alien interracial crossbreeding. In that knowledge, existed, the possible solution to the issue, since Osodon and Oosiah had inhibited instantaneous visitation between each planet by forging consciousness to have to go through the birthing process. In a sense, Osodon and Oosiah caused everything about the nature of the design to slow down, which clogged things up. So, it was part of the solution Kahlip, as well most of all Plaenellians, sought to speed things up again. From this concept of slowing things up, the interracial alien fighting began on each and every planet of sentient beings. So, it was thought, the many solutions to speeding up a slowing planet.

A Chapter for the Good, Gold & Gould

Kahlip took a night to be rekindled with the past and what he knew. He began reading from the Killian Dawn, and found himself ensnared by the past than a rekindling.

In the drive to speed things up, which ultimately began long ago with the advent of certain technologies, part of this effort meant affecting certain aspects of the planet to accommodate for what Osodon and Oosiah had done, for which they initially thought there was no solution. However, they were wrong. The beginnings of the Gould family in the times preexisting the Egyptians became part of the solution, as far as the gold aspect of the Plaenellian plan to affect what Osodon and Oosiah had done. The Gold effort began with understanding the nature of the weight effect in contrast to a slowing planet. Understanding this was better done in knowing how a washer with clothes in it that are unevenly set in the drum can slow the washer down or offset the spin of the drum, as it washes clothes. When the washer spins offset, it's time to reset the clothes within it to balance the drum to spin at its optimum. This was the value of the materialist view. If people understood that, the value of gold was to reset the weight of the planet because gold was cooling down, causing the slowing state of the planet, Gold might have never gained in such value, and mining it might have never become so important. However, this isn't something that is such popular knowledge, which made it easier to get people interested in gold enough to make selling it, and mining it that much more important. A washer with an offset drum, working harder to spin, will eventually damage the mechanism upon which it spins. In the least it slow down, then it breaks. Ayeraal, if it hadn't been for the early gold mining effort, might have slowed at an increasing rate through the years. This was why huge civilizations mined gold and made many things from the gold that was mined. However, the truth behind gold and treasure is that much more intricate and unbelievable than just merely getting it out of the ground. Gold needed to be redistributed around the planet for the true measure of the gold effort to come to fruition. It was one thing to get it out of the ground, but another to redistribute it around the planet, which essentially served the same purpose, as redistributing the clothes in a washer drum to get the drum to spin properly. However, this wasn't the only precious metal to which this needed to happen. Just about every precious metal needed to be mined and redistributed, as well as many other aspects of what cooled in the ground because of a slowing planet rate of spin. What made the most sense with distribution, was putting the precious metals in the form of money to ensure it got distributed evenly across the many growing nations. These efforts were just more of the effort to engineer a planet that was verging destruction with sentients beings upon it, which added to the weight, and slower rate of speed. Osodon and Oosiah hadn't planned on that; they didn't count on an intelligence that could devise a plan to compensate for what they did. The ants were a measure of what humanity could become on Ayeraal to ensure its survival. This is why every aspect of life on Ayeraal was important. It's why steel became the essence of the big building. It's why concrete was thought of, as a building material. And, it was in these processes that Faeverluhn didn't have, which became its downfall. Faeverluhn was a battle and attack that was easily won by Osodon and Oosiah, and that further proved to be a guide for which Plaenellians sought to engineer the planet of Ayeraal. The point to it was that it served, as a premise for the survival of alien consciousness upon Ayeraal, and anyone resistant to this state of planetary engineering was more than likely working for Osodon and Oosiah. This was why going green efforts and environmentalists were less than appealing. This was why big cities were created in various regions, as they were. What no one realized was that the bigger the city, the better it was to compensate for the lack of pressure by the ocean from the oceans that were drying up. Of course, this concept was more prone to the Secrets of the Keepers, but it worked to aid in the views needed to engineer the planet, as had been done in the time it began. However, it needed to be an ongoing effort without fail, if the processes were to succeed in the solution coming to fruition. This is what drove the Plaenellians to aid in moderating perspective because Osodon and Oosiah were strong to thwart the effort, as in the environmental effort that had been created. This was why true environmentalists were truly environmentally sound, because if it was truly smart to be environmentally sound, then engineering a planet was pointless. However, engineering the planet is what prolonged the life of the planet to give rise to these environmentalist opposed to it. Another aspect of big city projection was the purpose of stopping the ground from becoming saturated by rains for the ground had been dried enough that it had become stable enough to sustain its density and dryness. Big cities stopped the water from weakening these dense grounds, which could variably weaken the ground enough to enable lava flows hindered by the dense grounds. This was really the importance of bigger cities near ocean shores to create a density in the ground where the water table is higher nearer the ocean. It is an age-old engineering concept that to create density, high moisture content is needed for certain soils with less silt. So, these bigger cities act as density devices to create a shored effect to add to the density upon which the buildings are founded upon.

And, that was where the Gould family in the beginning possessed their initial importance. The concept of gold mining was maintained by the Gould family for many centuries through the ages. They weren't the only ones however, that served in this effort, but they were a majority of the beginnings of Gould mining.

Demitri Gould of the Gould family from the eleventh century were the mainstay for mining in the early European nations, which eventually branched off throughout the few coming years. Eventually, the Gould family migrated in all directions with their purpose of this mining effort, which didn't only include Gold, but various precious metals, and gems, as well. However, their early techniques were hindered by technology, but the purpose for mining would drive better methods to eventually be discovered.

Kahlip thought about one thing, after reading from the Killian Dawn. He was rekindled with something more sinister than what supposed humans had in mind for existing upon Ayeraal. He realized that planetary engineering was just the tip of the iceberg. If the mix of alien consciousness was to survive upon Ayeraal or Earth, it had better find a way to coexist and work together for their desired sense of survival. It was clear that Osodon and Oosiah hadn't done their worst yet. And, that reality was what Kahlip and the other Plaenellians were working to stop from coming to fruition. However, the darkness in the alien consciousness could be their worst enemy in this effort, which was why it was so important to seek the higher perspective or that which all alien consciousness possessed at one point before the battles with Osodon and Oosiah began, and before the very first planet was destroyed from this beginning battle.

The Chapter Race

Kahlip began to consider the legend of Roderick Caine, and what he did so long ago in protecting the Union from falling apart at the hands of Osodon and Oosiah's reapers. It was then that Kahlip thought about how important saving it was and what the union actually had become from the truth behind the various races coming to exist in North America at the time.

Underlying supposed humanity was the survival of each and every alien race that made up humanity. What this meant was that early on, surviving the years was important, and what every race could do was vital. For the Keepers of the Secrets or the Plaenellians surviving wasn't such a desire because they knew they would for who and what they were. However, the lack of knowing the heritage of each alien race on a planet of common ground was detrimental to such extremes that life and death were over exemplified concepts. And, this concept of the Race in a people in contrast to the sport race could be easily seen for what was a true measure of the race at all. This importance of the races was evident in the way humans viewed life. This was also something Kahlip picked up from the Killian Dawn.

For Killian in his day, perspective on existence wasn't truly formed yet because the various alien races were coming to terms with being stuck in a planet not knowing where they were going. Birth wasn't fully understood by this point. And, that was an amazing fact Kahlip was rekindled with, but it made sense. The various alien races had no known concept or idea of birth in the beginning. They didn't put two and two together to fully understand that when a male and female got together, that a baby could potentially pop out. This is ironically, where the concept of the Mother came from because women did the same thing as a moth in becoming a walking cocoon with no knowledge that she became with child because of the male. That was not to say that it did happen that a woman got pregnant every time she connected with a male. This is another reason why there was no connection made between having sex and birthing a child. And, that further made the woman appear, as the moth seemingly cocooning with no reason behind it. From this effect, could be the reason why males didn't take responsibility for children so long ago because it wasn't fully understood that males were in fact responsible for them. However, that defines the intent with doing so, and the true effect of the break in the Universes forged this desire to connect with the opposite sex in what would eventually be coined by the Aubrahteerians, as lust. However, that was the shortsightedness of the Aubrahteerians, which defined said male and female interactions in such dark way. This is why Aubrahteerians and the Anthrocytes were confused one for the other at times because of the nature of influence. It's why the Seyions thought about the Aubrahteerians and Anthrocytes the way they did. It was why the Seyions believed of the Aubrahteerians the way they did, as well as the Anthrocytes. It was why they thought of the Guardians of the Garden or Paradise the way they did. However, Kahlip knew what they had been through. And, it was that, which Kahlip knew about Mickey, as Osodon that bothered him so much about the Seyions. That was the point. Osodon had shown up, as Mick Ellis to reap the rest of the Seyions. This was also much confusion of the Killian Dawn for the Seyions. However, as Kahlip had come to understand, the Seyions had been reaped some years ago long before Mickey had been born to Ayeraal. And, Osodon had been fooled by a great many things about the Seyions that didn't exist on the earth in his time. This defined the battle with Osodon and Oosiah, where Oosiah was who was left to face in the remnants of that battle. It was just a matter of finding out where she was and who she was. However, in that was when Kahlip learned that Osodon and Oosiah weren't on Ayeraal to only reap the Seyions. They were there to begin with other alien consciousness upon the planet.

Kahlip thought about the last years of the Seyions on Ayeraal with a heavy heart. Sadly, he pondered how they seemingly died out, but he knew. Throughout their last years, Seyions had been slowly reaped by Osodon and Oosiah because of what they weren't able to give to the success of the various races on Ayeraal. Seyions had no influence on Ayeraal, as the Rosicrucians and the Poliglials or the Aubrahteerians and the Reiluians. Also included in that list were the Puhlosians. However, there were a couple other races that were on the verge of the next reaping.

Deep in the heritage of the Universes before the effect of Osodon and Oosiah, there existed, a race of sentient beings called the Daelosia Sichella of the Planet Daelosia in the eighth Universe. These Daelosia Sichella were the bi-species of their counterparts, the Daelosians. However, the Daelosia Sichella was actually the more influential race on Daelosia. And, in what some believed was the oldest race on Ayeraal or Earth was the heritage in the Africans who were made up of the Daelosia Sichella. And, ironically, sickle cell anemia or the description of the disease was derived from Sichella for their race and the consequence for some Daelosia Sichella born to Ayeraal. Sadly, the disease was a racial thing, which is why labeling the disease was derived from Sichella. Sichella became Sickle, as if the ch was turned into a k with a few letters being dropped.

Sadly, the truth behind the Sichella begins with their planetary reaping by Osodon and Oosiah first and foremost in the battle that began the Universal wars. The Daelosia Sichella and the Daelosians, as well, were the most revered of all alien races, which was once a fact among consciousness even upon Ayeraal in the days of yore, but by that time, they had become the Africans on Ayeraal; their beautiful and wondrous heritage had been lost. They had been under the attack of Osodon and Oosiah and their reapers. This all happened upon Ayeraal to the ignorance of many of the alien races present upon Ayeraal, after the Universal wars were seemingly over. Kahlip thought about what the Africans had gone through since their beginnings in Africa, and how much it hurt that what they went through, took them from being a revered race of Daelosian beings, to being considered animals and less than anything of what they once were. However, where Kahlip understood their anger and hatred with supposed oppression, they didn't understand that deep within the Plaenellians was the knowledge of who they once were. He could understand their hatred with being considered slaves. However, that was done with a purpose and for their protection to such extents that they weren't necessarily slaves, but protected individuals. This plight of the Daelosians motivated his drive to return things to the way they were. However, things had to be done first. And, protecting the Daelosian Sichella on Ayeraal meant everything, no matter how much they didn't like it. So, they were shackled, which meant that reapers couldn't come in and take them. They worked on farms and plantations to provide themselves with the duty of preserving the food to be eaten. One thing the storytellers missed in telling the stories of how bad the Sichella or Africans had it, was in the fact that the Daelosians were trusted to provide food for the table. They were the trusted protectors of the whites, which in a sense proved to be a valuable union of sorts. It was a symbiotic union between the Daelosians and the various other races that held them, as supposed slaves. The biggest point in knowing the truth behind the stories of the Africans, as slaves, existed within the fact that they actually could have killed their supposed masters, and ran free. However, they didn't, but the stories existed that the slaves were afraid to do that. The truth was that they weren't afraid. They knew they were heading for a better life in the New World. Sadly, the most popular story created was with a purpose. Osodon and the Reapers knew that if they could forge the lies of slavery, they could segregate the whites from the Africans, which is where the supposed hatred for the Africans stemmed. In turn, it was the reason for the hatred in the Africans for the whites. This battle for the Daelosians had gone well, until Osodon and the Reapers began purporting what the whites were doing as slavery. The reapers knew they couldn't get the slaves because they had been chained, most of them for long periods. So, they forged hatred in the Africans for the whites who would put them in chains by calling them by their hated label of slave. Africans began being called many other things, and hated most of all only because Osodon knew if he could create hatred in the Daelosians or those of African descent, they were that much closer to being reaped. And, to accommodate the plan in Osodon's battle design, President Abraham Lincoln, in turn, told the Daelosians of the north that they were never slaves to show the supposed ones considered slaves that they weren't slaves as Osodon's reapers maintained.

However, this was all a secret, well within the Keepers, but the Keepers were the ones working behind the scenes the entire time. However, for Ayeraal and her current condition, the Daelosian Sichella experience would never be the same, as was for all other various alien races. Life on Ayeraal was far different from what they were used to in its days of glory, let alone their own planets. Kahlip finished up with thinking about Roderick Caine again, who was, by all accounts Plaenellian, as equally, as his father was, which is why his father infiltrated the south to discover more of Osodon's plan. Then again, sadly, Plaenellian truth is merely the stuff of legend in itself or deep and silent secrets of the Keepers, which was another behind Abraham Lincoln, as well with Poliglian flair.

A Chapter to Lose

Unfortunately, the concept of war is something that makes sense from a certain point of view. However, only from the point of view of Osodon and Oosiah. Osodon and Oosiah had spent so much time creating the negative view of the Universes in consciousness, that at one point it seemed like they were winning in their efforts because the various alien consciousnesses were so willing to be reaped, giving in to the negative side or view of things. Unfortunately, Osodon and Oosiah had found a way to use the human concept against the various alien races present upon Ayeraal in a battle concept considered divide and conquer. Unlike what Plaenellians had hoped for in unifying the various consciousnesses on the planet with the human label, they didn't realize how that could weaken a consciousness, and forge a sense of darkness in them for the new label, which sadly, erased their alien heritage from them when this happened.

The way it worked was that consciousness thinking itself, only human was weaker than a consciousness understanding its deeper alien roots, and there were more of those human thinkers on Ayeraal than could be reaped in a single lifetime upon the planet. The planet was ripe with a harvest of weakened consciousness, and the worst part of it was that the human mistake wasn't an error in the choices they made, but in thinking, they were allowed to make mistakes. When really, it was the mistake of the Plaenellians that forged this sense of humanity, which would prove to be a valuable asset to Osodon and Oosiah. Even the term human meant that every consciousness was relative to the man, which is a very weak sense of consciousness. However, that was the nature of the Aubrahteerians and forging an all-encompassing label with which to refer to sentient beings upon Ayeraal or Earth. The Plaenellian mistake was eventually running with it, or not countering the human effort with something that could aid sentient beings upon Ayeraal to maintain a sense of what their individual true roots were.

However, that was the value in thinking that humans actually, begun on Ayeraal, but that was a measure of the true level of intelligence in consciousness. And, it was for this that Plaenellians fought so hard. Being Plaenellian was not at all easy. Actually, it was hard among a larger race of beings that forgot themselves, but this was happening in every Universe and on every planet of sentient beings. Kahlip knew the gripping effects of what is known as the highest levels of depression that existed in the various alien races. It was what caused their habits so to say. Their habits made them forget what it felt like to upon an alien planet. However, the Aubrahteerians had their way of looking at these habits, considering them the work of the demons and the devil. However, the Aubrahteerians had their habits, as well, in what would be their dogma. Too, this habit in the Aubrahteerians was sometimes worse because it forged some of the worst forms of social interactions between each other and the other various alien races upon Ayeraal. For Aubrahteerians, their sense of power was habit forming. They took advantage of the weaker alien races, coercing those races for their feeble senses of consciousness into their religions and dogmas. This sense of witnessing was a power struggle to forget their own sense of despondency for where they were. And, it was this power that Aubrahteerians sought.

Through all this, Osodon and Oosiah grew stronger. This was "The Killian Dawn 101". Instead of seeking the individual prowess, as in the various races, the Aubrahteerian power struggle, the other races with their drug and alcohol use, the Killian Dawn purported that a new perspective for the alien races was needed. Separate, the various consciousnesses were weak and feeble. Unified, the various consciousnesses could be strong. However, this wasn't something that was prone to the average sentient being. In the beginning, there was no sense of unity, and the harvest was ripe for Osodon and Oosiah, which too, was the greatest period of loss of potential consciousness. This meant that the most harvested individuals happened in the beginning when there wasn't a global plan on how to exist. This was what existed behind suicides of individuals that didn't understand what was going on. It was the incessant need to war, which happens to date. And, though wars really recycle consciousness, wars were in fact pointless, however motivated by the reaping population for Osodon and Oosiah, which purported the wars in secret. The reason was simple. Even though war eventually brought death, not all death through war was a harvest for Osodon and Oosiah, but they did get their form of reward, however.

This is really, what motivated the depression effort in Psychiatry. Depression and suicide was a potential harvest for Osodon and Oosiah, but that of course is a secret in the keepers. However, that was how the head doctors were important, other than for what darkness claimed they were. The point was that the darker one's view of life, the easier they were harvest by Osodon and Oosiah. This unfortunately was knowledge deeply ingrained in their Plaenellian offspring. It's as if Osodon and Oosiah's darkness spilled out into all measures of creation. The point was and what Killian tried to convey was that the various consciousness aren't separate, as they could potentially feel. Every manner of consciousness was connected, but to harvest consciousness, it had to feel, as though it was separate. This was what Osodon and Oosiah did for the planets they could be born to after escaping what they thought was jail, but it was their home. They just didn't have the right perspective themselves to be capable of existing as they were meant to. So their darkness would eventually become the confusion in alien consciousness or what they considered their harvest. Many alien races lost much when Osodon and Oosiah did what they did. It was what forged the horrors of mental illness. Sadly, this state of mental illness, as it progressed on Ayeraal was not as bad as it was on other planets in other worlds. It was the head doctors that took responsibility of those issues and sadly, weren't honored, as they should have been for their efforts. However, that was how separate and lost alien consciousness had become upon every planet, but that was what the Plaenellians fought every day. It was what their

efforts to solution were aiming for; it was why the solution was so important. And, that was the importance of Orinthalle Wilifer Loste of the Loste clan in the earliest beginnings of consciousness upon Ayeraal or Earth.

A Chapter Loste

Kahlip was reading from 'The Killian Dawn':

Killian wrote about Orin Loste in his book in brief, and he tried to shortly exemplify the life Orin attempted to have with so much darkness running rampant on the planet at the time. To some Plaenellians, Orin Loste was one of the first meager alien consciousnesses to possess strength on an alien world. Orin wasn't Plaenellian, but perhaps he did have some Plaenellian influence helping him in some way to this strength he supposedly possessed. The Loste clan was a small grouping of an alien race of Uhvians from the second Universe and the planet Uhvia. However, the Loste clan was too far from home on Ayeraal, and was lucky to have found each other, to form a clan to begin with. Many alien races weren't capable of finding others like them sporadically throughout the Universes. It was a little known secret that the Plaenellians actually aided them in getting to Ayeraal for their survival, as had been done for many races throughout the ages. There was nothing worse in the immortal Plaenellian than the knowledge of a dead race, of beings or those who had been harvested. Too, there were a set division of Plaenellians that made it their responsibility to aid surviving races to find homes or planets in which they could start over. However, there were those who were lost through these efforts of the Plaenellians. How these races were saved was intricate and nuanced, but a successful effort in degrees. This was where the Loste clan came into play, which was the influence of the Plaenellians Orin had to aid him.

The Loste clan proved to be a valuable asset in forging the Planetary Engineering Ayeraal needed for how the planet was changing after the battles with Osodon and Oosiah had come to an end. Although the battles weren't necessarily over, but they had become more silent. Uhvians were important for the early understanding of the land for the areas of the planet that were becoming more and more exposed for water loss. Uhvians were a dry planet race from their beginnings on Uhvia, which served, as a viable source of knowledge because the land on Ayeraal was unstable from the evaporation of water. Uhvians had the knowledge of what would happen and continue to happen, as the planet dried. Little known to the alien consciousnesses on Earth or Ayeraal that it was Uhvian influence that was a deciding factor in designing the early settlements and where these settlements should start. It was what big cities would become for where they began, which all started long ago. This Uhvian knowledge is what depicted that the stronger cities should be further from the water because the water source would eventually put these eventual bigger cities at the center of landmass because the water was receding and would continue to do so. And, it would eventually put these cities at higher elevations, as well because, as the water receded, the land elevations were decreasing the further from the cities the water went. This meant that the cities would be more protected and eventually come to exist at much higher elevations than at the water's level. It meant that eventually, these cities would come to exist on hills and mountains, which would act as a deterrent for any enemy. Grecian and Roman temples were founded on this concept, which was why they existed for long periods on the mountainous regions, after the cities progressed and changed throughout the years.

Because of their saving Graces, the Uhvians became one of the very first charitable peoples on their new home of Ayeraal. Aubrahteerians were believed to have gotten this sense of charity from the Uhvians, claiming it for themselves however. But, the truth was that originally, it was the Keepers who offered such charity in a dark world. It was the Plaenellians that showed the rest of existing alien consciousnesses charity and its worth on Ayeraal or Earth. However, the secrets lie in Keepers who really weren't known for being such things, as Plaenellians weren't known to exist, whose secrets didn't exist either. And, that was a measure of Plaenellian strength to exist when no one knows that they do. That was the Plaenellian measure of heart. Ironically, the Aubrahteerian race of beings on Ayeraal or Earth wasn't as supposedly loving, as they would eventually purport, but the Uhvian heart enabled them to come to think of their sense of charity they had, which would seemingly become what they considered an aspect of their religious dogma.

Sadly, around the beginnings of the two hundred fiftieth years the Uhvians arrived on Ayeraal was when their light eventually went out of Ayeraal. It was hard to get them to populate on Ayeraal when they were on it, so it was known that it was a valiant effort in the least. Eventually, they wound up getting recycled throughout the Universes, as Osodon and Oosiah had reached them across great distances through their influences on the other various alien consciousnesses that were being born on Ayeraal. This meant that the Uhvians were, continuing to be attacked by Osodon and Oosiah through the other races that eventually they died out on Ayeraal. But therein lied Osodon and Oosiah's battle plan of divide and conquer. Some Plaenellians claimed that what really motivated the saving of the Uhvian race was a secret relationship between Uhvian princess Aurotia, and a certain Plaenellian existing on the planet at the time of the last days of Uhvia. However, it was wholly conjecture when this certain Plaenellian thought responsible had heard about it, at least those were his claims.

Kahlip reflected on Princess Aurotia in that moment, which he realized was a potential aspect of his curse. It was what forged his disliking of becoming something from what his parents had done. He recalled how much it hurt when he had to say goodbye to Aurotia because he knew there would be an end for him. It was a curse of the Plaenellians or the Keepers to know such an immortal thing as love for just one creature. Though Aurotia had become such a large part of his heart, Kahlip had the immortal love between him and Kaera, which hindered any kind of a true love with just anyone. It was the Plaenellian effort to support a new consciousness to any planet they may come to exist. This was, in part, why Kahlip was the supposed good father he was because he was built that way. It was why he had to clean up after his father Osodon had done what he did, as Mickey Ellis. Plaenellians were made good parents, but that didn't say anything about parenting skill. This was the plight of the children of a Plaenellian parent. They think they have an awesome parent, but what they really have is a machined parenting thing that can do nothing but be a good parent. Plaenellians cannot be bad parents for the purpose they know existing behind what they do. This was the effort behind the Loste Clan, and the Uhvians in general.

It was some years after the Uhvians found a home in Ayeraal when Kahlip found Aurotia again. However, he couldn't do it again. He couldn't torture himself with another moment enduring that he would have to leave her again. The sad thing was that he knew her, but she didn't know him, but she did have something for him that she glimpsed. However, Kahlip knew what it was. He just couldn't do it again. So, he made sure to stay at a distance from her. Deep down in Kahlip too, was the knowledge that for how distant he could stay from Aurotia indicated how close Kaera was. The Plaenellian heart or what is sometimes considered lover's hearts were like magnets, when they were close; they only got closer because of their connection, which decreased the strength of another's heart. Kahlip instantly longed for Kaera in that moment, and like always in those moments, came the frustration for existing. He would be some kind of a sick thing if he enjoyed what was going on, which was also another measure of the Plaenellian heart, and what defined such a creature. Doing what had to be done meant so many heartbreaking decisions. And, that hurt almost as much as knowing how many races had died by that point. But Kahlip took something from that moment in understanding himself on Ayeraal or Earth for that lifetime. His time with Aurotia had taught him something, but it just could have been what kept both Lisa and Karen away from him.

The Chapter for the Races Lost

It was Sunday in the week, and a perfect day to relax. Unfortunately, for Plaenellians, there is little time to relax. Their hearts and minds are always seeking and knowing, loving and having to leave. On the porch by now, Kahlip was driven to find his grandkids, having knowledge of one, Karen, whom he deeply cared for. He knew what he needed to with his daughters; they just needed the desire to want to find him, as he didn't want to disrupt their lives. He had kept his eye on them, as they grew up, and he felt that he did what he was supposed to do. When they were growing up however, Kahlip got the feeling deep down, as though Mick knew they were Kahlip's offspring, which is why he eventually did what he did to them, which is what frustrated Kahlip most. With Mick being Osodon, he knew things that were happening, and in a sense, what he did was a measure of the reaping of his Kahlip's grandkids, if not his daughters, as well. Kahlip then considered the races lost to Osodon and Oosiah. The Seyion's were actually the first large alien race to go. Kahlip recalled the battle with Osodon and Oosiah long ago, when there was still a chance for the Seyions. This was why, in part, Amidestor was considered the prison planet. Further, it was why it was thought that prisoners escaped from the Amidestor to be born into Ayeraal's Universe. The truth was that those who did get to Ayeraal from Amidestor were alien refugees because the rest of the Seyion Planets had been destroyed. Anything now of Seyion descent in consciousness was little to none of the true Seyion race. Plus, any design of a planet existing where there might be Seyion consciousness was now so perverted that it doesn't wholly exist, as truly Seyion. However, Plaenellians knew the truth about things, and unfortunately, Seyions have been recycled through so many planets that there is really nothing of what their race was. Kahlip didn't like knowing that because it hinted to the fact that things might not be capable of going back to the way they were for the Seyions or many other races. In that moment, Kahlip sat emotionally facing the loss of the other races that were once so vital to their Universes. He verged tears for what he knew, but that was the measure of the Plaenellian heart, and how it affected Kahlip. What also hurt were the glimpses that things were permanent in every Universe, and that they couldn't be returned to their former glory, which hinted that even Ayeraal was going to wind up like its moon eventually. However, Kahlip couldn't focus too much on that. He had to keep the hope alive that he and his Plaenellian brothers and sisters could find a solution. He questioned though, where did that leave the races lost. Kahlip considered a possible solution, meant turning back time, returning everything to the way it was long ago. That would take too much supposed magic to achieve. In the face of what had happened, it seemed like the alien races were on the desired path Osodon and Oosiah had achieved for them. Kahlip only wished there was a God that could put everything back the way it was as if nothing ever happened. Kahlip wished the Aubrahteerians were right about God. Sadly, he knew they weren't which the value of their faith was. Sadly, Kahlip knew that whatever concepts about God the Aubrahteerians had about God were what Osodon and Oosiah had done to them, as equally, as they had done to the Seyions with their Master Seyion. Then, Kahlip had a thought.

He thought of the house built. There was a creator or a builder who organized all the elements, and upon a design, began to build. Now, the house being built was intended for a specific purpose with various rooms for their purposes, but the overall idea was that whoever should come to exist within it, should be enabled to do the same things to exist within said structure. That got him to thinking about the Creator of the design behind the Universes, since he knew deep down that Osodon and Oosiah weren't God. He considered that perhaps God was that homebuilder that got put out of the business because the opposing company, Osodon and Oosiah came in and destroyed God's business. Worse yet, Kahlip contemplated that Osodon and Oosiah had somehow come to knowing how to destroy God or they imprisoned God somehow, stopping the continuum the Universes was built upon. Kahlip then suddenly threw that notion out because he considered that wouldn't say much about the power in the creator or designer, and much less about God in general. But something had to be said for the fact that, everything didn't begin with Osodon and Oosiah. Even they were an intricate part of the design; they were nothing more than a plant in the garden of planets, as every other measure of alien consciousness. And, in that was where Kahlip found some sense of light, replacing his sadness and despondency for those lost races out there.

Suddenly, Kahlip was rekindled with the fact that that moment wasn't his first for regretting what happened to the alien races. His broken Plaenellian heart did truly start for him in losing Kaera or having to say goodbye so much, but it was made worse by what happened to those races. Then, Kahlip was then recycled through the machine of hurt and pushed out of it feeling like he didn't want to exist. What was happening to the alien races just made him so hurt for their torment that he just wanted to become nothing again, as before he was made Plaenellian to Osodon and Oosiah. Darkness was better than feeling his pain for the lost races. Darkness was better than knowing Osodon and Oosiah were doing what they were doing, enough to experience it through those alien races. And, that was what humans didn't get to know or understand with their supposed human thinking. Though everyone appeared the same, that didn't mean, every supposed human was coming from the same place, as sad as that was for Kahlip to know and understand. That led to another thing that humans would never see for their one sighted view of themselves on an alien planet, every other measure of consciousness was becoming, as they were, but not necessarily for their supposed human forms, but what lie beneath them. And, that was the deadly effect of Osodon and Oosiah, who knew that, would happen with an alien race born to another of a varied planet. Osodon and Oosiah knew that if the intelligence of a specific consciousness empowered it on one planet for what it was, and given the relative affect or the visitation between alien races and different worlds, the only way to destroy consciousness was to put it through the birthing process and through the consciousness designed for another planet. What this meant was that for Aubrahteerians, their makeup was a certain design, for Aubrahteery solely, but they could visit other planets and other Universes because of the immortality effect. However, Aubrahteerians for their essential makeup in consciousness wasn't designed to be born Ayeraalian or Uhvian, they could mix with them, but they couldn't truly exist, as one of them. This would assimilate with taking the measure of a tree out of a tree, and genetically mixing it with a flower. The desired effect wouldn't be a monstrous flower because the two weren't designed to become one. However, this was the sad reality behind what Osodon and Oosiah were doing. In other words, for what they were doing associated with the child that was born with a specific illness that died shortly after birth. As in the tree and the flower mixed, the seed from that would never get much bigger than a few molecules or atoms, but not enough to even be considered a successful experiment. That was the reality Kahlip and the other Plaenellians faced. That was how cruel Osodon and Oosiah were. To this end, Osodon and Oosiah knew that would happen to alien consciousness born specifically to another planet, which is torture in Kahlip's book. Sadly, this was what defined Kahlip's drive and desire to find a solution, but worst than that was motivated his habits. Kahlip hoped the Rosicrucians were right that smoking was bad, and that too much sugar was harmful. He was hopeful that certain foods were bad for the body over others, that way he could die from Ayeraal without being known for suicide at his death. However, that was the point. If one dies from too much red meat, weren't they committing suicide? Ironically no, as equally, as someone who smokes doesn't die from smoking. This was what is not seen in the Rosicrucian assumption that sentient beings on Earth or Ayeraal were dying from these things. What mattered were the consciousness and the effect of an alien planet upon an alien consciousness. Two sentient beings that die from a heart attack, doesn't mean that the heart attack is what killed them. It defines the two sentient beings were coming from a different Universe or planet. That's it. And, that they couldn't endure life on Ayeraal. And, that would be the value in honoring the alien consciousness or races that are born who die young because they cannot withstand the planet upon which they are born. This is why, unbeknownst to supposed humans who are really Ayeraalians, that birth almost seems like a revolving door because consciousness is dying and living at a specific rate and on such alien planets, which also defines the many Universes there are. How and why are simple. Consciousness regulates according to the number of Universes there are. The point is that consciousness cannot be in limbo. It will always be upon a planet in some Universe somewhere. It's the general rule of thumb in the underlying equation of creation, which defines the many more alien races there are. Why is simple. The potential for birth has to come from somewhere, and if there are more sentient beings upon Ayeraal or Earth, than in the earlier days, they had to come from somewhere. Consciousness isn't created. It is easy to think that, but Plaenellians know better. Consciousness isn't created when a man and woman join up. They are merely opening a door from another Universe and another planet. Unfortunately, the alien consciousness being born is not necessarily known for being capable of existing for a longer period of time. And, then, the parents are potentially set up to deal with their child on the brink of death. It hurts Kahlip every time he is rekindled with knowing that. He had cried many times for parents he had heard about concerning a young child they lost. He has shed many tears for the children that die so young because one thing their parents are saved from is in the knowing that their child potentially becomes much less when they die again so soon. Birthing and death take a lot out of consciousness, which is why it is important to appreciate people for who they are because they went through a lot to be born. And, that hurt Kahlip too, knowing how Ayeraalians or Earthlings treat each other, when they don't realize that for what they have become, is much less, than what they were on their home planet. The most frustrating thing Kahlip has ever heard is references made to the lack of intelligence in certain members of the gene pool, which is such a crass and heartless thing to say because it really is an ignorant comment. Ironically, the motivation to make such comments like that come from a dark place, which ironically, puts the commenter in the same effect of the gene pool.

The Chapter to Find

It had taken Kahlip an extra day to recover from going through the honoring of the alien races lost, which for him had been happening more and more lately. Now it was Tuesday, and Penny was nowhere around. He had the stressors of his financial situation, which was funded by the travel seasons, and the motel activity. He had his other side jobs, which were really pro bono because he considered it his charity effort. Ayeraalians needed more charity than they realized, but he was doing what he could, but that was also the curse of the Dawn Keepers and those secrets of the Keepers. There was much responsibility in Plaenellians and knowledge to be applied to their lives. Since Kahlip was aware of his daughters, knowing where they were and how they were doing, his grandchildren were his biggest concern. They had to be at the moment because he knew that Osodon was part of the door open for them. To affect what his potential in them would be, Kahlip had to find them. Granted Osodon didn't necessarily create them, as a new consciousness, they would still have to Osodon effect for being born to him. This was the confusion in the Rosicrucians or the scientists for claiming genetics. It unfortunately wasn't a matter of genetics, but an indication from where the consciousness originated. Kahlip did understand that importance of the Rosicrucians; he also understood why things like that were claimed by them. It was an easy understanding to settle the mind and heart of an alien consciousness to offer up some kind of genetic answer. Plaenellians knew better however. So, Osodon just might have given way to alien consciousness bent on purporting his influence, which wasn't a good thing. There was always some vile reason Osodon had children on any given planet or Oosiah for that matter. Kahlip thought about Penny in that moment, and considered that she had hinted about wanting to have children, but Kahlip had other plans. Besides that, he didn't expect such a thing from Penny for the life she had growing up. He knew on glimpse of what she went through. It was easy to see in her. Besides that, Kahnelle had disclosed her past to him, so he knew more than he could see in her. That was why her desire to have children seemed out of place with her. However, Kahlip did glimpse something in her that spoke of why she would want children, but he kept that to himself.

So, the motel was adding to his stress, at this point. He had been given the ownership over it because of some illusory details in Julius Mickey had instilled. And, because of the financial difficulty, and strain on him, taking over the motel wasn't necessarily profitable or a good idea. It seemed like travel, especially to the area was less, and less as the years went by. Kahlip had come to a point where if he didn't have an outside investment into the motel of at least five hundred thousand dollars, the motel was going to go out of business. It was that point of being potentially broke that he realized for his Plaenellian efforts, if he wasn't financially stable, his other responsibilities would suffer, as well. He needed someone that was like-minded to see the effort of finding the solution to Ayeraal and its sentient beings' solution, among all the other things that needed to be done. Kahlip knew, along with his fellow Plaenellians that life on any planet was never achieved by one. This was also a measure of what Osodon and Oosiah had done. In having to be born, for some eighteen years it put the newest member of Ayeraal into weakness and vulnerability. This was the supposed growing stage of new consciousness to any new planet.

Kahlip had gotten to the point where he just felt like giving up, but only one other time that he could recall. He was eighteen when he was faced with a decision. He had spent so much time with Mick at this point, and Lisa was becoming who she was from what Mick had done to her. Karen was an issue because Kahlip sensed the Amos effect in her. Kahlip almost just gave up on everything. He almost decided to just walk away from everything and go walk the beach for the rest of his time. But he made a decision not to, as he sat alone in some exclusive bit of forest. He had spent a night alone, considering living the rest of his life that way. Then came a moment of profundity for him. He sat internally searching when it hit him that he was worth much more than through what he'd been. So, he decided to return to life, and when he did Karen was more open to him, which was only worth little Karen at that point. Then, something changed with Lisa, but even that was only worth two little darlings. His life just seemingly snowballed from there, to where he was to date. And Kahlip then knew he was stronger for his current days because he had so much more strength than to contemplate giving up on the races of consciousness from many planets that needed him which would start with finding his grandkids.

Ignoring the financial issues, Kahlip had to put his efforts into finding his grandchildren. That was what was really important. He knew it. He had been doing little bits of research to find out what happened so long ago to the family that Kira and Mick started. Kahlip had watched his girls growing up and watched Lisa go downhill from a distance, but not necessarily Mick and Kira. Kira was another concern of his those years back, but eventually she just seemingly fell from the picture.

Kahlip had left when the fight between Mick and Amos was coming to fruition, and he regretted leaving for that short period because he wasn't as close to his girls, as he wanted to be, but that was when he knew Mick had taken advantage of him being gone. As he sat there needing to find his grandkids, he regretted leaving, but he had to, which only added to feeling as if he was being torn in a bunch of different directions.

So, before Mick died, as he told him he would, without being permitted a placement upon Ayeraal again, Kahlip saw him the day before he died. He went to him, when Mick couldn't possibly understand that he was slowly leaving the planet. This meant that Kahlip and the other Plaenellians took responsibility over ensuring that he wouldn't return. Mick didn't understand that he was being driven from the planet for his crimes against consciousness on Ayeraal and throughout all the Universes. However, this meant that Kahlip and those Plaenellians made

Osodon the responsibility of the other Plaenellians on a different planet. Deep down, the Plaenellians of Ayeraal knew they still had their mother, Oosiah with which to contend.

So, the day before Mick officially left Ayeraal, Kahlip visited him, which was something of an effort to do, as by this point, Mick knew all too well who Kahlip was. Mick wouldn't see him at first. And, in the end, Mick did give in, but under the premise that Mick wasn't Mick, but Osodon, Kahlip's father. So, it was in that moment, that father and son finally looked at each for who they truly were. Osodon spoke up, more cordially than Kahlip expected. "Son…what can we say to each other, that hasn't already been done? You know this isn't the first time for us." Kahlip and Osodon were on the front porch, as Osodon would let Kahlip into the house. Kahlip leaned against the rail of the porch heavily, as he stared at his father, and the father of all Plaenellians. "First…father, it seems like I am the only one that wanted to face you for everything that has been done. And, I have a feeling as if I am going to be the one to face mom, as well. But, you two do have to realize something. Father, you are not building anything. You are destroying something more wondrous than for what you saw it." Osodon looked at him when he said that. He felt angered when Kahlip said that. Osodon spoke up. "How can you be so indignant, Son?" Kahlip was shocked by his father's words. What was he talking about? Kahlip mentally questioned him with a stare. Kahlip finally spoke up. "Indignant, father… that's your argument?" Osodon looked harder at his son. He spoke up. "We gave you…our children a chance at existence, and you condemn us for it! How dare you?" Kahlip seemed shocked by his father's comment. "Father, at what sacrifice? Were we that important? Besides the way I understand things, we weren't even a consideration for what you two did. We came after the fact…as your consequence. You are twisting things, father. I know too much. Remember, I am one of the Elder sons. That might work on my younger siblings, but not me." Osodon took a moment to think upon what his son said.

He looked at him intermittently and thoughtfully. Finally, he thought he found a better argument. He spoke up. "We were sitting imprisoned, Son. You don't know how that felt." Kahlip turned from his father in anger and thoughtfully. When he turned back to look at his father, he unleashed so many years of hurt upon him in just words alone. He spoke with a very deep, heavy tone in his voice. And, with mounting anger in every word, he spoke. "No father…I understand too well. You have made us like you for we are prisoners of the same anger and frustration. However, ours stems from what you have done to the various races, as well as their planets. You don't know how hard it is to endure the pain and anguish of watching seemingly innocent beings being destroyed because of what you have done. You don't know the levels of love we endure for what you have done, father. See, father…yours was selfishness that you fought to get out of what you thought was prison. We fight to no avail to save them from the prisons you want them to exist within, just so you can feel free. And, that is the point." Kahlip stopped speaking. His mood lightened, as he eyed his father, the thing he didn't want to know he came from. He spoke again, with sadness this time, and emotion on his face. "Father, you despised them, and we love them. You wanted to kill them, and we fight to help them to exist. I hurt so much that I don't want to exist, but I fight that so I can fight for them…while you enjoy what you have done." Kahlip stopped speaking and there was deadly silence between them. Kahlip thought about one last thing. He looked at his father with a love and hate thing going on in his heart. He spoke, but he didn't look at his father he stared as far away from him, as he could. "Father, what you don't realize is that for what you have done, it will render you alone in all the Universes, as equally as alone for what prison you thought you were in with mom." Kahlip turned to him one last time and spoke again. "So, I need to know where my grandkids are…because I need to save them too. I know that you killed Kira…it's the only thing that makes sense about her leaving so soon." Osodon looked at his son, and shockingly,

Kahlip almost reached him…almost. He looked away from Kahlip quickly. He thought about the fact that he did kill Kira and how he had the body put into the ocean, never to be found. Kahlip thought about something in that moment. He spoke up. "You do realize that you murdered your own daughter? And, you want to tell me that you did this for us? You didn't know I knew about her, did you?" Osodon couldn't even face his true son. He stared away and out into the distance. He finally spoke up. "You will not do it, Son." Kahlip looked at him, not understanding him, as he didn't want to do anything to him. He knew coming there to talk sense was pointless, especially with his father, who was supposedly justified. Kahlip spoke up. "Do what, Father? I know you don't think what you did to Kira was murder, that you just sent her to another planet, as well, as my brother Amos…so what am I trying to do to you, father?" There was a moment of silence between them. Kahlip stared at his father thoughtfully. Osodon was dead silent for another moment before he spoke almost silently. "Make me feel guilty." Kahlip's mouth dropped open. He felt frustrated. He spoke. "You know, Father, you were made with love, but I am curious how you can exude such hatred. I would be better off for not knowing about what you have done, but see, Father, that is the point. I love them more because you could not. I won't be like you and give up on them. I won't destroy them just because I think I can. I am having hard time trying to save them when I think I cannot…FATHER!" Kahlip looked away from his father with a tear. He didn't deserve to see his emotion, not that it mattered anyway if he did. Kahlip spoke again sullenly. "I still love you so much father, that I cannot want to destroy you, though I know it may be easy. See… father…that is the nature of your offspring, father. We love too much…we have to, to counteract what you and mom have done. So, that is why I cannot stand here and waste time with you…I need my grandkids, and damnit…you are going to help me save them…damn you!" Osodon thought about what his Son said. He turned to look at him. Kahlip was staring hard into him. Kahlip was fierce in that moment, and for a brief moment, Kahlip was going to make his father show the slightest bit of love, even if it was the last amount, he had. Osodon spoke up almost silently. "There's only two left…one is north of here. The other is Karen, and she'll be around later." Kahlip barely heard him, and asked him for what he said. Osodon spoke again. "I'll write the address down for you." Kahlip spoke up loudly. "Damn right you will!" Osodon looked at him when he said that. Then, he turned from him and seemingly sauntered into the house solemnly. Kahlip followed him without permission.

A Chapter for the Win

Kahlip took the small bit of paper with a strong, stern grip that his father wrote upon with a shaky hand. Kahlip watched him write the address, and he could tell he affected him in the smallest way. In that moment, Kahlip knew that he had won something, even if it was just to get the voice of all the alien races out to his father. Kahlip walked away from that sad thing of a man, and didn't look back for he knew it was the last time he would do so on Ayeraal. Osodon actually watched Kahlip leave, but Kahlip ignored any sense that his father was watching him leave. Kahlip cared, but that wasn't what his father needed him to show. His father needed to understand that what he did was wrong, even for whom he was. Osodon needed to understand that he wasn't going to be a part of the solution, and that his Plaenellian offspring were going to have to make amends if they could. Kahlip left the house and nothing behind but the love he still gave his father, whom by certain points of view, didn't deserve it. However, Kahlip loved his father, even though he hurt him too many times. Kahlip left knowing his heart was still intact, even though there was no way for him to heal his fathers' whole being.

Osodon was left to think about a great many things when Kahlip had left him alone. Osodon, for a while couldn't get the image of his son walking away from him, as Mickey had been the one his entire time on Ayeraal seemingly running his show. But Kahlip woke him up to what kind of show he was running. And, it was that, which he questioned. Kahlip not only made him think about what he was doing, but what he had done, and what he just may have to do. He thought about his son, Kahlip with a kinder thought, than he had his whole existence, which motivated him to do what he did. And, now, for how he saw Kahlip and things he said, He considered what he would do from then on. Mick didn't do much since Kahlip left. He waited for that moment when the Plaenellian restrictions would ensue, and he would take his last breaths. Towards the end of the night, Mickey Dawn felt the cold rush of death overcome him. And he knew it was time. He went to his bed, unable to fully walk straight. He bumped into the walls down the hall, and stopped at the doorway to the bedroom and eyed his bed. He wished in that moment that Kahlip were there to tell him sorry. He thought of Kira and how he wished she were there so he could apologize. He finally decided to try to make it through the bedroom to the bed. He fell at the side of the bed and fought to get up into it. About a half hour later, he made it and eventually covered himself up. He drifted off to sleep at one point, thinking it was the end for him, but he awoke the next morning to find the sun and it streaming through the window, which is what woke him up. He looked around the bedroom, and noted that if the next day had come, then it was his day. He knew he was going to see Karen again. So, until he did, he needed to put his journals together to give them to her. He fought with death to do so, but he did it. On the chair next to the door, he placed his files, and he thought about having to tell Karen that she must find the remaining Anthrocyte power in the planet. He had to remember to tell her that before he died. It was important, and what Kahlip would need to assist in finding the solution. In the next moment, Karen was walking into his bedroom. He saw her and smiled, then drifted off in between consciousness and those early death moments.

Karen Dawn watched her grandfather lying in bed, attempting to breathe. This was it! His final moments! She knew it. Suddenly, he beckoned for her from the chair beside his bed. She stood slowly with her eyes on him. He turned his head the best he could to clear his throat. He wound up staring at the ceiling. When she was by his side, he moved his eyes slowly. He started to chuckle. He whispered in a raspy voice, "I've been here too long, dear Karen." Karen teared up abruptly. She didn't have enough time with him and she knew it. There was a long portion of her life where he seemed not to be in it. She teared as she watched his eyes and they seemed to fade in and out. He opened them briefly wider than he had for a while. He stared into her. At least that was how his gaze felt to her.

He said in a plain, clear voice. It was less raspy, but still a whisper. "Karen, those files there, I want you to take them. You need to find the Anthrocyte energy left here and access it. It might be the only…the only…" The files lay neatly stacked on the short round table by the bedroom door. Karen turned and eyed them quickly, and then returned her gaze to her grandfather.

Suddenly, he went blank for a moment. "Grandpa…Grandpa!" Karen said that loudly.

He came to again. He looked at her lovingly and with warm eyes. He continued to speak. "Karen, those files are the key to the Anthrocyte energy still here on earth. You need to take them, study them, and find it. I don't know how you will access it, but you must. I know you do not remember, but just learn from my journals. You must do what I say, dear…understand?" Mickey stopped speaking thoughtfully. He eyed his beloved granddaughter, thinking she was the last of the true Dawn Keepers. "Karen, you're…the last…." His voice was low, and broken. He was in and out of consciousness. He closed his eyes for a moment, as Karen looked on. "Grandpa?"

"I…am still here, dear Karen." He paused looking into her soft, light brown eyes. She had soft flesh adorning her high cheekbones. She wore little makeup at that point. She smiled at him with tears. "Don't cry now, dear. Listen, you have to be strong. Your cousins have been hidden for what you must do. If there was ever another hoard to arise here, your family could have hindered you from seeing what you need to do. You're the last… the last Dawn Keeper, Kiddo. Remember that, dear. And, keep your heritage in those files close, they are the keys…you need."

Karen nodded with tears in her eyes as she looked at the great Mickey Dawn while he died alone. Her grandmother left Earth a week before, and that was hard. But now she was alone with her grandfather. At least when her grandmother died, her grandpa was there too. She felt though that most of her grandpa left when her grandmother had. This was just too damn hard to do.

He continued to look at her. He smiled and added with tears, "You're so beautiful child, I love you dearly, and my beloved I know misses you as I will. I am going, Karen, but remember what I said. You take those files, dear. You learn about me and do us all some good. You have to find the 'ang'…"

All the while up to that moment, Mickey wanted to look into Karen's eyes and tell her that he was her father, and not her grandfather. He wanted to tell her that her grandfather is the one that saved him, which is why he started to tell her that she had to find the angel, where existed the remaining Anthrocyte energy which would help Kahlip and his Plaenellian brothers and sisters to undo what he and Oosiah had done. He wanted to tell her that her grandfather loved her more than he did, and he regretted it. But he didn't have the strength for the restrictions his Plaenellian offspring had put on him in leaving. He was in his most silent moments in parting with Ayeraal. So, Karen was left to feel the sadness for him, which he didn't deserve. He wanted to tell her that he abused her mother, and he did so wrongly, that he finally saw that, but it was too late. All he could think about was one of his eldest sons in that moment, and how he had saved him, even if he couldn't tell him. Osodon was amazed that Kahlip had reach him, but perhaps a little too late. In that moment, Mick shrouded a tear from Karen, but it was the spark of love Kahlip drew from him, and their conversation had been over the previous day. He thought about how he had told Kahlip that he wouldn't make him feel guilty, but Kahlip did something more than that. Kahlip made him truly love again. Mickey Dawn, for the first time felt love, that he glimpsed he may have possessed too long ago to remember, but his son had done it. Kahlip was his inspiration, and at his death, Osodon had made a decision to turn his heart around, and he decided he would do what his son said he couldn't, and that was to be part of the solution. Lastly, he regretted what he told Julius, and that was to be mindful of Lehmich, for he might attempt to steal her. He regretted telling Julius that, but Kahlip would have to work through that with Julius and Karen. There was nothing he could do about that now.

PART II

The Chapter for "I"

There is a sense of me in a team, but it is a measure of self-appreciation, and equally knowing that "I" doesn't make it alone in a team. This was the value of not giving up for Kahlip. He fought hard with his father some time ago, but he realized it was his brothers and sisters he couldn't give up on, let alone the various alien races and even the ones long lost to memory alone now. Kahlip operated on the notion that he would take responsibility appropriately, for what he could do, which he felt would add to the team effort. Never once did he think he was taking responsibility way beyond what he should. He took on his father once and finally felt like he made a point with him. Did it actually work, he wasn't sure, but he tried something. He at least did that whatever it was truly worth. But now he had his grandkids for which to worry. And, eventually Karen. Kahnelle was nice enough to go in his stead to France to reach Karen, when really, it should have been him to do it, but if Kahnelle could at least get her back to Florida, Kahlip could take it from there. As far, as his other grandchild, he had to find her, but he felt like he was at a loss when he got to the address and found that one of two things happened. Either Mickey lied, or whoever had her, moved away, but in either case, he was still on the hunt. While hunting, he couldn't help but think about his girls. He wanted to be with them. He had wanted a family for so long, and felt like he was only a few short steps away from that. In that desire to want a family, Kahlip knew why. He couldn't be close to Kaera and his Plaenellian brothers and sisters, as he wanted to. So, if he could make a family with which to give his heart to, he could have something that represented his heart and what his heart could do. That was why it was equally important to find his other grandchild, Little Lorande. Well, she wasn't little any more. She was roughly Karen's age, but she was his little granddaughter and would always be. Upon that knowledge, went the knowledge that Little Lorande had probably moved out and was on her own by now. But that meant finding her would be that much more difficult, if she wanted to be found. She might have even gotten married or something like that. Ironically, Kahlip didn't realize how close to her he actually was.

Katy showed up again at the motel, right on time. She said hi to Jonas who had just clocked in. She looked at Harvey who was ready to leave. Harvey looked at Katy cheerfully. Katy didn't return his cheer. She spoke up. "You're too cheery for someone that just worked a whole shift." Harvey smiled, as he looked at Katy for his crush on her. "I know…that is why I am cheery." Katy smiled and spoke. "I see." She clocked in and got the run down from Harvey about how the day went. Harvey couldn't stop taking glances at Katy while she straightened up the counter. She turned to him and spoke. "You know…you could be doing this before I get here." Harvey smiled and spoke. "Tomorrow…promise." He continued to look at Katy, as she worked, now, dusting a small bit of dirt from the counter. She spoke up. "How does this happen?" She then turned to Harvey who was still enamored by her. She looked away quickly, and then spoke. "Don't look at me like that. It's like you like me or something." Harvey stopped smiling, as a customer walked in. She turned to Harvey and spoke. "Has it been busy?" Harvey looked at her a second longer like he was before. He finally spoke, as she turned to him for an answer. "The logs are darn near empty. It's been quiet." The customer that walked in approached the counter. She looked at Katy and spoke. "Can I get some water? I have been walking for a while, and I am thirsty." Katy point over at the water fountain by the restroom door. She spoke up. "It's there." Katy smiled at the woman. The woman smiled back and spoke. "Thanks." Katy spoke up. "No problem…you can't go gettin' dehydrated." Harvey watched Katy interact with the woman. Katy was so attractive and her demeanor with customers and people in general was genuine and real. That was what Harvey liked about her. She was a short thing, but attractive. Her dark hair was a pleasant romp through a valley of orchids, his favorite flower. She always had a fresh smell to her no matter what perfume she was wearing. And her green eyes, and small, dark-rimmed glasses made her seem smart, but she was intelligent. He knew that. And, her voice was remnants of the ocean waves to him, as they crashed upon the shore. However, he had to enjoy her from afar, and he knew that. She seemed like she wanted to keep him at arm's length, and he obliged her, but he didn't mind looking, and she always told him not to look at her the way he did, but he ignored her, as always. However, it was those moments that gave him the notions that he had a chance with her, and that she was just waiting for the right moment. He didn't know when that would be, but he hoped it was soon. Katy watched Harvey leave. He was this awkward thing, tall and lanky, a bit pale for her with short brown hair. The guy was obviously different, and didn't know it. That was why she didn't mind him looking at her because eventually he would find out different he was. And, she didn't want to be the one to tell him that he is too happy for her. Besides that, Katy had something she'd been dealing with for too long. It was a family thing…a sordid past of sorts that she had never come to terms with. She thought about her mother who seemingly disappeared at one point. Then, Katy disappeared from the family she thought loved her. It was as if she was sold off, and used and trashed.

Katy went off to live with the Isaacs when she was eleven. Her mother went off to live wherever, and she hadn't seen her again for a long time. It hurt, and she never understood why, which is why she returned to the motel for a job. She wanted to be closer to her roots, even though those roots were seemingly destroyed. Katy never knew her father, and at one point, she thought she had a grandfather, but the situation was confusing because her grandfather was doing things with his mother and aunts that she didn't understand. That was why life with the Isaacs was that much harder. Then, Julius seemingly saved her when he gave her the chance at a job. There was some other man running the motel, but Julius was the one that hired her, and he really never saw the other man much. Then there was Harvey who seemed like he'd been working there forever. She thought about how much her grandmother hurt, and for what was happening to her mother and aunts was why her grandmother was so loving, at least that was what she thought. Her grandmother tried to compensate for what her grandfather was doing. At least that was what Katy thought.

Well her grandmother would only be in her life though, only so long. Katy remembered the police that used to come to the house. After her grandfather would talk to them, and smooth things over, he and her grandmother would fight, and eventually something happened to her grandmother. Then, her grandfather got a new one. She recalled the last time she saw her grandfather. They had come to see him and their grandmother, who was different somehow. He told them the stories of the past and how he was supposedly this big hero, but in real life, Katy hadn't thought much about him, other than for how upsetting he could be to all the family. So, his last hero story was her last. Her mother had seemingly gone from her years ago, and the Isaacs were the ones that brought her to see him. Her cousins were also there, which ironically would be the last time she saw them. She thought about her one cousin, Karen who stayed with her grandparents. And, Katy often wondered why that was, but she rationalized that Karen was perhaps the favorite.

But then Laura Isaacs explained a lot of things to Katy about things, as she had gotten older. And, though she explained things the best she could, one thing that didn't make sense was when Laura said that her grandfather a little off mentally. It was why Katy had come to live with them. She explained that Katy's grandfather didn't see things like most people did. At one point, Laura almost told her that her grandfather was really her father, but she didn't let it out. She explained that her grandfather though, did look at her for being much older than she was. And, to save her and her cousins, the grandchildren were separated from the grandparents, not so much her grandmother, but her grandfather. However, her cousin Karen slipped through the cracks and her grandmother maintained custody of Karen. That was why Katy's name was changed from what it was to Katy. However, when it was, Katy was young enough to accept that the Isaacs wanted to start calling her Katy. Her mother, by this point had no say in any concerning Katy. Katy recalled one thing with being with the Isaacs. She recalled how different things were, and Katy really began to understand being a kid. What Katy didn't understand was that her mother put her into the Isaacs household for how things actually were with Mickey. Lorande would have loved to have had been somewhere else than where her mother Lisa had seemingly dropped her, Frances and Karen off.

However, Katy was already stricken with the Mickey Ellis effect by the time she had come to live with the Isaacs. She had gone to a couple different psychiatrists since she was eleven till she turned eighteen and was seemingly on her own. Katy was supposed to have continued to seek therapy from that point, but she didn't go. Somehow, she began to take the Motel, as therapy, as confusing as that was.

So, Katy sat at the counter of the office. She was bored, when a customer finally came in. However, what was once a customer hopeful, became a man in need of directions. It was strange though. He was looking for directions to something called Heroes Hollow, to which Katy had no idea. She looked at him strangely. He looked at her with frustration. He spoke. "So… you don't know?" She eyed the man a second longer, thinking she might, but then she finally had to tell him that she didn't. The man spoke again. "Well…is there someone that might know?" Katy looked around. She smiled and without being as sarcastic, as she could have been, she spoke. "Nope…sir, I am all you got." The man spoke looking around. "Damn!" Katy spoke up. "Is there something else, I can do for you?" The man looked at her squarely and spoke. He seemed agitated. "NO…I guess not!" Katy had learned to take the good ones with the bad ones for the business. She spoke again. "We got rooms, if you need one." The man looked at her. Thoughtfully, he spoke up. "Well…I guess I could take one for a few hours. It is late." Katy began working on a room for the man. She asked him for his identification.

Then, she asked him the usual questions if he wanted up stairs or downstairs, if he wanted one or two beds. The man looked at her when she asked him that. "Two beds…are you serious!" He spoke, as he reached for his wallet and then handed her his ID. Katy looked at the man, and for the sake of how slow things had been, she had to take this guy's attitude. That was one thing Steve, the motel owner had told her. He said that if it wasn't too bad, then have understanding for the customers and their emotions, setting aside her own. Katy spoke up. "Well, sir, we're running a special on two beds. It's cheaper." The man looked at her, as she said that. Suddenly, his mannerisms changed. He realized how hard on her he was. "Hey…listen…I am sorry about how I talked just then." Katy looked at him and smiled. "No worries, Sir. I'll give you the cheaper rate, and then you can decide if you need the two beds or not. How about that?" The man looked at her and smiled. He spoke. "That'll be great. I will take upstairs if you don't mind." Katy looked at the man, as she was inputting something into the computer. "Not at all, Sir. I will put you real close to the office, and if I have someone that comes in, I will try to get your questions answered about that place you mentioned." The man smiled, as Katy handed him back his identification. She then asked for his payment and handed him his room key and other packet of information. She then told him his check out time. He spoke up when she said that. "I might need the room for a couple days." She smiled and said that would be fine. She explained that he would just need to come in before check out time and pay for another night. He agreed to that and took his key and thanked Katy for her time. Katy smiled and gave him the usual spiel about staying at the Muhndalay.

After the man had left, Katy felt a sigh of relief, and thought about the many Steveisms that had helped her throughout her time there working. She thought about the owner and thought a lot of him. He was so much better than the old guy that owned it, or Julius who ran it then. Steve was different somehow. She didn't fully understand what she felt about him, but it was just different.

He seemed to treat her differently for some reason. She thought about Steve on into the night. She thought again, about how the Steveisms saved her in that moment with that customer. And, as the night went on, Katy ate her lunch, which was a modest apple.

Katy thought about her mother, and how much she missed her, and how much it hurt that she couldn't be with her. She thought about Laura and Tim Isaacs, and how they tried to give her more of a childhood than she had when she was even younger than when they had her. However, the night progressed; she went into the same drab moments of hating her childhood, and then eventually her life. She thought about how she felt most of the time, in darkness and loathing. She thought about how she should have been seeing her therapist, but that didn't work out too well. There was just something about going to someone who, when you broke down their title, they became "The Rapist". She guessed that was why there was such a stigma about going to see "The Rapist". It was as if therapy was meant to rape one's mind, tear it apart, and find out something that would probably not make sense anyway. Too though, eventually Laura and Tim lost interest in her, which hurt. Katy thought it was because she didn't got to see "The Rapist", but they claimed it had nothing to do with that, and they even claimed not to know to what she was talking. But Katy knew they lost interest in her. Maybe she was too much of a job to handle. Katy hated her mother for giving her up.

She had come to a point where being around Steve was therapy, which was weird and unexplainable. Just being around him made her feel, so much better. She needed to be around him more, but she worked opposite the times he was at the motel. She upset Harvey one time because she went off on talking about the owner so much, that he had asked her to stop at one point. He claimed it was just too much to take. He asked if they could talk about something else. Katy just stopped talking at that point. Harvey regretted saying anything, but then it was too late. He realized his jealousy had ruined the moment.

So, instead of talking out loud, she just kept her thoughts to herself, and her and Harvey didn't talk for the rest of the hour until Katy left. Harvey would then watch her like a lost puppy, hopeful of his masters' return. Katy wouldn't even look back though. Harvey didn't realize it, but it was those moments that stopped him and Katy from getting together. It was those things he did, which hurt her. It didn't matter what she wanted to say, she just wanted to be heard. And, if he wouldn't hear her on what she had to say, then he wasn't for her. Besides all that, Katy was screwed up for relationships from how she grew up. Katy almost felt like there was no one on the planet that could relate to her, but maybe Steve with his wonderful Steveisms. It was odd, but Katy had a word for Steve, and it was her favorite word. It was relativity. What Katy didn't realize is that she was an unsung hero of sorts. Katy was a creature that was brought into Ayeraal because of a dying planet, well, that was the motivation for her birth anyway, but that would turn her into an unsung hero. Unsung heroes took responsibility with little or no support from anyone around them because Katy was, by all accounts, alone for whom she was.

A Chapter of Stars

At one point, Katy had taken to the stars for answers, though she didn't know why. Her hobby was the stars. She bought an expensive telescope just because she knew she wouldn't be spending money on anything else. She had been saving for it for months before she finally had enough to get it. The telescope was the only thing she really wanted. She loved to watch the stars and the night skies for hours. She would have her plate of snacks, usually cheesy chips, and peanut butter bread. She would go through two plates easy in the time she spent looking at the stars, which is really why she wanted to work in the daytime. She wanted more nights to watch the stars. There was something about the stars she loved. It seemed more like her home than the ground upon which she stood. It was odd.

But there was a particular night where she found out the most about herself, as she sat looking lovingly into the night skies around her favorite Augustine beach. She found that out about herself by way of the stars, but through someone else. Katy had been sitting in her favorite spot by the old house from her childhood, down the path of the rows of trees aligning the roadway. There was a large open field to the north, which suited her peace and tranquility. She had a lantern lit so she could see the area, but dimly lit because she didn't want to distract her scope from picking up, as many stars as it could. About an hour into her star gazing, someone walked up on her. She had her telescope set up and she had been following a line of stars to the east. There was something about those stars that intrigued her. A familiar voice rang out as she had her eye into the scope. She jumped when she heard the voice. The voice though, was barely audible. Katy turned in the direction of the voice. She spoke up. "Hello…is someone there?" Then she noticed a lone figure in the street lamps far away at the roadside. The figure was close, but it was the light that went far beyond the figure. She had to keep looking and watching the figure. She spoke again. "Hello!" The figure got close enough to speak again, sensing that the person they were talking to couldn't hear them. The figure spoke again. "I said…it's a nice night to watch the stars, isn't it?" The voice was louder that time. Katy heard what was said clearly. She spoke up with a raised voice. "Yes…" The figure got close, and when it was close enough, Katy held up her lantern. She noticed that it was the motel owner. It was Steve! Katy spoke in shock. "What are you doing here?" Steve spoke up quickly. "This is my spot!" Katy looked at him in shock. And, things just got weirder. He spoke again, as he came to standing a few feet away from her. "But usually, I come here during the day. For some reason, I felt the need to get out here under the stars. So, I followed my heart." Katy like the way he said that…followed his heart. She smiled at him. "Yeah…this is my spot too. I put the city lights behind me and I can get more stars in my scope. Sometimes though, I'd like to shoot that damn street lamp out so I could get more darkness." Steve laughed, as she said that. Katy turned around and looked at the dark skies. Steve was at her back. She felt him looking at her, pondering their chance meeting there at the beach. Eventually, he walked up beside her. He spoke quietly. "So, how long have you been gazing?" Katy turned and looked at him briefly. Then, she returned her gaze to the skies overhead. She finally spoke up. "Actually, I think the question would be when do, I stop gazing, because I have been star gazing mentally since I was a kid. I never stop thinking about the stars, which I feel like sometimes are my home." Steve thought about something, as she said that. He spoke up. "Well, you are right, if you think about it. We're in space and among stars. So, really you are enjoying being upon the planet you're on." Katy looked at him and smiled. She spoke up. "I see why you say that, but there is a lot more to it. It's not that simple." She stopped speaking and looked at Steve. "I am an alien here. I don't belong." Steve smiled when she said that. He eyed her inquisitively. "Alien, huh?" Katy returned her gaze to the skies, as he said that. She spoke up. "Yeah…my adopted parents wanted me to see a mind rapist when I was a kid because I told them I was an alien." Steve looked at her strangely. He spoke up. "Do you mean a therapist?" She turned to him and spoke. "No…I mean "The Rapist"." Steve chuckled because he realized what she was doing in saying it the way she did. He spoke up. "I see." He looked at her, as she stood looking at the stars. "Well, you do realize that in a sense, most of us are aliens." Katy looked at him quickly, then, looked upward. She spoke up in that voice that strained her voice because she stretched her neck. "Tell me something I don't know." Steve stood thoughtfully next to her. He looked at her, then upwards too. He finally spoke. "Well…did you know that there are other planets like this one that have gone through almost the same transformations, as this one?" Katy looked at him and then back up. She spoke. "Interesting." Steve spoke again. "So, you knew that too?" Katy looked at him, and then at the skies. She spoke. "I told you to tell me something I don't know." Steve thought about something. He spoke up. "So… you are just an alien. It sounds like you don't know where you come from." Katy looked at him thoughtfully. That was a smart comment. She eyed him another minute. "So…that's it…you are going to tell me where I came from because you think I don't know." Katy stopped speaking and eyed him. She spoke again. "That's what I don't know?" Steve smiled and sat. Then, he laid down in the grass looking up. "There are a great many things I can tell you, Katy that might remind you." Katy sat next to him, as he finished speaking. "So…where am I from?" Steve turned to her and smiled. "Well…it is a long story, Katy." Katy looked at him feeling the sense of relativity she had with Steve. "I got all night, boss." Steve turned to her and smiled. "Out here I am just Steve, okay?" Katy smiled again. She spoke. "Alright." She waited for him to speak again. "Well, you might be from Socudosuul, or Puhlosia, and then there is Uhvia and Maervuhn or Moarluhn. You definitely don't seem like the Rosicrucian type or Aubrahteerian type." Katy listened, as he spoke. She thoughtfully considered what he said. Most of all, she liked how she was feeling at the moment. She didn't feel so alien. She spoke up. "Who are the Rosis and the Aubries you mentioned?" He smiled as she said that. He spoke, as he continued to look upward. "Well, the Rosicrucians are what we have in our scientists to date. And the Aubrahteerians are the religious officials of today." Katy thought about what he said. "Well, I definitely ain't one of those. What about the others?" Steve thoughtfully turned to her, and spoke. "Well, there are the Uhvians, and the Puhlosians." Katy looked at him, as he spoke. She spoke up with interest. "Who are they?" "Well, the Uhvians are one of the oldest races. However, they have long since died out. They came from the planet Uhvia long ago. You could say that they were saved in coming here. The Puhlosians here are what you would consider the gay population." Katy chuckled when he said that. She spoke up. "I think Harvey is Puhlosian." Steve turned to her and spoke. "Really?" Katy thought about Harvey instantly. She looked at Steve and spoke. "Yeah...really...he is in the closet...severely." Steve thoughtfully smiled and looked upwards. He spoke. "I never gave it much thought I guess." He considered Harvey in the moment. "Oh yeah...I was talking about you to him one time, and he got pissed off. I think I reminded him that you weren't from Puhlosia. And, it upset him. I sensed his jealousy. I don't think he was jealous because I was talking about you. He is angry because he would rather talk about you more, but that might pull him out of the closet. I think he wants to use me to stay in the closet." Steve thought about what she said. He spoke up. "That's sad." As Katy sat there, she thought about something. "You know, that what you said about the Puhlosians being the gay population makes sense. I mean...look at it, only other gays can really relate to other gays." Steve thought about something, as she said that. "Yeah...what you don't realize is how things were long ago when every alien race was capable of interacting with each other in pretty much the same way it happens now, but just a shade differently. The difference now, though, is that everyone seems to be stuck with only an unknown point of departure. It's why you feel alien without anyone to relate to." Katy sat silent a moment, as he said that. She was amazed that he spoke to her heart, as he did. She thought about something, and spoke up. "Well...since we're talking. I always felt some strange connection to you or sense or relativity...it's weird, I know, and I probably shouldn't have said that with you being the boss and all." Steve turned to her and smiled. He spoke. "No, Katy, don't worry about that. It's nothing." As he said that, he considered something. He turned to look at Katy, and suddenly, he thought about Lorande. He had seen Katy on many occasions, but never did she strike him the way she did in that moment. "To be honest with you Katy that was nice to know...now I don't feel so alien." Katy laughed, as he said that. And, suddenly, Steve was reminded of Lorande again. That was Lorande's laugh. Steve knew it. He turned to Katy one more time. He studied her, and in one instance, he thought he knew where his last granddaughter could be found. It was right next to him, but he dare not say anything to her or even mention it, but he did think to talk to Lorande.

Steve looked at his watch and noticed the time. It was getting late, as it already hit morning time the next day. Katy noticed him eyeing his watch. She looked at hers. He spoke up. "Well, Katy, I have had the time of my life, but I have to get going." Katy thoughtfully considered what he said, and how sad it made her feel. She looked at her boss and spoke. "It was a good time, wasn't it?" Steve spoke up. "Yeah, Katy it was, but you know what, I would like to come back if you don't mind. When will you be gazing again?" Katy looked excitedly at Steve. "Well, I have these two days off. I will probably be back tonight." Steve appeared hopeful when she said that. "Great...it's a date then." Katy smiled, as she eyed Steve. She knew what he meant. She spoke with a hopeful chirp in her voice. "Sure." Steve left. Katy spent a couple more hours there with her telescope and the beloved stars. In that time, she couldn't help but think of Steve and what they had been through the last couple hours. She was excited that they found each other at that spot. Suddenly, life seemed to take a sudden turn for her. If not for Steve, for her definitely.

Kahlip got up the next morning late. He thought about stargazing with Katy. He couldn't believe that the stars brought him and his granddaughter together. It was amazing how it worked. Once up, he didn't even make the coffee. He couldn't. He needed to get on the phone and call Penny. He grabbed his cell phone and dialed her, and while waiting for her to answer, he went out onto the back porch and sat. He listened, as the phone rang and rang. Then her voicemail came on. He left her a message to call him. Now, he could make the coffee.

He went to the kitchen and started up a pot. Then, rested against the counter thoughtfully. He had been looking for his granddaughter not too long ago when he came up against a very hard dead end. He felt discouraged from that, but then, as if by magic, he found her. He knew it was little Lorande. He knew it. She must have changed her name, darkened her hair, but it was her. He knew it. He sat there against the counter thoughtfully. He couldn't get over the fact that he found her seemingly out of nowhere she just appeared. He smiled, as he thought about how they had talked into the wee hours. He really didn't want to leave, but he had to. He had to check on how Jonas was doing at the hotel. He'd been working the office and counter for his third week.

The coffee maker finished pouring a hot fresh, aromatic pot. Kahlip grabbed a cup and filled it with the proper condiments. Then, he added the most important element. The coffee took his nose prisoner, as he stood pouring the first delectable cup of the day. In the midst of that pour, the front door opened. Then the door shut, and Penny was in the house. She spoke "Kahlip!" Kahlip heard her voice, and looked up thoughtfully where he stood. He was staring at the cabinets when he spoke. "And, the magic continues…" He picked up his cup and spoke again. "In here!" He turned around with his cup in hand. Penny entered the kitchen. He walked towards her. Penny spoke up quickly. "What was so important? I got your message." Kahlip looked at her with a sense of excitement. He spoke up. "I found little Lorande!" Penny tried to hide it, but she looked at him, as if her balloon just got popped by that little neighborhood punk. That was it! That was what was so important. Kahlip could tell Penny didn't share in his excitement. He sensed she didn't share in the thrill. Kahlip took his excitement, his cup, and his appreciation for the fact he found little Lorande, and went to the back porch to celebrate by himself. Before he left the kitchen, he looked at Penny and spoke in a dull, plain unexcited tone to match her attitude. "That's all...I found only another important member of my family...that's it." Penny should have felt bad for her lack of excitement, but she wasn't good at lying about her feelings. She watched Kahlip leave the kitchen feeling rejected with his tail, seemingly between his legs. As Kahlip walked through the living room, and before he stepped out onto the porch, he was thoughtful that Penny wasn't turning out to be the thrill he thought she would be once. There was something about her that seemed she wanted Kahlip to fail at things, instead of succeed. That felt odd, but he couldn't feel anything different about her. He made a promise to himself that he would figure her out, or it would just have to be over. He didn't want the downer around that she could be. As he stepped out onto the porch, he realized that Penny seemed to be showing some kind of different shade of gray from the brightness she was once so full of. Penny needed to do something to get in tune with his life and what he was trying to achieve. Kahlip looked forward to the coming days where he and Katy could star gaze together. It was going to be the time of his life. He knew it.

✝

A Chapter for Us

Over the next few weeks, Kahlip met with Katy, as he said he would. He even started researching star charts. And, he bought some to give to Katy. On another one of those nights, Kahlip had an idea. Katy had been set up when he arrived. He greeted her warmly. "Hi Kat." That was another thing. He nicknamed her Kat, short for Katy. She liked it and it stuck. She looked at him and smiled. "Hey, Steve, did you bring the chips? Those cheesy ones?" Steve smiled at her and spoke easily and with excitement. "Of course!" He tossed her the bag. He spoke again, but he brought something else. He spoke again as he held up a long rolled, and what appeared to be, poster sized paper. Kat spoke up. "What's that?" Steve looked at her and smiled before he spoke. "Something else you don't know." Kat looked at him inquisitively. She became curious. Steve walked up to her and held it out for her to take. Kat smiled, looking at him, as she reluctantly held her hand out. Steve spoke again. "Go ahead…take it…it's yours." Kat felt more comfortable then. She never was comfortable with gifts. Since she'd been on her own, what she wanted was what she could buy, and that was it. Steve spoke up, as she took it lightly in her grasp. "You don't have to look at it now, but when you get a chance later on, take a look, and tell me what you think." Kat smiled, as she eyed what seemed to be a poster. She spoke up simply. "Okay." Steve looked around. Kat had everything set up. She even brought a cooler to sit on instead of standing to look through the scope. Steve spoke up. "So, brought drinks, huh." Kat smiled and spoke. "Yeah…and I thought we could use the cooler as a seat." Steve looked at the cooler at that point and spoke. "Good idea." Steve thought about something in that moment. He looked at Kat. "Hey…I figured out something else you might not know." Kat looked at him plainly, as he spoke. She thought about what he said. She spoke with interest. She was curious. He looked around thoughtfully at first. He appeared to be finding the words or something like that. He spoke up. "Well, I thought about something. It was what you said about telling you something you don't know." He stopped speaking to look at her. He was appreciating her for her look. Suddenly, he noticed that her hair was changing. It seemed lighter than usual, even in the dark under one dim lantern. Kat looked at him with interest. He felt it. He spoke again. "Well, I can tell you the story of the Universes. I bet you've never heard that." Kat looked at him and spoke finally. "Universes?" She was more than curious now. She noted how he spoke to her knowledge seeking side, which had become more awakened since they've been meeting on these late night rendezvous'. He looked at her and spoke. "Well, there was a time when consciousness on any planet was immortal. This meant that when you existed upon a planet, was where you existed always. There was no death and no birth, but you could visit other planets and other Universes then." He stopped speaking, noticing she was intently listening. He spoke again. "See, the Universes were much like the homes we exist within where all these Universes are part of a bigger structure. For example, the wires in your house are one Universe, then the pipes are another, and the walls were another, and so on. Understand?" Kat smiled and nodded. He spoke again. "However, at that point everything was fixed into a specific location. And, where there was this state of constant, consciousness could move between Universes and visit other worlds. Every Universe served a purpose in contrast to the others. Every manner of consciousness too, served in this regard. What is important to remember is that every Universe had its purpose." Kat thought about something, as he said that. She spoke up. "So…what happened?" Steve looked at her. He spoke. "What do you mean?" She spoke up. "Well, you said that there was no death and no birth. What happened that there is birth now?" Steve looked at her thoughtfully before he spoke. He recalled everything that happened in that moment. "Well…with every manner of consciousness, like I said, had a purpose. However, there were two individuals, a male and female that was angered for how things were because they existed beyond the single Universes in a state of what the Universes together made up. You could say they ran all the Universes, making sure everything stayed upon its continuum, till one day they decided that they didn't want to do this any longer. In other words, you could say that they stopped taking care of the house; it no longer began to function as one unit. Pipes began to leak they wouldn't fix. The wiring got old and began to show, in which fires could start. The walls began to get holes in them. They were letting the house go. Sadly, the truth of the matter is that they consciously were trying to change the Universes." Kat spoke up interrupting him. "Well, who were they…what are their names?" Steve looked at her thoughtfully. He spoke up. "For the sake of the moment, we'll call them Osodon and Oosiah." Kat listened intently, and tucked what he said neatly away in her memory. He spoke again. "Anyway, this was how the house falling apart makes understanding the Universes better. In the beginning, every consciousness coalesced. This means fit well together to produce the effect in being a unit, as in the elements in a house." Kat continued to listen intently. She seemed more intrigued at this point. He continued to speak. "Birth and death came into play when the water pipes burst, which kind of represents the birth and death thing where consciousness was now, instead of being filtered into the mainstream of the house, was crossing borders affecting the structure of the house. See, the water in the pipes that come out of faucets was like immortal consciousness that could cross the Universal boundaries the right way. Water is then introduced into the internal part of the house into the sinks and tubs or showers and becomes known. However, pipes that burst are the break within the Universes that forged birth and death of consciousness because it forged consciousness that was destructive. This is the same with wiring that can cause a house to burn up. Electricity running through the wall in things called conduit, eventually pour into what are known as outlets. Then, the electricity can be used properly, as in immortal consciousness that could visit other worlds the right way. However, the wiring became shoddy, and fires began. This is the plight in Consciousness going between worlds the wrong way, as in birth and death, to extents that it began destroying worlds because the potential behind immortal beings was being filtered through a planetary equation or makeup that was alien to it." Steve stopped speaking, and eyed Kat. She seemed to have a tear in the corner of her eye. Steve spoke up. Kat just looked at him. She couldn't speak for the moment. She wiped her eye and looked at Steve. "Kat…what's wrong?" Kat didn't speak. She looked at Steve solemnly. Steve spoke again. "Kat?" Kat finally broke her silence when he said her name again. Her mind was in the past. She spoke. "I had a friend when I was younger." She stopped speaking and eyed Steve thoughtfully. Steve looked at her for saying that. He thought he knew where she was going with that. She continued to speak. "This friend died in a house fire. It seemed an arsonist started it. So, when you said that I was reminded of my friend." Steve felt bad for her. Kat continued to speak. However, in her mind, Kat was reminded of her cousins who died because of the fire. She just didn't want to admit it to Steve. "This friend was family to me more than some mere friend." Steve looked at her compassionately. He felt an ache in his chest for her. Kat…I'm sorry." Kat wiped her eyes again. Steve thoughtfully looked at her. He spoke up. "Kat, this is why the Rosicrucians and Aubrahteerians were so important. It's why psychiatrists and psychologists are so important because they act as plumbers and electricians and firefighters and policemen, trying to aid the various alien forms of consciousness that exist on the planets in the Universes, as Osodon and Oosiah had destroyed the various borders between the Universes." Kat looked at him. She thought about something. She spoke up quickly. "So, I guess I shouldn't look at therapy as a form of mind rape." Steve laughed when she said that. He eyed her with a light heart. He spoke. "Unfortunately, what you are going through is the stigma attached to these professions, but it's why, which is important." He stopped speaking and took a second to enjoy the moment there with his granddaughter. Kat looked at him, as the hours ticked away into the night. There was a slight breeze in that moment. Kat brushed her hair from her face, as she looked at Steve. She listened. He spoke again. "Psychiatry isn't the enemy, Kat, you're right. These stigmas, against psychology were put upon the minds of people through what Osodon and Oosiah had begun and continue to date." Kat looked at him curiously. She spoke up. "What?" Steve smiled kind of knowing she didn't understand. He spoke again. "Yes, Kat, these professions were created upon the notions of acting against what Osodon and Oosiah had done. One of the best ways to thwart the effort of these effects is to create a stigma against them. Osodon and Oosiah began long ago trying to ruin these professions. They created the negative view behind them. The supposed crazy man doesn't want to go to someone that supposedly deals with crazy people for the effect of feeling crazy for it. See?" He stopped speaking for her understanding. Kat nodded in a half-hearted kind of way. She sat thoughtfully, looking at Steve. He continued to speak. "See, many of these professions were meant to empower people, but Osodon and Oosiah have twisted their purpose. Every time someone pokes fun at someone for their mental instability, that's Osodon and Oosiah. Every time someone thinks ill of a doctor, that's Osodon and Oosiah. Every time a supposed doctor fails at healing, that's Osodon and Oosiah." Kat looked at him strangely for what he said last. She spoke up. "That last one really got me. How can Osodon and Oosiah be responsible for that?" Steve smiled because he thought it would throw her off. He spoke up. "Well, Kat, doctors do make mistakes or do they. What if the effect on the person, for what Osodon and Oosiah, had done was too great? What if the individual with the illness had no chance at survival because of the effect of being on this planet is too much for them? I say that questioningly, but I mean it factually. Doctors are only helping, as equally, as shrinks are. The point is that we are all going through the torment for how Osodon and Oosiah wanted to take care of the House of all Universes combined. Too, if Osodon and Oosiah can create enough stigmas about them, any one of these professions will go away, which is what Osodon and Oosiah really want. They don't want Ayeraalians to succeed." Kat looked at him curiously when he said that. She spoke up. "Wait…Ayerians…what was that?" Steve smiled. He spoke up. "This planet that you stand upon is Ayeraal, which makes everyone on it, Ayeraalians." Kat still looked at him strangely. He smiled again. "Kat that is another thing you have to know, which ironically is what you don't know. So, there I am telling you something you don't know. This planet was named, Earth, however, that is the evidence of the state of consciousness on this planet. This planet was once the home of the Anthrocytes. They powered it, as well as every other alien race for their home planet. So, technically, we're Ayeraalians, not Earthlings, and sadly, not even relative to the Anthrocytes of old." Kat looked at him when he said that. She spoke up. "Wow…that is something I don't know." She looked at Steve in awe. She spoke again. "Wow… you are being wasted …Steve…how did you come to own a motel? You seem so much smarter than that." Steve smiled at her. He appreciated her sentiment, but he was humble enough to know better than to think he was worth more than what he was. That was when he was motivated to tell her about Plaenellians. He just looked at her and spoke plainly. "I can appreciate your astute assessment of me, but I am nothing more than what I am. Kat, we're all working to the same goal essentially, whether we do it consciousness or not, we do have our moments of weakness." Kat looked at him plainly. She spoke. "You are modest. I will give you that." she laughed and turned to the scope and took a quick glance in it thoughtfully. She considered something from everything he'd said. She turned to him quickly. "So, what's going to happen then? I mean…we're in a world of shit, pardon my expression. I get that from one of my aunts that I haven't seen in a long time ago." Steve automatically thought of Frances. He smiled, thinking yep, you sound just like Frances. He just smiled at her. She looked at him thoughtfully, as he just smiled. She spoke up. "What's the smile for?" he looked at her another brief moment before he spoke. "You just remind me of someone that I haven't seen in a long time. I miss her." Kat looked at him thoughtfully. She sensed his emotion, and glimpsed his big heart. He spoke again. "But to answer your question, that is the point behind everything I have said. All of us have to work together to get through these days." He stopped speaking thoughtfully. He looked at Kat warmly feeling his heart gleaming. He spoke up. "Kat, we have to seek the higher perspective behind all of us. These doctors and head doctors don't have to do what they do. Unlike what Osodon and Oosiah have started behind the stigmas and theses professions, these aliens from other planets come with a purpose, which is where doctors of all sorts are coming from. It's not about the money they can make, as much as it is believed. Think about it Kat, that the purpose behind moving money around, was intended, as well. Earning money is the side effect for their true purpose. So, they get to have the more expensive things… things that really mean nothing. It's about responsibility, Kat. And, they take a lot of it." Kat thoughtfully listened. She looked at Steve and spoke. "I think I see what you are saying." Steve thought about something in that moment, and he verged saying the most profound thing he could ever say. He looked at her with finality and opened his mouth. "Kat, what I am trying to give you is something that is applicable knowledge to help you, and ironically, this understanding underlies everything around you. It's what most alien consciousness on this planet cannot aspire to possess. Doctors don't have an ego problem; they have their defenses against those who would look at them for how Osodon and Oosiah want them to be seen. If Osodon and Oosiah had their way, Rosicrucians and Aubrahteerians wouldn't exist on Ayeraal." Just then, Kat thought about something, as he said that. She looked at Steve with a certain look. She spoke up. "Steve…forgive me, but this is something I needed. You are my therapist." Steve laughed when she said that. He eyed her warmly. She felt something in her heart, which she thought was long lost once. She spoke again. "Steve, I was just thinking about my mother. I held such hatred in my heart for her and what she did to me. She gave me up, after she put me through the hell of having a child-molesting grandfather. But I think I understand her a little bit better from talking with you. I see that our differences could have a very firm reason. I think I may understand what I thought was her weakness." Steve looked at her, hiding his emotion in that moment. Steve spoke up. "I am glad to have helped." Kat jumped from her seat and ran and hugged him. He seemed shocked at first, but he realized he was now getting that much closer to his granddaughter, even though she didn't realize who he truly is to her.

By this time, the sun was coming up. Kat and Steve both noticed. They decided that since the stars were disappearing, so should they. They packed everything up, and Steve offered to help Kat home. She thanked him, but admitted that she was only a few minutes away from home. They left together, and eventually separated. Steve went to his car. Kat went home on foot with her telescope in one hand and the rolling cooler in another. Before they parted, Steve asked Kat for another date in a couple days, for which Kat agreed. He smiled at her when he knew he had to leave her, and Kat felt his emotion and smiled back.

✝

The Chapter of "We"

Little did Steve know, his time with Katy and their many ventures star gazing, had helped her, enough that she began searching for her mother. Katy knew it would be a long journey, but one she wanted to endure because of how Steve had helped her to feel about everything. He helped her to find understanding. He also helped her to love herself more, which in turn, helped her to love others more. His aid also came in the form of what he didn't say, as well. Katy came to understand that things, for people on Ayeraal, as he called it, were hard already. What people didn't need was any excessive negativity from her because people were already suffering. Ironically, whether or not they were Ayeraalians, as he said, they were people, and aliens too were people because she finally came to understand what the people are. People aren't strangers; they aren't human things, even though they could be referred to as such. People were trying to exist, as she was. One thing she realized Steve tried to convey to her was that being is a matter of loving, plain and simple. And, that was what she was going to feel for her mother no matter what. And, Katy began with trying to contact the Isaacs whom tried to show her love, unlike what she thought. That was something, Steve showed her as well.

Kahlip was in the living room later that day. He was relaxing, and thinking about that night and early morning with Kat. He couldn't believe how he felt at that moment. Suddenly, Penny walked in the house. He called to her. She didn't answer, but later she appeared in the doorway to the living room. He looked up at her from the sofa. He spoke. "So, how have you been?" Penny just stared at him. She seemed like she was annoyed that he would even ask. More and more each day, Kahlip was beginning to notice things about her that made her seem like she was three different people in one. He looked at her with expectation. Finally she spoke. "I am fine!" She turned and stormed off. In that moment, as she stormed off, Penny couldn't help but hate having to put up with Kahlip. She pondered why she had to be the one to deal with him. She just wanted to kill him right then and there. She wanted to just do away with him. It was beginning to be too much for her to handle. She felt too angry around him all the time. She didn't like feeling the way she did. She thought about what her sister said about having to be patient. But she couldn't do that. Then, Penny had an idea. She had to leave the house instantly. She grabbed her purse and left without so much, as a word about where she was going. And, as always, Kahlip was left to wonder, but he was getting to the point where he didn't know if he could handle Penny any longer.

Suddenly, Kahlip's phone rang. He answered it. "Hello." A male voice answered him. "Kahlip…this will be the only time I can speak to you…I will not call again." The voice stopped, and Kahlip was left searching for an understanding of the voice. It wasn't recognizable. It spoke again. "We met a long time ago… in the early battle with Mick Ellis…just call me Dave." Kahlip looked around the living room, deeply thoughtful. "Okay Dave… what can I do for you?" There was a coughing sound in the phone, as Kahlip squinted to hear more clearly, what was in the phone. Kahlip spoke up. "Dave?" Dave spoke again. "I am here…but to warn you, Kahlip…about…the…gait." He stopped speaking with more coughing. Kahlip listened, as the man's voice was broken up, as equally, as were his words. The coughing eventually ceased. Dave then continued to speak. "The gait, Kahlip, be watchful of the gait…the gait is…" Suddenly, there was a gunshot in the background, and Dave stopped speaking abruptly. Kahlip spoke up. "Dave?" Suddenly, his phone went dead silent, as if someone hung up the other phone. Kahlip closed his. He looked around. He pondered what the man said about the gait. Be watchful of the Gait. Kahlip thought about that, but he would have to leave it alone because there wasn't much to go on from what the man that wanted to be known, as Dave, had said. Kahlip was in the least, curious about his strange phone call, but even that he couldn't ponder too much with little to go on about it. So, Kahlip pretty much had to go about his days, as if he never got the call.

Penny stood looking at her sister by the northern cornered wall at the mall, and Penny stood looking at her sister. She spoke up. "I can't do this any longer, Sis. I just cannot!" Penny spoke up. "Pen, you have to keep going." Pen looked at her sister with frustration. "You cannot take over for me? He won't know." Penny looked at her sister, feeling for her but helpless to help her. "You know why, Pen. I am busy with my own little thing going on." Pen spoke up. "Let's trade jobs!" Penny stared at Pen. "Don't be ridiculous, Sis. You know that won't work. You cannot do what I am doing." Pen spoke up. "Look what John Horn and Darion Knight achieved, Sis. We can too!" Penny looked at her sister, feeling hungry, suggested they go get something to eat in the mall. Pen agreed with her sister, and they entered the mall for a bite, while Pen tried to convince her sister that they should trade jobs. Eventually they got some food and Pen took her pleading with her sister to the lunch table. Penny maintained that she couldn't because she was needed elsewhere. Pen thought about something. She spoke up. "Let's switch for a day. How about that? Just a day." Penny seriously considered that. Her last statement made Penny really consider it. Pen spoke up. "Penny, we are doing this remember. I think I am failing with him. You need to take over for at least a day. You have to get me back on track with him." Penny thought about something in that moment. She spoke up. "Hey don't forget what *WE* already did for you, sis. Remember…you cut your hair, and we had to match it. We couldn't look different from you."

Katy finally made contact with Laura, who agreed to meet her in a couple hours. Katy had been getting ready to go. She was getting excited to see Laura again. After she put the last finishes touches on getting ready, Katy looked at herself in the mirror thoughtfully. She felt ready to face Laura. She thought about what she was going to say to her, but she finally decided that she would have to let the moments flow as they would. There was one thing she knew. She was going to apologize for how she treated her and Tim. For that, she was truly sorry. She finally realized that she and Tim weren't the issue. It was her the whole time. She left the house on her bike. It was an old ten-speed she bought at a yard sale, but it worked and well for its age. She was to meet Laura at Dugan Park at the corner of Phelps and Second in West Augustine. That was the park that Tim and Laura used to take her to when she was much younger. She recalled those days, as she rode through the many street blocks to reach the park. It was a nice day for a ride, and she was glad she chose the bike. Laura had offered to pick her, even after the way she treated them when she left after turning eighteen.

Katy finally reached Phelps and Second and noticed the park. She didn't see Laura's car but she went on to the park anyway. She put her bike in the bike rack and locked it up. She looked around and still didn't see any sign of Laura. Katy went on to the bench where Laura used to sit and watch her play. In that moment, Katy began to watch the children at play on the grounds where she used to romp. She imagined that was how Laura used to feel watching her. The children laughed and played, but suddenly, something Steve said struck her. She thought about the children that were playing. She thought about how seemingly innocent they were about what was going on. Suddenly, Katy seemed like she was experiencing another side of what Steve admitted to her. Suddenly, she felt for the children she watched, admiring their innocent romping through the sand of the sandbox, the swinging on high swings, and the plop of the teeter-totter, as one child takes the high ground, and the other, the low ground. Katy recalled herself at play, and how innocent she seemingly was. She thought of herself long ago, in contrast to what Steve said. Suddenly, she felt saddened by what faced those children or what they didn't know lie near to them in an aged planet. She thought about what she didn't know she faced at their age. She thought about a great many things in that time waiting for Laura. But the biggest thing about the moment was the future for those children. She thought about what Steve said more and more. And, suddenly, she wanted to be with him again to get some kind of perspective on the future.

In that moment, as she pondered Steve, Laura pulled up in her car. She watched, as Laura seemed to look around the park. She assumed Laura was looking for her. She stood and waved to Laura with a smile. Laura finally saw her. Laura parked and exited her car. She carried nothing with her. Katy started walking to Laura. She seemed nervous as the two of them closed in on each other. Katy was smiley and bubbly, but Laura was apprehensive. They finally reached each other. "Hi Laura." Laura looked at Katy when she said that. She wasn't smiling. She was emotionless. "Katy…I am sorry, but we're to have no further communications from now on." Katy looked at Laura in shock. Katy tried to speak. "But, I just wanted to apolo…" Laura interrupted her. "I know dear…but…you see… it is Tim. He hasn't been able to deal with the past. He wasn't comfortable with me coming to meet with you." Katy looked at Laura, and how she'd aged through the few years since she's been gone. Laura once had long blond hair. But now it had barely visible streaks of gray, and she was keeping it short. Laura had a few more wrinkles than before. Her lips seemed like they were drying. Laura looked at Katy only a few moments longer, before she started to back away from her. Katy spoke up quickly. "Laura…wait…" Laura turned to leave. Katy grabbed her by the arm. She spoke with a sense of urgency. "Laura, please." Laura turned to her and spoke with anger. "Katy…I AM SORRY, BUT I NEED TO GO." Laura struggled to free her arm, as she spoke. Katy spoke up pleading with Laura. "Laura…" Laura stopped struggling and glared at Katy. She spoke up. "Katy…your family has an evil to it that we were not made aware of when we decided to take you in. It has brought us grief since. Tim has health problems now…I feel like I am dying all the time…Katy, please let me go." As Laura said that, she let a single tear fall from her face. Katy watched it fall, as she begged her to let her go. Katy finally let go of her arm.

She was shocked by what Laura said, and it hurt. Katy stood there and watched Laura walk away. In the distance, a police officer approached Laura to see if she was alright. Apparently, he watched the whole thing, but Laura brushed him off. Then, the officer looked at Katy, who was wiping her own eyes at that point. She and the officer just shared a brief stare. Then, Katy began to walk to her bike. The officer watched her. Katy felt it. But eventually, she was too far away for the officer to see her. Katy couldn't help but think of things she didn't know about the family growing up. What was Laura talking about? Deep down and suddenly, Katy felt a stronger need to find her mother to find out what happened back then.

The Chapter for Lacking & Knowing

That night, Katy sat in her room, tucked neatly into her bed and cried. She couldn't get the images of Laura out of her mind, and what she claimed about her family. She mentioned Evil. It made no sense. Katy thought the Isaacs were strong people, which meant that there must have been something to this evil she mentioned. She knew there was something off about her family, but never did she once consider it evil. Katy had to find her mother, and now she wouldn't have Laura or Tim to find her. Katy suddenly, felt all alone, and it didn't feel good. Suddenly, she thought about Steve. She needed him. She instantly made her mind up to find him. Katy hopped out of her bed with determination. She threw on some shorts and a pink loose tee. She ran out of the house and to her bike. She unchained it and hopped on it and rode. She rode fast to the motel, the fastest she had ever gone on a bike. She was there in about ten minutes. She didn't live too far away. She hopped off her bike and saw Jonas at the counter. He wasn't busy. She ran into the office and up to the counter. She faced Jonas easily and with that continued determination. She spoke up quickly. "Jonas, I need to talk to Steve." Jonas looked at her for what seemed like her distress. He spoke up. "Sorry, Katy, he isn't here." Katy looked at Jonas quickly and thoughtfully. "I know…I need his address." Jonas looked at her at first, as though she was crazy. He spoke up. "Katy, that's against the rules…" Katy interrupted him. "I don't give a shit…Jonas…can you give me his address?" Jonas looked at her with surprise or rather shock at first. Then, noticing her determined gait, he gave up the ship. "Okay, kid, but it's your butt, not mine." Jonas looked up Steve's address in the computer. He wrote it down, and slid the paper to Katy. Katy grabbed it and ran out the door.

Kahlip sat on the back porch in contemplation. He sat quietly and alone. He was staring at the stars of the evening sky, thinking of Kat with a warm sensation in his chest. He felt so much for that little girl. It was so wonderful. He enjoyed their moments there under the stars, as they chatted. He smiled at times, as he thought about her mannerisms. He smiled for how much of his daughters she had in her personality and her face. She was a reminder of Lorande, but she could see Frances in her, especially her mannerisms. Frances had the mouth when she was younger. Kahlip remembered that, and actually, it became a staple thought with Kahlip about the dirty mouth his daughter Frances had, but he couldn't say nothing about it for what those girls were going through when they were growing up. He didn't fault her for it. As the night went on, more and more stars showed through the clearing skies. Suddenly, from the back porch he thought he heard a knock at the front door, which was possible considering how quiet it was at that moment, but instead of going through the house, he went to the front from the back. He walked slowly, and spoke. "I'm 'round here!" He continued to walk. Suddenly, he heard footsteps on the driveway coming towards him. He continued to walk. Then, suddenly, Katy appeared in front of him. He stopped suddenly and looked at her. He thought about how he was just thinking about her, then, she shows up. There again was that magic. He spoke up quickly. "Kat…what are you doing her…is everything okay?" Katy looked at him and then started crying hard before him. He couldn't help but go to her. She ran to him and they hugged, while she bore just about every tear she had to bear in his shirt. He spoke up. "Oh…Katy…it'll be okay." He helped her out of his embrace gently. He looked at her. Her makeup smeared. He spoke. "I know what you need… some hot chocolate and a good ear. I got some of both." He put a hand around her shoulders and helped her into the house. He spoke again. "Why don't you go into the living room while I make up a cup of some hot chocolate?" Katy agreed to that. He went to the kitchen, and she went into the living room. Kahlip couldn't believe that Katy was now in his house. He marveled over that fact, as he withdrew some milk from the refrigerator, and two cups, and a packet of cocoa mix from the cupboard. He was curious though that it must have been an emergency for her to get his address to need to talk to him. He finished up the cups of chocolate and went into the living room, where Katy had found his only family pictures he put upon the walls. She was standing, eyeing them intricately when he walked into the room. Katy was pointing to one, and she turned to look at him. Kahlip half smiled, as she looked at him. Her mouth dropped open. He spoke. "That's you…I know." Katy then turned to the picture again. Kahlip went to the end table and put the two cups down, and sat at the edge of the sofa. He looked at Katy, who was engulfed in the pictures on the wall. Kahlip spoke up. "I stole that one from your grandmother before she died." Katy turned to him with tears. He thought they were left over from when he found her in the front yard. She turned to him and spoke with emotion in her throat. "Why didn't you tell me?" Kahlip spoke up. "Katy, I only realized I found you on one of the nights that we spent star gazing. I didn't have time to tell you, but I have been more than motivated to contact your mother lately." Katy couldn't believe what she was hearing. She spoke up with excitement. "You know where mom is!" Kahlip looked at her for her emotions. He spoke again. "Now, Katy…I have wanted to show up in your mother's life, but I have held back. See, I have been watching over your mother for some time now. It's a long story, but to make it short, I have been Uncle to your mother, but that was what your grandmother wanted." Kahlip stopped speaking and looked at her. She thought about what he said. "It's complicated kiddo." Katy spoke up. Her heart was racing by this point. "But you know where she is?" Kahlip took up a cup of the hot liquid beside him. He stood and offered it to Katy. "Yes…of course, I know where she is, but I am kind of waiting to see if she will figure out that I am her father enough to want to find me." Katy took the hot cup delicately and eyed him for his words. She felt thrilled to hear that. She spoke up. "Well…I want to know where!" Kahlip looked at her thoughtfully. "Katy…that's not wise right now to try to find her." Katy studied him. She couldn't believe what she heard. At first, when she spoke, she sounded angry, then, her demeanor changed. "NOT WISE! Why not?" Kahlip spoke up. "It's another long one, kiddo." Katy studied him. "I don't understand." Kahlip stood and walked to the sliding glass doors. He spoke up. "It is long and complicated, Katy. I wish it were simple." He Stopped speaking, and turned to her. "Let's just say that right now she is safe because she is thought to be less of a threat. You see, it has to deal with who your father is, Katy." Katy studied him. She studied him at great lengths. She considered what he said. She spoke up. "And, who is my father." He spoke up, as he looked at her. "It's complicated Katy." Katy took a sip of the hot liquid in the cup. She continued to look at him. She spoke again. "I like complicated." Kahlip spoke up. "Perhaps, but what can you handle? That's the question." They shared a glance between them. Then, Kahlip thought about something. He spoke up. "Okay...you like complicated, then try to understand this." He looked at her intently, as he spoke. "My name isn't Steve, well, it is, but only because my parents didn't know they could call me Kahlip, which is my real identity...my Plaenellian identity." Katy looked at him. She studied him a brief moment. She considered what he said. She spoke up. "Kahlip, huh? Plaenellian?" Suddenly, she thought about something. She spoke up. "So, who is my father?" Kahlip smiled. He eyed her. He spoke up. "You are determined!" Katy smiled and spoke. "You're damn right." Kahlip smiled again, and spoke up. "And, you sound like your Aunt Frances." Katy smiled again. She spoke up. "I love that woman." Kahlip endured the sentiment through his granddaughter. He looked at her with a heavy heart. She felt something coming from him. She didn't feel comfortable in the moment. Kahlip spoke up. "Katy...I am going to tell you, but know that I do so with a heavy heart for what it means. I will say that is why it was so important to find you." Katy stared at him. She looked harder at him, as the moments passed with expectation. He finally looked like he was going to speak. He moved to take a sip of his hot chocolate. He continued to look at Katy. He finally spoke. "Katy...your father...is...Osodon on this planet...this time around. And, I am his Plaenellian offspring. His consequence you could say." Katy stared at Kahlip. She stood thoughtfully. Kahlip spoke again. "I know what planet you were born from." Katy studied him. She thought about something. She looked at Kahlip with finality, and spoke. "Why didn't you tell me then…that night?" Kahlip spoke up. "I had a hard time informing you that your father is the father of the demise of all the Universes. How in the world could I tell you that you were born from a planet that had been turned into a harvesting planet? It's Amidestor. How could I tell you that your father is your father because he wanted to harvest you with Oosiah…my mother?" Katy thought about something and spoke up. "Oosiah is my mother…is Lorande." Kahlip chuckled, as he eyed Katy. "No…silly, Oosiah is the one that is looking for you, and your mother's safety, is your safety." Kahlip thought about something. He spoke up. "Katy, Osodon fathers the children, and Oosiah reaps. That's how it works. And, Oosiah is on the prowl. To some of Plaenellians, it's like some sick game of cat and mouse for those two." Katy went to the recliner and sat thoughtfully. Kahlip looked at her with concern. He spoke up. "Are you handling okay?" Katy stared off into the distance. She thought about something. She spoke up. "So, my cousins…" Kahlip interrupted her. "You mean my grandkids… harvested. You…potentially harvested, had you and I not found each other. Karen is your only other cousin that hasn't been harvested. I was on protection detail for her, and got her safely away. Right now, I am working on getting her here. I am the one that bought her ticket to France…and unfortunately, Julius, who has been touched by Osodon too. I know it. If Julius isn't his son, and he engineered Karen and Julius', union for a double harvest… you know that two birds with one stone thing. It's sick. He was setting them up for Oosiah. Then, I got in the way." Katy thought about something when he said that. She spoke up. "I recall finding out about Julius and Karen being together, and it hurt, but I think Julius thought that I had a thing for him. I didn't. And, yet, I didn't confess what I knew about Karen, and I should have." She turned away thoughtfully, and sadly. She considered something.

Kahlip looked at her and thought about something. He felt her sadness for his own about her life. He spoke quietly. "Katy?" Katy turned around and looked at him the best way she could. She spoke. "You know, I didn't steal that money from the motel… it was Harvey…and I covered for him because his grandma was being kicked out of her house. And, I thought I could try to play on Julius' attractiveness, and that whole thing to distract him from holding it against me. But he fired me anyway. He did call me back to work though, but he never looked at me the same way. It hurt." Katy stopped speaking and let a tear fall in looking at Kahlip. "I don't even care that Harvey might have been lying…I liked the guy and didn't want to see him screw his life up. Me…I had nothing going for me anyway…I was in a much darker place then." Kahlip looked at her and considered something. He spoke up. "You are a brilliant young lady, Kat, don't ever forget that." Katy tried to smile, as he said that. But, in that moment, she realized why she felt so alien because her father committed the crime of having a child under nefarious means. It was one thing to have a child with a woman, married or not, but to work a child into having a child, is criminal. Katy felt the effects from it. She suddenly hated her father, against the love Kahlip helped her to have. She thought about something else in that moment. She spoke up with emotion. "I haven't felt better for being here. I always felt like I didn't belong." Kahlip looked at her. She spoke again. "And, don't give me that crap about life being what I do with it either. Cause I know that doesn't work." She stopped speaking and looked at Kahlip. He sat quietly. She spoke again. "My telescope is the only thing I wanted because I knew to not want for much because I knew I would never have it anyway." Kahlip looked at Kat with a smile. He spoke softly and warmly for the love, he had for her. "Katy, your life was the result without me in it, which is why I have been trying to find you. I had a conversation with your father before he passed away. In which case, I got what I thought was a viable address for you." He stopped speaking, and looked at her thoughtfully. He smiled, then, spoke. He felt so much love for her in that moment. "I knew

I had to find you somehow. And, I did…kiddo, you are more important to others than you realize. And, yes, you weren't born under the most Universal lawful means, but you have to turn that around. Understand." Katy tried to smile when he said that. He thought about something else when he said that and felt that emotion for her, which to him it wasn't supposedly human to feel that kind of or as much love, as he did in that moment. He looked squarely into his granddaughter's eyes and spoke. "There has never been a more beautiful, unlawful creature to this planet, as you are, Kat…don't forget that." Kahlip thought about something, as he looked into her eyes. He spoke again softly. "I have never seen so much immortal beauty in a creature, as you. And, if you want to know the truth, you have more courage than most to be born under the circumstances to which you were born. You have the courage to stand alone…knowing that you haven't much support here." Kahlip stopped speaking and thought about something. He spoke again quickly. "Well, you had my support, which you perhaps, didn't fully know or understand, but that is how it works, Katy. When we think we're alone, we're not necessarily in such a way that we're totally disconnected from everyone else. We might not be capable of touching, but we touch and connect in other ways through the space or distance between us." Kahlip thought about something, after he said that, and seemingly made Katy tear up by his emotions for her. He spoke again. "And, one last thing Kat, too, remember this, when you think you are alone, it just means two things." He stopped speaking to look and see how attentive she was. Then, he spoke again. "First, it means that is how strong you are from your true support system, and secondly, it shows how strong you can be, knowing how many people in a given area that are far less the level of being you are." Kahlip looked at her and thought about something. He spoke one last time before he took a sip of his hot chocolate to finish it up. "I know what I am talking about…Kat for what I went through in being born." Katy looked at him curiously. She spoke up. "How's that." Kahlip smiled thoughtfully. He looked at her gingerly and grinning, began to speak. "Because

Katy, my mother cheated on my father, got pregnant by some other man and then, in feeling guilty for it, wanted me born dead. She was Aubrahteerian, which meant she had religious guilt." Katy looked at him when he said that. She was shocked. He spoke again. "See, at least you had a mother, for however old she was, that was excited about you being born. You will never know what it felt like in the womb, knowing your mother wanted you dead. Then, ironically, I was almost born dead; my mother almost got what she wanted because I had the umbilical cord wrapped around my neck. So, I couldn't be born naturally. But the point is that there are many situations that we're born to, and we have to deal with it. For my mother, she had to finally come to terms, and she did so in silence, as she never told my father, but I knew. My mother had to get over the fact that she went against her Aubrahteerian virtue and religious views. And, after everything that she went through while I was in her, I loved that woman, and do to this day. She was the best mother I could have asked for. And, that was my courage Katy...it's one thing to know someone wants you dead, but it's another to stand and face your mother knowing that she wanted you dead at one point. It's what I had to face my entire life, and get over to say that I could truly love that woman." Katy looked at him in shock. She was floored, and suddenly, she didn't feel bad about herself any longer because she finally realized that someone else just might have it worse.

Kahlip and Katy continued chatting on into the later hours. Kahlip went on to explain that he lost her great grandmother when he was six years old. He explained that it was probably the hardest thing to do, but he did it. And that was to lose the woman that once wanted him dead. He admitted to Katy jokingly that he never valued "thou shalt not kill" from the Aubrahteerians more than when he was born, as it was his mother's value in that, which kept him alive after he was born.

A Chapter for Forgetting

Katy spent the night on Kahlip's sofa. He wouldn't let her go home, as he explained that it was way too late to be bike riding. Katy agreed to stay the night, besides; it's not every day a girl finds her grandfather. And, for probably the first time in her life, she felt like she was home.

Katy awoke the next morning to the fresh scent of coffee, which she really never understood, but somehow, she was enticed to try a cup. She walked into the kitchen where her grandfather stood, resting comfortably against the counter. She smiled at him. He smiled back. He spoke up. "You know, kiddo, it is nice to have you in my house...finally. I know I didn't say that last night, but that is how I truly feel." Katy smiled. She spoke up. "Yeah...well, it is nice to feel like I am part of a home." He smiled when she said that. He spoke up again thoughtfully. "Coffee?" He held up an empty cup for her. She spoke. "It's funny, but I never tried the stuff. I think I may have to now." She walked over to him and gently took the cup. She then, proceeded to stand next to him. She stood thoughtfully. She turned to him and spoke. "Is it true?" He turned to her and knew instantly to what she was talking. He spoke up. "Every word." She stood thoughtfully a brief second. She spoke again. "Do you know what I am talking about?" He turned to her and smiled. "Yeah, kiddo, you're talking about what I said about my mother." She turned and looked straight ahead. She thought about what he admitted about her great grandmother. She couldn't get over how amazing the story sounded. It was like something out of a book." Kahlip instantly thought about something. He turned to her thoughtfully. "You know, there are those who write the books, those who read the books, and then there are those that live the books." Katy turned to him and smiled, as the coffee seemed to ready. The coffee pot made that sound as if it was going through the last bit of water in the hopper.

Thoughtfully as they turned around to the coffee maker, Katy spoke up. "I want to live the books." Kahlip smiled at her, as he handed her the sugar. He spoke. "You already are, Katy and you don't know it." Katy poured some sugar into the cup. Kahlip then began to give her some advice on preparing a cup of coffee. He spoke. "Since this is your first cup, I would suggest creamer. I have some flavored stuff in the fridge. I've been drinking it for a while, but even I drink it with creamer." She went to the fridge and retrieved what she thought was the cream. He smiled as he saw what she grabbed. He spoke. "Not the whipped cream. The coffee creamer is in the door. In the small bottle." Katy spoke up. "It might still be good with whipped cream." Kahlip thoughtfully spoke up. "Well, yeah, I suppose, but the traditional coffee cream is good too. Maybe you should try the whipped stuff." Katy thoughtfully spoke. "No...I think I will follow in footsteps of my ancestors." Kahlip smiled when she said that. She spoke again. "I think it is time I got in touch with my true roots." Kahlip thought about something humorously. He spoke. "You know, they say that was what was wrong with the cowboys. They were drinking hard black coffee without sugar or cream." As he said that, Kat took a sip of her coffee before she added the cream and before she stirred the sugar. She made this horrific face. She turned to her grandfather, when the awful taste in her mouth had left her. "Well, I'd say that whoever said that was very smart. I don't think I ever would have had coffee then." Kahlip finished making his cup and spoke up thoughtfully. "I don't either." When they had their coffee completed in their cups, the two of them sat at the kitchen table. Katy noticed that she never fully enjoyed the family dinner table. So, sitting to one now felt odd. She spoke up. "I like this feeling." Kahlip sipped from his cup. "What's that?" She looked at him thoughtfully and spoke. "The feeling of being home...sitting at the family dinner table. I never had that growing up. My life was really screwed up." Kahlip thoughtfully looked at her. He spoke. "Well, Kat, then you are in for a lot of firsts. However, do me a favor, please, forget how screwed up things were. It brings you down." She eyed him when she said that. She thoughtfully spoke. "I see what you mean." Kahlip took a sip from his cup, then, noticed her thoughtfully. He spoke. "See, I had to do the same thing for how I got here. To this day, I think about the plight of the Aubrahteerians and their guilt. I think about how when I lost my mother at six, I was left with a man that thought he was my father, but really didn't treat me as if I was his son. I felt thrown to the wolves. But I began to see something. It didn't matter how he treated me because he was more father than I should have had because my mother made him think I was his. And, there is nothing more screwed up than that. So, I don't look at life that way anymore. I appreciate everything he did do, and he doesn't have to feel guilty for not being a true father. See, you have a grandfather trying to compensate for what your father wouldn't do. That's what is really important, Kat... someone that can take responsibility for loving you because they should. My mother's husband didn't have to. So, I cannot blame him. Ironically, I am better off for knowing what I knew about my life growing up. Plus, there are bigger fish to fry, as far as that goes." Katy looked at him, as he said that and she took a sip of coffee. She then spoke up. "What do you mean?" He looked at her intently and with a sense of certainty. "Kat...there is a war going on, and you are part of it. We're all a part of it, and most don't know that." She thought about what he said. She eyed him over her cup. She sipped from it. He spoke again. "That's what we cannot forget, Kiddo. We're all battling the darkness within each of us, fighting for that brighter future, the new Dawn that speaks potentially of a better day." Katy looked at him with a confused gait. "What darkness are you battling? You are the brightest light I have ever seen!" She sipped from her warm cup in anticipation of his response. He smiled at her. "I thank you for your vote of confidence in me, but I battle with the darkness too in degrees. I cannot hate the war for not giving up on it. Kat, finding you was not giving up. Not giving up was fighting against being an illegitimate child. This is why I owe a lot to my father and your great grandfather, who I never got to know. That is the kind of hatred we have to stand and face. And, that is why you cannot look at who your father is, but what designs the kind of life you have to lead." Katy thought about something in that moment. She looked at her grandfather. She spoke. "You mean that I have to love the man attempting to destroy the Universes?" Kahlip smiled. He spoke up. "Now you are learning what it means to be a Dawn Keeper, kiddo. That's what love is Kat." Katy looked at him when he said that. She sat thoughtfully a moment. "Explain the Dawn Keepers to me." Kahlip looked at her when she said that. He thought about something. He spoke. "Well, let me do it by asking a question first." Katy looked at him for saying that. She had her cup in hand. She sipped and then spoke. "What's that?" Kahlip spoke up quickly. "Do you want me to say it, as if it were legend?" Katy spoke up. "I don't think you could talk of it, as if it were legend, grandpa." Kahlip smiled when she said that. She was right. He spoke up. "Well, to most it was legend, but to those who know better, know what's going on. Anyway, long ago, a new alien race was born and they were the Plaenellians. However, through what was in their hearts, they became Dawn Keepers in the effort of having a brighter future for all alien races, then, sporadically placed upon alien planets in all the Universes. However, the legend was changed throughout the years because of the parents of all Plaenellians. Osodon…and Oosiah had forged a change in the legend, and created something they called the Dark Treaders. But the Dark Treaders were nothing more than those who opposed them. Keep in mind I love Osodon and Oosiah, as my parents dearly. I have to treat them like I love them, but that doesn't always mean I do the same passive thing when they do what they do. Sometimes, they need me to treat them, as though they are doing something incorrectly. I swear, sometimes I feel like their parent, as we Plaenellians do sometimes." Katy thought about something in that moment. She spoke up. "That's confusing when you talk of Osodon and Oosiah being the Plaenellian parents, and then Osodon being my father." Kahlip smiled, as she said that because he understood her. He spoke up. "Well, you have but one concept to understand. And, that is reincarnation. It doesn't matter if you believe in it, some things are true whether you believe in them or not, but the point is, that we understand things on a more immortal level. This means that what humans, in consciousness have become, they don't see that far, which is the plight of all alien races. Because of what I knew in Mick Ellis for being Osodon, was how I knew how to treat him the way I did. Sadly, this lack of immortal sight is how Osodon and Oosiah have been defeating the various alien consciousnesses on the various planets. It's why the darkness seems to run rampant on all the planets. It's why we're seeking the solution to the Universes' issues." He stopped speaking and thought about something. He eyed Katy and spoke up in between sips form his cup. "Kat see, that is a measure of the death of consciousness. What you don't realize is the power inherent in the animals." Suddenly, Katy glimpsed something in what he said. She could almost anticipate what he was about to say. She spoke up. "I almost see where you are going with that." Kahlip sat thoughtfully. He considered what Katy was capable of understanding and hearing. What he could say to her in that moment was something he had so far back in his mind that it was in the way back of his mental closet. It was, however, something that hurt him dearly. It was something he knew he didn't want to know. And, unfortunately, he was one of five Plaenellians that did know it, which made Kahlip feel that much older than his Plaenellian siblings. Actually, in that moment was that, which made him think there was no hope for the Universes, but he had to fight that feeling. In that moment and silently, as he sat there with his granddaughter, he recalled something he would have rather forgotten. He spoke up, but to say something contrary to his thought. "Actually, I cannot really get into that right now because you already have so much on your plate, but perhaps at a later time would be more feasible. However, in silence he ached for the animals of Ayeraal. He sipped of his coffee while he sat in silence. Katy studied him, and what he seemingly, almost said. Together, they sat quietly, enjoying their coffee, and that moment together. Suddenly, Kahlip had an idea. He looked at Katy with a loving sensibility. He spoke. "Kat…if you really need a place to go…no wait...why don't you move in?" Katy looked at him. She was shocked to hear that. She looked at him, and thought about how she really didn't like living where she was. The neighbors were a bit erratic for her with their ups and downs, their relationship issues. She was only renting a room. She did have thoughts about asking him to rent a room, and that was before she knew who he truly is to her. Katy's face lit up, at the thought. She eyed her grandfather. She spoke up. "Really...you mean it?" He smiled, as he eyed her. "It's my idea!" Katy smiled, as she felt more whole as the moments went on. "I'd love to. When can I do it?" Kahlip smiled and spoke. "I've got today!" Suddenly, though, he made her think. Why was he seemingly trying to get her closer to him? Suddenly, she thought to question his motivations. She looked at him. She spoke up. "Why do you want to do this because I feel like I should be worried about where I am living now? It almost seems like there is something I should be worried about." Kahlip looked at her, and couldn't believe she said that, but she was right. He spoke up. "I can't get anything past you. It's funny, but I feel sometimes that we're in each other's heads. But you are correct. I got that feeling. I want you to live with me for your protection, but it's up to you." Katy looked at him when he said that. "I would love to move in to get to know you and stuff like that. If I am going to rent a room, I would rather give you the money." Her grandfather chuckled. He spoke. "Katy, you aren't going to pay me." She stared at him when he said that. He spoke again. "Katy...I know where you are coming from and I understand you, but you aren't going to pay me. Your love is payment enough." In that moment, Katy cried. Her tears flowed, as she looked at her grandfather. Suddenly, it seemed like she had every parent she ever needed in her grandpa. She looked at him and he gazed at her. He spoke. "Kat...I know you didn't learn this, but that is what family is all about." In that moment, he considered something, as he looked at her for her emotions. He spoke up. "Kat...do you want to know where the idea for the word family stems?" She wiped her eyes thoughtfully. She spoke with emotion in her throat. "Sure." Kahlip watched her speak and wiped her eyes.

Then, he spoke. "Family means the Foremost Awe-inspiring Meticulously Intelligent or Interesting Loved Youth." Katy smiled as he said that. He spoke again. "You don't have the family if you don't have kids. I know it starts with F, but it actually starts with kids." Katy smiled again, and continued to tear up. She spoke up. "I wish I had you my entire life growing up." Her grandfather got a tear and spoke. "I know what you mean, Kat. I wish I had you your whole life."

✝

A Chapter for Fire

Katy was all moved in now. She and Kahlip sat looking at her one box she brought over. Most of the move meant getting one of the extra rooms ready for her to take. Katy suddenly had a thought. She turned to her grandfather thoughtfully. He seemed to be thinking about something. She spoke up. "Is it too early to ask about the animals?" Kahlip turned to her easily and smiled. "Yep." She turned from him and spoke. "Thought so." Her grandfather spoke up. "However, it isn't too early for a lesson on the Rosicrucians." Katy turned to him again. "The scientists?" That was the moment her grandfather appeared to be the wise old man to her in that moment. "Yeah…and to learn something about fire you didn't know." Katy looked at him thoughtfully. She spoke up. "Fire?" Kahlip turned to the one box of Katy's belongings thoughtfully. He stared at it a second and began to speak. "It was long ago when the Rosicrucians began being born. Long before fire ever existed, the various alien consciousnesses began going through the stages of birth. See Katy, fire isn't a thing; it is a concept. It's magic, but why?" He turned to her thoughtfully. She looked at him briefly and thoughtfully. She didn't have an answer for him. When he realized that, he spoke. "Rosicrucians knew something that most didn't. They understood elements, but concepts inherent in elements, which is why they were a needed addition to the Ayeraal. Like in a car, which is engineered scientifically, every part of the car is a concept, when fitted together, form a symbiotic circle of sorts. But the point is that fire wasn't discovered; it was actualized from a concept inherent in the Rosicrucians. That concept was moving fast. See, cooking food isn't a matter of making it safe to eat. It's a measure of making something alien to something else, suitable for the two to mix. Do you realize that you can speed up a straw and put through a potato, but if you try to put that straw against the potato, and try to put it into the potato it will bend." Katy looked at him when he said that. She spoke. "No, I didn't." Kahlip thoughtfully spoke again. "That is fire Katy. And, that is why it wasn't discovered, as most believe. It's why consciousness is going up from what Osodon and Oosiah had done because of what the Rosicrucians brought to this planet. It's why they were needed because in a sense, Consciousness was becoming a dark uncooked, stationary thing, more easily consumed to individuals that were attempting to consume consciousness. In a sense, Osodon and Oosiah were cannibals of consciousness. See, they think that all measures of consciousness came from them in the beginning, and they wanted to retain that, which they thought they lost. They began to do that until we were born." Katy looked at him, as he spoke. She sat thoughtfully. Her grandfather stopped speaking and looked at her. He spoke again. "You understand so far?" Katy thoughtfully nodded. He spoke again. "See, in a sense, the birth to this planet is like a straw through a potato, and the sick are a straw that isn't going fast enough to make it through the potato, so they get stuck in the potato. Note that in old age is a sense of slowing down period for an individual, whose fire is going out or in another sense, the straw slowing down in the potato." He stopped speaking and looked at her. Katy thought about what he said. She eyed him. "So, even a ripe old age isn't a long life!" Kahlip smiled because she got it. He spoke again. "Yes…Katy, even in ripe old age, that is the straw slowing down. See, long ago, immortality meant something. It meant that one was moving so fast, that there was no way to stop moving. And, alien consciousness could visit other worlds and others of different planets because of this state of immortality. Unfortunately, now, that once moving immortal alien form is slowing down to such degrees that it cannot physically go from one planet to the next carrying the weight of its body. See, at one point, body, and consciousness were one, which is where the Rosicrucians or the scientists get their views. Unbeknownst to many, scientists do believe in the soul, but in a different way." Her grandfather thought about something and stopped speaking. He looked at Katy thoughtfully. He spoke again. "Have you ever heard she needs a fire under her butt, or he is fired up?" Katy thoughtfully eyed him, as he said that. She thought for a moment, and then spoke. "Yes, I think a time of two." He spoke up quickly when she finished. "That's the point. It's what Osodon and Oosiah are trying to do. It's why passion is associated with fire and love is romantic and passionate. Fire isn't necessarily an element, but a measure of a concept, which is what the Rosicrucians understood. Sadly, that understanding of fire, as an element, and a cooking tool, something discovered is an indication that consciousness is down or in darkness. However, I like to think that it is on its way up, equally for all alien consciousness on every planet it exists upon." Katy thought about something and spoke. "Well, I just became a little wiser I think." Kahlip looked at her and smiled. He spoke. "Katy, one thing you have to remember is that alien consciousness knows everything I am saying because it was immortal once, but can be again. Everything I am telling you is a reminder, so even you can get back to where you used to be. Remember, outside of Osodon and Oosiah, your kind is the only thing that existed. We Plaenellians weren't even a thought." Katy thought about something and looked at him. She spoke. "Do you remember what it was like?" He looked at her curiously. He spoke. "What?" She spoke again. "Well...what it was like not to exist." Kahlip looked at her thoughtfully. "Well, now Katy, that is the thing, I said we weren't a thought, that doesn't mean we didn't exist. We existed on another level altogether, but that hints to the curse of the Dawn Keepers." Katy eyed him when he said that. She sat thoughtfully and briefly. She spoke up. "Okay, Mr. technical, what was it like to exist where you were?" Her grandfather laughed. He spoke after another thoughtful moment. "Well, from where we were, we got to watch you all like we were watching television, to put it in a way you can understand." Katy thought humorously. She spoke.

"Did you get to have snacks and popcorn and all that? Was it like movie theatres?" He laughed at her because he knew she was being facetious. He shook his head, as Katy laughed. He looked at her in that moment. "Katy, I'll tell you this. You made it a pleasure being me." Katy stopped laughing and eyed him. She felt warmed and she knew it was because of him. She thought of something and spoke. "I know what you mean about fire because it is very warm to be around you. I think you could actually melt ice cubes for being near them." Kahlip smiled. He wanted to laugh, but she was being emotional right then. It was a nice moment. He didn't want to ruin it by laughing. He eyed her. He spoke up. "Katy…that's love and how powerful it can be." Katy got a glimpse of where he was coming from. She spoke. "You know, I think I can see what it must been like to exist where you did. It's like sun and fun all day. It is a lit up place and very warm, but comfortable." Kahlip looked at her when she spoke, and what she said took him back. He thought about being there again, not having to stress over making things right, battling Osodon and Oosiah. Though he felt the curse…he thought of what that was worth. He looked at his granddaughter. Suddenly, Katy thought about something. She looked at her grandfather. She spoke. "You don't really look at me like your granddaughter, do you? You have some higher perception of me, don't you? I am more to you than a granddaughter, aren't I?" Kahlip teared up when she said that. He thoughtfully and tearfully eyed her. He spoke with emotion in his throat. "Katy, you all are more to us than the labels we have to use to refer to you." Katy was warmed again inside, as he said that. He spoke again. "You all are worth so much more than you realize." He looked at Katy and cracked a smile through teary eyes. He wiped them. Katy looked at him, and realized something in that moment, but she kept it to herself for the sake of sounding crazy. Though she kept that to herself, she looked at her grandfather, who was becoming more and more to her through every passing moment. She noted that he was right in what he said about love being that powerful. At that moment, she was feeling so much light and warmth in that room with him, that it did almost feel alien to her, but she realized why. In her life, Katy didn't have such a loving being in her life. She didn't have love coming from any elder in her life, not as loving as her grandfather or whatever he was to her. It was then too, that Katy knew she was getting fired up.

Moments later, her grandfather suggested that they get busy readying her room. Of course, in his style, he made her aware of how much he thought of her, and how delighted he was to have her with him. But that was stoking the fire for him in her. It was adding another loving log to her fire, as an alien being she was to him. In that moment, as the two of them cleaned up the room, Katy swept, and her grandfather dusted. Katy thought about something. She glimpsed the kind of job he had with just her alone, someone that once verged being put in an institution. She got the message of being loving before, but there was something in that moment with him that seemed even more special. There was a man who never physically saw her, but he stepped up to being her grandfather, and played the part, as if they spent her entire life together. Katy was romanced by him in the best, most loving ways a grandfather could. She then reflected. She thought about growing up, and how who she thought was her grandfather didn't come close to love what that man in the room with her did. Suddenly, she realized exactly where her father once thought of, as her grandfather, paled in comparison to being a father. Her grandfather seemed to give her all the love of a father, and a grandfather and a brother in one. It was uncanny. Suddenly, she also realized how therapeutic love could be when it is true and pure, without expectation. Katy teared up, as she swept. She had never cried so much before her in her life, but then again, she was never touched by the pure essence of a love grander than what resided in that man, helping her cleaning his extra room for her to have. And, technically, all she had to go on for him being her grandfather was a picture and his word for it that that was what he is to her. However, as she thought about

it, she could look at the man and know it too. She thought about
how he had said that he had watched over her mother and aunts
their lives through. It made sense that she would seemingly slip
through the cracks so to say, and be hidden from him. Upon
that notion, she considered that her grandfather was going to
be reunited with his daughters, and she would eventually be
rekindled with her mother. If he could find her, then her mother
would find her way to him, she knew it somehow. At one point,
when she knew he wasn't looking, she stopped and just watched
him work. She noted his aged face, and long blond hair that was
graying in degrees, but the gray was hidden well. She thought
about the kind of energy he had to work so hard and do what
he did that he did seem alien to her. He didn't look like a man
with the kind of life and responsibility he described. He was so
much more than that.

✝

A Chapter & the Threat

In that moment, when Kahlip and his granddaughter were cleaning, Penny came home. She appeared in the doorway and watched them both silently. She couldn't help but wonder who the little punk of a girl was. At first glance, she was just another girl to get in the way of her and Kahlip. Damn! She slipped away from being noticed. She went to the bedroom and closed the door. From the room, Kahlip could hear another door close. He turned thoughtfully. Penny! Kahlip turned to Kat. He spoke. "I think Penny is home…you can meet her." Katy looked at him, as he said that. She spoke up. "That'll be nice." He felt her earnest sincerity in what she said. Kahlip left the room. Katy was busy tidying up her things on the dresser by this point. Kahlip walked in the bedroom and Penny was sitting on the bed, appearing flustered. Kahlip felt concern. He eyed her. He spoke up quickly. "Penny?" Penny turned to him with a certain look. It was hard for him to discern. But in Penny's mind, she was seeking control in herself for how frustrated she was at finding a little girl in her house, whom she knew nothing about. Kahlip had a thought. "Penny, that's my granddaughter, Katy. I call her Kat." Penny looked at him with frustration. And, before she let go of one angry word, she composed herself. Instead of saying that she didn't give a shit, she spoke alien to her feelings. "That's nice." Kahlip didn't feel the sincerity in what she said. She spoke, as if she didn't say what she really wanted to. He eyed her a moment. There went another strike against her. Penny would have to come to realize what Katy being in his house was really worth. She would have to understand what Katy meant to him. And, for right at that moment, Penny would have to try and be part of his and Katy's world. Penny would have to realize that life was all about the youth, and youthful is what Katy was. She was beloved to him, unfortunately, for Penny more than she was, which hinted to something he knew about Penny she didn't know, he knew. Unfortunately, for Kahlip, he gave Penny too much credit for self-control. Kahlip looked at Penny. After she told him that was nice, she went back to dealing with herself on the bed. Kahlip looked at her once more, but briefly, and he spoke with a hindered sense of frustration. "Penny...that is my granddaughter out there. And, she is moving in! You are going to have to deal with that. It seems to me you better start appreciating family because I am founded upon the notion that family is where it all starts." Penny looked at him and shrouded her anger and disgust for that...girl in that room. She looked at Kahlip, thinking if their time together was worth what she felt. She wondered if what she was trying to do was worth him. She thought about the falsehood upon which their supposed marriage was founded. She pondered if he even had a clue. He was such an idiot. Kahlip left the room after he finished speaking and looking at her another brief moment. Penny got this mean look on her face when he turned around. Her anger she controlled seemed to slip out when she knew it could. Kahlip returned to the room where Katy was seemingly finishing up putting her things in place. When she finished with him in the doorway, she went to the bed and sat. She looked around and then at him, as he was leaning against the doorframe. Katy felt so good at that moment. Her new room was so much better than what she could have gotten on her own, but she already knew the value of the man at the door, and he was worth so much more than a room. She smiled at him and continued to appreciate her room. Kahlip smiled and felt accomplished, but with a sense of reserve, as he knew that his love for that little girl on the bed came with knowing that he wanted to do more for her. At that point, he was doing what he could. He thought briefly of Penny in that moment. There was something behind her or more than he fully understood. He just couldn't imagine how at one point, things between them seemed genuine, then in the next, there was nothing between them. It was hard to understand. Penny was almost another person. Kahlip didn't like the feeling of having to be mindful of Penny and her twists and turns and seemingly high and low roller coaster personality.

Penny came from the room with a sense of herself and Kahlip that it had to work between them. She went to the extra bedroom and Kahlip was standing in the doorway. She peered over his shoulder with a smile. She spoke. "Hi...Katy" Katy turned to her and smiled. "Hi there." Penny was thoughtful that Katy was too chipper for her tastes. Penny spoke up. "You'll enjoy it here. Grandpa loves you a lot." Kahlip turned to her, as she said that. Katy smiled and spoke. "I know...but the feeling is mutual." Kahlip smiled, as she said that. Penny choked out a smile, as she said that. She gave Katy a kind of shrouded glare, which Katy didn't notice. Not that she let Penny know, anyway. Penny suddenly had a thought, since it was nearing noon. She spoke. "Why don't we all go to lunch?" Kahlip looked at Katy when she said that. He spoke up. "What do you think, Kiddo?" Katy looked at her grandfather and Penny thoughtfully. She spoke up. "I'd like that."

Kahlip drove. He spoke up. "So where are we heading?" Katy spoke up about a little diner that she knew of close to the beach. Penny spoke up about not feeling like being so close to the salty air at the moment. Kahlip looked at her and thoughtfully spoke. "Penny...you live in the salty air for where we are." As Penny looked at him for his comment, she couldn't help but feel more anxious about Katy in the back seat. She glimpsed that Katy verged spoiling everything. Penny had her plan for her and Kahlip, for which Katy was looking like the wrench in those plans. Penny finally spoke, but with a hint of frustration. "Whatever. Let's go dine at that little place." Katy seemed uncomfortable in that moment. Kahlip turned to Penny and spoke. "It'll be nice to try something new, right?" Penny looked between Kahlip and the road. She spoke up. "I guess." At that moment, Penny instantly thought about having to deal with Katy. As she sat in the back seat, Katy thought about Penny, and there was something about her that didn't feel right. Katy was feeling like her enemy or something. She didn't understand wholly what Penny had against her, but she thought it wasn't warranted. Katy sat uncomfortably in her seat, while the ride suddenly became a long one. As, she sat there, she couldn't help but wonder what her grandfather was doing with Penny. She was quite obviously, the opposite of him, not in the complimentary way either. They were too different to seem like they were compatible. Suddenly, Katy thought that maybe her grandfather was holding out for a better Penny, but it was confusing to consider. Katy couldn't do it. Then again, her grandfather was the epitome of love…forever enduring.

In that moment through the car ride, Penny couldn't help but think of what she had to do. And, what Kahlip didn't understand was that Penny was looking for his daughters, as well. Too, in those moments in the car, Penny did have to be thankful she wouldn't have to locate all the kin of Kahlip. Katy, his granddaughter was in the back seat. So, Penny began to feel better. She didn't think of already having one of the Kahlip clan with her. There, she guessed was some kind of solace to be had. Ironically, the rest of the afternoon went better than for what it started out to be. Lacking what Penny now accepted, Kahlip and Katy should have been mindful of the switch in Penny that made the afternoon better. It wasn't for something they should have appreciated, but forewarned them of a growing enemy within the house, which was gaining strength, as the days would progress.

When lunch had ended, the ride back to the house went easier. At the house, the three of them all relaxed on the back porch and enjoyed the afternoon in the sun. At one point, Penny turned to Katy and spoke. "I am sorry about the morning, Katy. I have been having a bad week." Katy looked at Penny and smiled, thinking that for what she felt about Penny, it was odd that Penny would find enough love to apologize. Katy spoke up. "That's okay…we all go through it at times." Kahlip looked at Katy, then, at Penny and smiled. Penny tried to pass something off as a smile at Katy and put her head back on the lawn chair. She spoke up. "This is nice isn't it?" Katy spoke up. "Wonderful!" Kahlip smiled at her and looked skyward. He spoke. "Better because you are both here." Katy smiled from what he said, and Penny stayed silent. Katy picked up her book that she had been reading for about two weeks now. Kahlip noticed and inquired about it. Katy spoke up. "It's pretty cool. It's called The Angel Chronicles. It's good so far. I guess it's about the perspective of the Aubrahteerians, as you referred to them once." Kahlip thought about what she said. He spoke again. "Interesting." He stopped speaking and considered something before he spoke again. "Personally, I am into Cara Wayne. My favorite is Dark is the skies." Penny shook her head in a pitiful gesture, and in secret. Suddenly, as he sat there, Kahlip began to slink into the digression pointing him towards missing Kaera. Kahlip felt like a widower, who had lost his true love. Sadly, that was the value in Keepers. Their drive to make things right would eventually put them back into the arms of their other half, the part of them that made them complete. So, with Penny and Katy there with him and everyone was silent, it was a good time to endure being the widower. However, he had to appreciate Penny for something, but sadly he glimpse coming to see the greater purpose behind their union.

The Chapter for a Deeper Look

Hard was the day, and beloved was that moment on the bed. Penny was there too, but almost seemingly not. It was then that Kahlip was left to remember the beginning when his kind were figuring things out and realizing why they had come to exist.

It was long ago when earth was argued of being a created, singular entity. Ironically, it was before even that. Plaenellians began being born when the first attacks on the Universes were made. This was when the safety net from Osodon and Oosiah's behavior went into action. Kahlip was on a planet that no longer exists now because of the attacks that worsened. But, that planet was then known as Anialam with such sub-planets, as Ahmimalia and Ahminallah. For Kahlip, those times, as most for all Plaenellians are the worst to remember because on Ayeraal currently, they are witness to the worst crime committed by Osodon and Oosiah. And, Kahlip really wanted to forget it. However, it was what currently drove him to push forward knowing everything that was going on, beside his separation from Kaera. It was this special memory or glimpse into the past that hurt the worst. On that planet, with him and a few other various races that were visiting Anialam at the time, Kaera was there too. Kahlip and Kaera were visiting, taking what was permitted then, as a vacation of sorts. Anialam was home to one of the most ancient of alien races, along with the races on the sub-planets. However, what was supposed to be a vacation turned into one of the most important visits by Plaenellians to any one planet. That was where Kahlip and Kaera learned of the pact between Osodon and Oosiah and the Elders of all the races. Kahlip instantly thought about the Rosicrucian notions of cloning in that moment, and those who fought it, didn't realize why it was so important. Kahlip and Kaera did however. They didn't understand that it wasn't sacrilege, but a higher form of creative therapy. It wasn't replacing any deity for what it's worth, but exemplifying the creation to want to be capable of recreating certain creative powers. If anything, it wasn't showing God any indecent behavior, but showing God that consciousness could take responsibility, and what that consciousness would do to take such responsibility. However, that was really what the battle between the Rosicrucians and the Aubrahteerians was really worth in those early times when science was seen, as evil. And, that was how dark the Aubrahteerians were for how they saw things. Religion wasn't as light, as it was spoke of.

As Kahlip continued to recall the past, he thought about how the pact Osodon and Oosiah had created, was broken by the elders. Well, that was how Osodon and Oosiah told the story, but the truth of it was that Osodon and Oosiah went against what they promised they would do. Osodon and Oosiah thought their supposed imprisonment came from what the Elder races had done. However, it was something prone to Osodon and Oosiah for what they were to all the Universes. In a cycle, Osodon and Oosiah were restricted from visiting the other planets, like all races could. They didn't realize that they were on a needed basis around the Universes, in much the same way a light switch functions. Once the switch is on, the electricity is enabled to flow, but there is a point when it has to be off. Osodon and Oosiah were that measure of electrical potential, until they figured out how to cheat their position amongst the Universes. Then, they became the exposed wire where electricity was jumping from the wire to various attractive elements. And, like electricity when it does that, they began destroying the various aspects of the Universes, but they didn't understand this, which was why extreme measures needed to be taken. Upon this notion was why the Plaenellians knew they had to take measures that are more stringent. Unfortunately, that would happen much later than the races upon Anialam, Ahmimalia, and Ahminallah needed. Near the end of the destruction of those planets, there was a measure of security for a specific number of those races. However, as they sought safety in each new planet they found themselves on, up to and including the point at which Osodon and Oosiah destroyed the doors between worlds, those races wound up finding their last resting place in Ayeraal. Unfortunately, there was a price to pay for these races, which would lose more and more sense of themselves and consciousness. It would force them to become something far less than what they were for their home planet.

As he lay there comfortably, Kahlip wound up falling asleep while he continued torturing himself, recalling what all alien races went through because of Osodon and Oosiah's destructive behavior.

Katy was up early the next morning. Waking up in her Grandfather's house was magic…a sense of serenity fell over her, as she woke up in matching sheets and a blanket, white walls and a carpeted bedroom floor. But those things were evidence of the love that propagated them in her grandfather. She sat up and stretched. She looked around feeling a sense of completion that she hadn't ever felt. In that moment, she glimpsed what her grandfather was trying to do for her. It was then that she realized what his message to her was in giving her the love he did. It wasn't about the material things, but the security of a family because the Universes represented a broken family…a fallen one. It wasn't too long after Katy realized that that she was out of bed and roaming the house for the kitchen. She thought about that cup of coffee the other day with her grandfather instantly. She had to have another. In that moment, when she walked into the kitchen, she thought about how it was made. Being sensible, she thought she could go ahead and make a pot before anyone woke up. Her grandfather might be surprised that a coffee rookie could make a good first pot without experience or knowing how to do it. She filled the tank with water up to the upper most fill line, and then put coffee in the little basket after emptying the old grounds. She filled the basket just like the old one seemed to be. Then, she turned it on. She looked for three cups in the cupboard and put them on the counter. She turned around and leaned against the counter, as the coffee maker seemed to begin with those strange noises.

In that time in waiting for the coffee maker to finish, Penny walked out of the bedroom and into the kitchen. Penny spoke up. "Good morning, Love." Penny went to the refrigerator and peeked in it. Katy looked at her and smiled, but then her attitude caused Katy to question Penny. Katy thought that couldn't have been the same woman from the day before. Was she taking happy drugs or something? For her personality, she seemed so much different from the day before, and there were things about Penny physically that seemed unusual, as well. It wasn't anything remarkable, but subtle. Katy couldn't put her finger on it, but it almost seemed like if Penny had a twin, that was who was in the kitchen with her at that moment. It was strange in the least. From the refrigerator, Penny went to stand by Katy. She spoke. "Ah...the first cup of the morning." Katy turned to Penny and smiled. She spoke up, thinking of that moment with her grandfather the morning before. "Yeah...I didn't really drink coffee before I met Grandpa, but I had some yesterday, and liked it." Penny glanced over at Katy, when she said that. She thoughtfully took in what Katy said. She stood there contemplating the moment. Then, the coffee maker had finished and both Penny and Katy turned around to their cups. Penny noted that there were three cups on the counter. She spoke up. "You thought of me?" Katy smiled and then spoke. "Yeah...I wasn't sure if you drank coffee, but I thought I'd take a chance. It worked." Penny smiled. Thoughtfully, she spoke as she glanced over at Katy. "I appreciate that." In that moment, Kahlip walked into the kitchen. He looked at his two favorite ladies in the house at that moment. He smiled. Things seemed good. He noticed something though. Penny doesn't drink coffee, but there in front of him, she was pouring a cup. He looked at her and then at Katy. Something was going on. Too, there seemed to be a physical change in Penny that he couldn't put his finger on. She seemed a bit shorter or smaller. It was strange. He ignored that for the moment, and went to two of his favorite women and hugged them equally, as they finished preparing their coffee. Katy and

Penny took their cups and moved away from the counter. Kahlip moved in and took the coffee pot and poured it into the last cup on the counter. He was thoughtful that Katy had thought of him and put a cup on the counter. Penny wouldn't have done something like that. Well, she didn't think of drinking coffee and she wasn't considerate of others that way. From the table where Penny and Katy sat, Kahlip heard them talking quietly between themselves. It was nice to see them so cordial, but it felt odd with what happened yesterday. He finished making his cup of coffee and went to the table. He spoke up. "So, what are you ladies doing today?" Katy and Penny looked at him thoughtfully. He spoke again. "I have to go to the motel today." Penny thought about what he said quickly. She turned to Katy, shrugged, and spoke. "A ladies day out?" Katy looked at Penny and then at her grandfather. She spoke with a hint of doubt about how that would go. "I guess so." Kahlip smiled. "That sounds good." About a half hour later, Kahlip told them he had to go get ready to leave. He got up and left the kitchen, as Penny and Katy began planning what they were going to do.

In his room, Kahlip picked up his cell phone and dialed some numbers. He waited for someone to answer. When someone finally did, he spoke. "Hey, it's I...Penny and Katy are going out today, but I'll be at the motel. You know what to do." He hung up without any kind of departing words. He then went to shower and dress.

Penelope sat reading something she picked up from the bookstore the last time she was there. However, Penelope was always there. It became her kind of second home. It was peaceful and serene and just plain quiet. Penelope had to find the love for books because it was either that or she fall into the trap that many strict moviegoers fell into. It was understanding that the true value of the story revolved around not necessarily seeing the story play out visually, but reading was, having to use the mind, which actually controlled the eyes. And, what was seen. The point was that books gave so much more than a movie could ever do. Knowledge and the capability for it were lessening, as time went on. Movie seemed to be where it was at because people were more visually oriented, than mindfully. At one point, Penelope stopped reading and thought about Kahlip. She thought about how far from him she felt at the moment, which didn't make her feel any better. She felt like a widow who lost her beloved. It hurt to know she wouldn't love again as if she could with him. That was part of the curse of the Keepers, and she knew it. There were many in her past, which indicated to her that she had lost her other half because no one could compare. She wasn't lucky to find anyone that could measure up. It hurt. So, Penelope had to find ways to replace love in her life with a different form of it. She did that with books. Deep down though, she knew Kahlip was somewhere out there, and eventually their paths would cross again. She thought about what that meant. She did have other ways to see her plight and that of her curse in Dawn Keeping. All too many times what became known, as humans had fought to regain their immortal selves, without fully understanding from where that desire stemmed. This was how dark sentient beings of any alien world became. They didn't understand that consciousness is immortal, which is one way to understand being without Kahlip for as long, as she had been currently. She and Kahlip were separated for their jobs, as Plaenellians that had to be done. So, this meant that they were both working wherever they each were. In that moment, Penelope knew that Kahlip felt as she did in some small way about being a widower. She just knew it. However, the immortal side of Plaenellians let them know that eventually the workday would be done and they would each be able to return home to the arms of their other halves. At one point though, Penelope broke down while reading. She knew better than to read something romantic when she was going through a period of missing Kahlip…when she felt most like the widower, longing for the love lost. And, at one point too, she regretted what Osodon and Oosiah had done which perverted the Universes. But that was another part of the curse in being a Keeper was knowing that the Plaenellian parents were what screwed things up for which their children were cursed to undo.

Penelope had to love reading to do what she did as her main source of income. Penelope was a ghostwriter for a few clients, but she also wrote her own stuff, but she did it under the name Cara Wayne. Cara wrote such things as Dark is the skies, and Kind is the light, and she wrote the Fiddler Series, which tied into the Happy by Day trilogy. Penelope began writing when she was a child such things like poems and short stories, which she kept to herself. That was until she could start publishing at eighteen. She kept her writing life to herself, even from her mother. Penelope really wanted to keep a low profile, and unbeknownst to her at the time, it was important that she do so. She wrote controversial concepts that for her day and age weren't necessarily accepted, but she wanted to throw the information out there that might make people think. Always it was meant to enlighten those who may have lived in a darker world mentally, which made sense for a lot of people on the planet currently.

Penelope was one of the lucky ones that had good stuff, which was seen by the right publisher. However, as any Plaenellian knew, things didn't happen by chance. There was a Plaenellian effort to undo what their parents had done, and everything that was done, worked sequentially. This was why Penelope wanted to keep her writing life a secret. Besides that, Cara Wayne meant something to someone somewhere. She knew it.

In all her books, Plaenellian knowledge was laced, but in such a way that it rarely got noticed, for what it truly was, but Plaenellians would get it if they were reading it. Penelope had been studying, which was what she had been doing in reading currently. She picked another author who piqued her curiosity for her romantic style. And, that was the thing about romanticism, it actually stemmed from the Roman times. Hence the Roman in the Romantics. Through what she read, and thought as she read, she had come to the realization that she would probably not catch up with Kahlip this time on Ayeraal. It was a sad fact she had to come to terms with.

A Chapter Under the Face

Over the next few weeks, things with Penny seemed, as though they were remaining on a continuum. Katy had come to like her. And, in what Katy thought was adoration; she thought Penny began to like her too. As time went on too, she began to see what Penny said about having that bad week because Penny made it seem like she was right about that first time they met. Penny and Katy were having what seemed like the time of their lives. The times were so good that Katy even began to think of Penny as Grandmother. And, she eventually began calling her that, even though Penny was so much younger than her grandfather. However, with grandfather went grandmother simply. And, that was the way Katy saw it. Penny even began calling her Kat, like her grandfather. Too, Kahlip began to forget the seemingly high and low in Penny, which was strange that it should just suddenly level out. However, with Penny's new mental state, it did make life better in the house. And, it seemed like Penny had made the changes she needed to for Kahlip and her to stay together. Had she not made those changes, Kahlip was going to have to let her go. However, as with both Lisa and Karen, Penny was someone worth having feelings for, which was a little unnerving to Kahlip, as he did have his widower sense in him over Kaera. However, he did have his Plaenellian heritage, which permitted him to understand the reality behind romance and loving relationships, due to the birth and death scenario to the planet. Deep down all alien races knew it or in other words, it was something lost to them for how consciousness was losing more and more of it, as time went on.

So, with this new sense of bonding that Kahlip noticed in Penny and Katy, he couldn't help but admire the changes in Penny that she made to come to such a state, as to seem more loving than he ever thought possible. He was reminded of the first time they met, and what that felt like. It was disappointing that she never talked to him about having such issues to deal with that might affect her personality. Then again, that was something he noticed. He and Penny just seemingly began on a whim. Suddenly, Kahlip was thrown into the memories of Kaerrie. Sure, he might have mistaken Penny for Kaerrie and Kaera, when she was really nothing more than a Penny. He might have made her out to be more than whom she was, he was following his heart, but sadly, that said nothing about love, but what he needed to do. He had a feeling about Penny, which was really the value of his heart, as it pumped Plaenellian blood and the knowing that stemmed from that.

On the surface, Kahlip was a married man, with his granddaughter living with him and his wife. However, he knew better and he wished he could be that unknowing at times, as to think he was just a married man. This was why there were so many levels to consciousness, and what defined the responsibilities of the Keepers. It was important not to get too hung up on things like love, being separated from their other halves taught them that. Kahlip had the father he didn't know to thank for that, in part, too.

Kahlip was born Steven Louis Alders, to Wilma and Parker Alders. However, Parker wasn't his father. His mother had an affair, for which she kept her secret. But in secret too, laid her guilt for such an affair. She dealt with that in secret until the day she died. So, Kahlip took from his life and how he had been born to a man that technically, didn't owe him anything, with much adoration for Parker because he lived not knowing the truth. At times, it did hurt a little that there wasn't more of a connection to Parker, but Kahlip eventually came to understand why. However, in that time, Kahlip was left to wonder why he didn't have such a connection to Parker. It wasn't until Kahlip came to the age of awareness in his Plaenellian heritage that he began to figure out that Parker wasn't his father. However, Kahlip would come to terms with himself, as some other's son because of his awareness he knew couldn't have been Parker's influence, as a father. In psychiatry, mental illness is given responsibility to the male parent of the offspring. And, Kahlip for what he knew of himself, as such a Plaenellian thing, meant he was possessive of mental illness in certain circles. However, there was a secret in psychiatry that no one knew about, as the mental sciences were an idea in Plaenellians for what they knew about the consequences for certain measures of alien races born to Ayeraal. From that, there were two ways to identify an alien consciousness born to Ayeraal in contrast to a Plaenellian born there upon the planet. Plaenellians weren't actually mentally incapable, as mental illness made certain alien consciousness on Ayeraal as sentient beings. Ironically, this was why psychiatry blamed the male parent for mental illness because it was the male side of the parent door that enabled Plaenellians to be born, and certain races that were more easily prone to mental illness, as an effect of being upon an alien planet or that of Ayeraal. This was how he knew Parker wasn't his father. And, what he knew his mother had done so long ago that he couldn't talk about with her for her death. But Kahlip knew better than to mistrust his heart, and what he knew. And, it was science that actually assisted him in understanding that his father wasn't his father. Kahlip never let what he knew of his mother's affair affect what he felt for Parker or his mother or even his real father. This was the value in being Plaenellian, as Kahlip was. His true father and mother were how he got to Ayeraal, and Parker was there for male support because Kahlip or Steve, as he was known to Parker needed a male role model. However, Parker did think of Steve, as his son with some kind of understanding that Steve was an individual in contrast to himself or just different from his old man. He never questioned the differences between him and his son, like Steve was the result of an affair. Parker just went on to try and be the breadwinner, as most males thought for his generation.

However, for a long time Kahlip was upset because Parker claimed that his mother was the one with the mental illness. However, her supposed mental illness stemmed from her guilt for how Steve was born. That was why she shouldn't have kept it to herself because she dealt with the guilt in silence, and it screwed her up mentally. However, if Parker were keen enough, he would have figured out that his son wasn't his son for his peculiarities because Steve's real father had the same peculiarities. Now in psychiatry, Steve had a condition, but he knew better for what he knew which ironically, made him more alien to everyone else than supposed alien consciousness did. That was the point however. Steve's mental state wasn't because he had any kind of condition. Steve's condition was being Plaenellian and alien to Ayeraal and knowing it.

This was why there was a purpose behind the mental sciences, which Kahlip valued. If he was seemingly normal, he might have had his feelings hurt for being considered mentally ill. However, Kahlip was as purposed, as science for what it was. Early on in the times when alien consciousness became more in tune with Ayeraal for what it was becoming, there were more and more mentally ill patients that were being killed by the religious sect or the Aubrahteerians. Ironically, something had to be done about that. So, the Rosicrucians were valued for their efforts to subdue the battling between the mentally ill and the Aubrahteerians. However, this defined whom the Plaenellians were in contrasts to the truly mentally ill or those alien consciousnesses afflicted by such an alien planet, as Ayeraal. This was another aspect of the curse behind Dawn Keepers nor Plaenellians and why they fought so hard to return things to the way they were once in all the Universes.

For what he knew, he had his granddaughter Katy who could verify him, as an individual and what a prominent citizen he was. She was for all intensive purposes his testament for who and what he was, not because she fully understood his Plaenellian heritage, but the fact that he wasn't mentally unstable. Ironically, Katy would have accredited him with being more stable emotionally and mentally than she was. Besides that, Kahlip, as her grandfather had been the most loving being to her in an insane world where there were more people that cared less for each other. So, when he explained the alien affect in all measures of consciousness, it actually made sense to explain society that way. She knew it made her stronger. Ironically, to deal better with Penny when they first met. Had they met weeks before, Katy would have done to Penny what most of society did to each other. She might have flicked her off and told her to have a nice day, but for the love, Kahlip showed her, Katy had become a better individual. And, for that, she was thankful. It really did help her in opening up to Penny for as hard as that had been at first. However, Katy and Penny were having the time of their lives.

Penny and Katy found themselves at the salon early one evening. It was another girl's day out. Penny had her hair up in pins getting her haircut. Katy was having her nails done after her manicure. Katy turned to Penny and smiled. She spoke. "I just wanted to say thanks, Penny. I haven't had such a good time ever." Suddenly, Penny considered something. Suddenly, the reality set in that what she was trying to do was actually working, as she knew she could do it. However, those made her want to stop.

The Chapter to Feel

It was later that night when Katy and Kahlip were asleep. Penny stood on the back porch thoughtfully. Her heart that she wasn't supposed to have was catching up with her. Of course, of her two other sisters, Penny Rose was supposedly the weakest. That was what Pen had said once, but ironically, she used against her to get her to take over where she was failing in the plan with Kahlip and his family. That was something Kahlip didn't know. When he had been planning and plotting against Osodon and Oosiah, Oosiah was behind him attempting to undo his efforts, up to and including infiltrating his family for their eventual undoing. The story went that Darion Knight had disappeared and went into hiding to begin forging the plans against the supposed Dawn Keepers. However, that was the value of Osodon as Almichen, the Dawn Keeper. The truth of the matter was that Oosiah was behind everything. John Horn actually had nothing to do with it, but perhaps provide her the ability to have her three daughters, who became the Horn sisters. And, each of them were named Penny. There was Penny Rose, Penny Lynn, and Penny Ray Horn. Sadly, Oosiah didn't realize when she was naming Penny Rose that she was doing so for her mushy heart, which would prove to be a detriment to Penny, for what their mother wanted to accomplish through them.

So, Penny Rose was left to consider how she and Katy had connected, and she didn't fully understand her mother's hatred of Kahlip. On the surface, Penny rose had an idea that her mother, Lilly Horn had gotten burned by Steve Alders when they were younger, but Penny Rose didn't fully understand the whole Oosiah concept behind her mother. As far as being mentally coherent, Penny Rose just thought Steve or Kahlip had burned her mother, forcing her to want to take her revenge out on him and his family. No matter how her mother tried to explain, what she had between herself and Kahlip, Penny Rose just didn't get it. And, for her mother, as such a creature, she loved her dearly and didn't want to oppose her. So, she worked diligently to appease her mother. However, Penny Rose was having doubts about helping her mother bring down Steve and his family. There was something about that little Katy that had struck her just right. She felt such controversy in her heart for what her mother wanted her to do, that she felt her heart aching at the thought of Kahlip going through the hell her mother had planned. There were times she wished she were born with no heart at all. That way, she could do what her mother wanted without doubting what she had to do. There was something in Kahlip that she actually began to like. However, she was stuck with her mother's revenge plan, whatever that was. However, she was growing tired of the cloak and dagger, as it was. There were moments where Penny Rose would have just liked to be born into a normal family, without the apparent darkness inherent in her mother. Life doesn't seem like life, and she verged telling her mother that very thing. Life wasn't about the inherent darkness in her that vengeance was important. No matter what her motivation, Penny Rose was slowly losing her loyalty to her mother, and gaining it for Kahlip, and that little girl he had nicknamed Kat. Suddenly, Penny felt her heart bursting with feelings she never knew she had. Suddenly, she felt alive and light. She felt amazing. And, it was in that moment that she thought about telling her mother and her sisters that she wasn't giving up what she found with Kahlip.

Penny Rose thought about when she was younger and what life was once and growing up with her mother for who she was. Penny Rose was a different girl before her mother tried to afflict her with her vengeance. She thought about that in that moment, as she was alone on the porch. Penny Rose actually enjoyed being who she was, until her mother made the switch with her and her sisters. Then, all of a sudden life was different that it was purposed it be so different. And, for a girl of thirteen, which was when her mother decided it was time to take the fun out of life, life then became that much harder. Penny Rose thought about how much darker her mother's view of life had become that she shared with her and her sisters. It seemed like her mother were on a continuous low, and it never changed, which the continuity was nice, but Penny Rose wished it were at a higher level. Her mother's view was just seemingly so very different from the way she saw things. However, Penny Rose didn't give in totally to it. And, she sensed her mother's frustration with her over that. Penny Rose did resist, which was very different from her sisters, who were so seemingly willing to be loyal without question. Her mother said jump and they did it, without thinking for themselves. Sadly, Penny learned a lot from that. And, she learned a lot about herself enough to know that deep down, what Kahlip had coming he wouldn't be prepared for. And, her mother was so well versed in that valor and secrecy thing that Kahlip eventually wouldn't have a chance. On a tearful note, Penny made up her heart and mind. Suddenly, something struck Penny in that moment. She thought about Kahnelle and what he'd been to and for her. Suddenly, she thought about the accident so long ago. And, she thought about something her mother said, since she'd been out of the accident. And, what she once said before the accident. In that moment, Penny Rose realized why she had the accident. She fell into one of the lawn chairs and cried. She shed more tears in that moment than she had memory for her entire life. As Penny Rose sat there, she glimpsed that her mother tried to have her killed, but that went back to what her mother said before she had the accident. Then, what she had said to her after the fact, and shortly after, she came out of the coma. That had been shrouded from Kahlip that Penny Rose was even communicating with her mother since the accident. It was that part of her life she was trying to keep from Kahlip, and it had worked so far. Up to that moment where Penny Rose was feeling like she couldn't continue aiding her mother in bringing Kahlip and his family down. Penny Rose thought about that, as she sat there in loneliness on the porch. And, the hour was growing later and later, but she couldn't help herself out of the disparity in which she found herself. It was in that moment that she knew what she had to do, in the face of another potential threat by her mother because Penny Rose couldn't do what she wanted her to do. In that, made Penny Rose the rebellious child to her mother. But see, that was really the plight of everyone involved, as far as legends go. On the surface, what was happening was one big case of social drama; however, the true characters to the plot understood that life was more than mere human relations were. They understood that there was something underlying the destruction of the Universes, whether it was Osodon and Oosiah doing that or whether it was their Plaenellian offspring trying to oppose them; the story underlying everything was there whether anyone could see it or not. And, Penny wasn't given the whole story, but a few minor details from her mother. So, she knew that Kahlip was Kahlip because her mother knew him, as such, not Steve for how everyone else may know him.

Suddenly, Penny Rose had a thought. She wanted to get to know this evil man, as her mother so eloquently had referred to him once. As Penny was finding out, Kahlip wasn't as evil, as her mother made him out to be was. Suddenly, Penny Rose realized that she was given an opportunity to really do what lie in her heart. She was given the opportunity to save Kahlip and his family, in an effort to become a hero of sorts. Though she lost a lot from the accident, she didn't lose her heart, and she glimpsed something in that moment. She glimpsed a longer history behind her. It spoke of something far grander than she ever thought possible deep within her. It didn't make sense at first, and then suddenly, Penny Rose remembered something. Suddenly, she had awakened wholly from the accident. She finally came to terms with, as the light bulb went off over her, that her mother wasn't trying to kill her, as Penny Rose, she was trying to kill her, as Kaerrie, Oosiah's Plaenellian daughter. And, it apparently worked because for a long time, she didn't recognize herself, as Kaerrie, but strictly Penny. She thought suddenly of Kahnelle for how he had looked after her, as she lay in that hospital bed. Suddenly, she glimpsed something in him that spoke of betrayal. It didn't make sense. He had gotten her and Kahlip together, but in that moment, she realized that he did that, after the accident. He did that under the premise of her, as Kaera, Kahlip's supposed other half. But she questioned that though, because even Kahnelle referred to her, as Kaerrie. Suddenly, it didn't matter now. Suddenly, Kaerrie, the Plaenellian daughter of Osodon and Oosiah was awake, and in the right place to protect Kahlip, unbeknownst to her mother or sisters.

The Chapter in the Tear

Suddenly, Kaerrie, for the first time since she arrived on Ayeraal, she felt so good about being where she was, which was the value of her mother, Lilly and her sisters, who were mean to her growing up because she was so different than they…she had a heart. That should have told Penny Rose that she was above the darkness inherent in her family that festered like a sack of infection on an unhealed wound. Suddenly, Penny Rose or Kaerrie finally saw that even her mother Lily was just Lily Horn, and that she really didn't understand herself, as Oosiah. Suddenly, she saw how the darkness inherent in consciousness was working to affect the light. Suddenly, she realized that to do what Osodon and Oosiah had done, they had to forget whom they were to cause the destruction of the Universes. Suddenly, Kaerrie felt more alive in that moment than ever before. And, suddenly, she heard noises coming from around the corner of the house. First, it was a subtle, lone voice. Then, she heard footsteps. She remained quiet to hear any other noises. And, before she knew it, she was faced with her two sisters. She sat looking at them. She sat in shock. She spoke up. "What are you two doing here?" Penny Lynn spoke up. "Checking up on you." Penny Rose looked at her two sisters quickly. She spoke up. "How did you know I'd be outside?" Penny Ray smiled and looked at Penny Rose. She spoke up. "We didn't." Penny Rose thoughtfully eyed her two sisters. Penny Ray spoke up to Penny Lynn. "One of has to switch with her!" Penny thoughtfully questioned what that meant. She eyed them equally, but she knew. She stared suddenly coldly at them. She had to. She was building strength against what she glimpsed they would do. Penny Lynn looked at Penny Rose. She smiled and spoke. "Sis, it's time to give up your place. I am back, and I will take over for you. You were only supposed to do this for a little while." Penny Rose stood up. "I am not ready to leave." Penny Ray spoke up.

"You don't have a choice, sis. Mom said…" Penny Rose spoke up, interrupting her sister from finishing her comment. She had frustration in her voice. "I don't care what mom said!"

All the while, from behind the sliding glass doors. Katy watched the three women arguing. She barely heard them speak for the glass of the doors.

Penny Lynn spoke up quickly. "Sis, it's time…I am back and you can go. Or else…" Penny Rose spoke up loudly. "Or else what…you will try to kill me again?" Her two sisters eyed each other. They returned their eyes to their sister. They spoke up together. "Penny…" Penny Rose spoke up. "Penny nothing…you two…I know everything. I finally know. I know it was mom that tried to get me out of the way. I know you two had something to do with it. And, I know why. So, no, I am not going anywhere."

As she stood by and watched, Suddenly, Katy fully understood what was going on. She realized that Penny hadn't been one person, but perhaps three different people at intervals. It was uncanny, as she watched what appeared to be triplets with no distinction between them, except perhaps their clothing. Suddenly, Katy felt motivated to walk out of the house and address the three of them, when she should have went and woke her grandfather. She didn't do what she should have done, but exited the house. And, that would cost her greatly.

The three women turned to look in the direction of the sliding glass doors that began to open. Penny Rose thought about something in that moment, and her worst fears were recognized, as she looked at Katy walking out. Penny Rose spoke up. "Katy, go in the house and lock the doors!" Penny Lynn spoke up. "Yeah, Katy…go in the house like a good little girl." But before Katy had time to do anything, Penny Ray lunged at her, grabbing her and confining her arms and mouth. Penny Lynn withdrew a gun. Penny Rose and Katy looked at the two women in shock. Penny's heart sank. Penny Lynn spoke up. "Now, you two are going to be quiet or this gun will go off, and we will escape." Penny Lynn looked at Penny Ray and spoke. "Take the brat to the car, bind her, and with a gag, shut that damn mouth. Me and Penny Rose have to switch clothes." Penny Rose looked at Katy with a breaking heart. Katy looked at Penny Rose. Penny Rose spoke up. "Katy, don't worry…it will be alright." Katy tried to free herself, at least her mouth to no avail. Penny Ray took Katy to the car, as instructed while her two sisters were left at a stance against each other. Penny Lynn spoke up. "Now, sis, this can go easily, or the other way." Penny Rose didn't want anything to happen to Katy, so she was going to do this easily. Penny Rose started to undress, giving the illusion that she was willing to cooperate, What she didn't realize was that for what she said, her sisters had to do things with her that weren't necessarily going to be in her favor. All the while, Penny Lynn kept thinking about the fact that they now had Katy, one of Kahlip's granddaughters in custody. They were definitely going to be in good with their mother. As far as Penny Rose, she should have died in that accident.

Penny Lynn took her sisters clothes and held them while she directed Penny Rose to go to the front yard. Once in the front yard, she too, was bound and gagged in the backseat of the car with Katy. Penny looked at Katy who seemed frightened. Penny turned to her sisters who were casually chatting while Penny Lynn put on her clothes. She threw the clothes she was wearing on Penny Rose's lap. She turned to Penny Ray and commented. "You know what to do." Penny Ray smiled, as she turned to her bound sister and that man's little, precious granddaughter. She chuckled then and spoke. "Yeah…I do." Penny Lynn left the front yard for the back yard, while Penny Ray got in the car and drove off with her two passengers. Penny looked at Katy who had a tear running down her soft, young cheek. She wasn't crying because she was afraid for her life. She was crying because she was hurt, and the thought of never seeing her grandfather again hurt too much to bear. Penny Rose looked over at Katy who was crying. It touched Penny Rose that she regretted everything she had become that would put Katy in such a position. However, what Katy didn't know was what Penny Rose was actually doing there in her grandfather's house. Unfortunately, Penny looked like one of the bad guys in the whole mess, that she didn't think she would be able to get Katy to understand that she wasn't like her sisters. She didn't know if Katy could believe that she was actually working for her and Kahlip…for their survival. Suddenly, Penny Rose had tears of her own. Katy turned to look at Penny Rose who was bound, just as she was. Suddenly, she saw the woman next to her, and though she looked like her sisters, she didn't look like her sisters. Katy recalled how the past few weeks had gone with Penny, as she looked at her. Penny could only imagine what Katy was thinking at that moment. There they sat, both bound and gagged, tears on their faces, but when things should have been their worst, Katy actually found comfort in the fact that Penny was there with her. That was what the last few weeks had done for her in contrast to Penny. She wasn't just her grandfather's wife. She was her grandmother. Katy knew Penny was the good one between the three. She knew their immediate past wasn't a falsehood, put on by that woman next to her. Katy knew she loved her grandmother, as much as she had loved her grandfather. And, Katy knew that the woman next to her loved her dearly. Katy had seen it, felt it, and lived it. Katy, at that moment, wanted to be able to speak so she could tell her grandmother that she loved her for what she thought was her coming end. And, somewhere deep down, that woman next to her was feeling responsible for the situation in which, the two of them were. She wanted to be able to tell her that it wasn't her fault, that she did love her. Most of all, Katy wanted to tell that woman next to her that she thought of her, as her grandmother.

Penny turned and looked at her sister, driving the car at an elevated rate of speed. While she was distracted, Penny worked to try and free her hands, as Katy looked on. However, the big clear packing tape was hard to escape from, as it couldn't be ripped. It had to be cut. Katy used it on many boxes, tearing it; if it was the good, kind was hard to do.

Back at the house, Penny Lynn went inside the house, as if nothing was wrong. She went inside recalling being there before. She was rekindled with those days, but Penny Lynn had learned something about what she had to do to gain Kahlip's confidence, but she knew that it was going to be hard. Penny Lynn didn't have her sister's kind heart. She didn't have what it took to make a man feel like she loved him. Even though she knew, the consequence with her mother if she didn't do what she needed to. It wasn't enough motivation to get the job done, but Penny Lynn was going to try to do it, no matter what it might take. At least that was what she thought. Penny Lynn just wasn't designed to fake love.

The Chapter for the Plan, the Wrench
and the Cursing of Penny Rose

Kahlip awoke the next morning to a quiet house. Katy's door was shut. He noticed in passing it. He went on to the kitchen to make the morning coffee. He thought about what he and Katy and perhaps Penny might do that day. Kahlip withdrew three cups from the cupboard and put them on the counter, as he finished preparing the coffee maker. He went and got the creamer out because he knew Katy would like that. And, Penny would too perhaps. He leaned against the counter and recounted the days since Katy moved in. He was so happy to have her in the house. And, she became so much to him in the short time they first started watching the stars. He thought of those times with a smile. He thought about their first meeting. He smiled wider from that memory. He loved Katy, as he anticipated he would upon finding her. He couldn't recall a moment that was any more important to him that didn't include any one of his family members in it. Katy was one of those who became such a larger part of the picture of his life. It was an awesome feeling.

The coffee maker finished brewing. He turned and made a cup for himself. He thought about those two who the other cups were for. He smiled, at how they waited for their owners to awaken. He took his cup and went to the back porch for a morning stint in the early morning sunshine and air. It was a routine for him. He liked to greet the morning outside. And, he really liked his back porch, which was really a simple thing, and not too extravagant. Kahlip wasn't complicated, as far as that went. As he made it to the porch, he noticed that he could perhaps cut the grass and do some minor weeding. He noticed the time and wanted to wait till nine that morning. He knew Mrs. Carlysle was home and she liked to sleep until nine. She claimed the lawn mower would wake her up, and asked him that he not start it up before then. Kahlip obliged her. She was one of the good neighbors, not that Kahlip had bad ones, but Mrs. Carlysle was more personable than the others were. Mrs. Carlysle was, of sorts, a royalty of a certain alien race Kahlip had come to love so long ago. But that wasn't necessarily the important thing because everyone was equally important, no matter whom they were once or could be again.

The time slipped by. Kahlip had cut the grass after nine. He finished up in the yard and was thoughtful that he hadn't seen Katy yet or Penny for that matter. He eyed his watch. It was a little after noon. How odd! He went into the house after putting the lawn mower up in the shed. He noticed that seemingly, no one was awake. He went to Katy's room and knocked on the door. She didn't answer. He knocked again, but he still got no answer. He cracked the door open and peeked inside. He noticed her bed was empty, but had been slept in. She must have got up and left early while he was working in the yard. That was strange that she didn't say good morning or goodbye. Kahlip thought about Penny. She wasn't even up, but at that moment, she walked out of the bedroom. She smiled at Kahlip and spoke. "Good morning, dear." Kahlip looked at Penny curiously. He spoke up. "Katy apparently left…she didn't say anything to me before she left." Penny eyed him when he said that. She spoke easily. "That's odd." She walked past him down the hall, heading for the kitchen. Kahlip eventually followed behind her. He spoke up. "There is coffee in the kitchen. I don't know how good it is now, but you can try it." Penny spoke up instantly. "Oh dear…that's okay…I don't drink the stuff. It's gross." Penny entered the kitchen and Kahlip stopped in his tracks. He stood looking in Penny's direction, as she entered the kitchen. He became thoughtful that just the other day, Penny and Katy had coffee. Suddenly, Kahlip considered something. He spoke silently, "Damn…she's back. Here goes the roller coaster."

He walked in the kitchen after her. He spoke up, as he eyed her. "Dear…you just had coffee with Katy the other day…you didn't act like it was gross." Penny turned to him thoughtfully. "Oh yeah…I suffered through it with Katy for her sake. I wanted to bond with her. I used it as a tool. So, if you see me drinking it again, it would probably only be with her." Kahlip looked at her, as she spoke. He felt better for her answer. He contrarily thought that maybe he wasn't getting back on the roller coaster. What she said made sense. Penny, however, hid her distress from that moment. She thought about how Penny Rose was supposed to stick to the plan. And, drinking coffee wasn't part of the plan. There was a whole scheme behind using three girls alike to infiltrate Kahlip's family. It was agreed upon that whoever had to play at Penny would only do certain things, and drinking coffee wasn't one of them. Damn her. Suddenly, Penny anticipated what else Penny Rose had done to destroy the plan. She noticed one thing. Buying pink outer garments was one of them. Penny Lynn hated pink, but her sisters didn't mind it, but if one didn't like something, then it was out of the plan. Another was using the kind of hairbrush Penny Rose had been using. Suddenly, Penny worried about other things Penny Rose had done that might make it harder on her to do what she needed to with Kahlip. Penny Lynn didn't think about that when she decided to take over for Penny Rose. She only hoped Penny didn't start eating fish or make claims to liking it. Suddenly, Penny thought about how Penny Rose would be laughing at her because of what she knew had done. Suddenly, Penny had a very nervous sensation in her stomach from anticipating what she potentially faced with Kahlip. Damn! Suddenly, she realized why it seemed so hard to do. She and Penny Lynn had switched before, and all along, Penny Rose had been straying from the personality they created to fool Kahlip.

Kahlip suggested that she and Katy join him for perhaps an afternoon at the mall. He wanted to do some light shopping for the motel, and needed something that he could only find there at the mall. Penny looked at him for his suggestion. She spoke up. "Well, do you want to wait for Katy? I mean…she didn't say where she was going at all or when she'd be back." Kahlip spoke up when she said that. "That's what I mean…it doesn't make sense. It's almost as if someone came into the house and kidnapped her." Penny eyed him when he said that. She chuckled lightly. "Oh, but we know that didn't happen. I mean the house was shut up tight when you awoke this morning right." Just then, as she said that, Kahlip thought about something. He went looking for his keys. Suddenly, he had the information he needed to find out what was potentially going on. Penny looked at him, as he seemed to be on the hunt for something. Penny followed after him. She spoke up. "What are you doing? Where are you going?" Kahlip didn't answer her, but he eventually found what he was looking for. He held his keys up to Penny. Penny stared at him. She spoke up. "So, why is that important?" Kahlip looked at her. "Penny, Katy told me she didn't want a key to the house, that she wouldn't need them. She wouldn't take one from me even if though I offered it to her." Penny still didn't understand to what he was pointing. Kahlip spoke again. "If the house was locked up tight, then Katy couldn't have left on her own because she needs a key to lock the door. Here are my keys. And you have yours, they are hanging." Penny stood thoughtfully in contrast to him. Suddenly, she felt nervous. She felt panicky. She stared at him for something to say next. All she could think was, "Curse you Penny Rose." Then, something to say struck her. Moments passed as Kahlip stared at her. He was thoughtful of something amiss. He stared at her with an accusing gait. Penny spoke up suddenly. "Wait...I did make her a key. You didn't know it, but I eventually got her to take one from me." Kahlip stood there looking at Penny. He rationalized Katy being persuaded to take a key, when, as he recalled she was adamant that she didn't need one. He spoke up. "Well, how did you do it...I mean...get her to take one?" Penny looked at him with a sense of relief. She spoke up. "A woman's sensibility I suppose. You know how it is...a woman needs a way to get in to her house. And, we are considering this her house too, right?" Kahlip thought about what she said. It made sense. He was just disappointed that Katy didn't talk to him about it. In that moment, Kahlip noticed the shirt Penny was wearing. And how good it did look on her, as Katy said it might when she bought it. He spoke up. "That shirt does look good on you, as Katy said it would." Penny looked at the shirt and spoke. "I hate pink!" Kahlip looked at her when she said that. He spoke up. "That's not what you said when she gave it to you. You said it was your favorite." Penny thought about Penny Rose in that moment, and how angry she was getting from the stress that was put on her at that moment. That was the importance of having a plan. "I know, but I said that for her benefit." Suddenly, Kahlip thought about something. That fell right in line with being fake, as if she felt like she had to impress Katy, which didn't make for a strong relationship. Kahlip thought, "Yep, back on the roller coaster. How disappointing." He turned from Penny and went to the kitchen for a cool drink, and a thought alone. Penny stood there watching him walk away. She had several thoughts about what she wanted to say to Penny Rose. Suddenly, she realized Penny had been working to destroy the plan for a while now. She pondered how things were going to go. And, suddenly, she became thoughtful that they just might need Penny Rose more than they thought. She anticipated another talk with Penny Rose eventually. Penny Lynn sensed how hard things were going to be with Kahlip. She pondered instantly what other things Penny Rose did to destroy the plan.

Kahlip entered the kitchen with his cell phone that had been at his side since he worked in the yard. He always had his cell phone at his side when he was out of the house. He just had taken it off yet. He withdrew it and dialed some numbers. He waited for a response. There was an answer on the other end. Kahlip spoke up. "Doug…it's my granddaughter, Katy. I think something has happened to her. We need to investigate it. Can you get started right away?" He waited for a yes and then hung up. At that moment, Penny walked into the kitchen, as he hung up his phone. She thought to ask whom he was calling. She felt nervous. Suddenly, she instantly envisioned the plan falling apart steadily. She didn't want to be in the house for being caught. She became paranoid suddenly, and with good reason. Kahlip glimpsed that the woman in his house knew where his granddaughter was at that moment, but worked diligently to make him think otherwise. He didn't like feeling that way about Penny, but he sensed something about her, he didn't like. She was suddenly, a very dishonest person. His trust in her was gone.

✝

A Prelude ll

So, Kahlip had his job to do, even though, every day since Katy supposedly left, he hadn't stopped wondering what had happened. Things with Penny had gotten worse. He found out things about her that seemed alien to the girl he knew long ago, just before they married. So, he had to put his mind into that job and considered how it could be done. In that understanding, he pondered if it could be done or if what happened was permanent, and that consciousness was stuck upon earth within its Universe until the end when the planet would be incapable of birthing any more consciousness. For what Kahlip knew, perspective was a key to understanding the power behind knowledge. And, Knowledge was the key to finding perspective.

Kahlip then realized something from that, which he knew. With the addition of the different consciousness from all the Universes, it wasn't enough to solve the one problem that forged a manic union between consciousnesses on one planet in the first place. From that, he then, realized that somehow, what was happening on the Earth was simply a complex reaction to the problem. There were hoards of varied consciousness from varying planets coming to exist upon one place. And, consciousness or not to what was happening, they were using what they knew from the Universe they originated. Suddenly, Kahlip thought about the book. There was something in there about how the various consciousnesses could have been an effort. However, Kahlip knew one thing the book didn't possess. That thing it was missing was the information on how no various consciousnesses were necessarily working together, even though it may have seemed like it was.

Kahlip thought about something. He considered something he experienced on another planet in another Universe with the similar problem. However, things weren't so amicable. In that, sense of obligation from what he knew, as Plaenellian in nature, Kahlip began to contemplate the beginnings for all consciousness on their respective planets. And, for where he was, he contemplated Earth's beginnings. He contemplated the Anthrocytes and what they had in a planet long before their dreams, hopes and lives were destroyed by the addition of alien consciousness to their Universe, which became added to their planet...eventually. Hence went the Secrets of the Keepers. Hence, Kahlip's reflection, and his loneliness at what he considered was the top.

At home and in peace...sort of...Kahlip heard a knock at his door. Distractedly, he heard it. It was subtle, but that could have been for how distracted he was. He went to the door and putting a hand on the knob, turned it, and slid the door open. Beyond the threshold was an older version of a young face. He stared and smiled. He spoke. "Well, hello!" The woman at the door smiled and spoke. "Hello, father."

Lorande awoke one morning, startled from a dream. She woke up to her bed alone, as it had been the case since the divorce. She didn't know what happened, it just happened that Karry didn't want to be married any longer. She thought about how that affected their daughter, who was named for her mother. Instantly, Lorande thought about the dream. It was odd, Lehmich was there for some reason, and so was Frances. She thought instantly about how Lehmich saved them from the nightmare at the house. She thought Lehmich was her uncle. She'd been told that, but in looking back, there was something else that did not make sense. In looking harder at what was going on, Lehmich saved them. It was as if he had a watchful eye on them. Why would her uncle have kept such a watchful eye on them, ensuring their safety? Something did not make sense. She thought about how she was the mother to her daughter, and how she too felt that she had to keep a watchful eye on Little Lorande growing up, ensuring that her offspring made it in such a dark world. She thought about the predator numbers growing every day. She thought how concerned she had to be with strangers, and their reasons for getting close to her daughter. Suddenly, Lorande had a notion that didn't make sense. She thought of her mother, who had now died five years to the current day. She wondered if Lehmich was still around. Suddenly, she had a notion to find him. She didn't know why. She just needed to see him again. She thought to call Frances. She pondered what she was doing at the current moment.

Frances ducked from being hit. She spoke up with anger. "Damn, Frank, stop!" In the midst of the fighting, her phone rang. She walked away from Frank to get her phone. She answered the call with the button and spoke. "Hello!" Lorande spoke up from the other end. "Frances…hi!" Frances eyed her husband with frustration. She was almost out of breath. She spoke again. "Lorande…not a good time. Frank is…" Frank picked up the lamp from the nightstand and threw it into the wall. There was a loud crash. The light bulb exploded. Lorande heard the commotion. She spoke up with a sense of urgency. "Frances, I am coming over!" Frances did not have time to discuss the issue. She spoke up. "Okay!" She hung up the phone, turning to walk out of the room. She yelled in her husband's direction. "I am not cleaning up after you, Frank!" Frank thought about something and yelled back at her. "You screwed him, didn't you?" Frank heard her, as she walked down the hall. "Yeah…and now I am pregnant!" Frank then sat thoughtfully on the bed. Frances went to the Kitchen. After grabbing some orange juice, she went outside on the front porch. She wanted to be able to greet Lorande when she arrived.

She sat thoughtfully in one of the old wicker chairs. It was the one that could take only her weight because it was so old. That ensured her she would always have a seat at her house. No one could get mad at her for not letting him or her sit because the chair was just too old. She sat easily in the chair, sipping her orange juice. She was enjoying the moment. It was the first sense of peace she had since she was woke up with a drunken Frank at three in the morning. She thought about how he was so self-righteous to think she couldn't screw anyone she wanted, the same, as he'd been doing for the last year. She knew about Tina and Marjorie. He didn't know it, but she knew. She thought about that, and what if he'd gotten them pregnant. So, she didn't use some kind of control, what was the big deal?

She took another sip of her juice and sat patiently waiting for her sister. She thought about Lorande and her divorce. Maybe that was what she should have done? Frances thought hard about that. After five minutes more, Lorande pulled up in her new car. At the same time, Frank came walking out with a gym bag. Frances looked at him, and then at the bag in his hand. Then, she looked back at Frank. She spoke up sarcastically. "What…are you finally leaving? Why didn't you leave after Tina…or Marjorie?" Frank looked at her, as if she shouldn't have known about them. Then, he thought about how he had to pay for Tina's abortion. Frank spoke up, as he gripped his bag a little bit more. "I'll stay if you abort it." Frances eyed him sternly. She could not believe what he just said. Her mouth dropped open. At that moment, Lorande was walking up to the porch. After another moment, Frances spoke up, but calmly because she was done shouting. "Frank…just go. I am not a murderer." She turned and looked away from him. She didn't look back, as he walked away. She didn't even look at him when he got in his car and drove away. Lorande watched him leave, and then when he was gone, she went to Frances. She spoke up with concern. "Need a hug?" Frances turned to her with a smile. She spoke up. "What…after throwing out the trash? It was something that needed to happen a long time ago." She stopped speaking with a smile. Thoughtfully, she spoke up. "Lorande, I am pregnant."

Lorande's mouth dropped open. Her eyes grew wide, and shock kept her from speaking. She looked Frances over and finally spoke. "Well…you do not look it!" Suddenly, Lorande thought about Frank. She spoke again. "Wait. You're pregnant, and Frank is gone. What's right there?" Frances eyed her sister, as she spoke. Thoughtfully, she had words of her own. She spoke, as she looked beyond the porch. "It's not Frank's child." Lorande looked at Frances with wide eyes. "Oh…now that makes sense… sis." Lorande thought about something, as she eyed Frances. She could not believe that Frances was pregnant. Something in that did not make sense. Something deep down was telling her Frances wasn't pregnant.

Frances turned to Lorande. "Lor, Frank's cheated. When I found out, I should have left him, but I thought to give it a try anyway." She stopped speaking and looked beyond the porch. Thoughtfully, she spoke again, as Lorande took in what she said. Lorande sat beside her. "I know what you mean…divorce is not necessarily an option that is easy to accept." Frances turned to her sister with a tear. She thought about her mother. Lorande wanted to tear up with her. Thoughtfully, Lorande spoke up. "Frances…I have been thinking a lot about Lehmich lately. I don't know why, but there is just something there I cannot figure out." Frances ran a cool hand through her dark hair thoughtfully. She turned to Lorande. She looked at her briefly for her long and straight blond hair, thinking back to those times at the Muhndalay. "Lorande… that was a long time ago. We've grown so much since."

Lorande looked at Frances easily. "Frances, did you ever consider that our father is not our father?" Frances eyed her sister when she said that. Thoughtfully, she looked Lorande in the eye. "What would it matter, Lorande? We're older now. So, we didn't grow up having a father." In that moment, Frances thought about lying to Lorande about being pregnant, but she considered how close Lorande was to Frank's sister. Frances did not want Deirdre to get wind that she wasn't. She was done with Frank and wanted him to stay away. Frances understood that lying to Lorande wasn't necessarily trusting her sister, but that last fight with Frank wouldn't let her think clearly.

Lorande thought about what she said. She looked at Frances briefly and then away from the porch. She spoke. "But…Fran… what if we did?" Frances turned to Lorande quickly. "What?" Lorande turned to her sister then with a thoughtful eye She spoke. "You heard me." Frances put a finger in her ear and moved it about a bit, then spoke. "Nope…got peanut butter in my ears… what was that?" Lorande smacked her on the knee. She spoke. "Frances!" Frances laughed. She eyed her sister lovingly. She spoke. "What exactly do you mean…what if we did?" Lorande looked at Frances, as she spoke, then away from her. "Frances, isn't it strange that our uncle seemed to come to our rescue?" Frances thought about what she said. "So…?" Lorande looked at Frances when she said that. "So, why was he keeping such a close eye on us?" Frances thought about what she said. Lorande thought about something, and spoke up. "What about the past do you remember?" Frances thought about what she said. She looked at Lorande, and then out and away from the porch. She sat thoughtfully, silently reflecting on what Lorande considered the past. "Lorande, the past is a blur to me. There is much I didn't understand at that point." Lorande thought about something. She spoke. "Do you remember the Ellis'?" Frances turned to her and spoke. "Yeah… Mick and Kira" Lorande spoke up again. "Do you recall the man that saved us?" Frances sat thoughtfully. "What was his name… umm…Steve?" Lorande spoke up. "Yes…but what you do not know is that I remember mom talking to some guy named Steve when we were kids. She was on the phone. The overall impression I got was that whoever she was on the phone with was our father." Lorande stopped speaking thoughtfully. She spoke again. "I never asked her about it, but I wanted to." Lorande eyed Frances as she stopped speaking. She spoke again, as she thought about something and spoke. "Then, after our mother leaves us for dead, this man Steve shows up to save us. It's almost as if a conversation between them happened that we didn't know about." Frances was starting to see where Lorande was going with that. Frances considered what her sister said. She looked to the street and they watched a couple cars pass. She spoke, as she watched a red truck roll by. Frances spoke up. "Wouldn't that be something?" Lorande looked at her thoughtfully, and spoke. "What's that?"

Suddenly, Frances reached deep within her heart and considered what hurt her for so long. Suddenly, she realized her anger and frustration stemmed from the fact that she didn't grow up with a father in her life. The man her mother was married to was definitely not the father he was made out to be. Then, Frances considered something. She turned to Lorande and spoke. "Why the secrecy, Lorande? Why didn't he just admit to being our father?" Frances stopped speaking and considered something. Lorande thought about what she said. "Think about it, Frances. Think about what was going on. Our mother leaves us for dead. Then, in the midst of this new man that seemingly saved us, all we could talk about was our mother." Lorande stopped speaking and thought about something. She spoke again. "Would you have accepted that he was our father, if he would have admitted it without our mother to back it up?" Frances thought about what she said. That made sense. She then considered something else. "So, what are you proposing?" Lorande thought about what Frances said. She stared at her sister at first, then, spoke. "I think we should find him." Frances thought about what she said. She stared at her briefly. She looked out and away from the porch. She spoke up easily and curiously. "How?" Lorande thought about what her sister said, but she hadn't thought that far ahead. All she had was the idea. Lorande thought about something else and spoke. "I don't know why, but I think we might want to start looking at the Muhndalay. It's an odd feeling."

The longing for Kahlip continues, as equally as the frustration with her mother over Roger continues. Penelope just got off the phone with her Mother, later one night when she asked her if there was any way she could appease her mother and show up for breakfast the next day. Penelope reluctantly agreed, but her mother said that morning would be real important, and that she would really like to have her at home. Penelope had to appreciate the request. If her mother didn't care about her, she wouldn't have asked. Deep in her mind was the fact that her mother was trying to get her over so she could maybe convince her that Roger and her breaking up was a mistake that Penelope couldn't make. She put that out of her mind for the moment. She thought about Kahlip instantly. She let his memory fill her, but it hurt that he wasn't around, and that was when she was filled with thoughts about the curse of the Keepers. It was then that she understood what it meant to be her, not necessarily her mother's daughter, but her. She thought about whom she truly is, as Kaera, the Plaenellian born Kahlip's wife. Consciousnesses or sentient beings on earth didn't understand that it really had it much easier than they thought. However, she did understand the alien effect and existing upon a planet that it shouldn't have come to exist upon. However, going to work only to come home to one's home and loved ones wasn't that bad after a small amount of time away. For Kaera and Kahlip, this time apart was the same as going to work in the morning with one difference. The hours of work were years, and coming home potentially meant on a planet in another galaxy. For Kaera, she had only hoped that their "coming home" would happen on Ayeraal this time.

Kaera had glimpsed coming to terms with being away from Kahlip so long because of work. She thought perhaps that she had to focus on that, which would take her mind off Kahlip, but she always seemed to get to where she was at that moment. She always came back to him mentally, and then emotionally. She did consider that perhaps the problem was that work wasn't time consuming enough to take all of her attention, which didn't make sense for the amount of darkness upon Ayeraal in the minds of the masses of sentient beings.

Kaera's job was perspective or public relations. She had been with Thermal Oil for a few years now and really got started with them over a few incidents where their drilling supposedly caused a few neighborhoods' grief over their drilling methods. Kaera's first job was to subdue the frustration from the residents about what was going on and there were always environmentalists to deal with. The good thing about tomorrow was that it was Sunday, but she thought about Monday when she had to go to battle with the officiating committee on ethics for a new project Thermal Oil was taking in the Congo. It was a big deal because Thermal Oil was being subcontracted to drill in the deepest parts of parts really unknown. Penelope was supposed to present her case to the committee, which governed projects existing outside of the United States to ensure that the United States would in no way receive flack for Thermal Oil's US Roots if something went wrong in the Congo. Relations between Africa and the US have been quiet and peaceful for so long. It was that, and too, the US government wanted to keep track of what others were doing outside of its borders, as well, as inside them. Plus, as many knew, many privateers have been the plight of many US discontents or countries that blamed the US for its privateers. Essentially Penelope was the public relations department to the official US public relations department.

That night, Penelope slept on the next morning with her mother. She wanted to prepare herself for her mother to bring up Roger again, but before long, her thought and dreams flowed over into the missing of Kahlip…again. Then, she was awake for the next hour, but she would eventually fall asleep…again without him.

PART III

PART III

✝

A Chapter in Peace

Kahlip had been on the phone for five minutes when he came to a point where he had to end the call. They had been talking about Katy. And, how Katy hadn't shown up for work on her last few shifts. Kahlip had to hire someone else. He spoke with finality. "Doug, I will have to call you later. I have someone at the door."

Kahlip invited the woman inside. He smiled at her, as she took his invite and walked passed him into the house. She looked around, eyeing the interior décor. Kahlip shut the door slowly, as he kept an eye on her. He was reminded of the girl of yesteryear, and wondered why it took so long to finally seek him out. He invited her into the living room, as she stood waiting while he shut the door. They walked to the living room casually. They sat comfortably on the sofa. Kahlip thought about something, and he asked the looming question. And, the woman thoughtfully looked at him and smiled. "I waited so long because it took me that long to finally understand." Kahlip eyed her, as she spoke. He spoke up when she finished. "So, Karen, how have you been?" Karen smiled at him. She finally spoke. "I have been confused about a lot of things. I have been trying to make sense of the past." Kahlip looked at her when she spoke. He was attentive to her mannerisms. She was reminiscent of her mother. He thought instantly of Lisa, and then, something else. He spoke. "How about your sisters?" Karen lost her smile. She sat thoughtfully a brief moment. She eyed him sadly. "I've lost contact with them." Kahlip instantly thought about Lorande and Frances. He spoke up. "Well, I hope they are okay." Karen thought about something instantly. She looked at the father she never had growing up. She spoke up. "Why, father? I just want to know why?" Kahlip knew the day would come when he would have to answer that question, but it wasn't a one-word answer. It was complex. He reflected on the past thoughtfully. He thought about what he wanted from it. He thought about what he wanted from Lisa. "It was your mother. It was Darion. I could make all kinds of excuses. In the end, I had just had to leave. You had your mother, and the rest of the family. Besides, there is much more than you realize about the past, and what was really going on." Karen eyed him, as he spoke. She considered what he said. She was curious about what was going on. She spoke up. "So, what was really going on?" Kahlip eyed her thoughtfully. He pondered what he thought she could hear. He considered her, as his daughter. He thought about how knowledge of Seyion heritage had long since died, and he thought about how well she could even accept the truth. Karen spoke up in that moment. "So…" Kahlip eyed her. "Okay…I'll tell you." He sat back in the sofa. She anticipated his coming words. He spoke quickly again. "Knowing everything takes that to the beginning, where the truth began instead of what humanity has come to believe." She listened intently, as he spoke. "In reflection, Peace once existed upon Earth. However, that was so long ago, and that was information only well within the Secrets of the Keepers. To these Keepers, Anthrocyte history is not mere legend, but a memory of what earth used to be in contrast to what it had become."

He began to explain everything to her, but in the back of his mind laid Katy and his broken heart for her being gone. Once long ago, there existed the peaceful, loving Anthrocytes. They were gentle beings that existed on a plane of consciousness too high to actually be remembered, but not for those who keep the secrets. They existed on a planet called Ayeraal or what is now considered Earth. Ayeraal was the understanding of their home from the uniform consciousness between Anthrocytes. This is also the proof that earth was made up of varied consciousnesses from various planets and Universes, simply because it had to be agreed upon what to call the planet upon that which they existed. This was not the case with Anthrocytes. It was just kind of understood what the planet was named and everyone understood it. Ayeraal and the way of life upon it were not taught. Anthrocytes did not have to be taught anything of the planet upon which they existed for they existed, as one with it. This is the difference between them and consciousness upon earth in its current state. Sadly, consciousness in its current state was degenerative in contrast to what existed within the Anthrocytes. However, there was knowledge within the Keepers that where consciousness seemed degenerative, that was simply because of the various planets from where they originated. Anthrocytes for their knowledge and way of life did actually, exist in what many thought was a Heaven type scenario, which is where, from a certain point of view, the concept of Heaven stemmed. Again, however, that was knowledge within those who kept the secrets, and had the perspective.

The Anthrocyte way of life was a design of a perfect world. And, that perfect world was easily understandable in seeing that Anthrocytes were part of the ecosystem, never affecting it. However, the planet was spinning at a much higher rate, which defined what it felt like to exist. As with the planet and the higher rate of speed, there was no darkness within the Anthrocytes. It could be said that the nature of a planet's health is indicated within its physical appearance, and within the inhabitants upon it. That meant Ayeraal was in its healthiest state when the peace and tranquility existed within the Anthrocytes and they existed upon Ayeraal. There was no thought to their demise, and in that was a strong sense of belonging.

A day in the life of Anthrocytes was not just one mere day because everything seemed as though it was on a continuum. The higher rate of spin within the planet would not allow for day and night distinction. There were actually no dark spots on the planet in the form of shadow, but again, there was no darkness within the Anthrocytes. Their lives and existence upon Ayeraal was based upon the connection with everything, and everything was known within each Anthrocyte. Where humans have to be taught to think tree, Anthrocytes knew what everything was. This was easy to understand from understanding one's house self-built or having designed one's interior. Anyone that has done this knows why things go together and fit so well. The point was that Anthrocytes lived or existed within a house they felt as though they designed and created. That's the power of building one's house. They felt like they built the planet that there was nothing needing any change. However, this kind of a connection could only come from the planet, as well, about the Anthrocytes. To the planet, the Anthrocytes felt like part of it. It was a perfect sense of unity and within each Universe, there was this tranquility of consciousness upon their respective planets. The Anthrocytes and Ayeraal were one body in existence, which associates with any organ within the body in contrast to the body itself.

This state of the Anthrocytes to Ayeraal was what created the sense of peace within Ayeraal's Universe. The Anthrocytes were a compliment to the planet itself, which was the case for all planets and measures of consciousness to them. There was such a sense of completion within the Anthrocytes stemming from this union between Ayeraal and them that an end to it could not have been foreseen. At this point, unity…true unity between consciousness and a planet was complete and a state of perfection had been created.

Kahlip stopped speaking. He eyed Karen. She was immersed in the ocean of his words. She sat looking at him when he stopped speaking, considering what he said. Kahlip then spoke up. "That's why it is easier for all manners of consciousness to just think they are only human upon this planet. Kahlip thought about something he had not said. Karen thought about what he hadn't said. Suddenly, she had a glimpse. It was something from the distant past, far distant than her beginnings on earth this time around. She quietly spoke up. "So…I am…like you." Kahlip looked at her with a sense of sadness and the hope that she was wrong. He studied her briefly before he spoke. "I hope not for that would mean you possess my curse." She looked at him strangely for saying that. She pondered what he meant. She spoke. "Curse?' Kahlip stood and walked to the window thoughtfully. He spoke, as he eyed the world beyond it. "Yes Karen, to be me is a curse. You don't understand the ramifications. Never once did I think that I would have offspring that would know the things I do." Karen stood and looked at the back of his head. "Some things aren't in your control or designed by thinking it." Karen stopped speaking and looked at him. She spoke up after she thought about something else. "You think I was easily fooled. You think I am engulfed by this human concept. Well…you're wrong. I know there is more to it." Kahlip thought about something, as she stopped speaking. He spoke up. "So, you know of Osodon…" Karen interrupted him quickly. "And, Oosiah…yes, I know." Kahlip turned to her and spoke. "You are cursed." Karen studied him quickly. She felt lighter inside for having talked with him. She spoke up. "Father…how do you think I knew to find you?" She stopped speaking thoughtfully, and looked harder at him. "We all play the game, Father." Karen stopped speaking and looked at him.

Kahlip stared back. Kahlip knew what she meant. In a board game, each player has to become his or her piece on the board, essentially becoming part of the game, but each knows what exists beyond the game. That was the Plaenellians. And, that defined the humans that played the human game, thinking that was exactly what they are. Humans think they are the checkers on a checkerboard, which is red in contrast to black, and vice versa. Instantly, Karen thought about something. It was something she hadn't told her father. "Father, it's why I got into Psychology and Psychiatry. I am helping to down the awareness in my patients about their anxieties about being born to a planet that is alien to them." Karen stopped speaking thoughtfully. She looked at her father and considered something else. She spoke again. "That was the worth in the study of the mind. We have always been working towards the forgetting of other worlds by consciousness on this planet. That's been my area of expertise. It's why criminals are criminals, and the mentally impaired aren't prone to the lack of controls of this planet. The criminal element is subjected to prose of an ordinary world. And, I am talking the hardest of criminals who have fewer controls put upon them, that they go wild."

Karen stopped speaking, as she eyed her father. Kahlip turned to her. He looked at her with a sense of appreciation for her, more than he ever had in any one individual. Suddenly, he thought about her sisters. He pondered the reality behind them and his curse. Karen spoke up again. "You think I fell into the mind trap of humanity. Dawn Keepers and Dark Treaders and the legend was created to down the knowledge of consciousness from the Seyion planets. That is why it is legend. I know that." Kahlip took a lasting look at his daughter. "Okay…okay…I get it. You have my curse. And, if that is true, then you understand why it is a curse." Karen looked to the floor before she spoke. "Yes, I do." She looked to him for solace from her feelings. She spoke. "But it feels less like a curse when you have someone that feels what you do." Kahlip turned away from her. He thought about Lisa instantly. He spoke up with emotion in his throat. "I thought I had that in your mother." Karen thought about what he said. She looked at him and spoke. "I know you did. I finally realize that." Kahlip turned to her thoughtfully. "I see that I have that in you, however." Karen thought about her sisters. "You will have that in my sisters, too." Kahlip considered what she said. Suddenly, he thought about something. On one hand, that was good, there was solace in numbers. However, on the other, many Plaenellians in one area was not necessarily a good thing. He did not like the implications.

Karen thought about something. She spoke up. "Father, I do have to go. I have a few other things to tend to." Kahlip looked at her solemnly before he spoke. "And, you will return at some point?" Karen smiled, as she felt his yearning for their connection. She eyed him with a bit of a tear in her eye. She instantly considered not having him in her life as a child, and how hard that was. "Yes father…I will. I cannot lose you again. Besides, in the end, you are my Plaenellian brother." Kahlip smiled when she said that. He felt better for her having to leave. Ironically, Kahlip stood now, with a stronger sense of peace than he had before. He never realized, as Plaenellians never really do, that one's offspring could actually be cherished and appreciated. However, that only went so far.

Lorande drove, while Frances sat comfortably in the seat next to her. Well, she wasn't comfortable inside. She spoke up abruptly. "Lor, I got to be honest." Lorande looked between her and the road. Frances noticed she was trying to keep her attention on the road, as well as her. She spoke again. "I am not pregnant, but you cannot tell Deirdre. I want Frank to think I am. It's over between him and I." Lorande looked at Frances one final time. She spoke up. "I knew you weren't." Lorande, then looked at the road with finality, as she thought about Deirdre. "Don't worry Fran, I won't tell her." Frances smiled and spoke. "Good…now I feel better." She sat thoughtfully a moment before she spoke again. She turned to her sister lovingly and spoke. "Lor…I hated lying to you, but…" Lorande interrupted her. "Don't worry about it. Had you not said anything…" Frances then tried to finish her sentence. "You would have told her." Lorande looked at the road. She sat thoughtfully, as she drove. She finally spoke up. "Yes, but I'll tell you why." Frances turned to her sister and listened intently. Lorande continued to speak. "It would have been another stab at Frank Deirdre couldn't take. Deirdre thinks too highly of him sometimes that she doesn't realize his flaws." Frances listened intently. She thought about something in that moment. Lorande continued to speak. "She makes him out to be the victim. He doesn't have to do a thing. I would have liked to tell her that you two are no more because he is not so perfect, as she thinks." Frances smiled. "You don't have to do that." Lorande drove comfortably as she listened to her sister say those words. She thought about how Frances had been treated in her life by the sad state of men that she let linger. She considered something. She spoke up with her eyes on the road. "You know, sis, this might be a time to look Ray up." Frances turned to Lorande with a smile. She chuckled and Lorande turned to her. "What?" Frances just looked at Lorande, but she knew what that meant. "Ray? Lorande, come on." Lorande spoke up. "He's charming…funny…witty."

Frances shook her head and spoke. "Lorande…" Lorande quickly spoke again. "He's hot!" Then Frances burst out laughing. She spoke when she stopped laughing. "Ray…hot?" Lorande looked between Frances and the road. Frances spoke again. "Thanks, Lor, but I will be fine. I'll find him on my own." Lorande looked easily at the road. She considered what her sister said. She knew what Frances would find on her own. It was the same sad thing every time.

The Chapter in a Word

Kahlip hung on the phone, as he heard Doug say those fateful words. He didn't want to hear it, especially from someone like Doug. Apparently, his mother had been harvested. It killed Kahlip, but with that, he knew Oosiah was closer than he thought. Osodon and Oosiah were always the curve in the graph of the harvest.

And, the word was Keepers, and they were very important, but not until the demise of the peace and tranquility between consciousness and its planet. The Keepers of the secrets had to be instilled with the knowledge of their purpose, and that purpose was the height of many frustrations within them. Kahlip knew that about himself. Sadly, all Keepers had the knowledge of what was, which in a sense, was a curse in itself. It was hard to maintain the knowledge of what was in contrast to what is now. It was hard to be capable of seeing the end of something, knowing what could have happened that might have kept everything on a continuum or maintained its survival. In the end, the Keepers had Osodon and Oosiah, their parents' to blame, which was perhaps the hardest thing to accept. It didn't feel good to know that one's birth and creation was a consequence or a security measure whose purpose was to counteract what wrong had been done.

That word was also destitution. Keepers were destitute. This meant they did not have a planet to call home. Their next planet was their goal, which added to their curse because if by some chance, they found their other half, they would probably be separated from them, as soon as they left their current planet or station. Keepers had the knowledge that their home was the culmination of all the Universes, which indicated their chances of finding a sense of belonging. This is what it meant to harbor the control of their parents. It's kind of like the blood within the body, which has to be a part of everything, but in that, it will never truly understand its origin. It just is. It has its duty and it is always moving, indicating that it will never find a home. It is believed the blood dies off and new cells are grown. Sadly, Keepers never die; they always know what they know from one planet to the next. Before they came to exist, consciousness upon any planet never died…until their parents did what they did, which indicated the difference between consciousness of any planet, and the Plaenellians, otherwise known, as the Keepers.

The word was also intent. Unlike the average consciousness appearing upon any planet or due to the breakage between Universes, Keepers existed with intent from one planet to the next. They were always searching for that solution to the problem, affecting the Universes due to the control in them over those Universes for their parents' activities. Unfortunately, the birth of the Keepers didn't affect what their parents' had done. The sad thing was that they had to forge their intent to affect the Universes. Sadly, what their parents' had done set the Universes on a downward spiral or had set them on a course of destruction. At one point, the Universes were set upon from a blueprint, which indicated everything to keep them eternal. However, their parents added an element of chaos within them by affecting the blueprint. Removal of planets from any one of the Universes offset the initial balance and introduced the break between them. This was the initial crime of Osodon and Oosiah.

In Osodon and Oosiah was the word. That word is jealousy. Many of their Plaenellian offspring hold contempt for what they thought was their jealousy in their parents for other consciousness existing in Universes they could not exist. By doing what they did, opened up the Universes to them. Many thought it was because they transferred planets between Universes. Actually, they might have had it right; that was perhaps their method. It was their reasoning and motivation that was important. Osodon and Oosiah were like the inventor that wanted to be a bigger part of the invention. A light bulb was a universe all its own, but Osodon and Oosiah were invasive, and had to have their hands in it, which meant the light bulb was never going to work. Osodon and Oosiah were also like the inventor of the car who could not see a finished product that it never came to work independently. They were also like a bear at a picnic. Once the bear arrives, the nature of the picnic is gone. This is why the Keepers were like the fence for what the bear has done before on previous picnics. They were the effect that made the light bulb work.

One of the last of words was damage control. With the invasive properties behind Osodon and Oosiah's looming presence within the Universes, the Keepers were present to ensure the prosperity of life on all planets. However, this implies another secret within the Keepers. And, that secret exists within the premise of staying power of consciousness on any planet upon which it is born. Keepers were the regulators for consciousness and its presence on a planet. In a sense, Osodon and Oosiah had opened the crack in the ground that swallowed up things of the surface. They were like the sinkhole, and in the right place, what existed upon the surface would fall inwards. However, that was the case without Keepers; but similarly, they were the affect between worlds, as well. This hinted to some potentially dark things for the result of a consciousness that was not supposed to be born to a planet specifically. Sadly, this is the case of the child born with illness upon any planet. The various nuances are, however, endless with respect to what is within the realm of the Keeper prowess. This means that Keepers in certain combinations maintain the safety net for consciousness born from specific planets. This allows for the seemingly random scenarios of children born with terminal illness.

Sadly, it is easy to identify a random consciousness from a planet of a different Universe by their lack of understanding, their hurt, and their pain from loss. This was the pain of secret and curse within Keepers for what Osodon and Oosiah had done, but Keepers get the blame or feel the responsibility. That was the power in Keepers, however. Their parents could not understand the nature of consequence, but their Plaenellian offspring sure do.

The last, all-encompassing word was responsibility, which was a secret to maintain. However, the true question was whether it was the Keepers responsible for who was allowed to stay born to earth, or was it their parents for doing what they did, which ensured that no one would stay immortal. But that was necessarily the point. When Osodon and Oosiah did what they did, their actions erased the immortal sense within consciousness and opened the doors between Universes. Part of their offspring, in curse was this knowing. That was what defined immortality, and destroyed the knowledge of life on other planets. Long ago, when the Universes were intact, consciousness was actually aware of the bigger picture. It was aware that life exists on other planets, and in other Universes, but that knowledge was based upon how firm one life was ingrained within its planet. John the doctor is not immortal. John the dad is not immortal either, just as equally, as John the friend is not immortal. John the doctor dies everyday he stops being the doctor. John the dad stops being the dad seemingly when there are no more children to rise. And, technically parenthood never stops, but what a child needs from their parent does; it changes to extents that the child becomes a parent. John the friend dies when John separates from his friends, for that friendship to be born again. In all this, John becomes so many things that there is a sense that since John is everywhere, there is not much that exists outside of where John is. In other words, since John is a bunch of different things for many different places, there is not much outside of him controlling his world. That was first, the destruction of immortality where John the person had to become so many different things than the one thing he truly is essentially. Secondly, that was how the knowledge of life existing outside of John died. John the doctor has to be the only doctor because if he is not, then someone else is getting his money from his patients. So, no other doctors exist outside of John or that which he is willing to recognize.

It is the Keepers that take responsibility for this death and loss of knowledge of life on other planets. However, attempting to rectify a situation does not necessarily indicate that Keepers did what was done to the Universes. It just means that now they have the duties of cleaning up the mess. To some Keepers, that describes a curse.

The Chapter of Dear Hope

Kahlip picked up his phone. It was Doug. He answered it with a meager hello. They were on the phone for a couple sentences. Doug wasn't in a good place to talk for too long, but he wanted Kahlip to know that he was doing alright.

Karen thought about her father, as she drove away. She then thought about her sisters. Suddenly though, she thought about her daughter. She pondered what Karen had been doing. She thought about the fact that she left her. She pondered why she ever did that. She thought about Mickey and what he said so long ago.

Karen drove the next hour thinking about leaving her daughter with Mickey and how wrong she was, but thoughts about what she did were replaced with thoughts of Frances and Lorande, as she pulled up to Frances' house. She sat momentarily looking at the old house on bricks. Frances, she knew had been there for five years now, but she never stopped by. She looked around and didn't see Frances' car. She got out and walked up to the house slowly. She kept her eyes on the front door. She graced the steps to the front porch and stood thoughtfully a moment before the front door. She looked around and decided to knock. She knocked, but didn't get an answer. She knocked again, and suddenly, she realized Frances isn't home. She thought about her father and Lorande. She knew where Lorande was living now. She went back to her car and left. She had Lorande in mind now.

Lorande thought about something, as Frances drove. She spoke, as she turned to Frances. She had a loose hand on the steering wheel. "Have you thought about Karen?" Frances considered what she said. She sat thoughtfully, as she eyed the road ahead of her car. She spoke up eventually. "No…not in a long time." Lorande sat thoughtfully, as she thought about what her sister said. She spoke up. "She was our sister too, you know?" Frances thought about what Lorande said. She put her blinker on to get into the turn lane. As she turned right, she spoke. "Yeah…I know." Lorande sat back in her seat comfortably, as Frances said that. Frances was okay with everything that happened. So, she guessed she should be, but there was something that bugged her about losing sight of Karen. She turned to Frances and spoke. "I would like to see her again." Frances smiled and spoke. "I thought you would." Lorande thought about something else. Then, she thought of Karen. "I wonder where she is." Frances thought about what Lorande said. She pondered something she didn't think Lorande considered. She turned to Lorande quickly and spoke. "Is Karen thinking about us? Has she thought to come find us?" Lorande thought about what Frances said. She spoke up. "Someone has to make the first move, Fran." Frances heard her, and considered something. "Yeah…I guess you are right. But who are we going after…the long lost sister or the father we didn't have?" Lorande thought about something in that moment. She spoke. "What if the father will lead us to the sister?" Frances thought about what she said. She smiled and spoke. "That's hoping."

Hope, to many, was just a word. It was more than that. Plaenellians knew that more than any other did. They had to hope for the fulfillment of their duties. After all, hope was why they were an integral part to all things created. The Plaenellians were hope for all the Universes and planets within each. Kahlip knew that too well.

Kaerrie had left for the afternoon and Kahlip was left with a renowned sense of being, after talking with Karen. Then, there was the premise of her sisters, and the truth finally coming out about him, as their father. However, as he knew, he couldn't fall too much into the sense of being a father, knowing what he knew. Much more was at stake than his parenting skills and the relationship therein. However, it was nice to be closer to Karen, and then possibly her sisters…whenever that could happen.

Suddenly, Kahlip felt, as though he was being too distracted from his purpose. Then again, if what Karen had said were true, then she too had his purpose, and quite possibly, Lorande and Frances. Kahlip began to think about what could be done to affect the break in the Universes. He considered something else before he felt the frustration for what was happening. Lastly, he thought of Kaera. That's always how it went. Kaera was the last thing he had the chance to think about, but therein lied the curse, his and many others. He then thought of hope and realized how he didn't think in terms of when their reunion would happen. He thought about the fulfillment of their connection eventually. He had to have hope if he was to go on. He was going on the feeling that there had to be justice in creation for two individuals that were of the same essence, had to be reunited. Sadly, though, he understood that what needed to happen was that which was not. Perhaps that should have been his hope. However, he and the others had to make that happen. There was just no hoping that the Universes are fixed by some magical process. Kahlip wished it were that easy. It would have been nice if that were the case, and that life would be that easy. However, therein lays the curse. With that, Kahlip was reminded of something. Knowledge is not power. Knowledge was the key to being forced to act. If a road possessed a hole in it. Then quite possibly, someone could damage a tire or an accident could occur. That was the Plaenellians or those who saw the problem enough to having the potential to care enough to make things right. Someone had to know that a pothole was a potentially dangerous situation. And, in that knowing, made things right. Kahlip then thought about the other side of the curse in being him.

Doctors and Nurses came out at a time when they began realizing their potential. However, Kahlip knew why they came to realize this potential. Unfortunately, Plaenellian life was a lot more complicated than, a doctor realizing his or her birthright was as a doctor. Plaenellians were the doctors for the Universes. And, medical school for them was so much more advanced than, a doctor in the traditional medical school, which indicated another aspect of the curse of the Keepers. Kahlip considered the rise of doctors and how easy it was to become one in contrast to being cursed with having to repair the Universes.

Plaenellians have always known that consciousness was crossing Universal boundaries for centuries, and myriads of years. However, illness has never been at such a height, as it was in the current day. The knowledge in Plaenellians was so precise that cancer patients could be understood for their home planet, as with pretty much every intense illness. Common colds were something universal between all alien consciousnesses and planets not of their origination. Kahlip thought about something in that moment. Plaenellians were the ones motivating doctors back in the day and waking them up to what was going on, and that aided them in realizing their potential. Every aspect of human life was a means to assist alien life on a planet upon which it shouldn't have come to exist. That was another secret of the Keepers. Suddenly, Kahlip thought about Maervuhn of the sixth Universe.

Maervuhn was once a thriving world of alien consciousness with the potential for a doctor on another planet. Some would say that doctors have to be aliens for what they do, but the truth of the matter is that doctors are a high level, intelligible race of aliens that do not have the ability for emotion. It's not their fault, but that is what makes them valuable. Maervuhn was a peaceful planet. Kahlip thought about that. He thought about what it was like on Maervuhn. Well, that was before the damage to all the Universes. Now, Maervuhn was much like all the other planets with a mix of races upon it. However, this was where earth differed from the other planets affected by what Osodon and Oosiah had done. On earth, the problems for the various alien races could be fixed. This was the importance of fixing things, and resetting all the planets to, in computer language, their default settings, which would heal all worlds and return consciousnesses to their home planets, at least in theory.

Kahlip thought about the first hope for alien consciousness on earth and how that first hope didn't necessarily work out as if it was first thought that it might. Religion was that first hope for unifying all manners of alien consciousness. It was thought that a strong set of rules could contain the various differences between all the consciousnesses. And, for a time, it did work, but things for alien consciousness got worse than what religious dogma could affect. Then, it wasn't truly understood what consciousness, especially alien consciousness would undergo on an alien planet. However, the physical effects on alien consciousness were then discovered on an alien planet. Religion could not affect this physical effect. It was the job of Plaenellians to seek out those born from Maervuhn to appeal to their potential to begin to heal the consciousness that could not maintain a healthy existence upon earth. And, that was a secret of the Keepers. Kahlip recalled what that entailed. It was a grueling effort to try and find a Maervuhnian from all the various alien consciousness existing on earth at the time. Beings were dying form unexplainable conditions. Too, at that time, there was much political unrest. The Poliglians of Kroilon II hadn't made a strong enough presence upon earth yet to be capable of forging a political arena for alien consciousness to find some kind of hope. So, Religion was still the greatest asset alien consciousness had to pull from, as to be capable of any kind of a social organization. However, it was later found out that the alien consciousness from Aubrahteery in the Magnus four of the Eleventh Universe had gotten power hungry. Some had come to call themselves angels, but the majority of alien consciousness for the Magnus 4 clung to the ever-powerful religious dogma, which forged the eventual great houses of worship. Ironically, the Eleventh Universe was a vital aspect to the union of consciousness in all Universes, which was why the Plaenellians sought them out to forge some kind of a social order in what religion was in the beginning. However, it was found out that even Aubrahteerians were affected by the earth's living conditions. This was the point at which words like demon, demonstration and concepts of the like came out from how the Aubrahteerians were behaving. There was much confusion between the Aubrahteerians being less than what they could have been and alien consciousness from the third

Universe or the planet within it called Caamerahl. Still, there were some that lived by their sense of unity on Aubrahteery, so that effect wasn't universal between all Aubrahteerians, but those who found enough in themselves from their old world were the ones that called themselves angels. They lived according to the code of Aubrahteery, watching their fellows ruin the reputation of the Eleventh Universe. And, it had been ruined. Religion had gotten such a bad reputation that Aubrahteerians were appearing like the enemy. Religion was looking more and more like a path to power instead of the charity for which the Eleventh Universe had gained a reputation. And, the Eleventh Universe and the fourth Universe were closely relative, which was why the Poliglial race was sought by the Plaenellians to take over where the Aubrahteerians fell short. This was true enough, which was why their fellows began to look at them as fallen angels, which is where angels got a reputation at all. Though it wasn't the Plaenellian plan to hire angels to cure the ills of earth, certain ones that held to their angelic heritage enough from Aubrahteery. They proved to be an asset in Earth's Universe. And, there were records of people that weren't necessarily outwardly open about their Aubrahteerian heritage, but their view of alien consciousness was angelic. It was easy to see an Aubrahteerian first above all alien consciousness, which definitely contrasted the Caamerahlians.

Also known as the crime race, Caamerahlians were the most affected alien race born to earth. In a sense, it was the Caamerahlians who gave crime to all the Universes because they became the criminals of every planet to which they were born. Of course, this was not their fault. Well, it was, but only because they lost the control they had on Caamerahl. Also, Caamerahlians were truly defined by the crimes they committed. Some Plaenellians understood that most murderers were Caamerahlians. However, it was known that Caamerahlians were the most likely to rebel against the order, only because they were inept at order because their conscious design was based upon the planet, Caamerahl's makeup. However, criminals were made from the other races due to the nature of law design. However, it was easy to see a

Caamerahlian. Their home would most likely be a place called prison or jail. Another way to identify a Caamerahlian was by their repeat offender status. They just cannot seem to get it right to stay free. So, they wind up in the most relative place to Caamerahl, which is prison. Prisons were based upon the general makeup of Caamerahl or closely resemble the control Caamerahlians need. However, Caamerahl doesn't look like a jail of course, but the semantics of design are not too far off between Caamerahl and a prison. Eventually, Caamerahlians became to be called Cagers by some Plaenellians just because it shortened the referencing agent between Caamerahlian and Cager. Cager was easier and quicker to say.

From this understanding of Caamerahl, Kahlip understood that it was one of the most beautiful planets in all the Universes. For this control that it instilled in its inhabitants, Caamerahl maintained the most constant state functionally. This meant that it did not change according to the activity of its inhabitants, unlike the other inhabited planets of the Universes. This did not mean that the inhabitants of the other planets were a detriment to their planet; it meant that they could interact with their environment, but it changed in degrees to balance itself with its inhabitants. Caamerahl never changed because the balance between it and the Cagers were always in balance, no matter what they did. It could be said that Cagers only behaved according to the design of the planet. What this meant was intricate detail. Caamerahlians acted like the orange to the orange tree or the grass and weeds to any planet. They were extremely natural to the planet that one went hand in hand with the other.

However, in everything he knew Kahlip didn't like to think too much, about how daily life on the various planets was for each race. It added to the torture of the curse, remembering what used to be in contrast to what was now. That hurt. As he recalled the Caamerahlians, he thought about what torture they went through dealing with the lack of control on earth. Understanding that about them made him appreciate the death penalty a little better. Most human thinkers don't really understand that the death penalty isn't a penalty, but reprieve for those who have acted, as though they deserve it. Actually, it's a kind act to put them out of their misery for what really motivates them to perpetrate supposed horrible crimes. Kahlip thought about the Cagers and felt something for them, as Plaenellians would knowing what they knew about them. Caamerahlians were actually a peaceful race, but only in their element. This was what hurt as much as it did about knowing the true essence behind Caamerahlians. However, in understanding that, Kahlip was only reacquainted with his curse. And, in a sense, the Plaenellians were the greatest hope for all Caamerahlians, perhaps unrecognized by the Cagers or anyone else, but Plaenellians knew that too well. The plight of the Cagers was perhaps their greatest motivation to set things right.

Chapter for Fulfillment

Karen stood outside Lorande's door knocking. She'd been there for ten minutes. In the midst of knocking, she peered into the window adjacent to the door, but didn't see anyone in the house. After another five minutes, Karen decided to leave. She decided to go back and see her father. However, she had to go see one other person. She thought about Mickey and Kira. She wondered how they were doing. It has been years since she left. It had been too long since they said two words between them. Karen thought about why. She thought about Kira. There was confusion when she was younger about whom her mother was, but in the end, Kira put an end to the confusion. She thought about her daughter, Karen, and how she had done the same to her that Kira had done. Karen thought about her father and what Mickey did not know had happened between Kira and Lehmich so long ago. Then, he was Lehmich, but Karen finally knew the truth. Kira and Lehmich had a thing before Mickey and Kira finally got together. Then, she got stuck with Lisa, whom Karen was told was her mother, as well. Karen thought about not having a mother or a father growing up, but worse yet she had been lied to the entire time. She went through her entire youth thinking Lisa was her mother.

Karen returned to her car and headed for the beach. She withdrew from Lorande's driveway slowly. She drove off with Kira in mind, and her deep-seated frustration with herself for what she did to her daughter. She was headed for Hero's Hollow at this point, but her heart lingered with her father…and her sisters.

The premise of tomorrow brought forth a new vision of what could be, out of the ashes of the past. This was true for mere and supposed humans that didn't know their heritage previous to being upon Earth. It was in the unknowing that fulfillment could be found. Consciousness wasn't privy to knowing much beyond their supposed human roots. This was where fulfillment existed, but not for Plaenellians. It existed for those who didn't understand their loss, in contrast to what they think they gained in existing upon Earth. And, this concept of Earth is where the truth existed behind it. Take a planet with a formal name, such as Maervuhn. Maervuhn isn't made of Maervuhn; it is made up of various minerals, composite soils equal to what Earth was, which were called such things. However, one of the definitions of Earth was the ground that Earth was made of, which didn't make sense. The only way it made sense was if Earth too, had a proper name, in which case, it did, but no one understood that. And, that was what defined the planet as a home for various measures of consciousness that did not understand what the planet actually was. The point was that one does not pull a wire from one's wall and say this is my house, as equally, as one doesn't pull soil from the earth and call it earth. However, Earth was made a noun and a proper name at the same time. Ayeraal or what Earth once was is only a proper noun, not a general noun. The reason Earth is a proper noun and noun is for the quick general reference for one's placement, but this was not all there was to the earth. Kahlip considered that, as equally as all Plaenellians understood. The point was that Maervuhn was a planet

However, this was why fulfillment was only capable from the understanding of earth, as a noun and proper noun. It indicated the unknowing in the measure of consciousness holding to such lower concepts of a planet that was once called Ayeraal, once housing the Mighty Anthrocytes. Sadly, that was the secrets of the Keepers to know that what has become human consciousness was the confusion of many consciousnesses from many planets. On that premise, it was easier for Kahlip to understand why humans could find fulfillment, and his kind would never be capable of doing that. Fulfillment for Plaenellians was returning everything to the way it was once. However, lingering in the back of his heart and mind was the fact that what Osodon and Oosiah had done was permanent. That meant that everything was going to continue to decline through what little life seemed to be within all the Universes. In that moment, Kahlip thought instantly about Penny or Kaera, as Kahnelle proclaimed she was. Then, he considered what Kahnelle's ploy might have been. However, Kahlip thought of himself, as an individual of higher understanding. With that, it meant that he had to see the higher purpose in being with Penny, if there was one to see. However, something struck him about relationships. Relationships boiled down to one thing, and the essence of relationships was relativity and relating, Relativity creates a kind of feeling in each relating to the other. Penny seemed like she was of a different consciousness than Kahlip. There was just something missing between them. To Kahlip, Penny seemed like she had more human understanding than Plaenellian. That could only mean that she was, for all intensive purposes, a consciousness with a home. She was fine with human things and for that, it made relating to her that much harder.

Kahlip thought about how fulfillment was easier for Penny to find. She was fine with having the house and settling down with just the ordinary life. Communicating with her about higher concept was harder because she wasn't Plaenellian, as Kahlip is. Kahlip knew that much, which made him think about Kahnelle. Something in that moment struck him. It was a feeling. Suddenly, he considered Penny in a higher light. Suddenly, Penny made sense. Penny was from the Anthrocyte heritage of long ago. With that, Kahlip realized something. Penny wasn't with a home, but she was because she was still on the planet where she began. That was what made him realize that Penny is an Anthrocyte from the Anthrocytes of long ago. One thing about Penny was her ability to understand without wholly understanding what was going on. Kahlip thought about the Anthrocytes or what he had come to know about them.

One of the things about Anthrocytes Kahlip knew was how loving they were. Of the few alien races that had relationships on their respective planets, Anthrocytes were the most dedicated to their respective counterparts. Anthrocytes also understood something most alien races did not. They understood the value of both males and females in pairs. It could be said that Anthrocytes knew more the value of fulfillment than most because most races weren't designed to have the understanding of procreation or propagating. Anthrocytes did not reproduce either. However, they were one of the races most relative to the Creation Powers, which forged everything. With that, Kahlip understood that Anthrocytes were perhaps the parenting race of many other races. In other words, a lot of the other races came after the Anthrocytes.

After realizing that, Kahlip understood Penny. He realized why things between them were so amiable. Further, it was why she seemed so open to a relationship with him, even though the level of relativity between them was low. Deep within Anthrocytes was an ingrained sense of connection to the opposite sex. That was how Anthrocytes were built, which kind of took the thrill out of love. At that point, love isn't achieved; it was destined to happen because an oven cooks, as it was designed to. And, that was different from Kahlip seeking Kaera. Anthrocytes were designed to be capable of loving everyone. And, what he felt from Penny was just that. He could tell her anything and she wouldn't down him for saying it, but that didn't mean she agreed with him. It meant she wouldn't call him crazy, but there still wouldn't be a level of relativity between them. Kaera was the only one to whom Kahlip was truly relative because Kaera is Plaenellian, as well. With that, meant there were things that didn't have to be said. Kaera knew what Kahlip knew. It was just that simple. That was the importance of relationships.

From what Kahlip now understood, he suddenly glimpsed Penny and why their union was so important. Penny was of Anthrocyte Royalty. Suddenly, he thought about Kahnelle. Suddenly, Kahlip understood that Kahnelle wasn't necessarily working for Osodon and Oosiah, but against them. It looked more like Kahnelle wanted to keep Penny out of the reach of Osodon and Oosiah, but he didn't see why exactly. With that, he realized what he said to Penny about Osodon and Oosiah being her parents, as well wasn't wholly true. Suddenly, he realized why she looked at him the way she did when he said that. It actually made no sense to her. And, he finally understood why.

A Chapter in the Light

Kahlip began another day alone. Penny had gone out for the day. He sat up in bed and suddenly, he began to think about that day, and the seizure he had when he was fifteen, but he knew why. It was his motivation for it that ironically made him stronger. Amidst that thought about that day, he considered Penny, and what he was going through with her. He finally realized how different they actually are.

With this full understanding of Penny, Kahlip then began to understand why she lived, as she did. Penny was only trying to have the kind of life Anthrocytes were used to when they were the only consciousness upon Ayeraal. It was frustrating to watch her attempt to achieve this. In just the short time they were together, he had seen her go from accepting what was going on, to expecting certain things to happen. One of the greatest frustrations for Anthrocytes is no longer living, as they once did. Simply put, Anthrocytes were trying to find the light again.

Anthrocytes were at their very best when Ayeraal was only their home. The Anthrocyte way of life was a beloved one. Everything Ayeraal had become was less than what it was once. The saddest thing was watching an Anthrocyte attempt to exist with Ayeraal in its current state. Some Plaenellians believed that was where depression stemmed, enough that it could have a clinical diagnosis. Then, there were others that believed depression was the result of any consciousness born to earth, not of the planet they originated. Darkness was associated with this state of consciousness that existed in depression. This was also, why suicide was associated with depression. Death was thought to be capable of returning one to the planet of their origin. However, that premise wasn't fully understood with those supposed afflicted with depression, as Plaenellians knew, which meant it was a secret of the Keepers. However, with the many perspectives on the subject, there were those that believed that a suicide solution was nothing more than a means to further destroy the elemental makeup of the creation program. Some believed that one didn't necessarily return to their home planet, but another and forcibly. However, that was why suicide became murder of the self. It was murder, and thus wrong because of the former understanding about it destroying the creation program.

Just about every viewpoint within Psychiatry was coined through these secrets of the Keepers. It could be said that it actually began with the understanding of the Plaenellians. This was why there were many drugs used to affect the brain chemicals, because of the nature of consciousness from another planet were not affected by the drugs that worked on some other. This was why there were many supposed symptoms of mental disorders for the many consciousnesses from many different planets in the many Universes. That was why there were similarities between the supposed diagnoses. That was an identifier for who was who and where they were from. However, all this information was kept from the science books and medical journals, but to those who knew the secrets, held the knowledge.

From the secrets of the Keepers, many other forms of consciousness could be understood. Vegetarians could be understood. Even meat eaters could be rationalized. Environmentalists sometimes called tree huggers could be understood. But there was a sad end to the tale of understanding and perspective. It didn't put Keepers closer to the light, but further from it, which was probably the greatest aspect of the curse of the Keepers. For their knowing, that made them more adept at existence upon any planet for they carried with them the knowing of what was really going on behind all the Universes. There was nothing better for a Universe than a Plaenellian. Kahlip knew that too well. This was how and why consciousness upon earth was capable of existing upon Ayeraal for as long as it had. Plaenellians were attempting to prolong the life of consciousness and each respective planet until such time, as a solution to the breaks between Universes could be found. One of the greatest achievements in history for consciousness upon Ayeraal was the extraction of oil and proper burning. For the land that was drying out, this put the oil pockets in the earth at risk of being affected by the lava that was flowing closer to the surface of land. As more and land dried out, that meant that lava flows would change course as well. This was why oil drilling at the bottom of oceans didn't make sense for the most part. However, some was done to affect the oil pockets closest to landmass, which was the proof to why it was done. Landmass only appeared from the oceans that were drying up. Oil pockets closest to potentially drier regions had to be emptied for the safety of the area. If there was a pocket in deeper oceans, it wasn't a threat.

One of the greatest secrets of the Keepers was the knowledge they shared about the potentially deadly situations if these pockets of oil came too close to lava flows. For hundreds of years, the means to burn more of the fuel in the ground had been a concern for many Keepers for they knew what could happen with explosions in the ground if the oil and lava met. They knew this information because of what they understood about the planet when it was known, as Ayeraal. Oil and lava were higher concepts before the planet began to slow down. It took time, but eventually, through the use of primitive forms of this burning process, as in torches, eventually, the automobile would be built. However, the carriage had to be created first, as in the grand vision and motivation to devise the oil-burning engine that would drive the ridding of the planet of this oil excess in the ground. With consciousness upon the planet, as naïve, as it was, it was easy to get them in tune with the automobiles of latter days, but only with the early carriages, which was something else that most consciousness upon the planet did not realize, and was another secret of the Keepers. Getting from one place to the other actually was not a burning desire. In the beginning, most people were stationary thinkers. Beyond what was popularly believed people just did not travel. The truth behind this was that there was not much beyond what their parents had before them, and so on for the previous generations. Not only that, but the worst fact remains that consciousness just didn't think about moving around. There was no point. Everything they needed was where they were. If it wasn't nearby in walking distance, it didn't exist.

And, there was the light again. Early forms of depression made it harder to have the motivation to move around. This worked two-fold. Anthrocytes still being born to Ayeraal didn't have the motivation because they weren't driven to move. Why move around when wherever they found themselves was home. And, alien consciousness born to Ayeraal was so restricted for what they could do because they had to understand why they were on the planet in which they found themselves. So, if they did have the chance to move around, it was with much deliberation about where they did go, but not out of fear, but what they could actually do.

Another secret of the Keepers were the pioneers of long ago. The first pioneers were Plaenellians who taught their secrets to those who could have the courage to move around and discover things about the supposed new planet for alien consciousness. Plaenellians were driven to do this for their origination. Another secret of the Keepers was such that consciousness would have destroy the earth long ago, had it not been for Plaenellians, but only some of the elder Plaenellians knew this. The Elder Plaenellians were the first born to Osodon and Oosiah who were not consciously gifted with knowing, but they gifted with knowing from birth. It's kind of like the last born were those who knew less. It was like in Halloween where the first ones usually got the good candy, and the last got whatever was left. Ironically, though, those with more knowledge were granted more responsibility. Kahlip knew that all too well. As in, those who got the best candy were granted the rite of the best bargaining chip. Those who had the knowledge also had the advantage.

Those who had the advantage also had consequence for that advantage, which wasn't knowledge. The consequence for having the advantage was an inherent security system, which was taught to those seeking Psychiatry as a profession. Plaenellians not adept in their heritage or those who chose to abuse it fell under the effects of this security system. This was where electric shock therapy stemmed. Epilepsy was such a security system or an inherent means to level the power Plaenellians had. Many Plaenellians were confused with the angels from the Magnus four for this self-medicating electric shock therapy. It was where head doctors thought to utilize electric shock for what the Keepers shared with them. In the technical understanding of Epilepsy, it was the measure within Plaenellians against what light they omitted. It stopped the outward flow, and an inexperienced or young Plaenellian always was affected by this state of seizure, which is why Epileptic episodes are associated with seizures. The emitting of too much light was potentially detrimental to the outward environment of the one emitting the light. Seizures happen to inhibit the transmission of this light for what this 'Light' actually was. This was why the differentiation between light outside of the individual and what was internal sometimes caused the episodes. Seizures are a balancing of this effect. It's why flashing lights sometimes caused certain episodes. However, this happened in young Plaenellians for their inexperience. There were some Elder Plaenellians that also understood that young Plaenellians were out of there element where seizures occurred to the extent of death. The truth of the matter was simply this. Plaenellians projected an internal light so powerful, that if concentrated upon a power source, such as a movie picture screen or certain flashing lights, they could potentially inflict such power into it to cause it to explode. However, the younger ones understood enough to know that they potentially could blow light bulbs and movie picture screens. However, what would actually happen is that they would draw the power into them because the light internal would equal the power in the bulb. So seizures stop this from happening. And, that was the inner circle knowledge of Plaenellians.

Kahlip thought about something in that moment. This concept was where Dark Treaders or their stories were created. That was what made the legends of the Dawn Keepers and Dark Treaders and their battles. Dark Treaders were actually young Plaenellians that were born to the wrong planet for their purpose. However, Plaenellian birth was conscious on the part of the one being born.

And, that added to the frustration of the Elder Plaenellians. There were some young ones that took advantage of what they knew. However, they didn't fully comprehend the consequence inherent in them at birth to respective planets. That is how a young one from an elder could be determined. Especially in an autopsy of the body of an elder in old age. A young one will potentially die early in life from the effects of the seizures. Elders get to suffer the effects into old age, which isn't necessarily enjoyable, but withstood by the elder for their power. It's what designed the Elders. And, that was the light ingrained in them for what they were as a consciousness, or eventual sentient being upon a planet somewhere in the Universes.

Kahlip had been out of bed since he began thinking about Penny. He had gone through the kitchen and made coffee. He even took a stroll through the refrigerator for a quick nibble of some food. It was a piece of lettuce and cheese. He finally came to stop on the back porch in the latter morning breeze. Lastly, he thought about that day he had his only seizure. He finally understood why. He was young once, but at fifteen, he was still an Elder. From what he understood, his seizure protected him from the darkness around him. The proof existed in the fact that he was merely walking by those four individuals. His seizure didn't begin while he was watching a movie on the big screen and he wasn't looking at lights. It was in the daylight, and he was walking to his friend's car. He finished the morning, sipping his coffee, and remembering the good old days. Ironically, for what he knew, as a Plaenellian, the good days were when he wasn't sentient upon any planet. Ironically, the good ole days were the future when things would be, as they once were.

A Chapter to Revel

The most gracious moments were the sanctity of consciousness upon any planet. However, younger Plaenellians might see the current day and time for consciousness upon earth, as the time to glorify the lengthy time consciousness has been upon Ayeraal, but the Elders understood one thing that wasn't prone to most. It wouldn't last much longer. When meager consciousness was celebrating the small stuff, the bigger stuff was getting harder to deal with. There was so much small stuff that average consciousness celebrated. However, as Kahlip grew older, he understood that with age brought the understanding that his chances of making more of a difference were slimming. He thought back to the many strides consciousness had made on Ayeraal. And, where there was some light for it, there was still more darkness to come.

This was how revel led to revelation. Revel was the recognition of fulfillment or achievement, and revelation was the recognition of knowledge. It was harder to accept revelation than it was to revel over simple achievement, but the common phrase among consciousness upon earth was the statement of making it to one more day and not being six feet under. The revelations were what it took consciousness to achieve to be capable of reveling in their achieving life past one more day.

The early revelations were those that would see consciousness achieving a sense of knowing itself, and what it actually was. This defined the Anthrocytes from the rest of alien consciousness upon Ayeraal. Kahlip thought about that, as he readied himself for another outing. He had to stop by the motel and check in with how things were going. That day he wanted to take it off because he needed a moment to himself. And, with Penny's plans, he was left to his solitude. He did think about Karen and how it would have been nice to have her around that day. He understood that she had things she had to do.

So, he was left to consider the Anthrocytes in contrast to the rest of alien consciousness on the planet. Anthrocytes, as with all relative consciousness to its respective planet thought like the planet itself. This was the Anthrocytes and what defined a consciousness alien to them. Then, Kahlip considered something that forged an uncomfortable feeling deep within him. Anthrocyte consciousness was verging total breakdown. There wasn't a single consciousness upon the planet that wasn't partaking in some form of consumption. This meant that Anthrocyte heritage was or had lost its hold on Ayeraal. That hurt. It meant that more planets in more Universes had consciousness that did not think as if the planet did. And, that meant the eventual death of the planet. Suddenly, Kahlip felt frustration with Osodon and Oosiah for what they had done. There was nothing to revel about in that. Too, Osodon and Oosiah didn't have anything to worry about for what they did, and that added to his frustration. What Osodon and Oosiah didn't realize is that consciousness, unlike them, would go through what many sentient beings upon earth or Ayeraal would go through. Being human wasn't being human. It was attempting to find some relativity between so many various consciousnesses from many Universes. That was hard to do for most. With his final thoughts before he left the house, Kahlip considered the history of consciousness on Ayeraal. Suddenly, he figured that he could blame the warring humans underwent on Osodon and Oosiah, who probably ignored that fact. And, now they were in Paris, supposedly living it up.

Kahlip thought about Karen. He pondered what she really understood. Then, he pondered her mother. That led him to contemplate the curse of the true Keepers further. It was a sullen fact that Keepers or Plaenellians knew too much to enjoy being born to any planet. Why was crucial to understand. However, it was for what they had come to know about themselves that this was a curse. The Elders knew what the younger ones had to come to understand. So the Elder Plaenellians were seemingly born cursed, where the young ones had to, over time, feel the curse overtake them.

Kahlip thought about Lisa in that moment. He thought about why she wouldn't leave Darion for him, not that she really loved him, but convincing her of that, Kahlip could not do. However, this part of the curse, which Lisa had become a part, was part of the duties of certain Plaenellians. That was why Lisa would not leave Darion for Kahlip, but it was why she would have his kids, under the guise that they were Darion's kids. Lisa knew about Kahlip's many women, especially Kira at the time, but Lisa didn't mind that knowing she had Darion. She didn't mind meeting him a couple times a week, they would go to dinner, and then to his place. Kahlip thought about that. The point was that Kahlip wasn't in love with her, and Lisa knew that, although he tried to convince her of it. She always felt, as though he had ulterior motives behind his supposed affections for her. And, she was correct, which is the part of the curse Kahlip was afflicted with. Among his other duties, Kahlip was part of the group of Plaenellians that regulated relationships. Unfortunately, this meant that both he and Kaera had this duty, as with their other duties. However, this was the truest sense of the curse in Plaenellians. Lisa didn't really understand Kahlip this way; she just felt there was something telling her he didn't love her. And, she listened to that part of her, and they never became a couple. However, this was why Kahlip could not be hurt, unlike most. It didn't make him inhuman; it just meant that Kaera already had his heart. That was what made Plaenellians better for this kind of duty. And, why they had to separate from their other halves. However, deep within all of them, lays the secret hope that the next was the path to their other half. There were moments where they could see each other, but after their duties had been fulfilled to that point. However, sometimes their duties spanned lifetimes on many planets in many Universes. That was what Kahlip and Kaera had been going through. That was how long they had been separated. So, it was easy for Kahlip not to find something in which to revel, but that hope that Kaera was just around the corner. If he could persevere through the moment, he may just find her, and then keep her if only for a brief moment.

A Chapter for the Blue

It is said that the sky is blue, as the water is well versed within the ocean, which is what many do not realize. Science has come out to proclaim that the sky is blue because as water evaporates, even for its gaseous properties, hydrogen and oxygen will still appear blue. Capturing blue water isn't possible. When it is cupped within the hands, it is clear, as clear as a sky. It's ironic that the blue of the ocean and that of the sky is always so close, but yet so far away. However right science may be, for what it knows, the truth is truth to only those who keep the secret for the way earth once existed, and for who once existed upon it. However, that is also the sadness for those who should keep the secret for what died so the sky and oceans could become blue.

But long before their death and earth became earth, consciousness existed peacefully upon a planet once known as Ayeraal. However, the name of this planet would also be the secret for what is now earth was thought to be many planets, which indicated that many forms of consciousness had come to exist upon it. In their time, Ayeraal spun so fast that the entire galaxy existed upon a higher form of consciousness. Planets were planets without moons because moons were once planets. Universes were actually bigger then because the distances between planets were greater, which indicated that the Universal vibratory level was higher. Science also came out to understand that when something is hotter, its molecules are further apart. This concept was said true of Earth's Universe, and all Universes. This was the height of the existence of the Anthrocytes, whose true existence is the sad part of the secret and hardest to accept. Further, it is well known of the scientist that when something slows down, its part can be identified, as in a centrifuge. Centrifugation was a concept based upon the notions of what happened within the Universes, which also proves that the scientific mind is a consciousness of another Universe. This is also, why science seeks to prove the existence of life on other planets, and proves the hint that there are other Universes that exist with other forms of consciousness within them.

So, concerning the Anthrocytes, their existence was peaceful. And, according to science, the blue of the ocean is that of the sky. However, there exists the knowledge within those who would keep the secret that the blue skies were for what the Anthrocytes gave up. This meant that the life source of Anthrocytes equated with the water upon the earth. There is a reason scientists do not give value to sentient beings of possessing a spirit for they know the value of sentient beings today in the contrasts of the Anthrocytes of yesteryear. Scientists equate with a greater knowing from the Universe in which they once existed. That was the most important thing they had to share with the planet since their inception into Ayeraal's changing or slowing down. It was upon what they could base their science. And, that knowledge was shrouded within their science. And, that knowledge was that Anthrocytes were the higher state of consciousness upon the planet once long ago. Anthrocytes were what is now considered the internal spirit.

However, they existed upon such a plane, as to be capable of interacting with their environment on a less than physical plane or what exists currently upon earth. This is the state of spirit prone to thinking on earth or what once existed in the Anthrocytes. For what they know, scientists understand the higher state or spiritual state Anthrocytes were. This is why the know humans are possessive of spirit. And, the essence of their knowing what Ayeraal has become is why humans are more solid than Anthrocytes of old. This was the value in a planet that was slowing down. The consciousness existing upon its surface is always relative to the planet and how fast or slow it spins. Ayeraal is more solid not, thus, the sentient beings upon it will equal that. Sadly, that is a secret of the Keepers, and part of their curse. The curse existed in the knowing.

Kahlip thought about the Blues or the Anthrocytes from long ago, and what life was like for them. There were no boundaries for them. Ayeraal was spinning so fast that there were no physical limits, but yet, consciousness was separate from the planet. The planet itself was perceived, as light. There was no death and no birth, and only the continuation. This was how it was for all planets respectively, with minor differences for how each existed.

It could be said that the Anthrocytes were the Royals of all the Universes. They were the Overseers for the Universes. Kahlip thought about that. He also considered why Ayeraal was seemingly destroyed, as it were for this reason. Osodon and Oosiah didn't particularly like the fact that there was something more special in the Universe than them, but that was conjecture on the part of some Plaenellians for why Osodon and Oosiah did what they did. In the end, why they did what they did didn't matter. What was done was done, and had to be undone, if it could be.

Frances eyed Lorande, as they got closer to the motel. She felt an excitement deep in the pit of her stomach. She was anxious to see him again. She thought about that truck ride when she was a kid. It wasn't something that normally happens to a child, but not everyone shares in the same experiences. She had to appreciate what did for who was with her through the moments. And, Lehmich was there to save her from the carnage at the house. It felt good to know that. She thought about it again, and how her father saved her from the hell she was living in.

Lorande drove hoping they weren't reaching a dead end. She couldn't stop thinking that her father wasn't going to be at the motel. It was a distracting thought. Where would they go from there? That was her looming question, if their father wasn't at the Motel. About a half hour later and Lorande was pulling into the parking lot first, then a quaint space close to the office. Lorande and Frances looked around. The parking lot had a few cars in it, and a couple office attendants.

Frances and Lorande both opened the car doors at the same time. They exited at the same time, and they both felt hopeful of seeing what they wanted at the same time. However, it appeared as though the only thing to do was to check in at the office to see if he was staying at the motel. Frances turned to Lorande and spoke. "Are you going in to ask?" Lorande looked at her sister. She smiled. She knew Frances didn't want the disappointment of being told he wasn't there. Lorande spoke up. "Sure, sis, I'll go in." Frances felt relieved. She smiled a crack of a smile. She spoke up. "And, I will be right here." Suddenly, Frances had a thought. She thought about the house at the beach and Heroes Hollow. Suddenly, she felt urged to go there. Suddenly, she felt that was where they needed to be. She took a lasting look around before she went back to the car. Somehow, she knew their father wasn't there at the motel.

Frances was so certain that Lorande was going to exit the office and tell her that he wasn't there. She went to the car and got in. She waited patiently for Lorande with the car door open. It wasn't long after that before Lorande came out of the office with what news Frances anticipated.

Lorande entered the car. She looked at Frances with frustration. Frances spoke up before she could say a word. "I know. He's not here." Lorande looked at her strangely for knowing what she was going to say. Frances spoke again. "I just had this feeling. Then, I thought about Heroes Hollow. We should go there." Lorande felt anxious about going to Heroes Hollow. There was the memories of what that place meant for her and Frances that she didn't want experience again. She spoke up quickly. "Is there any other option, Fran?" Frances looked at her. She considered Lorande's hesitation. "No." Frances thought about what Heroes Hollow was to them when they were young. She looked at Lorande warmly. "Lorande…it's been a long time." Lorande looked forward in her seat. After a moment of recollection, she turned to Frances and spoke. "I know, Fran, but I still haven't gotten over it yet." Frances understood what her sister was feeling. She too had the memories.

Lorande thought about something and spoke. "Fran, do you remember the stories?" Frances looked at her sister when she said that. She knew too well, to what Lorande referred. Frances spoke up. "Do you remember the way it was?" Lorande instantly thought back to what happened then. She thought about her father, and how she and her sisters were left with their mother and those people. It was ironic, but perhaps they would have been better off had they been with their father. If they would have only known, Lehmich was him. Lorande thought about how she wanted to be with her mother so bad. Frances had the same desire. And, they guessed they got what they wanted.

Lorande thought back instantly to how it was growing up with her mother and Darion. She thought about the stories about the Dawn Keepers and Dark Treaders they were told when they were children. She then thought about how her daughter was told the same story. Suddenly, Lorande thought about something and the few questions for her father she had. One of which was the looming question about what happened back then. That was why she wanted to find him so desperately. She wanted to know.

Frances thought about how it was growing up. Suddenly, she realized something from her past, as a child. She realized why she was so seemingly angry all the time, and for what her attitude was attributed. She thought back to what Darion was to her, and how deep down, she knew he wasn't her father. She thought instantly about Lehmich. There was something about him, and that time in the back of that truck that she realized exactly who he was to her, but she was told the opposite. She thought about how she was still angry to date over growing up in the family she did. She thought instantly about Darion. She actually despised him for how she got treated. His sexual talk about her was unnerving all of the time. It was as if he knew she wasn't his daughter, and she got treated that way. There was no love coming from him. There was no caring on his part. She thought about how Karen had been molested. Frances knew about it, but no one else seemed to know but Karen, Darion and her. Karen wasn't saying anything about it. Frances thought about how she watched the whole thing from a Karen's cracked bedroom door. Karen was never the same afterwards. Frances knew why, but she never told Lorande so she would understand. Frances thought about how Karen had become an addition to the family after her mother and Darion got married. They weren't married for a long time, but then suddenly, it became important for them to be married, which Frances didn't understand.

Out of everything that had happened in the past, she and Lorande had been close. Now, together with Lorande, they were looking for their father. At least something had happened right in her life from how screwed up it seemed to be. At least she had Lorande growing up.

Lorande withdrew from the parking space. She backed up and proceeded out of the parking lot. Frances turned to her quickly, and spoke. "Do you remember how to get there?" Lorande smiled and turned to Frances. She spoke up. With a sense of agitation. "Sometimes I wish I didn't."

Frances knew all too well what she meant and why she said that at all. Frances felt the same way. It kind of bothered her that they had to use it to find their father.

The Chapter of Heroes & Union

It was latter morning. Kahlip had been working in the yard around the house. He was doing some minor fence repair on the privacy fence. He looked at his watch. He noticed that Penny should be home in a little while.

Lorande pulled up to the entrance to Heroes Hollow. She stopped briefly and thoughtfully. The past instantly came back to her. She hadn't been back to that spot since that time when she dropped little Lorande off. Frances sat thoughtfully herself. She recalled the past, as much as it hurt. After another minute or so, she turned to Lorande and spoke. "Are you ready?" Lorande turned to her, almost in tears from the hurt of the memory of what happened down that road ahead of them. She questioned if she was willing to almost relive those days, but then, she thought about what she may find down that road. She had to be brave enough to go. As she looked at Frances, she knew she was, as ready, as she could get. She spoke up. "I don't think that is an option, is it?" Frances smiled and spoke. "That's my sis." Lorande pulled the car forward down the darkened roadway. As in the past, trees still covered it with a canopy of vines and branches. Lorande wanted to race through it to get the drive over and done with, but she drove with moderate speed. She wanted to get beyond the anticipation for what was on the other side. She was driven to face the past, as much as it would hurt.

In another few moments, they reached the end of the road. Lorande stopped again and eyed the yard. Frances looked around for what she could see from the passenger's side. Their memories began. Unfortunately, the house appeared deserted. It was run down, as if there hadn't been anyone in it for years. Frances looked around thoughtfully. She turned to Lorande and spoke. "Looks like a dead end, Sis." As soon, as she said that, another car pulled up behind them. They both turned to look. They didn't recognize who it was at first. They looked harder to see if they could recognize the car, but it wasn't until the driver got out that they saw who it was.

Both Frances and Lorande got out excitedly. Frances spoke up first. "Karen!" They both approached her. They all hugged in a warm greeting and casually chatted about how each other were doing. However, there was something in the heart of each of them that needed to be addressed. For Karen it was finding each of them. For Frances and Lorande, it was finding their father, and Karen. In the midst of their moment, Lorande felt, as though they were being watched. She looked around casually, so as to not let on that she felt like she was being watched. She didn't see anyone and dismissed the feeling.

Karen spoke up. "I am so glad to have found you both." She smiled and eyed them equally. Frances and Lorande looked at her. Lorande spoke up. "So are we, Sis." Then, Frances spoke. "Yeah, this is nice." But each of them held to what really was important then. Frances finally broke the silence about it. "Karen, do you know about our father?" Karen eyed Frances, as she said that. It was funny that she should mention it because that was what she wanted to mention to them. Karen looked at them equally. She then fixed her eyes upon Lorande. She spoke up. "And, you know of him, too, Lor?" Lorande smiled and nodded. She spoke up. "It was me that approached Frances with my feelings about him." Frances looked at Lorande, as she spoke. Frances kept it to herself that she had a feeling about him when they were in that box truck so long ago. Karen looked at Frances quickly, then, she turned to Lorande. She spoke, as she looked at them both. "I found him!" She seemed excited when she said that. Lorande then looked at Frances after Karen said that. She couldn't believe what she heard.

Frances stood thoughtfully. She thought about something. She spoke. "He's still above ground, right?" Lorande looked at Frances and smacked her on the arm. She spoke up with her usual scolding tone when Frances was in appropriate. "Frances!" Frances turned to Lorande and spoke. "What?" Karen just laughed and replied to Frances. "Yes…he's above ground. He's in an above ground tomb." Frances and Lorande quickly glared at Karen, who was serious-faced enough that they thought he was dead. Suddenly, Karen burst out with laughter. "Gotcha!" Lorande and Frances looked at each other thoughtfully. Then, they turned to Karen and went to attacking her playfully. Karen attempted to get away from them, while laughing. Then, suddenly, the three of them felt like they were kids again, chasing each other playfully. That hadn't happened since they were very young. It felt good.

When the playfulness stopped, Karen caught her breath and finally spoke up. "Seriously though, he's got a place not too far from here. We can go there. Right now." Lorande and Frances looked at each other, as the playing stopped near the house. Lorande and Frances both had the same thought. There was no question about what they wanted to do. Frances spoke up. "What are we waiting for then?" Lorande nodded her head in agreement with Frances. "Yeah!"

Karen walked away smiling. She spoke up with a voice that followed her as she furthered herself from them. "Follow me." It took one second for either, Lorande or Frances to move when she said that. They equally turned in the direction of the car and headed towards it eagerly. Karen had already gotten into her car, started its engine, and was waiting for her sisters. In no time at all, the three of them were on their way.

It wasn't long before they pulled up to his house. The two cars were parked in the grass next to the driveway. Lorande and Frances couldn't stop eyeing the house, as they got out. The car doors were shut, and the three of them walked to the door. Karen knocked politely. Frances reached around her and knocked louder than Karen did. Lorande and Karen looked at their Sister. She gave them her famous eyeball look, and spoke. "What?" Lorande shook her head and Karen smiled and spoke. "The same ole Frances." Frances laughed and whispered. "But you love me." She blew Karen a kiss. Karen turned her head, as if she didn't see Frances' kiss coming. After a moment, and no answer at the door, Frances spoke up. "Is someone going to knock again?" She stopped speaking thoughtfully before she spoke again. "Not you Karen. They wouldn't hear you." Lorande Laughed. Karen smirked and knocked again. This time she pounded on the door. She turned to Frances. "Is that enough for you?" Frances shrugged and Lorande chuckled. Frances spoke up. "Love ya, Karen." Karen looked at Frances and spoke. "I hear ya." Frances looked at Karen and whispered. "Well."

From behind them, a voice rang out. "Can I help you?" It was a male voice. The three hopefuls of seeing their father, turned around. Standing before them, stood an older version of the face they once knew. Karen smiled. She walked around Lorande and Frances and went down the steps. She opened her arms to the man. Frances and Lorande stood by. The two of them thought the same thing. Frances then followed after Karen. Lorande finally got over the shock and left the porch. Frances hugged the man and Lorande finally got her turn. Kahlip looked at the three girls, as he felt moved by the moment. He finally spoke up. "It's been how long, girls?" He spoke specifically to Lorande and Frances. Lorande and Frances eyed each other. Kahlip thought about something. He spoke again. "Why don't we go into the house? We can sit and I think I have some coffee made." Lorande and Frances couldn't stop looking at him. Karen started walking to the house. Kahlip put a hand on Lorande and Frances' shoulder and spoke. "Shall we?" Lorande and Frances followed his suggestion. He walked behind them. He took a quick glance at his watch. He noticed that it was almost time for Penny to come home.

Once in the house, Kahlip told the girls they could make themselves comfortable in the living room. He asked them for their drink orders. Frances was the only one that said she would take coffee. Lorande and Karen said they were fine. Their father eventually joined them from the kitchen with two cups of coffee. The three girls were nestled on the couch when he took Frances' cup to her. He sat in the old recliner that he had planned to replace. Frances took her cup and sipped, waiting for him to sit. And, she was the first to speak. "What happened, father?"

Kahlip looked at her thoughtfully. She was a beautiful woman now. Kahlip then looked at the three of them equally. They had all turned out well and beautifully and seemingly strong women. "Well, I hope you have all day." The three sisters looked at each other. Lorande finally spoke up. "I do." Then, Karen and Frances spoke up agreeing with Lorande.

Kahlip looked at them a moment before he began to speak. "Well, it was your mothers." The three girls looked at each other. Kahlip continued to speak. "I don't know if they were too young or what, but they didn't want to become family." Kahlip thought about what he said. He knew different, but how could he explain it. How could he be honest without sounding as if he was talking about some kind of legend? Kahlip then thought about something and spoke up admittedly. "I really became uncle Lehmmy because it was a comment Lisa made when she was pregnant with you Lorande. I wanted to talk about being a family, and she brought up being your uncle." He looked at the three women on his sofa. Frances and Lorande sat thoughtfully. Karen thought about the fact that she and Frances and Lorande were half sisters. Kahlip thought about something and eyed Karen. "Karen, your mother didn't want to hear anything about being a family either. I really began to wonder what was wrong with Lisa and Kira that they weren't family minded." Suddenly, Kahlip knew he wasn't being totally honest with them, but he didn't want to sound like he was talking about something they wouldn't understand. Kahlip had already talked to Karen. He thought about something briefly. He looked at Frances and Lorande. Frances spoke up. "You know, I was angry for not having my father around. Darion hated me and I didn't feel too much for him either." Kahlip looked at Frances when she said that. "I had no control over that, Frances. I tried to convince your mother to leave Darion, but she wouldn't. And, for how close I was to your Uncle Mickey, I became Uncle Lehmmy. It's the way Lisa wanted it."

In that moment, Karen thought about something and spoke up. "But you weren't that close to him…were you?" Kahlip thought about what she said. He thought about the great, Mickey Ellis. He thought about the stories of the Dawn Keepers Mickey used on the kids. Kahlip thought about the truth behind Mickey that he didn't think the girls were ready to hear. What he didn't know was that each of them knew bits and pieces, but not enough to put the whole picture together.

Karen thought about something else. She thought of her mother. At the same time, Kahlip thought about Kira. He spoke, looking at Karen. "And, to hide my relationship with your mother from Mickey, You were a child of Darion's, unbeknownst to Mickey." Karen thought about her daughter in that moment. Kahlip also thought about her. "I tried to reach Karen, but somehow she got mixed up with this guy Julius. He then looked at Frances, speaking directly to her. "I think you had some influence on her because she moved to France with him for some reason." Kahlip thought about something else that he knew of Mickey Ellis. "If I know him, I'd say Mickey influenced the two of them. Somehow, he pushed them together." Karen thought about something. She thought about how she had been pushed out of her daughter's life through Mickey Ellis. Lehmich thought about how he tried to reach Karen, but not well enough. He thought about Mickey. Kahlip had been watching him his entire life. It was more like watching out for others around him. Suddenly, Kahlip wanted the girls to finally understand him for what he truly was. He thought it might give them some understanding about why Mickey did the things he did. He looked at his daughters equally. He felt the hurt form not being able to be the father to them; he knew he could have been, but he was what he had to be. That meant, depending on how he looked at it, cursed or not.

Kahlip eyed them with finality and spoke. "I want to share something with the three of you." They equally looked at him when he said that. He continued to speak. "I don't know what you understand about what it means to be on this planet, these human things, but Mickey Ellis, as with many other sentient beings are best understood for their true heritage. Mickey was as alien, as it got. Why is important." Kahlip looked at Karen abruptly. "Karen, I know we talked briefly, so you might understand this more." Kahlip then, looked at Frances and Lorande. He spoke. "I guess the first thing to do would be to find out exactly what you do know." They eyed him. Karen realized where he was going with that. Frances spoke up. "What we know?" She looked at Lorande. Kahlip spoke up. "Do you know anything of the Plaenellians?" Lorande looked at Karen. She spoke up. "And, you do?" Karen looked at her father and then at Frances and Lorande. She spoke up quickly. "I do because I am one." Lorande and Frances looked at each other. Frances then had a few words, but before she could speak, her father interjected. "The important thing to understand here is that all forms of consciousness on this planet is alien in some form or another." Kahlip thought about Mickey. "Sadly, there are those from other less desirable places." Frances thought about what he said. She spoke up. "You're inferring Mickey was one of those." Lorande spoke up. "I think I understand." Kahlip eyed Lorande, then Frances. He considered something. "Yes, Frances, that's exactly what I am saying." He looked at her and then Lorande. He considered something else and spoke. "The point is simple. Humanity is a concept to try and unify the various consciousnesses on this planet. This is something that we Plaenellians have tried to do for so long. Karen knows what I am talking about." Everyone looked at Karen when he said that. Their father continued speaking. "However, as everyone knows, unity has not been easy." Frances thought about something and spoke. "So, how did we get stuck here?" Karen looked at Frances, as she spoke, then she looked at her father. All three of them waited for his response. He was thoughtful about what he was going to say. He spoke up. "It's a long story, but in a nutshell, these two individuals, named Osodon and Oosiah forged a crack between the Universes. Now, at random, birth's happen." Lorande looked at Frances and then Karen and her father. She thought about something and spoke. "What doesn't make sense is that birth is the result of the male and female union." Kahlip thought about what she said, and he commented. "Yes, but what you are missing is that these cracks, in the Universes are what actually motivate sexual union, on every planet where there are sentient beings in every Universe. What is popularly considered lust is this motivation. You have to understand that the higher experience was consciousness in males and females before Osodon and Oosiah's behavior, which caused the cracks." Frances considered what he said about the males and females. Lorande spoke up, after she considered something. "So, you are saying that the true experience between males and females was sexual in nature?" Her father looked at her, then at Frances. "That is exactly right. What the cracks between Universes did was stripped the sexual connection between males and females that was present all the time. Each Universe too, had a connection with the others. Males and females didn't have to physically connect before the damage to the Universes had been done. Some of us Plaenellians think that was their intent in doing what they had done." Frances spoke up for confirmation. "You're talking about Osodon and Oosiah, right?" Her father eyed her warmly. "Yes. And, that is where the scientific minds of their Universe came in handy. They were capable of counteracting certain effects of the crack between Universes. Things such as illness and disease were affected. However, there are times when their medicine doesn't work, and people die anyway, and babies are born through the birth control effect." Lorande suddenly thought about Mickey. "So, what about Mickey?" Kahlip thought about her curiosity. He thought about how he could say what he had to in the nicest way. "There are many of us Plaenellians that believe the Seyions escaped from the prison planet, Amidestor in their Universe. This makes sense if you understand that the way the Seyion Universe is built, it is impossible for Seyions of the higher planets to fall through these cracks in the Universes this way. Amidestor is a boundary planet. Unfortunately, those same Plaenellians believe that was part of Osodon and Oosiah's plan. It was to use these Seyion prisoners." Frances thought about something. She spoke up quickly. "So, you're saying that Mickey was an interplanetary criminal?" Her father looked at her, then at her sisters. "Well, if you believe that he was from Amidestor, yes that would be true." Kahlip thought about what he said. He spoke again. "I guess you could say that I am one of the Plaenellians that believe all Seyions that come to this Universe is from the planet, Amidestor. That is the only way I can understand his behavior here." Lorande thought about something. She spoke up. "So, the legends of the Dawn Keepers are true?" Her father thought about what she said. "No, but the secrets of the Keepers are. However, the Keepers and the Dawn Keepers are very different." Lorande thought about what he said. She looked at her sisters. Her father saw her confusion. "Dawn Keepers were just pure legend, with really no truth behind them. The Keepers however, now there is truth in that. That truth exists in the understanding of what is really going on." His daughters looked at him. He knew he needed to explain. "Let's put it this way. Take the criminal or those who I consider Cagers. What makes you feel better, hating the criminal or despising them for the way they behave, or understanding them to know why they do what they do? It doesn't make sense that we have such a diverse human element, unless the consciousness behind the human element isn't truly human. What we consider human is the attempt to find unity on a different planet. However, on this planet, there are controls that certain consciousness find easier to adhere to, controls others cannot feel, as in the murderer or Cager." He stopped speaking and eyed them. They appeared to want to understand. He spoke again. "Let's put it this way. A man on death row is actually better off for his sentence. A murderer is so tortured with existence on this planet that he actually exists in misery beyond all sense of satisfaction. More times than not, when a murderer is put to death, they return to their home planet, where they find true peace. Jails were designed after the kind of control their planet gives them, without the bars." Instantly, Kahlip thought about Mickey. He eyed his daughters. "As far as Mickey is concerned, his type was deceivers here. He was witty and capable of escaping responsibility before it could be figured out that what he was doing was harmful to the planet." Frances spoke up. "He was a Cager, then." Her father thoughtfully spoke again. "No, unfortunately, he was a smart and witty Cager, which made him more dangerous. Again, that is why he was thought to be from Amidestor. The concept of Dawn Keeper was something only a Seyion could come up with, and one especially already imprisoned once. There is talk that Osodon and Oosiah got to the Seyions and filled their heads with concepts such as what revolved around the legends of the Dawn Keepers."

Kahlip noticed it was getting later in the afternoon. He noted that because Penny should have been home by now. He wanted her to meet his daughters. He had an idea, but it was too late to wait for Penny. He spoke up. "All this talk is getting me hungry. How about we go out to eat. I'll buy." He looked at them and waited for their response. The three of them agreed to his proposal. Lorande spoke up, as he left the room. "We can take the conversation on the road." Kahlip nodded and smiled and went to change his clothes. They left shortly after that. In that moment, as they were leaving the house, he thought about Penny. He wondered where she was at that moment. She should have been home an hour ago.

Karen and Frances were casually chatting outside when Lorande and their father walked out of the house. But before that, Lorande said something that made Kahlip think about something he hadn't considered for a long time. Lorande was sitting casually on the couch when he walked down the hall. When he came to the end of the hallway, Lorande stood. He eyed her and thoughtfully remembered Lisa. Aside from the hair differences and a minor height variation, Lorande was most like Lisa. She stood looking at him, as he walked up to her. He spoke easily. "Are you ready?" Lorande smiled. She spoke responsively quickly. "I am, but I thought about something, Dad." Kahlip smiled and then spoke. "What's that?" Lorande seemingly hesitated. She was fiddling with her hands. "Man troubles." She said that simply, but then considered something else. She spoke again. "I know I am a grown woman now, but it would be nice to finally have your input on relationships." Kahlip thought about what she said. He eyed her warmly before he spoke. "Unfortunately, Lorande that could potentially be a dark conversation." Lorande looked at him when he said that. He could tell she was in need of some perspective on her relationships. He spoke up. "We could take it on the road then, right?" Lorande looked at him. She seemed hesitant when he said that. She was kind of nervous. "Actually, I would like to speak with this between me and you." Her father eyed her, and suddenly, he glimpsed her nervousness and why she seemed so reluctant. She didn't want Karen or Frances there. She wanted to talk with fewer ears around. Suddenly, who Lorande is hit him. He smiled and spoke comfortingly. "Okay, then, what about after dinner. You could spend the night here, and we can talk." Lorande agreed to that. She and her father then walked out of the house where Karen and Frances had been casually chatting on the porch. Frances and Karen looked at them equally, sensing something was up. Karen spoke. "Are we ready for this? I am starving."

A Chapter in Darkness

Penny watched them leave. She stood in the bushes across the street. She stood questioning who those three women were with Kahlip. She stood silently by and let them leave. In that moment, somehow her age became a problem. Kahlip was an attractive man for his age, but something in their age difference struck her badly. Lately, she'd been thinking about how young she was, and what she wanted from life. She thought about how old he had to make her feel to be able to connect with him. She wasn't his age. She was young and full of life yet. She thought about the time she married, but she also considered under what conditions she married. Her internal clock was ticking, but too, she considered the fact that her kids were taken from her, and she had no mind to find them. Suddenly, she considered her sister, and how those were actually her sister's memories, not hers. She thought about the fact that she had been in a coma for so long that she hadn't really lived. Then, she got into a relationship at a very confusing time. She just wasn't ready. Suddenly, life with Kahlip wasn't going to work. She knew that much. She pondered packing up her stuff and leaving him with a note.

She watched them pulled down the road and out of sight. She considered how crazy she was for entertaining a relationship with him. When they were gone, Penny ran to the house quickly. Her thoughts revolved around hurrying to pack and leave before they returned. She didn't know how long they would gone or where they were going, but she would just hurry and pack up, write a note, and leave it for him.

It read:

Kahlip, I am sorry, but I have to go. I cannot do this anymore. I have figured out a few things, and I realize that I haven't begun to live. Besides that, I think I have come to realize that I am gay. I hope you can be happy. I am going so I can try to be.

Penny.

Penny left the yellow paper with her words on it, on the table. She tossed her house key on top of her note. She grabbed up the two bags her stuff made up, as she looked around not wanting to leave anything behind. She took a final look around, accounting for the memories that she realized did not mean much to her, as she thought they should. Suddenly, she heard a car horn and knew that was her ride. She walked out the door. She was ready to say goodbye, and as she thought about it while she was throwing her luggage into the trunk of the car, she realized that she may be screwed up, but something was driving her to a new life in California. She didn't understand it, but she was ready to find life's path for her. She only hoped Kahlip would understand.

Kahlip and his daughters returned from the restaurant late. Karen and Frances were ready to sleep. And, after rationalizing their day, both of them were ready to fall asleep. Frances actually dozed off in the car on the ride to the house. Kahlip parked easily in the drive, around the girls' cars. He was the first in the house. Lorande and Karen almost had to help Frances to the house… almost. Kahlip threw his keys on the wall on the hanger where he kept things like that when he walked in. Then, he went to the kitchen, but caught site of the yellow piece of paper on the table with a house key atop it. He picked up the paper and held it loosely. He read it, and chuckled. He whispered as he put the piece of paper down on the table. "Another Puhlosian admission. I never would have guessed that about her." But as he thought about it. He realized she couldn't be gay. So, he knew she was lying about that or saying that just to make him feel better about breaking the relationship off with him. If it was one thing he knew about Penny, she was Plaenellian. He knew where gays came from, and it wasn't Ayeraal or the Plaenellian heritage.

That did give him a thought into the vast regions consciousness came from to exist there on Ayeraal, but that was contemplation for another day.

Kahlip went to see to his daughters. Frances was curled up on the couch. He took one look at her and smiled. He thought of a blanket for her. He had an extra one in the hall closet. He went and got it and covered her up. She smiled incoherently and she wrapped herself up in the blanket when he put it over her. Karen sat in the recliner, appearing tired herself. Kahlip noticed and he spoke up. "Karen, I have a sofa in the family room that folds into a bed. You can sleep there if you would like." Karen thought of his proposal. It was late and she didn't feel like driving home. She spoke. "I'll take you up on that." She stood and stretched. Kahlip showed her the way to the family room. He assisted her in making the bed. The sofa was a small white fluffy thing that sort of reminded her about little fluffy bunnies, but it actually turned into a bed big enough for two adults tightly lying beside each other.

When they were done, Kahlip spoke. "Goodnight, Karen." Karen stood looking at him momentarily and thoughtfully. She finally spoke up. "Goodnight, Dad." He left the room, after gifting her, his smile. She took that to dreamland with her for what she anticipated would be the most relaxing nights of sleep she'd had in a while. She had hoped the disturbing dreams would stop now that she found her father.

Kahlip returned to the living room. He was looking for Lorande. He supposed that her lack of presence in the living room meant she was on the porch. And, that was where he found her. He spoke, as he stepped onto the porch. "There you are." His words were comforting to Lorande. She didn't understand why, but that one sentence from him meant the world to her at that moment. She spoke up with a cheerful voice. "Yeah, here I am." He sat next to her on the white, plastic lawn chair. He thoughtfully spoke, as he comforted himself in the chair. "So, what was that you wanted to talk about?" She looked at him when he said that. The moment finally came. She anticipated that moment since they made plans to talk before they left the restaurant. It was something she thought about, as they ate. She had a sudden nervous feeling in the pit of her stomach. She suddenly didn't feel comfortable in that chair. She looked to her father, attempting to smile. Kahlip noticed her reluctance to speak. "So, what about these relationship things, you wanted to talk about." Lorande instantly thought about her mother, and what she said when she tried to talk to her about the subject she had in mind for the conversation with her father. She thought about her mother's indignant attitude, as if she just realized Lorande was so much lower in class than she was. As she thought about that in that moment, Lorande realized how much harder life with her mother was from then on.

After moments passed since he asked her what he did, Lorande spoke up quickly, as if the damn just broke open. "I am just going to say it. I tried talking with mom about this, but she didn't want to hear anything about it. So, I am just going to say it." Her father eyed her when she said that. She looked at him and she spoke with finality. "I am gay, and I have been my entire life. Or maybe I'm not; I'm just so confused about many things." She felt so relieved to say that. She stared at him, waiting for his response. He looked at her thoughtfully. Then, he noticed that she had a tear. He spoke up with concern. "Why the tear?" She looked at him thoughtfully, recalling how her mother hurt her when she said that when she was younger. She was afraid she would get the same thing from her father. Lorande spoke up softly. She looked out and away from the porch. She seemed to be searching for the words. Her mother's hatred at that moment long ago, still stuck inside her. Her father spoke up. "Lorande?" Lorande turned to him. She was crying at this point, but Kahlip understood why. He thought about the damage various consciousnesses from the various Universes collided with each other on Ayeraal. He spoke up softly and warmly. When he said her name, she felt instantly comforted. "Lorande, it's not that bad." She looked at him when he said that. She questioned his words. "Not that bad..." Kahlip spoke again, interrupting her. "Lorande, what you don't realize is what many people don't know. It's why there is such hatred for the concept of being gay." Lorande looked at him. She wiped her eyes. Kahlip thought about something before he spoke. "Lor, I wanted to thank you for something." She looked at him questioningly. She spoke up. "What's that?" He heard the remnants of her emotions in her throat when she said that. He spoke again. "You have given me a chance to put my knowledge to work." She looked at him strangely. "Yeah, what you don't realize is that gay men and women are Puhlosian from the second Universe." She looked at him even more strangely when he said that. He chuckled for her confusion. "Lorande, you think that everyone so accepting of gaiety was so willing to accept it?" She stared at him. He continued to speak. "Basic understanding comes from the knowledge of what is really going on. Not many say what they know or why they seem to accept the gay population so easily, but that is the truth." Lorande thought about something. "But what Mom…" Kahlip interrupted her. "Lor, I know the kind of person your mother was. Let's just say that most sentient beings are from other planets in varied Universes and those planets, conceptually are alien to Puhlosia. Most consciousness was based upon the male to female creation concept. However, this is where hermaphrodites come from. Puhlosians are both male and female for their consciousness. This means that Puhlosians defined singularity or wrote the book on it." Lorande listened intently. She was trying to understand him. He continued to speak. "You see, Lorande, the hatred for gay men and women are the jealousy for how Puhlosians were built. Heterosexuals aren't adept at love and the same sex. Deeply ingrained in the consciousness of Heteros is the break between the male and female. Gay men and women are special. And, since there is a lot of hatred towards them defines how many more planets there are that are possessive of Heteros." Her father stopped speaking and looked at her warmly. He thought about something. He spoke again. "Lorande, what you don't really understand is that it is an honor to have you in my life. You Puhlosians, above everyone else are so unique that your kind is revered by us Plaenellians." Lorande suddenly felt so light. It was warmth that began in her chest. She teared up she was so happy. She never felt whole as she did in that moment. Kahlip thought about something in that moment. He spoke up. "I can tell you are about to really enjoy existence from now on. And, you just remember that I told you. And, Lorande, never forget this one very important thing." She looked at him more intently when he said that. He paused for effect. He took in the emotion he was feeling at that moment. "Lorande...you are my daughter, and I will never discard anything about you that makes you who you are." Lorande began to cry because she was so happy. She never before felt so loved than at that moment. She jumped from the chair and darted to hug him, as he sat. He spoke up, as he stopped her from hugging him. "Hold on. It's easier if I stand." He stood, and they embraced. She cried on his shoulder. He held her never more lovingly or any one as tightly, as he did his daughter in that moment. "I love you kiddo. And, I always have. It hurt not to be your father."

The Chapter for the Rift

Kahlip slept that night under different circumstances. He was alone on one hand in his bed, but not in his house. He finally had his daughters with him, even though they were women at that point. As he lay in bed alone for the first time in years, he thought about life when they were growing up. He thought about how he felt all that time when he wanted to admit to them about being their father. He recalled how hard that was. And, in sleep one moment, the night went fast, and it wasn't long before he was up, while everyone else still slept. He had made the coffee and waited for enough to brew so he could pour a cup. Then, he went outside to greet the new day. The clouds were gone and the blue skies were there that morning. He looked around, took a deep breath and exhaled, and appreciated his existence more than he ever had before, but that was short lived knowing why he had become anything at all.

Osodon and Oosiah might as well have just ripped the Universes open by their bare hands for what they did. Kahlip thought about how the Rift between Universes began, and the consequence and he finally had understanding in himself. He finally realized why he knew what he did, which added to the curse of the Keepers. Suddenly, he realized that being born to every planet where consciousness came to exist had taken its toll. And, that was the biggest part of the curse he endured every day. Mentally, it took Kahlip and any other Plaenellian time to adjust to a new planet for Plaenellians do not have the luxury of being born between a home planet and an alien one. This was what defined Plaenellians as the only race of consciousness without a true definable home. However, in the curse defined a certain sense of mental stability not prone to any other race of beings. Plaenellians were born of love and understanding, which defined them, but that love was empowered by knowledge. Knowledge is power, and that is how. However, with an outward flow of love for all consciousness, the Plaenellian heart was broken most of all and too easily. This was what made Plaenellians the epitome of the heart on the sleeve thing. And, that made them easiest to fall for just about everything, which meant that they were more apt to relate to every manner of consciousness because they once existed upon every planet where consciousness existed. So, when they moved from one planet to the next, as in death, they had to become something else mentally.

This was eventually what science would come to find as electrons jumping between molecules. It is why they would go at such long lengths to see the molecules at that level, but that knowledge was elementary. From that, this is why life on Ayeraal and one's job isn't a job; it's a way of life. This is why scientists spend so much time in the lab, but they don't stop being the scientist. They live as a scientist would. Kahlip considered that. He thought about the preacher, and how he doesn't stop being the preacher when he leaves his church for home. He lives, as a preacher would. And, those that do not are falling away from their heritage because they've been away from their home planet or Universe too long.

Kahlip thoughtfully took a sip from his coffee cup. In that moment, he realized why what Osodon and Oosiah had done really hurt. It was like taking a book apart, and putting it back together using pages from different chapters to make new chapters. In so doing, Osodon and Oosiah could enter the story instead of being invisible behind the scenes. The previous story may or may not have made sense, but it definitely wouldn't with two elements that were never supposed to be in it. That was Osodon and Oosiah. And, what they didn't realize was that would destroy the mental stability of the characters of the original story.

Suddenly, Karen burst through the doors leading to the rear porch, sweating and shaking, with an onset of tears. Kahlip appeared startled. He stared at her. As soon, as she saw him, she ran to him. She appeared as a frightened child. Kahlip held her tightly. She wept in his arms. Kahlip merely wondered what had her so emotional from an apparent, deep slumber. He spoke with a parent's soothing voice. "Karen…what is it?" Karen squeezed him tighter than she ever had anyone. She was more than hurt. Kahlip noticed or sensed some deep kind of hurt that seemed like it has been tormenting her since childhood.

Eventually, she eased her grip and looked at him with the saddest of eyes. Kahlip almost glimpsed her pain, but he still had to ask. And, to do that, all he said was her name when she interrupted him. "My daughter is Mickey's daughter." Kahlip heard the words he never wanted to hear, but he knew that eventually he might. Mickey Ellis was the worst for what he knew was the child molester. Mickey began torturing Lisa when she was real young. That was part of the connection Kahlip had with her. He acted, as a kind of barrier for her and Mickey. That was why it was harder to leave Lisa with him around, but Kahlip knew Kira was around at that point, and he thought she could keep his habits under control. When he left Lisa, after she had been taken back to the brother that used to molest her, Kahlip had to leave. Kahlip couldn't watch what he knew might happen, but Lisa said she had Mickey under control. The sad thing was that Kahlip knew that about Seyions when they were outside of their element. Seyions weren't permitted the sexual experience, as most races weren't for their home planets. This is actually why child molestation is a problem on Earth or Ayeraal, and why laws against it became what they were. When alien consciousness on Ayeraal in the beginning had been mixing, child molestation was the worst. And, the worst of it happened within families. The essential thought behind sexual union between children and parents was the desire to bring consciousness from their home planet to Ayeraal. However, in some instances, the Rift between Universes was blamed for this state of molestation too. However, those cases seemed to be more reserved for cases of lust between adults. It was understood by Plaenellians that the Rift between Universes forged the strong sexual desire between adults. The religious or angels form the Magnus 4 justified this sense of lust through their concept of marriage, where children would be born to a male, and a female. However, this was where the

Seyions differed from the angels of the Magnus 4, as in most alien races. Marriage was only truly important to those born from the Magnus 4. However, this was why it was important for Kahlip to befriend Mickey in the beginning, and follow him thoroughly to keep an eye on his behavior. Kahlip lost track of Mickey when he left him the last time, after he and Lisa had been reunited. And, Karen just made Kahlip plainly aware of how well Lisa had Mickey under control.

Kahlip spoke up. "I am so sorry, Karen." Kahlip thoughtfully stopped speaking. He looked at Karen, and spoke again. "Here, let's sit." Karen followed his suggestion. They each sat in one of the lawn chairs. Karen sat heavily for her emotion. Karen looked at her father, as he spoke again. "Karen, I trusted your mother, you must understand this. I fought with her not to go to him. I fought with Mickey not to do what I knew he might. I was powerless in the social arena, as it were. Then, I came to a point where I had to leave. I could not stay and be some outsider, as much the uncle I was made out to be." Karen looked at him. Suddenly, Kahlip had a thought. "Karen, you may be a young one, Plaenellian perhaps, but not an elder." Karen looked at him, and realized how much it mattered. Karen spoke up with emotion in her throat. "The past has been the essence of my nightmares." Karen thought a lot about how many sleepless nights through the years she had growing up, after her mother and true uncle had been reunited. She thought about having Karen so young. Then, how Mickey and Kira stole little Karen from her. Of course, Kira didn't know Karen was her daughter at that point. And, she wasn't mindful of what Mickey was doing. Kahlip thought about what had been done through the past with the various consciousnesses born to Ayeraal, which Osodon and Oosiah never cared would happen. Kahlip sat looking into the eyes of his daughter, and the damage done to her and Karen was just one in the seas of perversion that had sailed the oceans of Universes since their inception. Kahlip thought about something. He spoke up. "I suggest you get in touch with your Plaenellian heritage, Karen. It may be the only thing that will save you. I tried to use mine to save others, but the perversion between Universes is too strong. I don't know what else to do, but what I am doing." Karen thought about what he said. She looked at him with a thought. "What are you doing?" Kahlip thought about her question. He eyed her thoughtfully. "I have a book. It was written a long time ago by an individual that I thought was of a certain heritage. I realize now exactly who he might have been." Karen looked at him, as he spoke. "But what are you doing?" Without beating around the bush any further, He spoke up plainly. "I am seeking a way to reset the Universes and close the Rift between them." Karen looked at him with a confused gait. He realized in that moment that she wasn't adept in his knowledge for what he was. He spoke again. "Karen, there is quite possibly a way to seal the Universes and return things to the way they were. I am seeking the solution to the problems inherent in all the Universes, which encompass, quite possibly, the issues you're having." She eyed him thoughtfully. She spoke. "So, what of this book you mentioned?" Kahlip thought about what she asked. He looked at her, and finally spoke up. "The book is the Killian Dawn." She looked at him for saying that. "Mention of that book was familiar. She didn't understand how, but then she thought about something from the past. She spoke up, wiping her eyes. "I think you may be on the right track with that." Kahlip thoughtfully listened. He looked at her warmly and with the love for her, as his daughter that he wished he could have showered her with growing up. Kahlip spoke. "Why do you say that?" Karen looked at him, as she thought about what she had heard Mickey say long ago. "Uncle Mickey mentioned when I was younger about getting his hands on it somehow. He mentioned that it was a detriment to the plan." Karen stopped speaking thoughtfully. She looked at him and spoke again. "He didn't say it to me, of course." Kahlip eyed her more intently when she said that. He spoke up. "Do you remember who he said it to?" Karen looked at her father and thought back. She spoke after another moment. "I cannot recall." Suddenly, Kahlip thought about how Mickey had mentioned it to him a long time ago, glad that he never found it. He probably would have had it destroyed. Karen, it was a good thing he never found it. It actually holds a lot of important Plaenellian knowledge-based concepts. He might have been able to undo us Plaenellians with it. Karen looked at him when he said that. She considered what he said with intense deliberation. She spoke up. "What do you mean?" Karen looked at her father with expectation. He stared back at her for the implications of what he said. He spoke up. "Karen let me explain. It has everything to do with the dying."

✝

A Chapter in the Dying

The morning had progressed. Kahlip and his daughter spent the latter afternoon talking until Frances and Lorande awoke. Kahlip had begun talking about what dying truly meant. He started out by saying that death was very real, but always only a door to another place and time. "There was some conjecture that alien consciousness on planets elsewhere in the other Universes was wholly that…truly alien in mind and body together. However, there was the truth that alien consciousness between Universes was relative. As in the angels from the Magnus 4 who wore fur and feathers of color, but they still wore fingers and toes, and in many ways resembled a human type upon Earth. Conceptually, their ways of life were almost the same, as Ayeraal with a few minor differences. Until the Rift, they did not know death either, as in the other Universes. They had their ways of dealing with that even upon earth. What they considered falling was dying from their Universe to another. It wasn't till long after the Rift that any manner of consciousness really figured out what was happening and why their loved ones seemed to be disappearing. As in what happened in the beginning on Ayeraal or what is now Earth." Karen thought about something as he told the tales of death and dying. She spoke up. "So, there were people just dropping and no one knew why." Kahlip continued to talk about the old ways that first dealt with the whole dying thing. "Even upon Ayeraal, there was no such concept of death and dying. However, with a death, meant the Rift had been cut deep in the Universes. If one manner of consciousness was leaving a planet, then another was being born to another somewhere. This was also, where the early forms of sexual unions began, which is the truest effect from the Rift. Lust eventually became a concept, which actually has deeper meaning than most give it credit for, but there is conjecture, too, that the consciousness of the Magnus 4 was responsible for its dark understanding. Too, consciousness from the Magnus 4 was also believed to be the ones that put a higher value on sexual unity, as well, which was where marriage stems." Karen thought about something, as he spoke. "So, you're saying that sexual intercourse was an aspect of consciousness here, like animals almost." Her father chuckled when she said that. He eyed his daughter before he spoke. "No one thinks about it because they think that for some strange reason, life or consciousness always understood what was going on. It didn't. Think about it. Immortals began dying. How could they ever come to understand that? Well, they didn't for a long time. And they didn't understand sex either. The concept of the Moth created the mother from the understanding that when a woman carried a child, she was like a walking and talking cocoon. She was a walking egg. So, Moth became Mother to early consciousness upon Earth." Kahlip stopped speaking when he said that. He looked at Karen who seemed intrigued by what he was saying. And, he made sense, but somehow what he was saying felt like something she already knew, but never before considered. He then continued to speak, as Frances and Lorande joined them on the porch. Kahlip eyed them equally and addressed them, as they came out onto the porch. "Good morning, Ladies." Frances held a coffee cup and whispered. "Morning." Lorande smiled and sat on another of the chairs. Karen spoke up. "We were just discussing death." Frances whispered again. "Great." She was, of course, sarcastic when she said that. Lorande seemed curious though. Kahlip continued to speak, as his daughters settled in. He did have to look at his watch before he spoke. He had work that day at the motel. He saw he had a half hour left before he had to start getting ready. He looked at his daughters when he spoke. "I have to get to the motel in about an hour. So we can gather here for another half hour, but then I have to get ready to leave. Karen spoke up. "Yeah, I have to get to that work thing too, but I don't have to be at the office until four." Lorande looked at Karen when she spoke. Lorande thought about going back to an empty house. She thought about her talk with her father, and how she felt. She ponder admitting

herself to her sisters, but she kept her mouth shut about that for
now. Frances looked at Lorande for some reason, wondering
when she was going to come out of the closet. Frances spoke up.
"Yeah, I guess I should go to work too. I manage the little deli at
the corner of fifth and First Avenue." Kahlip looked at Frances
when she spoke. He spoke up. "Hey, I might have a job for you
at the motel. I might be looking for an assistant." Frances looked
at her father thoughtfully. "I just might be willing to take you up
on that. Let me know." Kahlip nodded, as she finished speaking.
He spoke with warmth when he said he would. Lorande spoke
up quickly. "Who does your advertising? I am market director
where I work now, but I am looking for something to build a
stronger resume around. I know the Muhndalay has been around
awhile, but Augustine is working up to be a tourist spot. I don't
know, perhaps we can put it on a bigger map." Kahlip eyed her
when she spoke. He thought about how that sounded like a good
idea. Lately, he'd been thinking about expansion. "Why don't you
drop by sometime in the morning? We can talk about your ideas
in more detail." Lorande smiled and spoke. "Okay. I am free the
day after tomorrow." Kahlip spoke easily. He was intrigued by the
notion of working with her. "Sounds good." Kahlip noticed the
time and admitted that it was time for him to get ready. He spoke
up jokingly. "A half hour isn't, as long, as it used to be." They all
laughed when he said that. The four of them stood and stretched
randomly. One by one, they entered the house. And, it wasn't
too long before his daughters left him with warm hugs. Lorande
and Karen seemed to share some deeper appreciation for him in
the way they hugged. Their hug seemed tighter somehow, but he
knew why. When they counted on him to be their father, he was
there. When they truly needed him, he was finally available. He
got ready himself with his dark slacks, slick or shiny black shoes
and shirt and tie. He brushed his lengthy, aging hair and put it in a
ponytail. He was lucky though, as the deep blonde-hair shrouded
the grays for the most part. Eventually he left the house for the
motel and another day of work.

Sadly, to most Plaenellians, work wasn't work. Work was ironically for humans and with good reason. But that was the sense of dying that humans had, which Plaenellians didn't. To work, humans died and became what they did. In just about every profession or job, there was a sense of becoming what one did, which destroyed the person. And, that was what most supposed humans missed about what was really going on. Pursuing money was almost similar to seeking the shelter of another Universe, as in the birth of one consciousness to another Universe and planet, where their attributes only fitted them for that planet so much. Ironically, this happened because of the human effect in consciousness born to an alien planet. That meant that no matter how an alien consciousness tried to fit in, its true origins would show through in its behavior and point of view. This was how a scientist was kind of like a religious man where his profession was who he is or was evidence of his planetary origin. Scientists and Religious men cannot stop being what motivates them to their profession. How they treat people when they aren't on the clock is evidence.

Kahlip was going to the motel, but he wasn't going to work. His job defined part of his plan. The motel actually served as a measure of being able to see who was passing through the area, by seeing where people originated on the planet. All of his employees were instructed to keep a log of the states their customers originated. Kahlip did this because he was trying to evaluate the consciousness migration through each season. When he had a moment, Kahlip would evaluate the information the employees kept. He would look at the logs and get an idea of who was moving around and why.

This was the value in being random consciousness from alien planets in contrast to being Plaenellian. Scientists don't look at themselves for where they are going or where they are from; they consider what they could do wherever they are. The same was almost the same for the religious man with one difference. Their respective labs appeared different. The religious lab is the church. Kahlip considered that. Too, the average alien consciousness didn't ponder itself for where it was. And, unless there was, true purpose behind one's self, as in the politician, religious man or scientist, most consciousness was from the random planets of the Universes, which is why the mass of consciousnesses on Earth were less specialized and just needing of a job. Anyone for the most part could be taught many jobs with which to fulfill and needs.

However, the truth of what he knew behind the Poliglials, the Aubrahteerians and those scientists was evidence of the truth in their heritage or the race of consciousness they actually were. The point was that religion could die, and life would go on. The political arena could just disappear, and life would go on. And, lastly, the scientists could die off, and life would go on. Each alien race was thoughtful of having purpose, which is the desire to be scientific, religious, or political. Another part of the proof existed in how in the beginning, the religious reigned upon the planet. This was the value of the journal, the bible, and the political law book, which were all relative, and proved to be another measure of countenance for the presence of the race behind the book. It was for the dying effect that a record must be maintained. Too, that showed how each race left an aspect of them in the planet. So that as consciousness as it died and was reborn, it wouldn't have to begin at ground zero as, each race had to in the beginning.

Lastly, Kahlip considered the colors of Earth and how inconsequential it was. This was why racially speaking, everyone wasn't the same even of the same race, but the understanding for this was lacking. Alien consciousness was born across supposed racial boundaries on Earth. Sadly, consciousness would never really come to understand this. However, Kahlip knew that was a secret of the Keepers, and not prone to understanding of a seemingly human nature.

A Chapter for the Darkening

After a long workday, Kahlip wanted to partake in the human rituals of the end of the day. However, there was one difference between him and the other alien races. He slept less because of who he is. He could never darken to need so much sleep. It wasn't Plaenellian to need that much. However, he knew that related to the darkening of consciousness, as equally as darkness engulfed the planet. There was a time when true peace existed among the Universes. Some would blame the fall of the Universes or The Darkening, to age of the Universes. However, it was well known that true responsibility lie within Osodon and Oosiah and what they did for their reasoning. The truest irony exists in how much darkness exists for how much sleep consciousness upon Ayeraal or Earth supposedly needs. There is relativity between the darkness on the planet and the sleep habits of the humans on her surface. This shows that sleep is a measure of dying or what happens in consciousness when someone goes to sleep. Sadly, Ayeraal or Earth isn't the only state of the darkness needed to sleep. Consciousness across all the Universes experiences this need for sleep state or what has become known to Plaenellians, as the Darkening. When someone is tired, they aren't wholly exhausted and necessarily in need of sleep or rest. It is the sad state of the darkening effect, which actually creates this sleepy state. However, it is believed that the body is in need of a period of rest to regenerate, but the reality is that the body is continuing to darken in contrast to the consciousness of its function.

This is a hard concept for any Plaenellian to accept. It hurts to know that consciousness and sentient beings experience this form of darkness. However, as Plaenellians know, it is relative to the amount of darkness the planet experiences. To shroud the truth behind The Darkening, those of influence have lessened the effect of the sleep habits by claiming sleeping is a normal activity, and a prerequisite to a good night's sleep is six to eight hours. Part of the proof of The Darkening exists in the belief that over sleeping is evidence to a mental disorder considered depression. However, depression is nothing more than an advanced stage of The Darkening, which many scientists have purported as having a solution. So, Depression became something abnormal to sleeping six or eight hours. The point was what all Plaenellians knew, and that was the fact that depression is actually the evidence of The Darkening, even in sentient beings who sleep six or eight hours. The point was simple. What actually defined normal sleeping habits? The desire to sleep was, as all Plaenellians understood, only a measure of The Darkening. It was a sullen fact all Plaenellians lived with, as much as it hurt. Sadly, it hinted to one sullen fact. The Darkening wasn't only prone to sentient beings upon any planet, but the planets themselves. A deeper understanding of Ayeraal or Earth's supposed moon showed that. The moon doesn't spin or rotate. The essence of its planetary makeup indicates its rotation and spin, and the moon is dead or what was once a planet, which died and got caught in Ayeraal's rotation.

Now it's not their fault, but the great minds or the racial alien Hierarchies decided long ago to shroud a lot of knowledge behind the Universes and planets respectively. It was seen that future generations could prosper if they went forward without the regret of The Darkening or the knowing of it and what actually happened. And, without knowing, only Plaenellians knew of themselves. There wasn't another alien race or sentient being upon any planet that knew about the Plaenellians. It was seen that the alien races were going to deal with what they had to accept, and change the things they could. However, the Plaenellians sat behind the scenes trying to right the Universes, so that eventually things could go back to the way they were. This is why the understanding about the moon never went any further than understanding that it has always been a satellite to Ayeraal. There wasn't any consideration that the moon was once a planet. It was seen by the hierarchies that if consciousness on earth understood how far a planet could die, then their existence from the dying of Ayeraal would make life pointless if in the end, the planet was going through a Darkening or aging phase. It was understood that sentient beings needed to think they were all the same, on a simple planet called Earth. However, the secret behind consciousness upon Earth revolved around the existence of another alien consciousness, which gave rise to the Anthrocytes upon Ayeraal, but that meant a knowing of the deeper secrets in the Elder Plaenellians. And, that gave rise to the information in the Killian Dawn that could have exposed the truest secrets of humans on a simple earth. And, that deeper secret was the battle with Osodon and Oosiah over what was once the vibrant world of Faeverluhn or what is now Ayeraal or Earth's moon. However, this was the time when Consciousness and Universes were almost one, which meant that moving between planets meant walking through a door, which is why there is so much deliberation over how consciousness exists upon Earth now. However, that is a secret deep within the most Elder of Plaenellians, of which Kahlip is one. And, that was what he found shocking, that that information was in the Killian Dawn, supposedly one of the most fertile books for Dawn Keeper Knowledge. However, he was awakened to who actually wrote the Killian Dawn; it was one of his fellow Elders, and why it was kind of ironic that he should end up with it.

It was true that Anthrocytes were the first stationary sentient beings upon Ayeraal or Earth. However, that happened after the first battles with Osodon and Oosiah, which gives rise to the knowledge of exactly how old the Universes actually are. Further, that is why there is so much disconnection with how things truly were at creation or that they were even created at all. There was some purpose in not knowing this information, which is a majority of the reasons for the Secrets in the Keepers. Actually, at the close of that battle with Osodon and Oosiah, it was decided between the hierarchies and the Elder offspring of Osodon and Oosiah that it was better to stop the knowing in future states of consciousness. It was important that any and all knowledge pertain to each planet respectively for future generations of all alien races on those planets. That was the pact of the Hierarchies and the Plaenellians or what was decided would be the case. However, there were certain races more giving to the influence of Osodon and Oosiah, and that race was the Seyions, which is from where the concepts of the Master Seyion stem.

For what younger Plaenellians understood, only because they were born after certain events to take more control away from Osodon and Oosiah, alien races once had immortality only prone to specific planets. However, Elder Plaenellians understood that those conditions were the first of the wrongful acts perpetrated by Osodon and Oosiah in the beginning.

However, the once enforced pact between the Hierarchies and, the Plaenellians had been broken by the writing of The Killian Dawn, which was why many wanted their hands on it. Knowledge was power, and the kind of knowledge in that book meant too much power for the one that didn't have the information written in their hearts.

Kahlip sat with a cold drink in one hand and that book in the other. Suddenly, he thought about Mickey and the legends of the Dawn Keepers and Dark Treaders. Then, he thought about the Legend of Swan Lake. Suddenly, he realized what he'd always known. Mickey was just another who was trying to pad his path back to this planet. That was the true value of the Child Molester. A key to understanding the Molester was simple. Even the word molester had some nefarious truth behind it, which made child molesters more sinister than what others knew. It was commonly known what a mole could do in a yard. A mole is that little creature that destroys grass roots, as it boroughs through the yard. The key in that is the concept of roots because the best way to destroy a family heritage is through its roots. This was the value of the molester, whose ultimate purpose is the propagation with the youth of another's heritage to later infest that heritage by being capable of being born to it after their eventual death. It was like bread crumbs through a forest back to being born upon a specific planet. And, that mole was Mickey Ellis who had tortured his sister growing up, to later infesting Kahlip's roots. Of course, Mickey Ellis wasn't the only mole out there trying to get back to Ayeraal, but it did show that he was working with Osodon and Oosiah, as with others who knew how to leave themselves breadcrumbs, which is what he knew about Karen and Julius. Well, Karen definitely. Part of the proof existed too, in how Mickey and Kira didn't have children together. Kahlip then thought about why.

It was the turn of the next phase of the Osodon and Oosiah's plan. In becoming the Master Seyion to the Seyions, Osodon and Oosiah basically depicted the next Universe they wanted to affect to make theirs better, which is why they did what they did. For the many Universes, their place in all of creation was this little plot with which to exist. Then finally came to realize that they could take other Universes and add those to their and make theirs bigger, without fully knowing the peace and tranquility for feeling a part of the other Universes from the one in which they existed. It was like a landowner with a smaller territory set within bigger territories surrounding it. Osodon and Oosiah went out to the other territories and destroyed the owners of the other lands, which made theirs bigger. However, they didn't have to destroy all the people of the lands outside of theirs, just those who opposed the merger between the two territories. Sadly, this was the plight of the wars fought on Ayeraal by humans to date. Ayeraal, it was seen was their last ditch attempt to find some kind of stationary position on some planet in at least one of the universes. This was why Osodon and Oosiah got credit for the wars on Ayeraal, and why earth is such a mixture of consciousness on any one planet. This was the plight of kingships long ago, and what put the value of kin in kingship. Kahlip thought about that, which was probably one of the biggest secrets for Keepers. And, that was the defining plight of Ayeraal and her inhabitants, not the propagation of the human race, but a means to secure a place in at least one Universe. For some manners of consciousness, and this hurt Kahlip to know, but Ayeraal and her Universe was their last hope for existence.

That was another part of the value in being human, which no one seemingly knew, but the Keepers. Humans don't have a planet. The concept human was a derivative of the word man, but with intent. Kahlip thought about that. If Osodon and Oosiah became aware of what was really going on with Ayeraal, they could have destroyed Ayeraal's Universe, and the last hope for certain measures of consciousness. In other words, Osodon and Oosiah could never find out that those who they destroyed found a place on Ayeraal, and that they were now human. This was another reason Mickey wanted his hands on The Killian Dawn because it would have opened his eyes, and then the eyes of Osodon and Oosiah. Right now, Osodon and Oosiah were content with existing in some place called France. They didn't realize that if Kahlip hadn't destroyed the Amulet of the Keepers, Osodon and Oosiah could have awakened on Ayeraal and began working to destroy her for her Universe. This was really the value of unity on any one planet. That was the true value of battling the child molesters because child molesters were those who were attempting to destroy the roots of the essence behind the various consciousnesses on Ayeraal with letting in certain consciousnesses from specific planets that were intending the eventual doom of Ayeraal or those who had loyalties to Osodon and Oosiah. Kahlip thought about Mickey and how Osodon and Oosiah had been born, though what Mickey did to Karen, but it actually begun long ago for Mickey. That, which was also a measure of the value behind the Legends of Swan Lake, set things in motion for Julius or Osodon to later be born and then, eventually Oosiah or Karen.

PART IV

An Excerpt: The Piece & Peace in 'The Killian Dawn'

Kahlip had been reading. These were his notes from what he gathered over the few weeks of investigating.

Day one:

It is the premise of the people that we should be united. However, this will never be the case and we will never find common ground. The limits of other planets of other Universes will never permit consciousness of other planets and other Universes to find the same limitations. The reason is simple. With the now migrating consciousness between Universes, certain consciousness becomes more restricted and some become more or less free than their origin. The core beings of this planet, then, are restricted and even imprisoned by this free state of other consciousness. These would be the Anthrocytes. It is the premise of those who know, to take the steps to ensure a common ground beyond that of normalcy to ensure that the same liberties exist for all consciousness here. However, it is known that this will have an effect on this planet of the Anthrocytes, and within their Universe.

The Universes Defined

There are the many Universes in which consciousness came to exist. These Universes can be defined or understood in the knowing that they associate with a construction with various materials used to do so. Ironically, the many aspects of what is known as human activities are actually a predicate to knowing structure segregation due to the inherent knowledge in consciousness. That means that the house was a design of the institution of migration. Even the use of verse in Universe is a description for what consciousness knows enough to refer to where it exists, as but one Universe in the overall construct and what would be known as the encompassing purpose for all the Universes.

As in an abode, if but one element of the abode, as a Universe crosses its boundaries, for instance, water pipes get holes in them, the essence of the pipes will infiltrate the regions beyond its pipes or the house. The water will cause damage to the house to extents that perhaps might be irreparable. This includes the cases of house fire. House fire is potentially the result of wiring that has permitted the electrical content to go beyond the wiring system. Electrical current or the consciousness of all Universes is an associate, as in the water from leaky pipes. With this in knowledge, is why buildings began so long ago. It was the premise of what is known, as the Keepers, to forge an existence upon an alien world or attempt to regulate the various consciousnesses against the Anthrocytes for they suffer and have been since the induction of new consciousness or alien consciousness to their planet. We the Keepers, then, forged a measure of containment to adjust for this variation of consciousness.

Kahlip stopped writing thoughtfully. He considered something, and formed an idea. He thought about why the criminal was, as victimized by his containment in a jail or by his crimes. A jail system isn't anything different than what Universe they originated. This was where the idea for said system stemmed. The supposed criminal element is a measure of consciousness from a Universe where elements against the consciousness forge a peaceful existence, but in another Universe will cause its sense of control to become unstable without those controls of its Universe. The truth in that is evidenced within the core of laws in contrast to the lesser laws that really don't partake in the sustaining of consciousness. Drug users that believe they need drugs are this evidence, as in those who need food. Drug users replace the controls of their Universe with the drugs and combinations of drugs they can find in Earth's Universe. Drug users also include those users of drugs of a lawful, healthful nature. Kahlip considered that, and in so doing, finally saw his Plaenellian heritage at work. He thought of how that worked. And, he realized that was what made him Plaenellian. He didn't use drugs for his existence. He might have experienced the same sensations of someone that uses drugs of any nature, but he didn't react the same. This was also how knowledge was power. Plaenellian knowledge, he found was a great asset, but that went without saying. And, that alluded to his curse. He couldn't want for some disease to destroy him, because he was Plaenellian, and planets of various Universes are inept against his heritage.

He put his mind back in to reading and his note taking. In the back of his mind, however, there was the looming sense about Kaera and finding her, but there was doubt he ever would. But there was one thing ever looming beside that, which concerned Kaera. It was the weakness of consciousness. He thought about Mickey Ellis. He considered Julius and Denton Bean. He thought about how Mickey abused the rules.

A Chapter for Abuse and the Rules

Mickey set the mole in the heritage of the Bean family long ago. Mickey was the great, great, great grandfather of Julius Bean at one point, but not for Mickey's bloodline. At one point, Mickey Ellis was Trevor Dorese. Trevor Dorese molested Lily Bean, the daughter of a preacher, who would never force her to have an abortion because of who he was. Plus, Lily claimed to love the father of her unborn child even though he was years ahead of her. And, what she didn't realize or what she confused for in a supposed loving act was that of a molester to his victim, as in the mole to the yard. Being the father and preacher he was, Lily's father accepted Trevor into the family, but with certain hesitation, which really didn't go anywhere. And, Trevor and Lily met, of course, at Swan Lake. The greatest irony in that mix was that Trevor used the fact that Lily's father was a preacher, who professed a love for all children no matter the circumstances in which they were born. Kahlip thought about that, and how the Seyions were good for abusing the rules of the angels from the Magnus 4, as it was the angels who attempted to aid the various manners of consciousness on Ayeraal at unity through their religious dogma. And, religious dogma was abused by those who knew how to do it, as in Trevor who molested a minor child, without repercussion from her father, the prominent Preacher, Arturior Bean. Sadly, Kahlip considered the reality in the truth about child molesting. The fact that the word molesting begins with a mole was the proof behind what he knew. It proved that molesting a child is with intent that it be done. The very understanding of what was happening is why the word became what it is to date, and why it begins with the word mole. Forget the fact that Trevor Dorese was sick when he molested Lily, and knew he wasn't going to live much longer. He needed to place his breadcrumb in the forest for his potential return, but the definite eventual appearance of Osodon. Sadly, the proof of Trevor's premeditation to cause Lily with child could not be found. Trevor escaped consequence, but merely because that was the flaw in religious design and absolution. His reprieve was the forgiveness that was perpetrated in the second book of the most famous religious artifact, which shows that there was a second form of religious sect from the Magnus 4 that came to amend the original artifact.

But the thing most pertinent to Kahlip was the fact that he had to try and thwart the efforts of Mickey when they first met as kids so long ago. Kahlip had been trying to put the past way behind him. And, the truth was that Kahlip was still too young when he met Mickey so long ago to do any damage to his plans. Mickey was an old pervert way too young. Kahlip thought about the way Mickey treated Lisa and how he tortured her. He thought about the guise Mickey used in the legends of the Dawn Keepers. Sadly, the truth behind the Master Seyion was evidence of what the Seyions attempted to do. Especially, Mickey Ellis. It was called the deprivation of consciousness, as in many cases where death ensues at a very young age. The point was that unless consciousness is able to find some relativity or satisfaction with the planet upon which it exists, there would always be some kind of bodily roadblock and potential disease. This was the sad case of Mickey Ellis and a host of many other Seyions. Kahlip thought about that. Mickey Ellis was one who couldn't accept that he was human on this planet. He wasn't satisfied with trying to relate to consciousness for the sake of the planet. So, he brought with him his Seyion lifestyle or inhibitions for being upon Ayeraal. That was like Kahlip and his potential for Epilepsy. However, that defined who Kahlip actually was. Anyone that had to move because they didn't like the area, or had to change jobs because there was something missing around them knew this too well. Tattooists knew this more than anyone else.

There was a certain mental level inherent in the desire to get a tattoo. This was only because tattoos were a means for the wearer to find some kind of relativity with the planet. In other words, tattooists and those they put tattoos on, are not mentally and emotionally happy unless they can ink their skin. Sadly, these forms of consciousness have it the worst. Kahlip considered that. He then thought about those who didn't look too kindly on those who wore tattoos, which was nothing more than the evidence of the variation of consciousness. Those who didn't, like those who wore tattoos only meant they were from a planet where skin color was one set pigment, and didn't vary. Kahlip then thought about the Puhlosians, and their plight, which really hurt him, and what forged a harder job for Plaenellians who had to stop thinking of themselves, as Dawn Keepers. That name was ruined by a few Seyions who had a bad case of Osodon and Oosiah who were really the ones that knew their offspring were considering themselves Dawn Keepers. And, that was another abuse of the rules.

Osodon and Oosiah had begun, which Kahlip found out and a few other elder Plaenellians that their mother and father were doing things to counteract what they were trying to achieve. Kahlip thought about his parents' abuse of the rules. However, the Elder Plaenellians felt cursed from this because when they thought they were getting somewhere, their parents were there to throw in the proverbial wrench. The point was, and Kahlip considered this, their parents were attempting perpetuate the problems with so many vast consciousness in a given area or on a specific planet, which added darkness to the planet to slow the planet down. Hatred for the Puhlosians began in this way. In a sense, and Kahlip thought about this way too much, but Osodon and Oosiah were the ancestral beginnings for bullying. And, that was the proverbial wrench in the plan to make things right in all the Universes, which Osodon and Oosiah didn't want.

The Chapter of Reprisal

The reprisal for their offspring truly began in Greece where communications were evolving from the spoken word to the written word. Kahlip thought about that. Story telling was worth more than what Osodon and Oosiah wanted it to become. They knew that if the various consciousnesses could finally find common ground by communication and words, eventually they wouldn't be capable of pitting one alien race against another. Eventually, they knew, that there would finally be the common ground upon Ayeraal they didn't want for the various races from other planets. Bridging the communications gaps would close another door for them and their influence. It was very important that each race stay indignant to another's plight, as in the Puhlosian plight to have a say in what they became upon Ayeraal. Osodon and Oosiah took comfort in the fact that Puhlosians had to hide who they were out of fear. And they would get their way concerning the Puhlosians for hundreds of thousands of years. Gays and Lesbians would not be capable of self-admission in open forums. However, this meant many other races would also find much fear in such an alien place. And, what Osodon and Oosiah had done all this time, worked to this effect. Until the Plaenellians influenced the Rosicrucians or scientists from their home planet to aid, the many alien Races that were under this effect of Osodon and Oosiah, outside of who the Puhlosians were. There was no hope from the Rosicrucians for the Puhlosians. However, the Rosicrucians were capable of aiding many alien races upon Ayeraal. As in the many races that felt the physical effects from being upon an alien planet. One of the worst effects upon an alien race was the Vampire migration of the ninth Universe from the planet Valadad. And, it was easy to identify a Valadian by the slightest of blood disorder. And, sadly, it was Osodon and Oosiah that fought so hard to hush the Rosicrucians from aiding the Valadians, which was their proper name or their slang was Vampire. They did this by the uprising from the Aubrahteerians or those religious officials who had prominence around the time the Vampire Migrations began, which really defined the battles between the Rosicrucians and the Aubrahteerians. Unlike what they claimed about God being the healer, Rosicrucians were made out to be the devil incarnate. Ironically, the Vampire Migrations led the way for the concept of Blood Transfusion to come into being. It paved the way for the survival of many Valadians, as well those who just needed a general blood Transfusion, but it was the Valadians that urged the creation of the method behind the Blood Transfusion.

Vlad the impaler was the first to give reprisal for what was being done to his race of Valadians. Vlad fought with the Aubrahteerians many times on many fields and finally had enough. However, because of the influence of Osodon and Oosiah, Vlad became the vilest creature on the planet in his time. Osodon and Oosiah urged the nightmares of the Vampires to be born and ruined things for the Valadians for many, many years. The stories influenced behind the Valadian migration forged many monster stories for many years to come. This hindered the growth and prosperity of the Valadians on Ayeraal. However, the story wasn't told correctly. Vlad the impaler wasn't as cruel, as he was depicted. And, the bodies he supposedly put up on the sticks were dead already, but he did that to rebel against the Aubrahteerians who, through their hatred for the Valadians, would have seen them parish. Sadly, the proof of this hatred, as being motivated by Osodon and Oosiah, was contrary to their religious dogma of the Aubrahteerians. The Aubrahteerians have somehow always managed to be inconsistent with their religious views through the years, to such extents that it lessened their influence. And, that led the way for the Rosicrucians to take a stronger position on Ayeraal, but at that point, they had hid their heritage or that they were from Rosicrutia, and took the name of scientist, which paved the Plaenellian concept of conscience to be born. This was how science was a derivative of conscience, and why the word conscious became anything at all. However, among the Aubrahteerians, conscience was an evil thing, indicating that science was a derivative of a con. That is why to their religion, conscience had nothing to do with adhering to what God wanted. However, the irony is what science has done, and not what it hasn't. Many claim that science is evil, and that it was once the work of the devil. There are many that claim there is little validity in science if it isn't wholly true for everyone. However, not everything is relative to everyone at any one point, but that was a sad fact that was missed when the Aubrahteerians tried to down the influence of science. Kahlip had the chance to get more in tune with the Aubrahteerians, considering he was born to two of them currently. However, where his mother made him appreciate the Aubrahteerian heritage, his father destroyed his appreciation for it. In the least, his father made him appreciate his Plaenellian heritage that much more. And, sadly his true origin through Osodon and Oosiah. His Aubrahteerian mother on Ayeraal died when he was six. And, that left him his Aubrahteerian father, who really had no connection to him to such extents that he really had only his Plaenellian heritage to fall back on or support himself. It was his Plaenellian mental and emotional state that he was capable of succeeding. And, that didn't say much to him about his Aubrahteerian heritage, or how much love Aubrahteerians were lacking. In his time with his mother, he had come to see the Aubrahteerian plight early on. However, for him, as a Plaenellian Elder, Kahlip was rekindled with what he already knew about the Aubrahteerians. He was well aware of the Aubrahteerian or religious dissention. His father was the typical Aubrahteerian male who thought they ruled their females. This was where the religious submission by their females stemmed.

Sadly, the religious discontent the Aubrahteerians were creating was actually unifying the other races against them. Eventually, strong government was needed to regulate the dissention that was being created. And, the Poliglians were recruited by the Plaenellians to satisfy this dissention. And, since the growing armies of the various races paled in comparison to that of the Christians or the Aubrahteerians, the Poliglians came in and used religious concepts of code and regulation to establish early laws, which satisfied both sides of the fence. This is why government actually seems like it was taken strictly from religion or what seems to be the separation of church and state. However, this was why the Poliglians were chosen to step in between the Aubrahteerians and the other races. The Poliglians were the most politically minded and great at diplomatic solutions. Diplomacy took a more rational mind.

However, it would take years before diplomacy would ever benefit the Puhlosians. Marriage of Puhlosian partners wouldn't come out until way late in the hundreds of thousands of centuries that would have to pass before they could be accepted, as a race of beings, which is what wasn't knowledge prone to the average consciousness. Sadly, as Plaenellians knew, Osodon and Oosiah had been capable of doing that which they had done through what the various alien races lost in being born to alien planets, such as Ayeraal.

A Chapter in Family

It was Christmas time in the year 2014 before Kahlip finally got to feel like part of a family with his daughters. However, Christmastime wasn't what it was actually purported to be by the Aubrahteerians, too, his family he grew up in didn't prove to fortify the Christmas perpetuation throughout the year, which said much about the religious inconsistency. It also hinted to the dissension within Aubrahteerians. Forget the fact that Aubrahteerians hijacked a holiday to perpetuate their own intent. The proof of this existed in the fact that their Messiah wasn't born on Christmas, which proved the true essence behind what Christmas actually was. Even for its Aubrahteerian supposed roots, the reality behind Christmastime were something for everyone. The proof existed in how most religions their major holidays existed around the same time of the year, which showed relevancy between the reality of the holiday and what was really happening behind it. Elder Plaenellians or Keepers knew the religious dissension that surrounded their taking of the supposed holiday.

Christmastime wasn't a religious holiday at all, which is really, what Kahlip enjoyed most about it. And, the most glorious thing about it, too, was the fact that it happened when it was hot for regions that weren't under snow advisories, which proved that it wasn't a holiday relative to the cold, as in some beliefs. Christmastime didn't have to come with snow, and it really didn't have to come with presents because the feeling behind Christmas was going to come anyway. This was how the Aubrahteerians supposedly hijacked the holiday. And, what was most inherent about the holiday itself.

Christmastime had Universal roots, as far as a holiday. However, to justify the feeling behind Christmas, the Aubrahteerians claimed their Messiah was born that day.

However, most that could partake in the Christmas bug knew that they didn't feel the way they did because someone was present that wasn't present before. The Christmas bug came from the relief of the Universes from the influence of Osodon and Oosiah, which is why the holiday actually had Universal roots. Christmastime was a holiday for all planets in every Universe where the celebration varied, but the feeling behind it did not. In this way, the Aubrahteerians were actually frowned upon by claiming such things, as they did about the truth in the holiday. However, those who understood it, knew how to celebrate it and to what extent. They knew enough to give even the Aubrahteerians or the religious a kind thought that day. And, to most Plaenellians the fact that the Aubrahteerians did this showed exactly what their influences were concerning Osodon and Oosiah.

Part of the proof of this revolved around what most races were lacking throughout the year. And, yearly, there was relief for these races for the most part in each holiday season, which forged the various alien consciousnesses to be more giving, instead of the taking that was present most of the year.

Since it was their first year together, as a family, Kahlip had made one simple request of his daughters that Christmas. He only requested that they come and stay with him for the week before Christmas and the week after to which, they all obliged him. It worked out because they all lived in close proximity. So, they didn't have to change much about their lives. However, when he made this request, he found out that Lorande didn't partake in the holiday, and hadn't for the last couple of years. Frances disclosed that to Kahlip and Karen, to Lorande's dismay. Frances and Lorande had been the closest into their adult years than they had been to any other in their supposed family...for various reasons of course. Kahlip, upon being told about Lorande's distaste for the holiday, decided that she learn the truth behind what was supposedly a religious holiday. He then proceeded every night for that week up to Christmas Day, told them a little more about the story of how Christmas became a holiday, and why the Aubrahteerians decided to try to hijack it.

They celebrated that week, as they never had before. And Lorande, upon learning the truth behind the holiday, realized she could partake in it. However, it was the love her father had shown her that motivated her into celebration. She confessed that into her toast later one of the evenings before Christmas. They had all sat to dinner, after going out for the day, walking around town, enjoying St. Augustine that had been decorated for the season. The early evening, Kahlip and Karen cooked, while Lorande and Frances sat in the kitchen chatting between them and the cooks of the well-anticipated feast that evening. Karen cooked the homemade mashed potatoes and broccoli. Kahlip cooked the meat in the oven. It was seasoned steak, with a promise that it would be the best they'd ever tasted. As the day had progressed, and the meal was prepared, Lorande confided in Frances at a point in secret that she had always longed to have the feeling of family growing up. Frances then confessed that she felt her attitude growing up was because of the family she wanted, but didn't have. Frances spoke up at one point. "I was so attitudinal that my attitude had an attitude." Lorande laughed at her sister, and jokingly spoke up. "I know…I lived with you." Frances gave Lorande a glare, but she did it with a half-crooked smile. That was the thing about her sister. Frances deeply loved her. And, it was at that moment that Lorande decided to confess something to Frances she had held from her. Lorande looked at Frances with finality, and spoke. "Fran…I am gay." She said that so straight-faced. Frances eyed her and gave her a look, as though she had just been grossed out. Lorande turned from her regretting that she said anything. Then, Frances spoke up quickly. "Lor…I am kidding…you should know that." Lorande heard her, but she kept her face away from Frances. Frances spoke again. "Lor, actually, I was a little hurt that you didn't confide in me. You talked to mom first. Then, you tried to hide it by marrying and having a kid." Lorande turned and looked at her sister. She spoke up quickly when she heard those words. "You knew?" Frances looked at her sister. "Lor, as far as sister go, I am in love with you, as such. You don't think I would know. I have been the closest one to you. And, personally, I don't think I would have went to mom with that." Frances looked at her sister. She spoke up. "Well, I realized that too late." Lorande thought about something, as she looked warmly at her sister. "You know…as strange as dad's explanation for his understanding about me being gay, it almost makes sense." Frances looked at her sister. She spoke up, feeling a little bit hurt. "You even told dad before me?" Lorande shrugged and spoke quietly, as she looked at her sister with a squinty eye. "Forgive me?" Frances just shook her head and whispered. "Man…" She did consider what Lorande said about their dad. She spoke quickly. "What about what he said?" Lorande thought for a moment. She stared at Frances attempting to recall exactly what he said. After another minute, she looked at Frances with a determined, confident expression. She spoke up. "He said that gays and Lesbians were an alien race from another planet, and that I should be proud of who I am for whatever that is." Frances looked at her briefly and thoughtfully. "So…what are you then?" Lorande thoughtfully looked at her. "He called me Puhlosian." Frances gave her a thoughtful nod. She pondered what she said and spoke up. "And, what do you think?" Lorande eyed Frances briefly and quietly. She spoke with finality. "I think back to when we were kids, Frances. I think back and ponder reality. And, you know, all I can remember is how angry everyone always was for some reason. I remember how mom and Darion talked about their expectations of us for whatever that was. And, I never made any sense of it." Frances thoughtfully looked at her sister. She chuckled. "Do you remember…the…" She stopped speaking mid-sentence thoughtfully before she spoke again. "What was it…the story of the Dark Treaders?" Lorande spoke up. "Yeah… and what stories Darion could tell!" Frances then quickly spoke up. "Yeah…it was almost like he wanted us to become more a part of the story or something." Lorande just laughed. Frances looked at her thoughtfully and spoke. "So what about what dad said again?" Lorande looked at Frances. "Dad seemed earnest about what he said, but you know what, even though I didn't fully understand what he said, the love coming from him was more than I had gotten from anyone growing up...besides you. I think what he said seems feasible...he just seemed so honest when he said it." Lorande thoughtfully stopped speaking. She looked at Frances and spoke again. "I think he might be a good source to understand myself."

At that moment, Karen and their father walked out onto the rear porch. The night was winding down. Karen spoke, as she heard someone say the last words spoken. "Who?" Frances quickly spoke up. "No, we were talking about something dad said." Karen looked at her sisters equally, then at their father. "What did you say?" Kahlip shrugged and spoke quietly. "To whom." Lorande then spoke up. "Dad, I was telling Frances what you had told me about Puhlosians." Karen looked at her father with a curious look. He spoke up. "Oh yes..." He looked at Karen squarely and lightly when he spoke further. "Gays are actually consciousness from the planet Puhlosia." Karen looked at him when he said that. Then, she looked at her sisters. She spoke a simple word. "Oh." She then sat, as her father sat. Karen was next to Lorande, and their father was closest to Frances. Frances looked at her father and spoke. "So, where am I from?" Karen and Lorande laughed. Kahlip smiled thoughtfully. "Well, there is a good way to figure that out." Lorande and Karen stopped laughing and looked at Frances, then at their father. "You have to figure out your traits to determine that." Lorande and Karen seemed more serious, as their father seemed more serious. "Yes... there is a way to understand you on the highest level possible." All three of his girls were listening intently. He continued to speak. "It is the plight of the alien races that things have become what they have become on this planet. Too many do not realize their true heritage long before they were ever born here. They think this was their beginning, which doesn't explain who they are or come to know themselves wholly." Their father stopped speaking. He eyed Frances and spoke. "So what are your traits?" Frances was put on the spot. She didn't like to be put on the spot or in the proverbial hot seat, but she was among close family so it didn't feel the same. She looked up thoughtfully, as he said that. "Well, I think it is safe to say that I am not political or scientific." She sat thoughtfully again another moment before she spoke again. "I manage people for the deli I work in." She stopped speaking thoughtfully. She eyed her sisters and father. "You know…I am a manger." Kahlip listened, as she spoke and then considered something. He spoke up after another moment. "Ok…I got it. Are you a political supporter…do you value science, as a manger?" Frances thoughtfully looked at him. She spoke up. "I never really thought about it." Kahlip looked at her. He spoke again. "It's not important. But the point is that you can figure yourself out that way. You have to know that there are qualities of consciousness from specific planets here." Lorande spoke up. "So, you're saying that scientists and politicians are from a certain planet." Kahlip nodded and spoke. "That is correct. Just glimpsing the reality behind everything could be one of the most satisfying feelings ever. Knowledge is power, and that is how. That's how it works. You have to know first, then, apply. It's kind of like having the cure or ointment. It's only good if you apply it. Take Lorande for instance. Knowing that she is human and gay wasn't enough for her." As he said that, Karen didn't know about Lorande, and Lorande looked at her. Frances looked at Karen. Kahlip realized his mistake in mentioning it. "Hey, I said that because I mentioned that Puhlosians are gays from another planet, inferring that Lorande is gay." Karen looked at her sisters. "Yeah I caught that, but I will tell you something, I am a little hurt that you went to mom with that instead of me." Frances laughed and spoke. "That was just what I said." Lorande looked at Karen and shrugged. Frances spoke again. "And, that was what she did to me." Kahlip smiled, and suddenly, he felt the warmth his girls maintained through all the confusion growing up, having a mother that was less than what she could have been which was why he wanted her with him. Kahlip thought about something, and spoke. "Look at your Uncle Mickey." The three girls looked at him when he said that. All three of them knew of the Uncle Mickey effect. "Mickey

Ellis was Seyion, and look what he did." All three of his girls continued to think about what Uncle Mickey had done. "Mickey didn't mind telling you what he thought about what was going on." Karen thought about something, as her father said that. She spoke up. "I didn't realize until a few years ago that Uncle Mickey killed Uncle Amos…and he got away with it." Kahlip thought about something when she said that. He spoke up. "Your Uncle Mickey was surrounded by friends at that point…who was going to tell?" Kahlip thought about having to leave because he didn't like the family feud going on between Mickey and Amos, even though Kahlip might have had something to do with what went down between Mickey and Amos. However, he did warn Amos that what they were planning to do could be potentially deadly, considering whom Mickey was. Amos claimed he could handle it. Kahlip thought about something and looked at Karen. "You remember Amos most of all or should at least." Karen thought back and nodded. She thought about Uncle Amos. She spoke up. "Yeah, he was a really nice guy. I remember he was helping me get to Florida to meet with mom. He said he couldn't explain, but my mother would see me there. He told me he was my uncle. I don't know why, but I trusted him easily." Kahlip spoke up. "And, you were right to do so. Amos was a trusted friend…a brother almost to me." Kahlip stopped speaking and thought quickly of Amos. He spoke again. "Mickey's actions against Amos hurt deeply. Mickey was what most would consider mentally off. However, sadly, that was the effect of this planet to Seyions." Karen thought about something. She spoke up. "Wait a minute… so, what he thought about what was going on, was really what was happening?" Kahlip kind of chuckled when she said that. "Karen, so you honestly believe in what the religious folks say about hell and people are going there because of some sin? Think about that. What the religious do every day is similar to what Mickey did and why. And, you think they are right?" Kahlip stopped speaking thoughtfully. He considered something and spoke again. "No, what Mickey did was ruined the name of Dawn Keeper. That's what he did. And, he proved that Seyions should not be born to this planet. They don't go crazy, as most think, but they are out of their element, and that forces them to see things that may be true or not, but it should not define their behavior or justify them to behave the way Mickey did." Kahlip thought about something, as he finished speaking. And, he had but a few more words to say about Mickey Ellis. "Your uncle Mickey, girls, ruined his chances of ever being born here again." He left the girls thoughtful of his last words. They looked at each other, and then at him. Karen spoke up. "He wasn't in any way related to me, right?" Suddenly, Lorande and Frances looked at Karen. They questioned what she said, as if she were crazy. Karen looked at them. "Oh, I forgot…you both don't know that Kira was my mother not Lisa." Lorande and Frances looked at Karen, then at Kahlip. Lorande spoke up quickly. "So, we're half sisters?" Kahlip nodded in her direction. "Yes. Kira and I shared a thing shortly before your Lisa and I got started. And, because of who Mickey would be to Kira, was why I asked Darion and Lisa to take Karen, as one of their own. I have been looking out for you girls since before any of you were actually born. You thought you were alone and that we weren't family, but I have tried to be the father to you all." Kahlip stopped speaking thoughtfully and looked at his daughters. He spoke again. "Kira was getting closer to Mick Ellis and I felt for the safety of Karen." He looked at Karen when he said that. "Karen was going to be your name when you were born. Kira and I had talked about that." Frances thought about something. She looked at her father and spoke. "So, I am curious about how Karen got be in the family." Kahlip took a long hard look into his daughters equally for their eyes. He sat thoughtfully before he spoke. "Well, it's a long story, and a short one, which do you want." Karen looked at her sisters. Her sisters looked at her. Karen spoke up. "We're on vacation. I'll take the long story." Lorande and Frances both agreed with Karen. Kahlip spoke up quietly. "Ok, here it goes."

Kahlip resituated himself for his chair. He took a deep breath and exhaled, thinking back that far about how it went down. He thought about Mickey, and then Kira and all the key individuals involved at that time. "Let me put it this way. Mick Ellis had this understanding that he and Kira would birth a child. So, he couldn't find out that she and I shared a love he wouldn't understand, which did produce a child." Kahlip stopped speaking to look at Karen directly. "You, of course." Then, he turned to his other two daughters, and continued to speak. However, this is where it gets sticky. "A pregnant teen wasn't something Karen's parents wanted. Forget the facts that who she thought her real parents were weren't hers..." Lorande thought about something, as she heard him say that. She interrupted him. "Wait...you're confused, you said Karen, but we're talking about Kira." Kahlip smiled as he eyed them. He spoke up. "I forgot to mention that. Kira wasn't her real name...it was Karen." Karen's eyes lit up and she spoke. "So, I am my mother's namesake?" Kahlip smiled. "Yes. As it always should have been." Kahlip took a moment to share it with Karen. He thought about his time with Kira when he called her Karen. As that moment drifted away, he got back to the story. "You see, Mick had it in his mind since he was a little kid, and this is what I heard him say that he and Kira were going to be together. Mick was always older than I was, and Karen was closer to my age then his, but he just mentally figured things that way. We had us a kind of love triangle, but me and Amos tried to ward off Mick from the girls man more than just Karen herself, especially your mother and his sister, girls." Kahlip looked at Lorande and Frances when he said that. He continued to speak. "This was why Kira and I would have our thing first, she would get pregnant and then move away to get away from Mick. However, going back to what I said about her parents, my parents would take her in. Well, it was my ex-stepmother, as my mother died early in my life. I got to stay close to Kira, but eventually Mick found out about her and where she was, and this was after the baby, but it kind of worked out because my stepmother and her new husband were moving. However, I had always warned them about Mick and what he could do to Karen. Shortly after that, he found her, and it didn't matter because then they were moving. In all this, Lisa, your mother had started something with a guy named Darion, who would change his name to John Horn, and then back to Darion. It was a screwed up mess. Anyway, Lisa and Darion had taken you, Karen, but really, Darion was the one that harbored you. Lisa was still living at home, but in a relationship with Darion. By this point, she was old enough that she would stay over at his place for nights on end, but because she was trying to get away from Mick. Amos was getting tired of Mick by this point. Mick was unbearable to live with. He would do things. He would say things, which were a little unnerving. But that was really irrelevant. Anyway, in that time with Lisa, Darion, and you Karen, Lisa, and I had gotten close. And, I don't know if it were the fantasy world that Karen helped to create between Lisa and me, but Lisa began talking on occasion about having more kids, at least two more." Kahlip thought about something and stopped speaking. He sat a moment looking at his girls. "There is something…your missing…oh that's right." His girls looked at him strangely when he said that. He looked at them and spoke. "Sorry, I missed saying something." He looked at Karen when he said that. "Your mother was told that you died in child birth. She had been lied to, but for a good reason. She was protected from Mick. If Mick had known that, you were born and to Kira and you weren't his, you wouldn't have survived babyhood. So, I met with the doctor that would birth you. I implored him to go along with having you die at birth. I won't go into details about how I did that, but it took a lot of coercing and eventually it took him to meet Mick, to be convinced. Anyway, that was it." Karen thought about something. She looked at her sisters. She spoke up, as she turned to her father. "Dad, Darion molested me." Kahlip thought back. Suddenly, he remembered something he hadn't in a very long time. "No, Karen, that wasn't the Darion I had come to know. The Darion I entrusted you with was very kind and loving. He was a good man and a good friend. He was closer to me than Mick and I was." He looked at his three daughters. "And, what I didn't know at first was something so profound when I found out." He stopped speaking and looked at them for effect. "Darion Knight had an equal twin with very little difference between them. No one knew this because no one found out. Even Lisa didn't know. It was his brother, John Horn that molested you, if anyone did. And, now you girls know why I tried to get Lisa away from Darion. It wasn't for Darion that I did this, but his brother to whom no one would ever know had switched places with him, and lives his life secretly. I only saw bad things happening from this." He stopped speaking and looked at his daughters. Their mouths were draped open. They sat in shock. "And, that was why many people hated Darion Knight, his brother, John, had made him look bad in everyone's eyes. By the time Lisa realized what was going on it was too late. That was why I had to rescue you two. Amos had already intercepted you, Karen, and had you on your way to Florida. By this time, Mick was older and further down the dark Seyion path, as always happens the longer they spend time on this planet." Kahlip stopped speaking. He looked at his daughters. "Do you recall that night, the night we all left in that truck?" Lorande and Frances looked at each other, then at their father. "How can we forget?" Kahlip seemed to gather his thoughts. He looked at them thoughtfully. "Well, John horn had finished with Darion who I later found on the coast trapped by his brother in a completely different world. At one final point, John and Darion switched places. I told Darion that Lisa and I had the two girls; at least I thought I was telling Darion. I found out eventually that I told his brother, but at that point, it didn't matter. John was already set about what he was going to do." Kahlip stopped speaking and considered something. He looked at his daughters with finality. "You see, John Horn was heavy into Government, but not at high levels. At that point, John was set to go into a merger with a secret organization on gene experiments. However, he felt that his past needed to be erased, which is when I found you and Lisa was set to be killed, as well. But that is really conjectured at this point. Anyway, what is real is the nightmare happening when I found you two. However, it wasn't whom you thought. John Horn was part of a mercenary group long ago. And, he did want you two killed, but went after everyone that once met John or whom they thought was Darion. Remember, Darion was actually at the coast by now." Karen stopped him short. "Wait, how do you know all this?" Kahlip looked at his girls equally. He considered something before he spoke. He even got tears thinking about what Karen said. He finally spoke. "All I can say to that is this, Karen, and to you two. It was my job, as a father to know the kinds of situations you were in. I wanted to eventually be a family. And, I think I earned it. You see, girls, a father's job doesn't stop when the mother is around. I knew you all would need me when I wasn't. And, I know things have happened to each of you that I would have liked to have not happen, but what did happen didn't kill you. And, now here we all are. Besides that, I did consider that Mickey was subdued at this point. But I counted wrong, I guess." Karen thought about something when she was younger. She looked at her sisters, then at her father, as he said that. "Dad, I remember you and mom talking one time. It was long after what happened to Uncle Amos." Kahlip thought back. He briefly recalled what she mentioned. He spoke up. "So you caught us talking? Well, that was one time you did. There were many times when I popped in to check on you all and find out how you were doing. However, because you were that much closer to Uncle Mickey, He couldn't find out about the fact that you were all my kids. It might have been detrimental to your lives. So, I stayed away, but, as close as I could be." He stopped speaking and eyed his daughters. He looked at each of them as he spoke specifically to them. "Lorande, I saw your first kiss to that redhead, so I knew about you before you confessed it to me." Karen and Frances looked at Lorande. They both spoke to Lorande. "And, you never said anything to us?" Kahlip smiled and spoke. "Wait girls, you all have secrets from each other that I know about." He stopped speaking and eyed Karen and Frances. "Karen, I know you almost got engaged, and then found out that Tommy was cheating on you. How did you find out about that?" He then looked at Frances and spoke. "Frances, I know it was you that stopped the drugstore from being broken into. Then, that night you got your first kiss." He stopped speaking and eyed the three of them. He spoke again.

"Do you all want me to go on?" He stopped speaking and smiled at them. He considered something, and spoke again. "You see, girls, I made a commitment to you all. And, a secret commitment to me, and a pact with you three you never knew about. So, I actually have a list of things I know about you that you each don't know I know." His daughters looked at him in shock. Karen thought about something, as they all had something to be more thankful for than they realized. Kahlip spoke up suddenly. "It's what being a father is all about and what family means to me." Kahlip thought about something, as he said that, which brought tears to his daughter's eyes. He spoke up again. "Hey, listen, on a different subject, I have to shop for the three of you. What do you say we all go shopping tomorrow?" The three of them liked that idea. And, for the first time in their adult lives, they all felt like kids again, or how their childhoods should have gone. Karen looked at her father, and realized somehow that she finally had a sense of what home was. Frances and Lorande too, felt the same as, Karen. Karen finally felt the sense of loneliness disappear, which she had for too many years.

The Chapter Relative & the Killian Dawn

Christmas had gone, but not without the first true and honest appreciation in his daughters for what Christmas actually meant. Karen, Frances and Lorande had a deeper sense of belonging that was growing more and more, as they spent time with their father. Karen was, really still trying to figure him out. Lorande and Frances got a glimpse of the man they had come to know, as their father since that time in the truck. Lorande was thoughtful that her father finally seemed real with who he was now, instead of being Uncle Lehmmy. As far, as Frances was concerned, she finally had her attitude adjustment in her father. And, the irony, he didn't have to spank it out of her. She gave it up willingly for the love he gave her.

For Kahlip, his daughters could have a bigger responsibility to the planet and each other, as well the other alien races upon the planet. However, that was their responsibility to accept, and in their own time. With his first real Christmas celebration under his belt, and the new year had begun for him with his daughters, Kahlip knew that it was time to get down to business. However, Kahlip knew that he was always on the clock.

As much as she didn't want to admit it, Penelope knew what was going on that was hard to accept on one hand, but not on another. She thought about the many relationships long past that had happened on the planet, she thought of the current ones, and the potential relationships. And, then there was her. She went to her mother's for breakfast that morning, reluctantly, of course. Roger was the last thing to whom she wanted to talk. Her mother seemed unable to accept that Roger was gone, and she had moved on. It was sad her mother hadn't, but she thought she knew why.

She arrived at her mother's house early. Her mother was still asleep. She used the spare hidden key to get in. She started cooking while her mother slept. She knew though, once she started cooking, her mother would smell it and wake up. However,

Penelope didn't expect someone else to wake up first. Her mother, she guessed was into her next relationship, which was perhaps why her mother couldn't accept that Roger was gone. In some way, she wanted her daughter to live unlike she did, not making the same mistakes in men. However, what he mother didn't realize was that she actually wasn't. Her mother had a different guy every two months. And, Penelope guessed that was fine for her mother, but Roger was a long year before it ended. And, Penelope had no mind to get into another one any time soon, save for one man specifically, but she didn't see that coming soon.

Penelope looked at the man with his head and upper body deep into the refrigerator. She spoke up. "And you are…?" The man stood quickly when he heard her voice. He bumped his head when he stood, as he got startled. He really didn't notice anyone in the kitchen when he walked to the refrigerator. He turned and looked at the woman that spoke. "I am Mitch. You must be Penny." Penelope smirked. She hated Penny. "No, I don't care what my mother has said. I am Penelope. Not Penny got it." Mitch eyed her for her long dark hair, her blue eyes, and long legs. He smirked and spoke up. "That was exactly what she said you might say. Okay…I got it, Penelope." Mitch stood there eyeing Penelope. She went back to cooking. "If it's any consolation, she also said you were attractive, and she was right." Penelope shook her head. "It's not." Penelope shuffled the scrambled eggs in the pan. She felt his eyes checking her out. She spoke up. "What?" Mitch looked at her for another minute when she said that. He thought about the little girl in the woman standing before him. "You don't remember me, do you?" Penelope stopped with the eggs and turned to look at him. She stared a moment, for what she considered his sleep shorts, his short dark hair, hairless chest, and thin frame. She looked a bit harder, noticing something familiar in him. He spoke again. "I am the one that got you to appreciate your name that you wouldn't let anyone call you anything but your whole name. It's me." Suddenly, Penelope remembered him. "Mitchy…?" Mitch smiled. "Yep…that's me!" Penelope went to give him a hug. He greeted her with open arms. "Hey Kiddo." They squeezed each other warmly. Penelope spoke up, as she let go of him. "Wow, this is great!" Then, she thought about something. "You were why Mom wanted me over for breakfast!" Mitch smiled. "I guess…I am nothing special." Penelope slapped him on the arm. "Hush. You were the greatest thing since sliced bread when I was a kid. I wanted you to be my father, but mom explained that you had to leave." Mitch thought back to that time. He recalled how hard it was to leave. He held back from her seeing his tears. He quickly changed the subject and spoke. "I am going to wake your mother." Mitch walked away with his red and black shorts on. She quickly spoke up. "Tell her not to come to the table in curlers. I don't feel like laughing." He waved in recognition to what she said. Penelope watched him leave, as she thought about the time when she was a kid and had Mitch in her life. Mitch was everything she wanted in a father. She remembered what her mother said when he left. "If you love something, set it free, if it comes back it was meant to be." She thought about how he came back. She thought of her mother, and how patience had worked for her and that ole saying. Suddenly, she thought about Kahlip. She guessed she had set him free, she was just waiting for him to come back. She guessed it didn't matter if they were too old to walk; she just wanted to see him again, look into his eyes, and say I love you. Until that happened, she knew she must go out and live if that was what she could call it.

She had breakfast done and on the table. She had just put the last plate on the table when Mitch and her mother walked out. Penelope instantly recalled what it was like growing up in her mother's house. Mitch was so much a part of their lives that it was commonplace to see him in the house. It was really like old times with one difference. Instead of her and Mitch racing to the breakfast table, it was her mother and Mitch. And, of course, she came to the table in curlers.

Penelope had even the juice poured at the table, awaiting them, just like her mother had done when she was little. Penelope spoke up, holding back her laughter, as they sat beside each other. "It's nice for you two to finally make it to the table." Her mother shrugged and smirked. She looked the table over, and then eyed

Penelope. She spoke with a groggy voice. "Looks good, Penny." Penelope was about to put a spoon in the eggs and dip some out. She stopped, looked at her mother, and spoke. "Mom…do you do that just to get at me?" Her mother smiled. She eyed her daughter warmly and spoke. "Love you…" Penelope stayed silent a moment and then went to digging at the eggs to add to her plate. Her mother spoke up. "You know…you were named incorrectly. You should have been a Penny, but your father and I compromised. I could call you Penny and he could call you Penelope." Penelope looked at Mitch, as her mother said that. She looked quickly at her mother and spoke. "Besides, I didn't laugh at your curlers." She looked back at Mitch. Her mother spoke up. "Well, I called you Penny…Penny." Penelope ignored her mother for that comment. She continued to look at Mitch. She spoke up. "Can you help me out here? You agree, as my father did about what I should be called." Mitch looked at Penelope, then, her mother. Her mother looked at Mitch. They gave each other a look, to which Penelope inquired. "What was that look?" Her mother then, scratched the itch on her face with her left hand, as Penelope eyed her. She finally noticed the ring. She spoke up quickly. "What is that?" Mitch spoke up, as he smiled at first. "I asked her last night… got down on one knee and everything." Penelope looked at them equally. She spoke up. "It's about time." Penelope looked at Mitch thoughtfully. "You know, I never stopped considering you my dad." Mitch thought about what she said. He spoke up. "I know, kiddo, and I never stopped missing my daughter." Penelope took in her eggs with a side of emotion in her throat. The next few moments were spent with quiet eating. Penelope thought about something looking at Mitch and her Mother. She finally spoke up. "Set a date yet?" Her mother spoke up. "Not yet…he just asked me." Penelope thought about something. She spoke again. "I want to have a date. I don't want to get my hopes up." Mitch thought about his condition. He thought about what the doctors said, as he sat there looking at the girl that didn't know he is her father. Her mother sat looking at her thinking that she didn't know if they could get married soon enough.

It was three in the morning when Kahlip got a phone call. He didn't awaken at first. His phone rang three times before he finally heard it. He stirred in bed, thinking it was too early for the phone. It rang one more time before Kahlip at least picked up the small, well-lit, little noise box. He looked at the screen thoughtfully. Suddenly, it stopped ringing, but as he looked at the screen, he noticed who it was. The number was all too familiar. He thoughtfully put his heavy head back into his very soft pillow. He stared at the ceiling waiting for another ring. He knew it was coming. It was just a matter of when. Then, after only another moment of staring at the ceiling, his little phone rang again, lighting up the area of his room around the bed nicely. He answered it quickly. "Hello, but it's too early." He listened for the voice on the other end he knew would be coming. A young, soft female voice spoke a few subtle words for which Kahlip responded. "Do you really think that is necessary?" Kahlip stopped speaking and listened. "Yes, this is me…who else would it be?" He stopped again and listened to the voice on the other end. He spoke again. "Okay, but I am not leaving right now." Another stopping point and then he spoke again. "Well, there is no way I am leaving until…" He was interrupted. He listened intently for a brief moment. "You know…this is frustrating." He listened again, as he sat up in bed. His feet hit the floor. "I know it is for you, as well." He was listening again. Then, he spoke with more subtle frustration. "I cannot help that." He stopped speaking and listened. He sat thoughtfully, as he endured the woman's soft voice. He spoke again. "You know…it's for your voice that I can entertain these conversations, but I'll tell you something. You should just go ahead and hire me full time." He stopped speaking and listened. "Okay…I will be there, as soon as I can." With those final words, Kahlip hung up the phone. He sat at the edge of his bed thoughtfully. He considered working at the motel, and in some ways, he wished it were the only job he had, but he wasn't that lucky. The frustrating part was that he almost, didn't get paid to be beckoned by the Company, whenever they got themselves into a jam. That was the point, at which he thought about having an assistant, when he needed to take off suddenly in an out of state trip.

He had to consult with "the book" suddenly, but first, he had to wake up. He sat at the edge of the bed attempting to find the motivation to stand. The book was hiding far from him, as he sat on the bed at that moment. For some reason, he just wanted to lie back down and close his eyes for a few more hours. Then, with a burst of drive, he stood and went over to the dresser, opened the bottom drawer, reached in, and then withdrew the book. He looked at it briefly for its cover, then, carried it out of the bedroom.

He went to the kitchen in a silent rush to the coffee maker. He threw together a pot of coffee, then, went to the back porch with a hot cup. He sat easily and tabled his cup. He sat back in the chair and opened the book. He was thumbing through it at first, glancing between pages without really reading anything in particular. Then, he found what he sought. He began reading into the next hour, which he needed to do to deal with the problems the Company was facing, per Vicky on the phone. With thoughts of Vicky, came considerations for Kaera. He had never officially met Vicky. He only had those moments on the phone with her, but they were sweet interludes of peace, which was the value of her voice. Then, her voice took him to considering Kaera, who he had met once upon a time and missed dearly.

So, he read, trying not to think about Kaera, but that was hard to do. After many stops and starts, he finally finished, after finding what he needed to in the book. He sat back with his coffee, thinking about his speech Vicky needed that she could read in his place. This time, the Company only needed a speech written that Vicky was supposed to read to a group opposing the Company and what they were trying to do. It was always some environmental group that really didn't understand what was going on. Kahlip gave thought to the Company's activities and how much resistance it had received through the years. And, to an unknowledgeable crowd, filled with fear from that lack of knowledge, the Company had problems on their hands. Kahlip thought about the last time he wrote a speech for Vicky, without his wit behind the reading of the speech, Vicky came up with great resistance, which was why she wanted him to brief her on it this time. She needed to fully understand the point of view with which the speech was written. For Kahlip, that was the value of The Killian Dawn. Kahlip regressed mentally to the time long ago when the planet and consciousness on it, really had no perspective on the planet itself or themselves in contrast to it.

Long ago, fear was a killer or what thrived in consciousness lacking knowledge. Kahlip actually needed that book less than he gave himself credit for because of the amount of knowledge, he did possess. That was what most sentient beings upon Ayeraal lacked, which heightened the fear. The mix of consciousness on Ayeraal or Earth made their biggest mistake in forgetting their heritage or their alien origins, which Plaenellians could never escape. However, much had been done to bridge certain gaps that currently, alien consciousness or humans could act in many various ways in contrast, one to another. However, for those Keepers who knew better, understood why and that humans weren't merely human, which is from where the concept of Planetary Engineering stemmed. And, it was that, which Kahlip took from The Killian Dawn.

With so many various forms of alien consciousness upon the planet, there was really a lacking in them for where they were. And, with the many problems stemming from that, as in the Aubrahteerians to the Rosicrucians, a higher understanding for consciousness in contrast to planet was needed. Planetary Engineering was that concept needed, and was provided in The Killian Dawn. Mere humans don't realize that everything changes and certain things happen in these changes, even those things regarding planets with consciousness upon them. However, the Aubrahteerians were the ones most relative to the resistance of this concept of Planetary Engineering. And, the Plaenellians weren't giving up with that effort.

It was an idea born in the Plaenellians early on, with what happened on Ayeraal between the various forms of consciousness. Perspective about existence upon her was lacking to such degrees that fear existed for what happened. Until perspective was found, every facet of existence had been questioned, which to date isn't knowledge based in reality. This meant that humans or alien consciousnesses have come to believe certain things once derived out of fear. Even Rosicrucians had certain levels of fear, which forged their perspective. Then, there were the Poliglians who were thought to be less fearful. However, even they possess a certain level, stemming from the fact that they think they have permanent residency upon Ayeraal. It eventually became Plaenellian knowledge that for the most part, the various alien consciousnesses would lose sight of their roots, and begins to believe they were part of Ayeraal. This is actually where the fear thrives, and why the concept of Planetary Engineering was so important. However, until the Plaenellian plan to return all Universes to their original states would come to fruition, and a solution to the Universal issues could be found, the various forms of alien consciousness on Earth would go through great turmoil without perspective and the higher point of view.

Kahlip's hobby was perspective. In his down time, Kahlip would offer his services to companies that had a weak public relations department that needed help addressing the public. Though Kahlip really didn't have down time. The Company, as he thought of them, was just one of those companies that had a job to do, without the support of the people. Kahlip was brought on to aid in this respect. Kahlip understood that for many alien consciousnesses, the way of looking at life on Earth was greatly similar without true understanding. This lack of perspective was what forged the problems of certain groups and lobbyists. It's what forged the plight of the weak and the strong. Ironically, the weak were those who knew more, and the strong knew less. This said everything about muscle to knowledge, which was why muscle was hired.

The Chapter of Unsound Fact & Sound Fiction

Kahlip sat one night thinking alone in the solitude of his back porch. The night was easy and the sky clear. He thought about the effort consciousness had been on since it became stuck on Ayeraal. He considered certain secrets of he, and his fellow Plaenellians. In a sullen twist, things and reasons were shrouded by what one knew or understood. All Plaenellians knew this however. And, ironically, fiction was more accepted than fact. However, fact and fiction had been reversed. True fiction was more easily accepted or seemed to make more sense. However, it was eventually passed off as fact. It's like in a true story that some might believe or take as true, which may or may not have fictional roots. However, Planetary Engineering was a concept that many would never understand was the underlying root behind how individuals existed upon Ayeraal. The argument existed on whether or not fire came first or the desire to cook with it? Was the wagon created before the desire to transport? Was the motorized car created to transport people in a more advanced age? Most would say that fire was discovered, then, used to cook. They would claim the wheel was created, in the early stages of designing modes of transportation. Lastly, many would argue that the motorized engine was the result of this desire to transport many people at once and do it at a faster pace. However, the ability to motorize a vehicle wasn't based upon the notions of traveling the world or one's country. This was where fact and fiction came into play. It was easier to have the potential, then, discover what to do with it. Fire, the carriage or wagon, and the motorized engine were all concepts stemming from necessity, than mere discovery. Fire wasn't actually discovered. It was recognized, as a potential in the planet upon which consciousness existed. Alien consciousness for its placement, or certain ones understood fire concepts. This was how fire wasn't merely discovered. Eventually consciousness was born that understood the essence of fire and introduced it into societies, which gathered in certain areas or in what was considered early cities or townships and villages. Part of Planetary Engineering possessed the ability of fire. This knowledge of fire was brought to Ayeraal or Earth by way of the earliest Rosicrucians. However, those of whom are incapable of accepting the concept of Planetary Engineering; fire was found by mere chance. However, one solid fact remained that if fire didn't come to exist when it did, certain facets of human existence on Ayeraal would have differed, which shows a kind of conscious effort to possess the ability of fire.

Another facet of progress in consciousness was the necessity of consciousness placed around the planet in specific locations. This meant that the need to transport showed a sense of Planetary Engineering in consciousness. This meant that for its worth and need, the planet, as it changed required more masses of consciousness in a specific region, as opposed to others. Migration wasn't the result of curiosity and discovery, and those supposed early discoverers weren't merely trying to discover new lands. A simple mind might take discovery, as fact. However, the reality in the land migrations happened, not for mere and simple sights set on freedom, as in the pilgrimage from England to the Americas, or any other European Nation to the Americas. It was Plaenellian knowledge that the people needed to spread out from the understanding of Planetary Engineering. However, most just think they are moving around because that is their choice to do so. However, it was a measure of destiny that one should have a destination, with which to come to an end, which still differed from fate.

Planetary Engineering had another aspect to it. With a planet changing as Ayeraal had been for so long, the potential fuels in the ground needed to be harvested for the safety and security of masses more numerous than of yesteryear. However, the understanding of most is such that gasoline was the byproduct of the need to drive the engine or fuel the torches for sight when it was dark. Actually, that was unsound fact, and the truth enveloped sound fiction. The engine was the byproduct of the need to burn off the fuel stored in the ground. This by the way are why the diesel engine was created, and whose engines applied to heavy transport of materials. It was seen that more oil could be used up in diesel engines, but adequate amounts to satisfy the burn-off because of the nature of goods transportation. The byproduct of a heavier fuel, such as diesel fuel was the transportation of these heavier good. This is why there is such a necessity to burn off fuels in the ground at a specific rate, and diesel fuel satisfied this need. Alien consciousness on earth had existed too long on the planet, which posed a greater threat to the planet, which was continuing to dry out. That put the lava in the ground, at a greater risk to the oil in the ground, and both posed a severe threat to the sanctity of alien consciousness on the surface. The point was that it didn't matter if humans have a place to go or not, the oil in the ground had to be removed and something had to be done with it or else the lave flows, as they got closer to the surface, could mix in the wrong way with the oil. That was unfortunately, sound fiction.

Another piece of sound fiction was the fact that Volcanoes formed because the planet is drying out. This was an early nightmare for many of Ayeraal's inhabitants. It's really a matter of compression. As the planet dries or becomes solid, its soft inner materials are going to be pushed out. This is why Volcanoes erupt for the drying effect in the area, which forces more lava from inside the planet to escape the surface. And, this was what eventually came to happen because Planetary Engineering couldn't happen any faster than it did. This was why the gas-burning engine finally came to fruition when it did. This is why it is sound fiction because sentient beings upon earth do not realize that every aspect of life and the way it is lived is a measure of trying to keep the planet going, as opposed to destroying it. Ironically, there are those who opposed this process of Planetary Engineering out of fear. However, in so doing would have caused their earlier demise than the prosperity. This is why greenhouse gases are less of a threat than most give it credit. However, this is, again, done out of fear and what alien consciousness or human consciousness upon Ayeraal is lacking in awareness. To the finer point, greenhouse gases are less of a threat than remaining oil in the ground to a greater physical region. And, it was this premise upon which Planetary Engineering was further developed.

Years ago, it was understood what was happening, which is really where Planetary Engineering began. The greater minds involved in gas production from oil, even those minds associated with the construction of the engines that could burn this oil off were part of the minds that were touched by those Plaenellians who knew what would eventually happen to the planet. This information was part of the Killian Dawn, and why Kahlip couldn't destroy it. It had further plans for the planet when each stage of the drying process came to fruition. And, Volcanoes were part of that. Sadly, Ayeraal's moon was evidence of where Ayeraal was heading when the two would eventually mirror each other, excluding perhaps, their size.

Another part of the Killian Dawn involved turning ocean water into drinking water. Even the use of animals and harvesting them was an aspect of the Planetary Engineering plan. Vegetable Farms would become an aspect of Planetary Engineering because of the need to bring water to that area of the planet, and keeping the soils fertile enough to plant. This would not allow these portions of the planet to dry out because farmers would water the ground on a routine and seasonal basis. It isn't mere chance that the greater farms exist in regions where the farms thrive in the spring and summer months until the cold weather, hits to suppress the drying effect. Then, the farmers plant seed and water the next spring and summer in an attempt to keep life in the region with the water and eventual vegetation. It was all a part of trying to keep the planet alive. Food, ironically, was a byproduct of this attempt to engineer the planet. However, most minds could only accept that they were farming and eating out of self-need.

There was much alien consciousness didn't understand about the nature of the planet and what true survival meant. Even the growth of cities and placement of these cities was important to

Engineering the planet. In effect, cities were actually a means to suppress the water evaporation in specific regions, contrarily to the concept that with so many city streets and parking lots, water couldn't be properly filtered into the ground. It was actually the reverse. Water could not evaporate for the city's parking areas and streets. There was so much more to perspective concerning the planet and its survival along with sentient beings than those beings fully grasped. This begged the question of which was purpose, stopping the water from evaporating with huge squares of asphalt and streets, or the roads and parking lots, cars and trucks needed to drive on. A simple mind would believe that it was the need of the cars and trucks that would drive the creation of streets and parking lots. However, one fact remains. If there weren't streets and roads, water evaporation would happen at a faster rate. It was all part of Planetary Engineering. The point was that pitch, which was used in early roof construction, was almost the same stuff used in roads, with aggregate rock, as a variable between the two. It isn't mere chance that major cities exist in regions where the potential for water evaporation is the greatest, but that was perhaps the reason why the cities seemed to be dying out of a lack of awareness to this fact. Pride should exist in the bigger cities for what is really going on. If it weren't for these bigger cities covering the planet, which really acts, as a thermal blanket, maintaining moisture, then the planet would probably dry out faster. For as dry as those regions were, there were still the water effects deep in the ground. Ironically, too, these bigger cities and their massive weight worked to suppress this moisture, as well in being the blanket. But it also suited another purpose in suppressing lava flows. Lava flowed underground as well as waters flowed above ground or the path of least resistance. The bigger cities suppressed the flow of lava, which is actually thicker than water, but that was mere sound fiction to most or unsound fact, but truth to others. However, the ultimate reason for Planetary Engineering, as a great secret of the Keepers, was the fact that planting farms was so much more than just an effort to keep a specific plot of land wet. Where this is true...it is actually more than that. Ayeraal was potentially a computer itself. In much the same way a computer is built, farms were plotted. Every computer element has a specific place within it. That is for its optimum potential to actualize. In much the same manner, as computer chips are placed and motherboards exist, so do these various farms. The reason why oranges don't grow in cold places is simple, but that infers that it isn't good to put the motherboard near to the power coming into a computer. For this reason, Apples do not grow good in the south. This is why apples have a more fleshy appeal to them, and oranges are more liquid, but also why the color orange is associated with heat. This is also why peaches grow best closer to a more moderate climate further than the true south, but also why the peach relates more to an apple than an orange with its tougher interior. The reason is this sense of Planetary Engineering that these things have been discovered as needing a specific place upon the planet to thrive, which also indicates that, unbeknownst to most intelligence, these things together, these fruit and vegetable farms, work together to counteract the slowing measure of the planet for their placement. However, the greatest effort in this form of farm engineering per the planet is for what the planet becomes from this effect. It becomes a machine of sorts in contrast to the other planets for where the elements, as in the fruits and vegetables, are placed. Understanding this should instill a stronger sense and support of these farmers or individuals that operate and function on a higher level than what was previously thought of them. However, most accept the farmer as a businessperson, but that is too far from the truth. They are so much more. So, in essence, this also explains how the watering effect works and for what these farms actually exists, as an element of a machine, In other words, these farms with their crop, are a computer part that has to be replaced seasonally. So, the water produces the wet ground while the element is in place, as a kind of weld in the computer that keeps the chip in place. But once the watering has to stop, it is time to replace the crop, as in a computer chip that has gone bad. This equates to a computer chip that has to be exhumed, and another put in. Due to the magnitude of the crop, it takes a season to exhume it, then to replace it after that cooler season is over, when watering needs to be done again that next year. Aside from a measure of saving the planet, these farms act as an aspect of something even greater…the means to save a Universe, and perhaps even the Universes.

Monday came for Penelope with an abrupt stop. Her Sunday went better than her last few with Mitch now in her life again. For some reason, she was thoughtful that Mitch came back in her life at just the right time. If it wasn't for her it was her mother. Monday she went and addressed the committee. She gave her usual speech about the necessity of the drilling to relieve the pressure inherent in oil pockets associated with jungle region along with the reassurances to the committee that all ethical measures have been taken to relieve the US form any negative publicity. As she left the committee, she considered how frustrating the lobbyists and environmentalists were. Environmentalists don't understand the necessity of releasing this pressure in contrast to volcanic activity in the growing number of volcanoes on the planet. There were at least two hundred to date. The point was that either the oil pressure was released in these supposed Eden type regions or there wouldn't be any regions because when lava hit them, the areas would explode. It was quite obvious that consciousness upon Ayeraal really didn't understand what happened to the moon, which is really, where the influence of the Plaenellians became most beneficial. It was the lessons of the moon and what happened to it that really forged an example for the Plaenellians to go by with the inherent consciousness upon Ayeraal. The moon then, became the unknown example for what do when existing upon a planet, and what must be done to continue to exist.

Kaera thought about the kind of resistance there had been throughout the years, downing supposed progress by lobbyists and environmentalists, which wasn't progress but a matter of life and death for humans on the planet. Sadly, those environmentalists didn't realize that Ayeraal was in a much better state than when humans first came to exist upon it. It was a bit too late to begin to fight for it through their means. What they thought of as tearing up the planet was a matter of life and death surgery for the planet. Kaera thought about that. She thought about it with a tear for what her parents did to the Universes, which caused the degrading states of planets with alien consciousness upon them. Sadly, that was the darkness in consciousness upon an alien planet. Kaera thought about that too many times. And, when she wasn't, she was thinking about Kahlip, hopeful that there was a solution to the destruction of the planets. Sadly, that was what the Environmentalists didn't realize. The planet and for what humans were attempting to be upon it, wasn't destruction if they lived a certain way. Ironically, environmentalists were looking more and more like representatives of Osodon and Oosiah preventing certain supposed environmental destruction, which would help the planet and consciousness upon it.

A Chapter for Solution II

Kahlip took a more intensive look into The Killian Dawn later that Monday night. He was in the living room, with one lamp lit, and an easy listening piece of music playing. Time was progressing, and with that progression, went the chances for a solution to the planet's ills. Perhaps the most frustrating thing about environmentalists was the fact that the degradation of the planet didn't begin with technology. The planet had been degrading long before technology came into the picture. This meant that it was the mere darkness within the various alien consciousnesses that forged Ayeraal's condition, not technology. Technology wasn't anything, but a means to help the planet. The point was that the very argument Environmentalists made came from a dark place to begin with. There, of course was the darkness, which was darkness in consciousness just from the mere fact that alien consciousness was alien to Ayeraal. However, that darkness could be overcome with a lighter view of one's self and where one is, with some exclusion, as in the Cagers.

Technology was only part of the solution, as in the burial of trash, not to hide it, but to put back into the planet, that which was once taken out, which environmentalists also didn't realize. However, they ran on logic, and what was taken from the planet couldn't be put back in any other way. However, what they don't realize is that there wasn't anything that couldn't be put back into the planet, even if it was in some other form, as in plastics. Plastics, ironically, were another part of the solution, but that was to some as sound fiction, as well. However, it was truth. The state of plastics in the ground forged the relief of the explosive properties of fuel. There again was the perspective of the sound fiction concerning plastics being a detriment or a benefit. However, what was known by Plaenellians or what existed, as a secret of the Keepers was the fact that if consciousness on the planet the moon once was did what was being done on Ayeraal, the moon wouldn't have become a moon at all. Plaenellians weren't going to let what happened to Ahvenshurr, happen to Ayeraal for what Ahvenshurrians didn't know back then. It was another secret of the Keepers that alien consciousness on Ayeraal was made up of a certain number of those from Ahvenshurr or in other words refugees from Ahvenshurr. This is what really gave depth to the Universes, and what being anything at all really meant. Part of the solution to Ayeraal's issues with consciousness upon her meant an awakening of sorts or a relieving of the darkness in its sentient beings. Part of the plight behind humanity was in the thinking that their humanity was all they had. They didn't understand themselves for their alien heritage, and thus great fear exists in them because they perceive death is their end. Death wasn't what motivated the survival of the planet, not for the Keepers. What motivated the survival of the planet and consciousness upon it, was simply that with more habitable planets, it forged a greater awareness and experience for consciousness. As in Ahvenshurr and what it meant to exist there was an entirely different level of experience, as a sentient being. Kahlip remembered his days upon Ahvenshurr. Ahvenshurr, in its day, wasn't too much different from Ayeraal or Earth. It too, in its beginnings spun faster, as Ayeraal did, but the experience was shades better, which is why Osodon and Oosiah chose it for destruction above many other planets.

Kahlip thought harder about the solution to Ayeraal's woes, as he considered what happened to Ahvenshurr. He really didn't want what happened to Ahvenshurr to happen to any other planet, let alone the Ahvenshurrians, who got split up between all habitable planets when Ahvenshurr finally became inhabitable. It hurt him the worst, knowing that Ayeraal was beginning to look a lot like the moon does now with all its moon craters, or what Plaenellians understand, as old volcanoes from the days of Ahvenshurr, the planet.

Kahlip teared up, as he remembered Ahvenshurr. It housed him a few times, and he enjoyed being upon her. Losing Ahvenshurr was a great blow to the Plaenellians, but probably he and Kaera the most, as it was the place of their last time together. Sadly, his memories of Kaera were associated with the destruction of Ahvenshurr. They would never see it again for what it once was, and he really didn't want to recall what it was to him or what it felt like to be there because the memories were too painful, which is what motivated the Ayeraal effort. That was also, why he thought he would find Kaera again on Ayeraal because many Plaenellians were attempting to tackle the Ayeraal problem and defense against Osodon and Oosiah. Suddenly, Kahlip thought about his granddaughter, Karen, and then Julius. He thought about how carefree they were, now living in France. He thought about what they thought they were, as the Master Seyion or playing as such. What they didn't realize was that they really didn't want the responsibility of being Osodon and Oosiah, which is who the Master Seyion actually was. Osodon and Oosiah have been playing head games with many alien consciousness on many planets. What Kahlip didn't get was how the Seyions were that naïve to be duped by Osodon and Oosiah, as they were. It hurt really, as Kahlip considered that. And, it hurt that the head of the Plaenellian family was also its enemy. This was why the solution had to lie in Ayeraal to all the Universal problems. Kahlip just had to find it. And, that was the greatest secret of the Keepers. Things on earth could be done that would satisfy the needs of many Universes, which is why consciousness exists upon it, as it does. In that moment, Kahlip glimpsed the solution, but only glimpsed it. He thought and thought about solution possibilities. However, the solution was but a glimpse at that moment.

Too, at that moment, his daughters walked in for a surprise visit. He heard them calling for him from the Foyer. He called back to them from the living room. He looked up, as they entered the living room. The three of them noticed the ambience, and commented on it. They went to sit around him. He looked at them, as they sat. He spoke up. "So, to what do I owe this pleasure?" He looked at them equally and warmly. He was glad to have them there, even for as late, as it was at that moment.

Frances seemed too cheery for the hour when she spoke first. "What are you up to?" Kahlip turned to her and considered something before he spoke. "I am studying, actually." Lorande spoke up quickly. "Oh yeah…what for?" Kahlip turned to her and smiled. "I should actually be asking the three of you what you are doing here." Karen spoke up, as she looked at her sisters. "Well, we've been talking about the fact that we've already missed so much time with you, that we wanted to pay you a visit." Kahlip eyed the three of them. "That's wonderful, but I am just here studying." Lorande looked at him, as he said that. She spoke up. "Can we help?" Kahlip looked at them thoughtfully. He spoke easily. "Okay…the truth is that I am studying for a solution to the Universal problems, and that of this planet." His daughters looked at him with intrigue. Thoughtfully, they then, looked at each other. Frances spoke up, as she turned to her father. "Solution… to what problem?" Kahlip looked at his daughters when she said that. He was thoughtful of the back porch. He spoke up. "Hey…I have some torches for the back porch; we can light them, and talk outside. It's a nice night for that." His daughters agreed to that.

Kahlip took the torches from the little standing chest by the wall of the back of the house, as Lorande, Karen and Frances set up the lawn chairs. He set them in the ground and lit them. He, then, looked at his daughters thoughtfully, as they comforted themselves upon the lawn chairs. The mood had been set, the torches burned and the ambience was enhanced with his daughters there with him. Kahlip became thoughtful and figured it was about time to tell them the truth. He figured it was time they knew their true selves, as opposed to what they got when they were younger. He looked at each of them before he spoke. "It's time to tell you the truth." They equally eyed him for what he said. Lorande spoke up. "Truth?" Kahlip eyed Lorande first and spoke. "Yes, Lorande. You need to know this before I explain solutions." He thought about something before he spoke again. "There is a chance that each of you are Dawn Keepers, but not for what you had as examples growing up. Dawn Keeping according to the Seyions was a perverted concept. Dawn Keepers, girls, don't have enemies for what it takes to be one. Dark Treaders were individuals that opposed their fellow

Seyions, and that was it." He stopped speaking and eyed them for their understanding. He spoke again, as they anticipated his next words. "We Dawn Keepers are about love and it strictly. See, there is an understanding in us for all alien consciousness not present in the average sentient being on this planet. So, when I told you about being a Dawn Keeper, Lorande, remember…in the truck that time?" Lorande thought back. It was so long ago, but she vaguely recalled. She spoke quietly. "I think so." Kahlip looked at her warmly, as he spoke again. "Well…that is what I meant. I couldn't be honest about everything for what was going on, which is why I was just Uncle Lehmmy. However, you three are my daughters, and you come from the same place I do. You are Plaenellian as I am or in other words, we are Dawn Keepers. However, the Seyions have ruined what it means to be one. Any more now, we recognize ourselves for what our true Heritage is." Kahlip stopped speaking thoughtfully. He looked at them equally. "Lately, and for the Seyions destruction of Dawn Keeping, we have had to rely on our true heritage, which defeats the purpose of looking at ourselves, as Dawn Keepers." He stopped speaking and resituated himself in his seat. He spoke again. "We became Dawn Keepers because it helped us forget why we do what we do. You see, we were born out of the consequence for our parents. Osodon and Oosiah. They forged the break between Universes and mixed the various consciousnesses on the various planets in the various Universes. And, they had a plan, which was to do many things, and those things are the conversations of many of us. But one thing is true. We exist because of their mistake." Lorande thought quickly of the conversation about her Puhlosian heritage she had with him, as he spoke. She looked at her father and spoke up quickly. "What does that say about me?" Kahlip looked at her thoughtfully. "Yes…Lorande, I remember our talk. However, Puhlosians are born that way on this planet. They bring their heritage with them. It sounds to me like what you are going through is relinquishing the influence of the Puhlosians, as if that was the last planet you encountered before being born here. If what you think of yourself were true, you wouldn't become gay. See, there are many of sentient beings that use influence in certain situations to aid in getting through them. I had glimpses of you, as Plaenellian, as I am." Kahlip quickly turned to Karen, who was already aware of herself. Lorande and Frances hadn't had the talk with him yet. He spoke up. "Karen...I know we talked about this already. And, you know things. So, I don't really say this to you, but I think you already figured that out, right?" Karen nodded, then, turned to her sisters. She spoke. "You two don't remember, but when we were kids, I knew myself for my Plaenellian heritage, which made the past harder for me. I knew who our father was then, but I was told that I must keep it a secret. The battling with the Seyions was that much easier. And, that was all for the solution to what Dad brought up." Lorande and Frances thought back to when they were kids. Frances spoke up. "I knew it! I knew then, but I hid it too!" Everyone looked at Frances for her excitement. "I realized you were my father then, in the truck, but I guess I didn't understand what it felt like to be near you enough to proclaim it. Besides, what I was hearing was contrary to what I felt, which added to my frustration." Kahlip thought back on what she said. He spoke subtly, "Yes, those were hard times, and I would have loved to have been honest about everything, but unfortunately, we had to handle the Seyions with kid gloves." Kahlip stopped speaking and looked at Karen. Karen understood what that meant wholly for her profession. Kahlip felt the adoration for his eldest daughter, and what she had become. He was so proud of her. He spoke again. "You see, Lorande, Frances, consciousness on this planet is alien to the original consciousness on this planet. This state of difference is detrimental to it. And, lastly, with such difference, there is a sense of darkness inherent because the various sentient beings have a hard time relating to each other because they are so different. This is why I knew of you what I knew. I had no doubt, which is why you will probably find it in yourselves to continue what we started here so long ago, and that takes me to the solution." He eyed them before he said anything further. He considered them for his feelings, but what they were and how important they were to the sentient beings upon Ayeraal, unlike what many alien sentient beings on the planet fully grasped. They each eyed him thoughtfully in return. It seemed, as though there was a moment of silence. For his daughters it was the anticipation of understanding the solution. For Kahlip, it was about finding the ability to relate to his daughters, which many parents didn't get to have because of the rate of various alien consciousnesses born to the planet. Kahlip did not have that problem. His daughters are like him, cursed with the Plaenellian heritage, and the knowledge of the Keepers. And he just found his next words in that understanding.

He finally spoke, breaking the silence. "For you my daughters, specifically you, Frances and Lorande, Karen has already gone through this, but you will find your job to do here. You will come to understand whom you are and what you need to do. This, Lorande, is why I reacted to you the way I did when you seemingly made your confession. It's not that you are from Puhlosia in heritage, but you made a pit stop, and took a liking to the Puhlosian way of life. You have a deeper, richer heritage, which I think you will find more rewarding." He stopped speaking and looked at them. He was enjoying being with them. He wished those moments started long ago, but therein was the truest sense of the Curse of the Dawn Keepers. After enjoying the moment, Kahlip came to realize that he had things to say because it seemed the girls were finally ready and open to understanding their true Plaenellian heritage. He spoke up. "So, to this solution, isn't really too far from what has been happening all this time. However, the time is growing short not to be precise and on the mark for what to do. Many of us come to aid in keeping the peace or those that have the planetary functions to achieve, while those who seek the solution do what needs to be done. And, considering our conversation, I think the three of you serve the functions of the planetary processes, while those who seek solutions, can get done what we have to do. Plus, considering that it seems you serve a seemingly natural existence, your mere presence on this planet serves it, as if you are a normal part of the function of the planet, but made manifest in a body. For instance, the planets work because of us, as in the rain and snow, even the sunshine. I don't know if you have ever heard the stories of the Prince of Rain, but it's like that." The three of them about what he said. Lorande thought about something. She turned to Frances. She spoke up. "What…like the queen of fire?" Frances turned to Lorande quickly and smiled. "That's right cool summer, and don't you forget it." Kahlip smiled at them for their banter. He spoke up. "Yes it is something like that." Karen suddenly chimed in. "I got into psychiatry and psychology because of the nature of the various alien consciousnesses having a hard time dealing with being upon an alien planet. Actually, that is where studies of the mind stem, but it has gotten so much negative feedback that its value has been lost through the years, when it has given great comfort to the most alien of consciousness here. It has helped many to deal with being upon an alien planet." Frances looked at Karen. She considered something. "You know, that is what I remember about you. You always had too much understanding for those who seemingly had mental problems. Your profession makes sense." Karen smiled, as she looked at her father. She spoke. "Now you fully grasp the value in what dad is saying." Kahlip eyed Karen when she said and he smiled. He felt the connection with them that seemed strongest at the moment. Kahlip added something to accent what Karen said. "Head doctors have always gotten a bad rap because of the nature of that which isn't visible. And, Karen can vouch for this, but head doctors are reaching for understanding the true heritage behind the one seemingly afflicted with the mental disorder, which is only disorder because their alien heritage varies too widely from their home planet and this one. However, head doctors have always tried to do only the most good, but that goes without saying." He looked slowly at Karen with a sense of warmth in his chest for what she tried to do professionally. He spoke up. "I know of the battles you face and the scrutiny, kid. Don't ever think you aren't appreciated, Karen. I appreciate what you are trying to do." Karen teared up. She thought about the ethics committees she had faced throughout the few years she's been in practice. She thought about how psychiatry was really a thankless job. She spoke up. "Thanks, dad." Frances spoke up; as good as, she was for most emotional moments. "Yeah, sis thanks for keeping the crazies off the streets." Lorande slapped her in the arm. Frances turned quickly to Lorande and spoke. "What?" Lorande spoke up. "You darn near ruin a good emotional moment, Fran." Lorande turned to look at Karen, as she spoke further. "I see the good in what you do, K. Don't forget that too." Karen wiped her eyes, as Frances thought about something. "K, you know my emotional weakness is my attempt at defense. I appreciate you sis, you know that right?" Karen smiled, as Frances said that, which made her tear up even more. She thought about something and spoke. "Frances, you know that is more emotion than I have gotten from you ever." Lorande spoke up quickly. "Yeah." She laughed. Frances looked at her sisters, then at her father. She spoke. "Yeah, well, if I would have had a father in my life, I might not have turned out this way." Kahlip looked at Frances when she said that. He spoke. "I see…blame it on the dad." Frances laughed. Everyone knew she was joking. Karen and Lorande joined in on the laughter. The mood was light for moments after that, which felt good to all of them. To them, as well was that long awaited moment where they could connect with the man, their father, who they never really got to know and appreciate. To each of them, as well, never before was there a sense of the appreciation for who they were, as individuals. Kahlip knew he was lucky to have his only three daughters born from his heritage, where they could actually connect, and for each of them to make that much more sense, especially to each other. In that moment, Kahlip thought about something, as he looked at Karen specifically. He spoke up. "Here's something I think you should know Karen." Karen looked at him for saying that. She thought about what he said. She spoke up with curiosity. "What's that?" Kahlip paused in the moment thoughtfully, as he looked at her, also thinking of Mickey Ellis. He finally spoke up, as if what he had to say was hard to do. "Karen…Mickey, and Kira filled my granddaughter, you daughter Karen with such lies about her parents. She was told you died in a car accident, hit by a car in front of a bar." Karen heard him thoughtfully, considering what he said; it didn't make her feel any better. Karen, however, knew not to dwell on the past. She thought about how Mickey and Kira seemingly stole her daughter from her, convincing her that she was young and that she needed to go out and experience life, as they had done with her sisters, Frances and Lorande, who both had their children named for them, only to have them stolen. Karen didn't want to remember that. She looked at her father, regretting the past without him, and had he been able to be there, life might have been different. "Dad, that was such trying times…I was young…we all were young." Kahlip looked at Karen when she said that. He knew she was pushing her strength forward so she didn't have to recognize the hurt from what Mickey and Kira did to her and her sisters. Her own mother did that. Kahlip thought about Kira, and Mickey's influence upon her. Kira was someone with a bright future, outside of Mickey's influence. Kahlip thought about that. He thought about how he and Kira connected, and how he tried to keep her away from Mickey, but he eventually found her. He eventually got his hands on her, which perverted her. He thought about something in that moment. He looked at his daughters and spoke. "My daughters, my wonderful daughters…what I don't think you realize is the problem that really begins here…it's why it is important to set things right, to find a solution to the breaks between Universes." They eyed him for saying that. He continued to speak. "Mickey Ellis tried to recreate the world he was from in another Universe and on another planet. Kira got caught up in the Seyion fantasy here and was lost to it." Lorande and Frances sat listening, thinking of their mother. Frances spoke up. "So, what about our mother?" Kahlip turned to Frances and Lorande and spoke. "She too was caught in the influence and unsound heart of Mickey, a victim of the breaks in Universes. She fought him however, at first. But eventually, he won out. Sadly, that is what has been happening to the females of this planet for too long." Kahlip thought about something, as he sat there. He spoke up. "I wanted a life with Kira, which I thought she wanted too, but then I found out that her heart was heading in a different direction. Then, Lisa and I got closer, and I thought I had found a home with her, but I was wrong." Kahlip thought with finality about lingering in the past. He spoke again. "But you know what…we cannot linger in what used to be or might have been. I have three great and wonderful daughters from my past, and that is what really matters." All three of his daughters smiled when he said that. Their hearts were touched that their eyes should drop water. They all got up and went over to hug him. They never before had such love than what they had in that moment from a man that couldn't care much more than he already did.

Lorande thought about something when she returned to her seat. Frances spoke up, as she returned to her seat. "So what about this solution, dad?" Kahlip waited for them to get comfortable in their seats before he spoke. "This solution I am trying to find. We have been working all this time to find the solution to the problems inherent with alien consciousness upon it. However, we have been only successful at achieving a solution to the immediate problems facing consciousness here. We have been capable of locating the Universal solution. I think it is here, but there are others that think the other planets hold the answer to the Universal breaks." Kahlip stopped speaking thoughtfully. He looked at his daughters, as he considered how much more relative alien consciousness had become through the years. However, the real problems were going to get worse, and he knew it. Alien consciousnesses or humans were in for the worse times for them on this planet, and they didn't know it. Kahlip thought about that. He looked at his daughters with finality, as he spoke. "I guess what I am trying to say is that consciousness on this planet doesn't realize what is coming. It doesn't realize that there are no more quick and easy solutions to its problems. Okay…so we took care of the oil in the ground problem. We took care of the certain other issues, like dealing with the earth's inner material coming out onto the surface, desert regions are growing, but the worst is yet to come, which is why the Universes need to be repaired." Kahlip stopped speaking and looked at his daughters. Frances spoke up, before her sisters could. "So, how can we help?" Kahlip looked at them thoughtfully. He considered what they said. He spoke lastly. "Girls, the problem is that there are many more planets where consciousness can function, intelligence can prosper, as we do on this one, which is why I think the solution to the problems exists with us here on Ayeraal. After this planet is destroyed, consciousness here will be filtered into the remaining planets, and things only get worse from there." He looked at them, as he said that thoughtfully. Then he said something that made them all think. "We Plaenellians have always known that it was Osodon and Oosiah's intent to destroy this planet with the consciousness that would come to it, which is why we're doing what we're doing." Frances thought about something. She spoke up. "Well, what's wrong with having another alien planet to go to once this one is gone." Karen and Lorande looked at her. "Fran, he already gave good reason to save this one. The other planets won't permit us the chance to save the Universes."

Karen, Frances and Lorande all got a glimpse into their father's nightmare…the Plaenellian nightmare. He looked at them equally. He thought about something and spoke. "What you don't realize, my daughters, is that the truest, most heinous intent behind Osodon and Oosiah was the destruction of consciousness. That is what this really all about. What you see in darkness in consciousness on this planet is the destruction of it. This is the one planet that will make or break alien consciousness. We Plaenellians are protected, which is why we know so much. We also know that Osodon and Oosiah are working to find a way to undo us, as well." And, now his daughters had something more to think about. Kahlip thought about something, as he sat there with them upon his last words. He spoke up. "I think I have come to realize that this is why we Plaenellians are so important to each other. I need things I haven't considered. I need ideas about what to do." He looked at them equally when he said that, and with expectation.

Karen looked at her father, when he said that. She thoughtfully looked, then at her sisters. She finally spoke up. "I need some perspective on human history…real perspective, dad, but I think

I can help." Kahlip looked at Karen first, for what she said. He looked at his other two daughters, as lovingly. He spoke up. "Well, the only way to get that is the understanding of then and now, but before I get into that, I just wanted to clarify something." He stopped speaking and looked at his daughters. He spoke after another brief moment of silence and glances into his daughters, as individuals. "Mickey Ellis wasn't evil, don't be mistaken about that. However, what we're attempting to do is save consciousness, like Almichen and Ahrveyais. See, that's the point. Osodon and Oosiah wanted consciousness to mix, as has been done all these years, but in the effort of destroying it. You see, Osodon and Oosiah didn't like that all the measures of consciousness were what they were, they didn't like something that seemed bigger than they were, so they went on this binge to destroy it. What you don't realize is that much alien consciousness has become so dark that to Osodon and Oosiah, it has become nonexistent to the point that it is or seems, as though it is uncreated. Mickey is a stage of the destruction of consciousness, as with many others. He is probably back on his home planet, but less than what he was before being born here. And now, since being here for a while, he will be less than what he can be for Socudosuul, his home planet. So, make no mistakes about it, I love Almichen for what he can be, but it's the Osodon and Oosiah affect against consciousness I have a hard time with. You don't understand how much it hurt to speak to Mickey before he left this planet. It hurt a lot." His daughters felt his pain. Suddenly, they all saw his efforts through life, as it pertained to Mickey Ellis. Their father had gone through great lengths to help him. They each adored their father that much more. Karen broke the emotional moment, and distracted them from the moment that seemed to turn heavy. "So, dad, what about that perspective." Kahlip withdrew from his emotions. He looked distractedly at Karen. He spoke. "Yes…the, then & now."

A Chapter for Then & Now

With the torches lit, the mood was set, and his three daughters had settled in for a good tale. Kahlip then began to speak about the past, going as far back, as when consciousness began to mix on Ayeraal…

"Humans to date don't realize how much different the individual experience was here in the beginning. However, as all parents had experienced in parenting, sometimes relating to their offspring wasn't the easiest thing to do. See, the Anthrocytes of Ayeraal begun having children, as were all measures of consciousness on every planet with sentient beings, which was Osodon and Oosiah's punishment in having us, their Plaenellian offspring. So, what alien consciousness was seemingly cursed with for what Osodon and Oosiah had done, they ironically, reaped the rewards of their actions too, which they didn't realize would happen. The difference, we Plaenellians were born to counteract what our parents had done, where alien consciousness had only to deal with being parents to their children for their respective planet. Now, if you come to understand things, as I, you'll understand how hard that was for the various measures of consciousness on the various planets. It was a mess. Imagine a religious child born to a scientific minded set of parents. That was the Rosicrucian child to the Aubrahteerian parents, and vice versa. Imagine a Rosicrucian child born to a Poliglian or Reiluian. The various mixes were detrimental to all the planets, which was the sad design of Osodon and Oosiah. Now, for Ayeraal and the Anthrocytes, was the greatest attack upon any one alien consciousness on any planet. Osodon and Oosiah had the greatest hatred for the Anthrocytes. And, what you girls do not understand is the Universal wars, which happened long before Osodon and Oosiah were left to destroy the barriers between the Universes.

Before Osodon and Oosiah had done what they did, the Universes were more like territories of one planet. There were what we have here, as ambassadors between planets, there was visiting another planet, and really interacting with each other in a more peaceful way. But that was the thing. Osodon and Oosiah couldn't do this. They were stuck in the castle so to say, as the function for this way of alien consciousness to exist. They were almost like the child that was restricted from going outside to play with their friends. They could only sit at their castle windows and look and watch the other children play. Then, they got notions. They got ideas about how they could get outside, which had to begin within the castle, so to say. The only thing they had to occupy themselves was each other, and their pets. And, that was where their ideas and notions arose. If they could get their pets outside, then they could follow. It was a good plan, and I don't say that from my point of you, but it was what actually worked for them.

However, this took a very long time to achieve, all the while all the alien consciousnesses shared life and peace, but that only angered Osodon and Oosiah that much more. See, the various Universes had doors to each other Universe. These doors were the proper way to visit another Universe. Osodon and Oosiah needed to destroy these doors, forge the birth aspect to a specific planet to begin their plan. However, that took a long time to achieve, as well. This is why humans question how they came to exist upon the planet, which sadly, is the evidence that Osodon and Oosiah's plan is working. The more consciousness forgets about its origins, the more uncreated it becomes, which it doesn't even realize. Then, it can be harvested by Osodon and Oosiah, which is their ultimate goal, until we came into the picture, and began working against them. The biggest thing is to remember that human consciousness on this supposed earth is the uncreated early consciousness inherent in the Anthrocytes."

Suddenly, Kahlip teared up. He thought about what the Universal wars felt like, even though his understanding of it wasn't experience. It was inherent knowledge, which was the value of the Plaenellians, and what defined their hearts. It took the highest sense of love for every manner of consciousness to first endure what sentient beings to go through on alien planets and what that would be to experience them, then to still find feeling for Osodon and Oosiah. Kahlip let that feeling slip away in him so he could continue to explain things, as they happened in the beginning. His daughters looked on and thoughtfully, as he seemed to become silent. He eventually began to speak again.

"See, the purpose inherent in Osodon and Oosiah was running alien consciousness through the various planets, which would refine each sentient being on a planet, which would degrade the consciousness, and then eventually the respective races for each planet. For instance, Anthrocytes looked a certain way, but supposed humans for their Anthrocyte heritage are a lesser state of what they once were. The Anthrocytes went through the many changes through the years with alien consciousness being born into their realm and the Anthrocyte perspective. Anthrocytes were beautiful blue tone skinned creatures, but they would eventually lose their color because of the deadening of the Anthrocyte Heritage with alien consciousness, as their offspring. This was the state of things for myriads of years until there came an all-encompassing point when the last of the blue skin tones were gone. However, what you don't realize is that for that to happen, Anthrocytes had to become red blooded. And, that is the concept of Red thru Black or the darkness of consciousness upon an alien planet. See, Anthrocytes were not dependent upon oxygen in their blood. As with all the immortal beings on all the relative planets, breathing wasn't a concept inherent in any sentient being until the Red thru Black concept came into being. This is where the knowledge inherent in the stories about immortals, as not needing to breathe stem. The blue bloods or Anthrocyte blood had turned black before it became red, when the full and complete transformation to the human forms from the Anthrocytes of yesteryear. And, now, there is only one other time that the Anthrocyte heritage shows through. It is a very depressing time, especially for us Plaenellians or of those Elders, as I am one. That is the time of death of the consciousness from the planet, when their bodies become relative to the bodies of the Anthrocytes before they needed oxygen. Ironically, the body becomes associated with its true Anthrocyte Heritage at the end, which is why all bodies on this planet go through the blue stage. Sadly, to some of us Plaenellians, we understand that the Anthrocyte heritage has already been harvested by Osodon and Oosiah. It is in us that believe that, who fight hardest not to believe it or see it. It is unheard of to give up in finding the solution, or not to see that things can be overturned. This is what I face knowing, for who I am. It is that depth in knowing, and what that feels like."

With saying that, their father stopped speaking, and emotionally tried to compose himself. It was easy to see what he knew had its price and took its toll on him, but it wasn't too long before he started speaking again.

"So, we Plaenellians push on, and continue to work for the benefit of the alien races. And, we dealt with knowing what the Anthrocyte heritage would become here. Sadly, what many think of as evolution was the changes that consciousness would go through throughout the history of consciousness on the planet. They sadly think it is normal, but it is not. However, we do understand why they think that way, which is another of our frustrations. Sadly, we know evolution is an elementary concept, but one that hints to the fact that consciousness is losing the truer sense of itself. It's like saying that the effect of Osodon and Oosiah is alright, we're going through evolution, and that is okay. But it's not okay."

He stopped speaking again and looked off in the distance, thinking to then. His daughters eyed him, considering what he must be going through. He was thoughtful of the Curse of the Dawn Keepers and Almichen had no idea what being a true Dawn Keeper meant. It wasn't about power and control, and lightshows and amazement in an audience. It was about love and keeping the light in darkness. It was about Plaenellians taking on Osodon and Oosiah and stopping them from the reaping or harvesting. He looked back at his daughters, thoughtful of the time. It was so much later than when they first arrived. He considered something. He spoke up. "It's late; do you have to get home? Do you want to sleep over? We can finish in the morning, perhaps over coffee." The three of them looked at each other. Karen and Lorande didn't have anything pressing in the morning to get back to. They each offered they were willing to take him up on that. Frances, however, was thoughtful about a breakfast meeting she had in the morning. She spoke up. "I have a breakfast meeting to attend, but I can be over after that." Lorande thought about something, and had an idea. Lorande spoke up. "Well, since you have to leave, I guess I can come back when you do, Frances or I can come back in the morning early. It's just that I came with Frances. I'd like to have my own car here." Karen turned to her father and spoke. "I guess it's just you and me." Her father smiled. "I guess so."

Kahlip put the torches out and left them in place. His daughters went on into the house. Kahlip arrived shortly after them at the door to say goodnight. Karen had already done that and was lying on the couch. He wished them a goodnight a warm hug and gentle smile, and the appreciation for them always. He went to the living room, where apparently, Karen had already fallen asleep on the couch. He looked at her and smiled. He cherished that woman on the couch for who she had become. Thoughtfully, he went to the closet in the hall for an extra blanket for her, covered her up, and then went to bed himself. He never before slept with such a sense of satisfaction from something he did. Being a part of the couple that could permit such beauty and strength on a planet was so fulfilling to him. He slept that night easiest than he had in a long time for his children; his adult children now had made it through life's turmoil to see their time age on such a planet. But then he had to be real with himself. As the Plaenellians his daughters were, it was not such a feat that they should become adults.

Morning came sooner than later. Kahlip had beaten Karen up that morning just as the sun showed itself on the horizon, but as he made breakfast, some peppered eggs, salt bacon, and sweet hickory sausage, Lorande came knocking. The aroma of the food filled the house lovingly and boldly. He went to answer the door, smiled at Lorande, as she stood smiling herself and bubbly beyond the threshold. She spoke up. "Morning, dad." Suddenly, she got a whiff of the aroma running rampant around the house. "Wow, smells like breakfast!" Kahlip smiled and spoke, as he motioned for her to enter. "You are just in time." Lorande entered the house easily and steadily. She had high hopes for her day and showed in her step. She seemed extra confident that day and more chipper lately. Her father spoke, as he shut the door. "I have to get back in the kitchen, if you care to join me, you can. Karen is still asleep on the Lounge." The lounge was the couch he sometimes referred to, as the lounge. He continued to speak. "She was tuckered I suppose." Lorande looked at her father for his words. She kind of chuckled to him. He eyed her. She spoke. "Tuckered?" Her father smiled in her direction. He spoke up. "Yeah...sleepy...extra tired." Lorande looked at him for explaining. She spoke quickly. "Yeah...I know tuckered...I was just taken by how you said it." Her father seemed thoughtful, as he finished up with the eggs. In the medium sized flat pan. He considered the word he used for how tired Karen was. He thought about something else, but was rekindled with Sharon who liked to use that word a lot. He spoke up, as he put the eggs in another bigger bowl. "Tuckered was something someone I knew once used a lot. She had a lot of other supposed Southern words that she used. I guess I was thinking about her when I spoke of Karen still lying on the lounge." Lorande looked at him and smiled. She considered what he said quickly. She spoke. "It's nice to feel connected to someone like that...that they would show up in your life later on in some way." Her father put the food on the round kitchen table, as he continued to banter back and forth with Lorande, one of his favorite daughters. He had three favorites. He spoke quickly and completely off subject. "Hey Lorande." Lorande looked at him, as she helped put silverware on the table. "I just wanted to tell you that you are my favorite, but don't tell the others...okay?" Lorande smiled. She looked at him and spoke.

"Okay, dad." Lorande smiled inside and felt warmth she hadn't ever. Suddenly, she missed having him in her life when she was a child that much more. She knew of course when he said it that he was just kidding around, but it still felt good to hear him say it. She didn't mind not being the favorite.

As soon, as he said that, Karen walked in the kitchen feeling warm inside. She looked at Lorande, then at their father. She spoke up quickly. "Man…I was having this dream I was walking through a five star restaurant at breakfast. It smelled so good. Then, I woke up and the aroma didn't end. So, I got up and here I am. Ready to eat." In her aiding the breakfast table setup, Lorande had actually set four places. Karen and her father noticed, but there would only be three of them, at the table. Karen spoke up. "Four places, Lorande?" Lorande looked at her watch, and spoke. "Wait a second…hold on." Karen and their father looked at Lorande. Suddenly, the doorbell rang. Lorande spoke again. "There you go…Frances, right on time. See, Frances' meeting canceled, and she woke me up this morning with a call. So, I knew she'd be here…I just didn't say anything…Surprise!" Lorande went to get the door, as the other two sat. They heard Lorande answer the door from the kitchen and then Frances' voice, as she greeted Lorande. Then, they both eventually entered the kitchen to sit for breakfast. Frances took one look at the table and spoke with surprise. "Wow…big breakfast." She said that, as she implied by her reaction that Lorande had mentioned a breakfast of sorts in the kitchen. Karen and their father greeted Frances, as she sat to the table. Frances reciprocated, greeting them equally. Their father spoke up. "Well…dig in." They all began the morning meal with great anticipation. Silverware was hitting serving bowls, forks were scraping plates, and food was being enjoyed with a certain varied appreciation. The three girls, never before really had a family breakfast, but it was something that their father wanted to share with them, at least once.

While they ate, and finished eating, their father spoke up. "So, shall we continue the conversation now?" He eyed the three of them. They looked at him, then, each other. Karen spoke up first. "Yeah…that sounds good to me." Frances and Lorande spoke up in agreement with Karen. Their father spoke up looking between the three of them. "I think I had just mentioned evolution, right?" Frances spoke up. "Yes, you just seemed to finish with that, but I was curious what you were thinking about when you stopped talking." Their father looked at Frances thoughtfully, remembering last night. "I was thoughtful of the Curse of us Keepers and how Almichen had no idea what being a true Dawn Keeper meant. It's not about power and control, and lightshows and gaining influence. It was about love and keeping the light in darkness. It was about Plaenellians taking on Osodon and Oosiah and prohibiting them from the reaping or harvesting of consciousness." He said that, as he then, eyed his three daughters. He spoke quickly again. "See, girls, there were those who took advantage of certain other alien consciousness here that was seemingly weaker. And, that is still part of the "then". However, it seems it still happens now, and that is all too true." He stopped speaking, and thoughtfully, he eyed his daughters before he spoke again. Frances thought about something. She eyed her father, and spoke. "I just cannot believe how familiar it sounds about the harvesting thing you said. It's like I recall that or something." Her father and sisters looked at her, as she spoke. Their father spoke up. "I am glad to see something strike you that way." Frances spoke up. "Well, it kind of sucks to be rekindled with knowing something as that." Lorande and Frances thought about what she said. Their father spoke up. "Welcome to being rekindled with you heritage." Frances looked at him for saying that, and spoke. "Thanks, dad." She said it with a humorous tone. Karen and Lorande smiled. Considering the conversation, the mood was still light. Their father spoke again. "Welcome to the Curse of the Keepers, girls, as you will all see in your own time."

Their Father paused a moment thoughtfully. He eyed them, as he got back in line with explaining the concept of then. Suddenly, he considered a great misperception about some facet of life on the planet early on. He looked at his daughters. He began to speak. "Now at that time, the Aubrahteerians had control over viewpoint, but it wasn't until the Rosicrucians came that people woke up to what really might have happened. See, then, the Aubrahteerians, being born into the Anthrocyte heritage, began to change the perception of what the Anthrocytes were. The door to the world of the Anthrocytes the Aubrahteerians considered the Garden of Eden and sometimes Paradise. However, it really became a perverted concept until the planet began to dry up and then, what was once considered the Garden became lost. However, one thing is clear from all sides. The Garden of Eden was the door to and from this planet to others. Now, some think the Dinosaurs were the pets of the Anthrocytes, which had to be destroyed in order for consciousness to come to exist here. However, this is erroneous to consider. The Dinosaurs were Osodon and Oosiah's way to get out of the castle. However, this little trick wasn't the same on every planet in which they came in contact with, but here on Ayeraal, these pets of Osodon and Oosiah because of their makeup grew to be so huge. However, for the nature of what they became here was evidence of the hatred Osodon and Oosiah had with the Anthrocytes. They wanted the Anthronyls or the Dinosaurs to harvest the Anthrocytes or to eat them up and destroy all manner of consciousness here. What they didn't consider is that the Anthronyls would not be capable of surviving the makeup of the planet. Though it seemed as though they lived for many years on the planet, they didn't and died off without really serving their purpose, as consciousness survived here." He stopped speaking thoughtfully. He looked at his daughters, as they seemed to be intrigued with what he was saying. He then, continued. "This is why dinosaur bones are found in deep regions of the planet because of how long ago, they died off. Dinosaurs weren't discovered, their reality was uncovered for what happened so long ago. The only thing is, we Plaenellians do not possess the knowledge of how Osodon and Oosiah did it, got their pets out of the castle so to say, and we only know what they did. This is another way to understand that we were born after the effort of Osodon and Oosiah…not too much long after however." He stopped speaking and looked at his daughters. They seemingly sat in shock and amazement. Frances spoke up first. "Wow…all I can say is wow!" Lorande spoke up. "That makes too much sense." Karen chimed in. "I always wondered why I thought often of what happened in the beginning. I often pondered the beginning." Their father looked at them equally. "Well, my daughters, now you should way ahead of the Rosicrucians who rely on carbon dating and stuff like that, and concepts of evolution to explain things to a lesser consciousness. You three have the complete and utter beginning for life on this planet." He stopped speaking and looked at them before he spoke again. "Now you understand why destroying this planet is so important to Osodon and Oosiah. Now you know what happened to Ahvenshurr, my daughters. This was how Ahvenshurr became caught in the Ayeraal's rotation for how long ago it died, and took to migrate closer to the Ayeraal. Notice the size of the moon. It is smaller. However, it was bigger at one point. For its current size though, this means that for it to dry out and die, as a planet, it had to have been two times the size it is now. However, it didn't die out like many other planets from what Osodon and Oosiah had done. We Plaenellians had been born to it to try and revive the planet, counteract what they did to no avail. It was the last time I saw my female half, Kaera, which was why it was hard to accept that it had died. Its fate at the hands of Osodon and Oosiah had come to fruition." Their father seemed extremely saddened by what he said. He stopped speaking distractedly. He turned to look beyond the dining room window. His daughters looked at him, as he stared through the window. Karen spoke up. "Well, I see some dishes need to done, and a kitchen needs to be cleaned. Lorande spoke up. "Yeah." Frances stood and began to gather plates and silverware. Suddenly, the kitchen was buzzing with activity. Eventually, Kahlip stood and began helping to clean up.

A Chapter for the D-Rift

In the midst of cleaning, Kaerrie showed up. She walked in on the effort in the kitchen. She stood silently at first, as everyone seemed distracted and didn't notice her. She watched Kahlip thoughtfully, then, noticed the other women in the kitchen, with many various thoughts about who they were. Eventually, Lorande became less distracted and finally noticed her. She stopped what she was doing, and spoke. "Hello!" She was a little surprised. Then, one by one, her sisters stopped and turned their attention to the woman at the doorway to the kitchen. Karen poked her father in the shoulder. Kahlip wound up drying dishes and putting them away, when he finally understood they had a visitor. He finally recognized that Karen was trying to get his attention. He turned to look in the direction of the doorway. He spoke up. "Oh…hey there." He dried his hands and put the towel on the counter. He walked over to her. She spoke, as he got closer. "Can we talk in the back yard?" Kahlip smiled at her. He spoke easily. "Sure." He turned and told his daughters that he would be back in a minute. Kaerrie had left the kitchen. She beat him to the sliding glass doors. She walked out and waited for him. As she stood, she noticed that it seemed like he had a party or something, as the torches were placed around the porch and still in the ground. She pondered what he'd been doing since she left. Kahlip finally came out of the house. He looked at Kaerrie with a smile. Kaerrie felt saddened that she had done what she had in leaving. She looked Kahlip squarely and with great emotion, she spoke. "Kahlip…I am sorry." Kahlip smiled. He eyed her warmly. "For what?" She looked at him for his playing dumb. "You know what. Kahlip…I left." Kahlip thought about something, as she said that. He finally spoke up. "So…does this mean you are back…to stay?" Kaerrie looked at him. She knew the obvious answer. She spoke up. "Of course." Kahlip smiled, and spoke. "Then, the way I see it, you took a vacation without me…a needed one. Did you figure things out?" Kaerrie looked at him before she spoke. "I did." Kahlip looked at her with a genuine smile for he knew what she went through. He spoke up. "Well, your little vacation gave me the chance to get caught up with my daughters, which is who you saw in the house." Kaerrie thought about what he said. She looked for a chair for which to sit. Kahlip followed in suit. She thought about something and spoke. "I take it there is a lot behind them" Kahlip looked into the living room through the sliding glass doors. He spoke. "Yes…much. It's a long story, but I think they are like us." Kaerrie sat thoughtfully. She looked at him for what he said. She thought about something else. "What about us, Kahlip? Why is it always us?" As she said that, she thought about something. "And, I take it; you figured some things out for yourself?" Kahlip smiled and spoke easily. "Yes…Kaerrie…I finally realized who you are." He thought about something, as he said that. "I finally came to accept those who came into my life, instead of expecting someone else. I finally realize that if we achieve what we seek to; it will put us all right with each other." Kaerrie smiled when he said that. "Do you recall Rosicrutia, then?" Kahlip smiled, and thought about their time with the Rosicrucians. He spoke up. "That was our last time together on any planet." Kaerrie thought about that, as he spoke. Suddenly, something struck her. He doesn't recall. He doesn't remember why she and he are together. She spoke up. "Kahlip, you don't remember, do you? You don't recall the reason why we're together." Kahlip eyed her when she said that. He just plainly looked at her, as if he should remember, but didn't. He thought about what she said. He turned to look out across the yard. She sat looking at him for a response. She thought about something in that moment, as she waited. While they chatted, in the background beyond the glass doors, his daughters were checking them out. At one point, Kaerrie could feel eyes upon her. She understood their curiosity. She smiled, as she noticed. Then, she could feel the eyes disappear. Kaerrie then, focused on Kahlip. "It's part of why I came back, Kahlip." Kahlip looked at her. He slowly glimpsed something when she said that. As he looked at her, he recalled something else. She still looked at him, as he seemed to be thinking. "Kahlip, it's what was continued with Kahnelle, but that perhaps, which you have forgotten." Suddenly, Kahlip thought about Kahnelle and what he considered was a teaming up by Julius, Karen, and Kahnelle. He spoke up, as he eyed Kaerrie. "I remember that Kahnelle seemed like he was working with Julius and Karen." Kaerrie thought about what he said. She spoke up. "Then, there is something you are missing, Kahlip." He eyed her strangely, as she said that. She looked at him plainly. "Kahlip, you don't recall, but for a long time, Mickey had been telling the tall tales, influencing Julius and Karen, how do you think they eventually got together? Mickey has been the designer of the past few years for them before he left this place." She stopped speaking and thought about something. "Mickey Ellis, Kahlip, is…" Kahlip interrupted her. "…is Osodon." Their final words were said at the same time. Kahlip looked at her. She thought about something, and spoke. "Worse yet, Kahlip, Ahrveyais isn't who she thinks she is. Almichen is her other half, But Mickey was not Almichen, and Ahrveyais is actually Reyanne of the Reiluians. Osodon had entrapped her on Socudosuul since Almichen and Ahrveyais had been harvested. That is why the story about Almichen and Ahrveyais being the closest to the Master Seyion exists, as it does." Kahlip eyed her for knowing something more than he did. She saw that discontent in him that he didn't know about what she said firsthand. "You couldn't have known about that, Kahlip. You were on Maervuhn when this all went down. Kaera was somewhere else. And, it was I, Kahnelle, and a few others. However, we learned something then…enough that a few of us got together and formed the Union League." Kahlip looked at her strangely when she said that. She spoke again. "Kahlip, we've been working secretly because if anyone found out, it might have been our undoing. That was why it seemed Kahnelle was working with Julius and Karen. He isn't, but that's on the down low, please." Kahlip thought about something. He looked at her, and spoke. "So, what's the aims of the League?" Kaerrie looked at him for saying that. She knew he eventually would be curious. She spoke up. "Kahlip, we're working together to pair up Plaenellians with their opposite half. You and Kaera are on the schedule, but we're working at our pace...alright?" Kahlip looked at her. "So, what does that mean for us? What about those things you said you figured out?" She thought about what he said. She eyed him. "Kahlip, I said that because it was my way of getting back to you, but now that I have let you in on the League, I cannot leave any longer. You kind of have to be under my intensive watch." Kaerrie stopped speaking, as she seemed to be distracted by something. Kahlip spoke up. "What's wrong?" She looked at him first before she spoke. "Kahlip, the League discovered that there are those of us, who have changed loyalty. They are actually working with Osodon and Oosiah. They have become swayed for their purpose. They are working against their inherent nature...our Plaenellian nature." She said that heavily. When she finished speaking, Kahlip thought about what she said. He thought about something else. He spoke up, thinking of his original question. "What does that mean for us?" She looked at him, and considered her answer. She spoke up. "Kahlip, I think what I am trying to say is that we have to create the illusion that we are in a relationship. Part of the League is protection too. If we are disguised, then you are protected, Kaera is protected, and the league can continue to work. It all goes hand in hand." Kahlip looked at her, as he thought about something. He spoke. "Not too long ago, Kaerrie, I had thoughts about you. Then, apparently, I found you without warning. What's up with that?" Kaerrie looked at him for saying that. She considered what he said. She spoke up quickly. "Well, I guess we all have moments where we're connected to others or are perhaps aware of who will come our way from that connection. It could be that simple." Kahlip thought about what she said. He looked at her. Kaerrie thought about something else. She spoke, as she eyed Kahlip. "Kahlip, a whirlpool doesn't spin forever, and a tornado doesn't either. Eventually, that which is adrift will eventually get caught in the spin of the whirlpool, until the whirlpool comes to fruition. The drift is the key in that. We Plaenellians are adrift, so to say. And, we do sometimes get caught up in the whirlpool, which distracts us from our path we are on, where it sometimes seems, as though we are adrift. However, if we can take a step back far enough, we can see where we were heading, and that we were not really adrift." Kaerrie stopped speaking, as she looked at Kahlip. Suddenly, she was reminded of how close they had become once. She considered her heart in contrast to Kahlip. She considered what she really felt for him. And, though she wanted to say it, she kept it to herself, but she recalled how they had made a deal once that each of them would try to find each other because of how adrift they were from their true halves. Kaerrie looked at Kahlip with sudden longing eyes. She became thoughtful. Kahlip was the one she wanted if she couldn't be with hers. She would, in the least always try to find him. It just so happened that the league was currently supposed to be working to get Kahlip and Kaera back together. Kaerrie's heart was torn in that moment. She wondered if Kahlip felt it too.

Suddenly, as Kahlip sat looking at Kaerrie, he was reminded of something. It was long ago, and that current moment was reminiscent of it. Kaerrie suddenly appeared so beautiful, so enticing. Kahlip couldn't help but notice. Suddenly, everything about the moment was nothing more than him and her.

Kaerrie looked at Kahlip with thoughts of being closer to him. She felt herself wanting to be right next to him. She wanted his seat to be big enough for two at that moment. She suddenly spoke up. "Kahlip…do you remember?" Kahlip looked at her when she said that. He thought about what she meant. He studied his heart intricately, and quickly. Looking into her eyes though, he knew who he'd found. Suddenly, Kaerrie spoke up. "Kahlip, part of the reason I had to leave was because I had to separate myself from you. I was getting to where I am right now. And, I didn't want to get to that point. I wouldn't let myself go through it again." Kahlip looked at her warmly. He spoke up. "But we were already married, Kaerrie. I had shown my intentions with you."

Kaerrie thought about what he said. She looked downwards, while she turned inwards. She thought about how her heart was torn into so many directions in that moment. She spoke up. "I wanted to leave the League for you. If I left, I didn't have to think about losing you again. Every time we separated, a piece of me went with you. But eventually I gave in and accepted that I may only have you for a short time, but I could make it the best time possible." Kahlip looked at her, as she spoke. His heart was suddenly and seemingly ripped in two. A flood of memories came to him about their pasts together. And, in that moment, Kaerrie seemed like the one. He looked at her lovingly, and in such a way, as to cause her to speak up. "Kahlip…that look kills me. You don't understand." Kahlip seemed distracted by what she said. He looked at her. He couldn't…not look at her. He spoke up. "Well…I apologize, but I am not in control here. Suddenly, I am just lost between me, you, and the past." He stopped speaking briefly. He looked at her with the same hard loving gait before he spoke again. "Kaerrie…I remember perhaps more than I should." She thought about something when he said that. She spoke up. "See…that is what I am talking about. I want to run away right now because the thought of losing you for this moment is scary." Kahlip eyed her warmly when she said that. They finished the next few moments straying hopelessly in each other's eyes. However, what lie between them both lay something so secret, which was really the essence of the reason for those moments.

Kahlip seemed to break the silence. "You spoke something of drifts…what was that exactly?" He stopped speaking briefly. He thought about something, as he took her beauty inwards with his eyes. "I mean…I think I know, but I wanted to hear you say it." She looked at him when he said that. She eventually spoke up, after she got through her heart and that moment with him. "The tides are actually created from the rifts in the ground, which eventually create the whirlpools. Many do not understand that tornadoes are created from this effect too, but on a gaseous level. This is why most tornadoes happen in lands of higher elevation or in regions where the gaseous region or atmosphere is shallower. A tornado in Florida means the land is becoming higher in elevation in contrast to the water. Whirlpools don't happen in the deepest parts of the ocean. They happen where the distance between the oceans bottom and the surface allow for a connection to the open skies. And, for this is a reason." Kahlip eyed her when she said that. "So, you're talking about the fact that whirlpools open up at the bottom where the ocean's floor becomes visible." Kaerrie spoke up when he said that. "Sadly, there is a reason. It's the reason why in space, there is a sense of space air. However, the molecules of oxygen and hydrogen are so far apart that it is too hard to create a vacuum with the lungs to obtain the molecules. The lungs are too small that they would close, and never be capable of opening again. The reason we know this is because of the whirlpool effect in space. The whirlpool effect is what galaxies or solar systems are based upon...but you should know all this." Kahlip looked at her, as she spoke. He thought about what she said last. "I do...I do, but I love to hear you speak." She shook her head, as he said that. She spoke up. "See...that's also what I am talking about." He looked at her, as if he didn't know to what she was talking. He spoke up. "What?" She looked at him warmly. She finally spoke. "Your charms." Kahlip smiled when she said that. He spoke again, as he admired her. "Well..." In that moment, Kaerrie felt such a sense of unity with him that she hadn't felt with anyone to her recollection. She looked at him. She was thoughtful that they should have been made for each other. Kahlip spoke up. "So, what's next?" Kaerrie was thinking of a bed when he said that, but what came out of her mouth was far different. She thought about Kahnelle in that moment. "I have been communicating with Kahnelle over these past few weeks. He's in France working on Julius and your granddaughter." Kahlip thought about how she considered Karen his granddaughter. Suddenly, he thought about his and Kaerrie's age difference. He spoke up. "You know...I never before really considered our age difference before now." Kaerrie thought about what he said. He spoke again. "You're the same age as my daughters." Kaerrie thought about that, but it didn't matter. She thought about something and spoke. "You know, as well as I that age doesn't matter. It never did for anyone. What makes the difference is the relativity." Kahlip thought about something, after she said that. He spoke quickly. "Yes, but that really only means something or is relative, as you said it, to us Plaenellians." Kaerrie smiled and spoke. "Yes…perhaps."

Kahlip thought about something, as she said that. He spoke up. "So…wait…the rift is the effect in the tides, which, concerning space would almost be the same thing, as the rifts between Universes, causing the galaxies or the spacial whirlpools." She eyed him, as he spoke. He spoke again. "Now…you're talking my department. Kaerrie…I am searching for the solution to the Universal rifts, where you're department, it sounds like, is dealing with those of us drift from planet to planet." He stopped speaking and thought about something. "We're both on the same continuum, but different levels. I am dealing with stopping the effect of the rifts, and you are dealing with aiding those of us who cannot find our other halves or stopping the separation between the two." Kahlip thought about something. He looked at her with a renewed sense about their relationship. "That's our relativity, Kaerrie…do you see it?"

The problem was that Kaerrie saw it too clearly, and she didn't need him to see it, enough to point it out. She was just reminded that they had a strong connection, but for where they were both headed, Kaera was his destiny because they both were working to the same goal. Kaerrie finally understood how to let him go, when the time came. She became saddened, and he noticed. He spoke up. "What's wrong?" Kaerrie teared up, as she eyed him. "Kahlip…I do see it, but we will have to say goodbye at some point. It's that point that I am having a hard time with." Kahlip looked at her for saying that. He felt for her, but he thought about something. He spoke. "Kaerrie…we have to appreciate this time we have, and we cannot forsake it for the fact that there will be an end. We have to go forward. Besides… you know, as well as I do, that our kind exists because of what

Osodon and Oosiah had done. We shouldn't have even become sentient beings for what we truly are." Kaerrie looked at him for saying that. He looked at her when he said that. He considered something else. He spoke up. "Kaerrie...we should really cherish what we have because it isn't usual that an Elder and the youth of our kind should be what we have become to each other." He stopped speaking, and thought about something. "See...I am an Elder...and what I know, you have yet to gain. I am not talking about our planetary ages either. As far as our kind, I was born long before you, and that meant that I would know much more than you would. You younglings have to learn from us too what really happened. It's kind of like here on Ayeraal, where the future generations have to learn about their ancestors. And, our Plaenellian knowledge exists in the times before that." He stopped speaking thoughtfully. He considered her other half, which was even more relative to her, than he was. He spoke up. "Kaerrie, what you are missing is your true roots. Where I can open my heart to you...there is another that will force your heart more open than what you think it has done with me. It's that, which you cannot see. It's that which makes you feel, as you do now." Kaerrie thought about what he said. She looked at him thoughtfully. What he said made sense, but matters of the heart don't make sense.

The Chapter of Malaise

As their father and that woman sat outside talking, Karen, Frances and Lorande sat chatting and contemplating who she is. Many ideas were thrown around. Frances had the most discomfort with her. There was just a certain level of uneasiness in her heart when she looked at her. It didn't make sense. Lorande thought she instantly understood the woman, and Karen just wasn't sure about the situation. Karen spoke up when Frances hinted about her discomfort. "Frances…it's his life…we don't really understand who she is to feel uncomfortable with her. Frances looked at Karen when she said that. She knew Karen was right in some way. Karen spoke again. "Besides…he's the dad…and don't know better than he for his choices. Too…you guys might have them all wrong." Lorande looked at Karen when she said that. She spoke up. "K, I don't think so…they are married." Karen looked at Lorande easily when she said that. "I know that, but married to her." As she said that, Karen thought about something. She looked at her sisters. "Have you guys ever questioned the ring on his finger? We've been getting together for a while now, and I have never thought to ask him about the ring he wears. I guess I just automatically assumed that because of the fact that it seems like he lives alone, that the ring he wears…is really, just a ring." Lorande and Frances thought about what she said. Lorande spoke up. "I've never talked with him about the ring on his hand. It does resemble a wedding ring, though." Frances thought about something. She looked at her sisters and spoke. "I know he is married, but I just thought that he would bring it up in his own time. He's obviously not living with the woman." Frances stopped speaking thoughtfully. She looked to the door of the kitchen where they sat chatting. She spoke again. "I think that woman is the one he's married to, but they are having problems." Lorande spoke up, as Frances said that. "So, you're saying that they are separated?" Frances continued to look at the door of the kitchen. She spoke simply. "Yep." Karen thought about something. She looked at Frances and spoke. "Awe...the protective daughter." Frances reached over and slapped Karen on the arm. Lorande laughed. Karen rubbed her arm, as she eyed Frances. She spoke up. "You know...the oldest is usually the protective ones over their divorced parents." Frances quickly looked at Karen. "Not always, sis." Suddenly, the three of them heard the sliding glass door open, and after another second or two, it was shut. Lorande spoke up. "Hush...here they come." Frances looked at her sisters, while Karen looked to the kitchen door. Frances put her head in her hands thoughtfully, with her elbows resting on the table. She didn't know what to think. She felt confused about the fact that her father was in another relationship that wasn't seemingly working the way it should be. The door to the kitchen slowly creaked open, and Frances heart began to flutter at meeting the woman. Karen spoke up suddenly. "Hey, dad." Lorande chimed in, and Frances' head arose. She got up, and suddenly she needed to go to the bathroom. She spoke, as she stood from the table. "If you'll excuse me for a second...I have to use the restroom." Lorande and Karen looked at each other. Kahlip watched Frances leave the kitchen. Kaerrie was curious about all three of his daughters. She looked at Lorande and Karen, thoughtful that she would meet the one that left for the bathroom eventually. Kaerrie walked up to the table and introduced herself to the two at the table. "I am Kaerrie." Karen and Lorande smiled at her. Karen spoke up first. "I am Karen." Kaerrie looked to the other. "I am Lorande." Kaerrie thought about both of them. Karen seemed like the woman's woman, and Lorande seemed like a debutante type. Kaerrie spoke up. "It's nice to meet both of you." Karen and Lorande smiled. They reciprocated her sentiment. Kahlip walked up behind Kaerrie. He spoke subtly by pulling a chair in which she could sit. He went to the counter, seeing a dish out of place. Then, he sat in the chair next to Kaerrie. Kaerrie looked at him and smiled, as he sat. Kahlip thought about something in that moment. He spoke up. "Hey...what do we think about going out for the day? I don't know, perhaps to dinner and a movie or lunch and a movie." Lorande spoke up. "Well, I can probably meet you for dinner later, and then perhaps a movie, I do have something I have to do in a couple hours. I will be free after six tonight." Karen looked at her sister, as she spoke. She spoke up, as Lorande seemed to finish. "I will be free for dinner too, but I have to leave in a few minutes." Frances entered the kitchen, while Karen finished speaking. Everyone looked at Frances. She spoke up. "What?" Lorande spoke up. "Dad was suggesting that we go out for the day. What do you think?" Frances looked around. She spoke up. "Well…I am free all day." Kahlip thought about what she said. He spoke up, as Frances neared the table. "Well, then, you can hang out with me and Kaerrie until tonight for dinner when your sisters can join us." Frances sat. As she listened to him speak, she sank into the seat with a plop, as he said that, hinting to a day out with that…woman. Great! Frances spoke up. "That would be nice." Kahlip looked at Kaerrie and smiled. Lorande and Karen looked at each other, then at Frances. They knew she was subtly being sarcastic. The uneasy feeling in her was already settling in nicely.

After another moment there at the table, and when it was decided that Lorande and Karen would join them for dinner, Karen and Lorande left. Frances Looked at Kahlip and that woman. She spoke up. "I am going to have to go home and freshen up, and maybe take a shower. I definitely want some fresh clothes on." Kahlip turned to Kaerrie when Frances finished. He spoke. "Well, that will give us time to freshen up ourselves." He turned to Frances. "So we'll see you back in a couple hours, then." Frances stood and spoke. "Yeah…about that." She hugged her father for where he sat and spoke, as she let him go. "I will see you soon." Kaerrie spoke up quickly, as Frances walked away. "It was nice to meet you." Frances spoke up, as she walked away. "You too!" She yelled that from the front door, as Frances moved with a sense of urgency. She had to get away before her mouth might have got her into trouble. It was bad enough that she was going to be stuck with the woman the rest of the day. She only hoped it wouldn't be, as bad as she foresaw. Frances opened the door to leave, and as she did, on the other side was a man standing and poised to knock. Frances opened the door before he could. He stood with his fist in the air, as if he was just about to put it on the door. Frances stood looking at the man. Frances recognized his face from long ago, but she couldn't put a name to it. Frances spoke up. "Hello." The man spoke. "Hey…is Lehmich here?" The man put his hand down. Frances looked at the man strangely at first. Distractedly, she spoke aloud. "Dad…" Her father heard her and came from the kitchen to the front door. Kaerrie stood at the doorway to the kitchen. She watched the scene transpire. Kahlip spoke up, as he walked to the door. He spoke up quickly. "Hey man…come on in." Kahlip then looked at Frances. He spoke up. "Thanks, Kiddo." Frances looked at the man another second before she spoke again. "Okay, dad. I am going to leave now. I'll see you like I said." Her father spoke up. "Okay." Frances walked away, passing the stranger at the door, which she knew once, but couldn't place him. The stranger walked in, as Kahlip offered. Frances heard the door shut, as she walked further from it. She got in her car and left, but very curious about the face she recognized in the man at the door. She pulled from the driveway, with her thoughts hung about that face she recognized, and it wasn't for five miles away from her father's house that she was able to lose the curiosity about the face she saw.

Inside the house, Kahlip, Kaerrie, and Sedious went to the living room. They sat. Kahlip was curious about the visit, as equally, as Kaerrie was. Sedious looked at them while they sat. He pondered his words, before he let them out. "So, I take it we got Almichen off the planet in a timely manner?" Kahlip looked at him for saying that. Kahlip thought about something. He looked over at Kaerrie, then back at Sedious. "First things first. You don't really need to keep the Sedious thing going. I lost Lehmich long ago. Next, this is Kaerrie." Sedious looked at him for saying that. He looked at Kaerrie, instantly being rekindled with who she is. "It's been too long, sis." Kaerrie smiled and spoke quietly. "I know." Suddenly, he thought about using his real name. He looked at the two of them, as they sat comfortably on the sofa in contrast to where he sat. "It's been so long since I have been referred to, as that." Kahlip studied him. He spoke up. "What… Kahel?" The man in the chair looked at Kahlip. "Yeah…" Kahlip looked at him a brief second before he spoke again. "Well, you'll have to get used to it again. I have." Kahel sat thoughtfully. He considered Amos or, as he knew him, Korrehl. Kahel spoke up. "I cannot get Amos out of my head, and what Mickey had done to him. You didn't get to see it, but I did. You left." Kahlip thought about what he said. He spoke up, "But you know why I had to." Kahel looked at Kahlip. He considered what he said. He let his gaze fall to the floor. He continued to think about what Amos did for everyone, especially for Kahlip in protecting Karen, and getting her to Florida. He thought about the fact that Amos was left to face Mickey and lost in that battle for what that meant. Kaerrie spoke up, as she looked at Kahel. "Kahlip didn't know this either, but Mickey was Osodon, Kahel." Kahel looked up at her thoughtfully. He considered what she said. He then turned to Kahlip. "What?" Kahlip looked at him before he spoke. "Yeah…that's right, and it makes sense." Kahlip stopped speaking and continued to look at Kahel. He spoke again. "You know about harvesting, Kahel. Osodon and Oosiah harvested Almichen and Ahrveyais, then, took their place. However, it seems as though Oosiah isn't Ahrveyais, but someone else on the verge of being harvested." Kahel looked at Kahlip, as he spoke. He was thoughtful then, where Oosiah was in all this. Suddenly, he had a thought. He looked at Kahlip, then Kaerrie. He spoke up. "So, where is Oosiah in all this, and to what end are they working?" Kaerrie spoke up; at about the same time Kahlip seemed to want to. "It's about the harvest, Kahel." Kahlip suddenly interjected. "Think about it Kahel. You can figure it out." Kahel sat thoughtfully. He looked at them and then, it hit him. He spoke up. "So, you're saying that Osodon and Oosiah are harvesting consciousness until that there is no potential sentient beings upon the planet." Kahlip spoke up. "On any planet in any Universe." Kaerrie spoke up. "Kahel, this state of Alzheimer's that consciousness has here is a large part of the evidence. You don't want to know what they do on Maervuhn with those who are stricken with the equivalent of Alzheimer's there." Kahlip spoke up quickly. "The Rosicrucians have done well to shroud the truth behind the disease, but there are others who are in the state of being harvested, as well. The mentally handicapped are also being reaped. That is why they exist in the mental states they are in. Osodon and Oosiah have their reapers out there working diligently to do this. Sadly, it is our fellow Plaenellians that have changed loyalty upon the premise of having rule over all Universes without the various alien consciousnesses out there." Kahlip stopped speaking thoughtfully. He looked at Kaerrie, then at Kahel. He spoke heavily. "What's worse…our beloved parents want to get rid of us, as well." Kahel and Kaerrie looked at each other when Kahlip said that. He spoke again. "Something else you both didn't know." Kahlip stopped speaking and eyed each of them. "See, I thought Mickey was a reaper, I didn't realize he is Osodon. That was the true end to which I was working with him, but in either case, we got rid of the problem, but perhaps a bit too late." Suddenly, Kahlip thought about something. That was the crowd encompassing Mickey and Kira the whole time. They were surrounded by their reapers. He became thoughtful that Mickey was hopeful of Kahlip being a reaper. Now he realized what Mickey had tried to do this whole time, which Kahlip had been awakened to the fact that Mickey was Osodon. He considered how he didn't know, but he is an Elder; he should have known. Suddenly, Kahlip sat uncomfortably. Kaerrie and Kahel noticed. Kaerrie spoke up. "What's wrong, Kahlip?" Kahlip turned to her thoughtfully. "It doesn't sit with me too well that our beloved father had harvested Almichen, and I didn't recognize it, when I should have." Kaerrie thought about what he said. Kahel looked at him. Kahlip spoke again. "I should have been on top of my game…I just ponder what happened." Kahel spoke up suddenly, as he thought about what Kahlip said, and then what he considered about Oosiah. He spoke up. "And, that still begs the question of where is Oosiah." Suddenly, Kaerrie's demeanor changed...somehow. She suddenly got lovey-dovey with Kahlip. Kahel thought it odd or strange. Kahlip felt something different coming from her. It was odd. Kahlip honestly didn't like how it felt. It seemed out of place. Kaerrie spoke up. "How could you have known, Kahlip? Don't beat yourself up over it." Kahlip looked at her, as she said that. Suddenly, he felt weary about her for some reason, as if she was trying to hide something.

Frances had been home, but for a few minutes. Suddenly, she started thinking about that woman again. Damn! She moved about the house distractedly. She didn't know how to explain her feelings, but there was something about that woman that had her vexed. There was something familiar about her that she didn't like. It was frustrating that her father seemed okay with her, but she didn't. Perhaps it was a woman-to-woman thing, but she had to figure it out. Suddenly, she thought of herself, as needing to protect her father, which her father didn't know. Suddenly, as she found herself in her room and readying to shower, she felt the urge to call Lorande and talk to her about how she was feeling. In everything she was feeling, she realized that she needed to be around her father and that woman more and more. She needed to figure her out. Frances took with her into the shower her considerations for that woman. She couldn't get her out of her head, and she couldn't get her father's seemingly vulnerable state out of her heart. She felt for him suddenly. As Frances turned the water on, she thought about her father's age and the big difference between it and that of Kaerrie. Frances didn't like it. She knew that when a woman that young went for a man that much her elder, there was something the woman was after. Frances considered if it were money or something, as she stood under the running water. She knew though, her father didn't have the kind of money Kaerrie might have wanted, but suddenly, she began to pull from her Plaenellian roots. Suddenly, there was something higher in Kaerrie's game she was after with her father. Frances glimpsed it but only in a glimpse of something viler. Frances thought about that. Frances suddenly felt as though she needed to move in with them, aside from actually sleeping with them too, and every night. That was what she had to do, and Frances thought about that, as she hurried to finish showering. She had to somehow work her way into living with her father, and that woman. She quickly finished showering, and toweled off. She rushed to dress, while picking up the phone to call Lorande, but something stopped her from dialing Lorande. She questioned whether or not Lorande should know what she was up to or if for her protection too, that Lorande should be in on it. Suddenly, Frances thought about Karen too. Should she be in on it, as well? So many questions, but little in answers. Actually, she pondered if her sisters would even understand what she felt.

Frances was ready to leave the house. She grabbed up her purse and keys. She locked the door and went to her car. In that time, her phone rang. It was Lorande. Frances spoke up. "Lor… tonight…after the movie and we're ready to leave, I want to talk to you." Lorande listened intently and agreed to that. Frances told her that she was heading back over to their father's house, at that moment. Lorande and Frances eventually hung up with each other, as Frances got in the car. She drove steadily, as if she were on a mission. She had her father in mind, as she headed in his direction. She couldn't get to him safely, but fast enough.

A Chapter for the Up & Down

Kaerrie had just got in the shower. She needed to freshen up, if she was to go out with them for the day. She thought about how things were going with Kahlip, and she still felt good about herself, but eventually having to say goodbye to him. She had come to adore him in a short period of time. She put everything out of her mind, thinking about the roller coaster that she had been on since she got to Ayeraal this last time. It was quite a ride.

Frances pulled up to her dad's house as fast, and safely, as she could. She only hoped she had the time to get him alone so she could talk to him. She hopped from her car steadily. She jogged up the door with a sense of urgency. She didn't knock. She walked right in, but slower than when she got to the door. She relaxed herself, as she walked into the living room where her father had been looking for whoever it was that entered the house. Frances spoke up, as soon as she entered the house. "It's me." Her father called back. "In the living room!" He was reading through the book. Frances found him easily. She went to the recliner and sat. She looked at her father who was seemingly finishing up with what he was reading. He stopped and looked up at her. He spoke. "You ready?" Frances smiled and spoke. "Yep." She looked at him, as if something was wrong, in which case, it was, but not the impression he had to give him. He spoke up. "What's wrong, kiddo?" Frances hesitated. She looked at him and then at the floor, then back at him. "Come on, Kiddo…what's wrong?" Frances looked at him lastly before she spoke, knowing she had to lie to him. "I am getting kicked out of my house." Kahlip looked at her when she said that. He spoke. "What?" Frances looked at him and spoke again. "Yeah…my landlord sold the house finally, and I have to move, but I don't have anywhere to go." Kahlip looked at her and smiled. She looked at him solemnly. "Yes…you do, Kiddo." He stopped speaking and looked at her. Frances' eyes lit up. He noticed and spoke again. "You're gonna move in here with me and Kaerrie." Frances teared up, and her father noticed that too. Suddenly, the two of them began making plans for her to move in. In that time, they heard Kaerrie exit the bathroom, then, walk into the bedroom. Frances and her father continued to talk. "Yes...and I have the extra room luckily. And, there is the shed out back that you can use to store your extra things." Frances thought about what he said, and then about her reasons. She didn't feel guilty for lying about being kicked out because her father's safety was more important than her ethics and morals. After another moment of chatting, Kaerrie appeared from the bedroom. They both looked at her, as she entered the living room. She spoke to Frances. "Hello there, Frances." Kaerrie seemed in high spirits. Frances spoke up. "Hi." Kaerrie noticed how bubbly she seemed, as opposed to when she left. Kaerrie spoke up. "That's nice...you seem more chipper." Frances smiled, as Kahlip looked at Kaerrie. "Kaerrie...Frances needs to move in awhile. She's being kicked out of her house. It's been sold." Suddenly, Kaerrie's high spirits plummeted, but she did well to hide that fact, except maybe from Frances, but Kaerrie thought she had at least. Kaerrie spoke up. "Lovely, but you'll probably want to find something else, real soon, right? You seem like a woman that loves her privacy and solitude." As Frances looked at Kaerrie while she spoke, the first thing that came to mind was that she was pushing her to not move in at all. She also implied that Frances would be inept at living with someone else. Kaerrie didn't understand how wrong she was. Frances needed her own space because most people couldn't live with others, but not Frances, especially if she knew she was protecting her father. Frances thoughtfully considered what Kaerrie said. She spoke up. "No, actually I do rather well in groups, but I will eventually obtain my own space." Frances smiled at Kaerrie when she finished speaking. Kaerrie looked at her with a great attempt at a smile. Frances noticed, while her father seemed to be enjoying the moment for whatever that was. Frances became thoughtful, as she eyed Kaerrie. Kaerrie was acting perfectly to make Frances feel like she was doing the right thing. Frances looked at Kaerrie, and she realized that Kaerrie seemed nervous about her moving in. She was secretly upset. Frances didn't know if her father noticed, but Frances sure did. Frances felt good about what she was doing because the more and more Kaerrie didn't, the more she was being exposed for what Frances felt about her. However, Frances knew she had a way to go to figuring Kaerrie out…if she ever could. It seemed that right now to Frances, she was the only one that felt something about her she didn't particularly care for. One thing Frances, too, had in mind was a resounding thought concerning Kaerrie, as needing protection from something under the guise of being with an older man or she was using him in some way to get to something. Suddenly, Frances felt the need to get in touch with her Plaenellian heritage, as if that might be a key to understanding Kaerrie, who, herself is supposedly Plaenellian. Suddenly, Frances recalled the concept of higher brain function, but she kept that to herself for the moment. It definitely wasn't a good time to bring it up to her father.

After another moment of silence, and Kaerrie had gone to sit by her father, Frances brought up the day out, and what the plans were. As she posed the question, she became thoughtful of the man that showed to the house, as she was leaving. She spoke up suddenly. "Dad, who was that man at the house when I was leaving? He appeared familiar, but I cannot place him." Kahlip looked at Kaerrie, then at his daughter. He spoke up. "Just an old friend." Frances looked at her father when he said that. She didn't buy it. There was something more to him than he was letting on. She spoke up. "Then why do I feel, as though he was something more than that?" She looked at him curiously. Kaerrie looked at Frances curiously with thoughts about what Frances was digging for. And, Kahlip finally realized that Frances could endure a more earnest, and true answer. "Okay, Frances, his name is Kahel, and one of us. You did meet him a long time ago, but briefly from what I recall myself." Frances looked at her father when he said that. He then spoke again. "He was one that Mickey didn't know was like myself, attempting to stay close to him to counteract what I thought was Mickey's reaping habits. However, Mickey was not a reaper, as I found out recently. Mickey was actually the head of opposition." Frances thought about what he said. She spoke up. "Now, remind me of reaping." Kaerrie sat by listening, as the two threw words back and forth. Frances noticed that she almost seemed frustrated by the meager conversation. Her father looked at her warmly and thoughtfully before he spoke. He felt a light in his chest, as he looked at Frances. He finally spoke. "Reaping, Frances is what happens when a consciousness gets to a certain level of knowledge and understanding. At which point it can be exhumed from its form. This is because it has no foundation within its body. Essentially, it loses grounding within itself." Her father stopped speaking and looked over at Kaerrie, then turned back to Frances. Frances watched them share that glance. Frances thought about something and spoke up. "So, what defines the harvest?" Frances looked at her father, as she said that, but suddenly, something struck her. She spoke again before he could say a word. "Wait…a harvest is kind of an investment. Well, it's to invest, as in an idea where the harvest is the investment into a crop." Her father looked at her intricately when she said that. He spoke up. "Do you know where the word harvest comes from?" Frances looked at him a second before she spoke. She sat thoughtfully and took a quick glance over at Kaerrie. She finally spoke. "It seems to me that the harvest would be a combination of two words, harbour, and vesting." Her father eyed her, as she said that. He spoke up. "And, that is what I am talking about higher brain function, or the evidence of your Plaenellian heritage. It's the knowing in you that keeps you grounded, incapable of being harvested or part of the reaping." Frances thought about what he said. She eyed him a second before she spoke. "So, you are saying that reaping, in a sense, is the result of feeding someone a line of crap, so that way they can be harvested for the crap they've been fed." Her father smiled. He looked kindly at Frances, and spoke. "Well, that's not the way I would put it, but yeah." Frances smiled and then looked at Kaerrie. She turned back to her father and spoke. "So, being fed crap…believable crap is a way to undo someone's grounding, then." Her father looked thoughtfully at her. "That's right." As they spoke, Kaerrie became bored by such elementary concepts. Her father thought about something, as he eyed Frances. He spoke up. "This was the truest value of school. Do you realize that?" Frances eyed him and thought about what he said. And, judging the conversation, Frances knew exactly where he was going with that. She spoke up. "School was a means to forge grounding in consciousness." Her father smiled when she said that. He spoke up. "And, that is how to tell someone that is considered a potential part of the harvest. It is really, why school was created." Kaerrie seemed to get upset when her father mentioned that. Frances noticed, but it seemed to blindside her father. Kaerrie stood and seemingly stormed off. Her father and her watched Kaerrie almost stomp out of the room. Her father looked, then, back at her and spoke. "School was created to take the harvest effect out of consciousness. Back in the day, when there was no school, Osodon and Oosiah had an easier time harvesting consciousness." As her father said that, deep down she knew it was that Kaerrie did not want to hear. Frances knew it. She didn't know how she knew it, but she did. Thoughtfully, her father considered Kaerrie, and how seemingly, easily she was to upset, as if she were on some kind of roller coaster. It was uncanny, and her father thought about that, as he looked between Frances and the exit from the living room where Kaerrie had gone He glimpsed something in that moment. He didn't understand it himself, but it was but a glimpse into Kaerrie. Frances watched her father. She knew he was secretly studying Kaerrie, but as to why, she had no idea. Perhaps he glimpsed what she did in her. She suddenly felt closer to her father, than she had before. It was a good feeling. As she sat with her father enjoying feeling the way she did, she couldn't help but feel closer to him. Suddenly, however, she also discovered something about herself in contrast to her heritage.

Kaerrie stood thoughtfully by the kitchen sink. She leaned against it hard. She felt so angered and so powerless, at that moment. All she could think about was that woman in the living room, and how much of a wall she was becoming. His daughter was the only reason why they were talking, as they had been. Kaerrie didn't like it at all. She could barely stand the woman in the living room, and it took so much to be near her. She didn't fully understand why, but she understood that she didn't like Frances one bit. In that moment, Kahlip walked into the kitchen. He stood just beyond the door, eyeing Kaerrie. She had a glass of water in one hand, as an excuse to leave the room. Kahlip noticed, but he noted that it was pointless to ask her why she left. It was easy to understand that something had upset her. He just didn't know what. However, in one thing he knew…he wasn't good at someone's moods. Kahlip wasn't good at up and down. Kahlip was good at consistency, and communication. He spoke up. "Are you ready to go? It's about time for perhaps an early dinner." Kaerrie smiled at him, which was hard to do at that moment. She had to choke down thoughts of that woman with every sip of water. She spoke. "Sure." Her voice wasn't light, but gloomy, as she spoke. Of course it couldn't be, she had thoughts of a growing opposition in her new roommate.

The Chapter for Lowess

Frances gave Lorande a quick call, as they were getting ready to leave. She had to leave her a message, but Lorande had commented when she asked Frances to let her know when they were getting close to leaving, that she would answer the phone.

Kahlip and his daughter figured out whose car they would take out. Kaerrie made it plainly known that she wasn't in the mood to discern that. Frances sat in the back with Kaerrie and her father in the front. Her father drove. Of course, it was his car. Frances thought about something, as she sat looking through the window. "Dad, I was thinking back to what you said about being among the reapers. How did you know what to look for to know who the reaper may be?" Kaerrie definitely didn't want to be a part of the conversation or even hear it. She tried to shut it out. She closed her eyes to make it look like she was falling asleep. Her father spoke up. He noticed Kaerrie closed her eyes. "Well, it was long ago. And, reaping wasn't something prone to a lot of us early on. We had a lot to do to counteract what Osodon and Oosiah had done. Bear in mind our responsibility." He stopped speaking, as he came to a stoplight. It was another second of going through a green light before he spoke. "So, in this early time we were trying to figure things out. It was hard to do, and we hadn't pinpointed a means to do it. Bear in mind too, that our nature is inherent abilities, as well as intelligence. This means that our consciousness functions the Universes naturally. Well, with knowing that, Osodon and Oosiah began to work more diligently than they had previously. This was done in the hopes that they could counteract what we achieved. Remember that Osodon and Oosiah do not have any idea in what of us lies, which control to the Universes. Now, knowing that, Osodon had been able to come up with this concept of taking back what they think of is consciousness emanating from them. They do not realize they are stealing or harvesting that which doesn't belong to them. However, they can do this because consciousness was freed with no certain amount of protection." Her father stopped speaking, as he came to a stop sign. He looked to find his way across the street. As he moved through the intersection, he began to speak again. "See, our department is the Universes themselves. We don't influence the measures of sentient beings upon planets or in other words, it's not within our innate abilities. From that, it is easy to distinguish amongst those around us, who are influenced into certain behaviors. See, Mickey, I thought was one among the many plots on a graph of a certain harvest intended for the season. I didn't realize he was the beginning of the data, with Oosiah being the end of the data collected. That's really how it works. And, John Lowess helped us to see it that way. This is part of the information added to his book by Killian Dawn. Killian and Mr. Lowess worked closely when Killian was writing it. And, that information is within Killian's book. Basically, Mr. Lowess taught us to look, at the harvest, as a graph with all the choices for harvest as points in it. Then, he advised us that the farmers would be connected to the harvest or the tools to do the harvest. As a farmer guides the machinery through the fields of corn, he designates what gets harvested, through what the tool or machinery can do." Frances listened intently, as Kaerrie stirred in her seat. Frances thought about something, and spoke up. "So, the farmer is close, but distanced necessarily for those to be harvested. I get it." Her father thought about something, as she said that. He spoke up. "Here is something you don't realize. Osodon thought he had a reaper in me." Suddenly, Kahlip looked at Kaerrie upon a notion, which he wholly dismissed for the moment. He thought that was what I was doing for him the whole time. He counted wrong." Her father stopped speaking thoughtfully. He eyed the road ahead. He continued to look ahead, as he spoke again. "Frances, what you girls don't realize that for what he did do, was what you further inhibited from doing. I recognize the crimes against you, as they go, but what you don't realize was the wrench in his plan that you were. For what he did, he did less than what he could have without you all present. Now, mind you, that wasn't my plan, but what I hoped would be the case because I was powerless to keep out of his realm of harvest or out of the reach of his reapers. And, I showed him I wasn't part of his plan when I left, but again, unfortunately, I couldn't take you three with me." Her father stopped speaking thoughtfully. He realized that was what happened to Kira and Lisa, and a host of others. He drove silently after those last words, and he left Frances thinking.

Karen readied herself, anticipating the night with her family. She thought about the woman in her father's life. She still didn't know what to think about her or that she should have any early-formed opinion. Frances seemed though to have her heart and mind already made up. Karen thought about that. Suddenly, she recalled something from her childhood with Frances. She considered how Frances was a pretty good judge of character most of the time. So, maybe Frances was on to something. In the end though, Karen had to make her mind up. The woman seemed innocent enough, but therein her heart was something about Frances and her apprehension about the woman. Karen locked up the house and left quickly. She was actually excited about going out. It wasn't the usual humdrum to which she'd come accustomed.

Lorande was running late. She arrived at home, as fast and safely, as she could. She wanted to be at her father's an hour ago before they left. She had received Frances' message. She just couldn't get away from what she was doing. Frances' birthday was coming up and she was planning it that latter morning and afternoon when she left their father's house. The whole point was to get it done when Lorande knew where Frances was. She didn't want her popping in on her when she was planning it. Frances was good for that.

Lorande had been planning her sister's party for the last three years, and for the last two, Frances ruined them both by finding out certain details about the big day. This year, Lorande wasn't going to let on about any detail or permit her knowledge of any secret behind it. So far, her plan to maintain secrecy worked and appeared as though, it would. The last thing she had to do was coordinate with her father about the place to have it, which would befit his house. If he were big on the first Christmas, then he definitely would be over a first birthday together. So, Lorande left her house, as quickly, as she could. She, of course, had to find out where to meet them, as did Karen.

Kahlip parked. No one stirred to exit the car. Frances sat thoughtfully about her sisters. Kaerrie was still playing at sleeping, and her father sat, appearing deeply thoughtful. Frances spoke up. "Penny for your thoughts." Kahlip smiled and spoke. "Which penny for which one?" Frances chuckled. From the corner of her eye, she saw Karen park. She spoke up. "Oh dad, there's Karen." Frances got out of the car, and closed the door excitedly. Kahlip followed in turn. He was happy to see her and that she could make it. And, as soon as Kahlip exited the car, Kaerrie got on the phone so as not to be seen for doing so. She watched the three of them, hiding sort of behind the door of the car. She had to keep an eye on them so they wouldn't surprise her. She sat listening for the most part while she watched outside the car. Occasionally, she would answer simply with a word or two. And, after she heard the last words, she needed to hear, she spoke. "I don't know if I can do this." She hung up, as Kahlip seemingly made his way to the car. Then, she went into pretenses about sleeping again. As Kahlip walked to the car, he looked off in the distance; he noticed Doug and nodded in his direction. Doug nodded back. Kahlip then, proceeded to awaken Kaerrie, by opening her door and a slight shaking of her shoulder. Kahlip didn't notice, but she pretended to awaken. He just saw her open her eyes and stretch. He spoke up. "Sleepy?" She smiled and spoke. "Not now." He moved away from the car and let her exit. He closed the door behind her gently. Kaerrie looked around and noticed the restaurant. She spoke up. "Is this a nice place?" Kahlip looked in the direction of the restaurant. He stood thoughtfully and spoke. "It is wonderful." Karen, Frances and Lorande walked over to their father, and Kaerrie. Karen and Lorande greeted Kaerrie. She smiled at them at first thoughtfully. She spoke, almost, as if it was hard to do. "Hello, ladies." Kahlip looked at his daughters and smiled. He spoke up. "Shall we go eat? This place has been a home for me and seafood." Kaerrie spoke up suddenly. "Seafood...how wonderful." Kerrie was, of course, sarcastic, but only two of them really noticed it. Karen and Frances looked at each other. The five of them walked toward the restaurant. Kahlip took a quick glance over his left shoulder, as they walked in. No one noticed that he knew of, and that was good. As they entered, they were met by a server. As they were met, Kahlip's phone rang in a call that had to be answered. He told his group that he would find them, that he must take the call. Kahlip went outside.

Kahlip looked over his shoulder to notice anyone watching him, as he stepped outside. He was alone on the sidewalk by the restaurant and out of sight. There was a slatted canopy overhead with vines intermixed between the slats. He held the phone to his ear until he knew he could speak. It was another second before he spoke. "Hello..." Kahlip listened to the voice on the other end. He spoke again. "No...we're at the restaurant." He listened again. "Yes...she's here too." He listened for a longer period. He spoke again. "Yes he is in the restaurant, as well." He listened for another brief period before speaking one last time. "I am as careful, as I need to be." With those words, he hung up. He pocketed his phone thoughtfully. He looked around, then at the restaurant. He realized what he was going through was what he would have had a lot sooner, had he his girls with him their entire lives. He returned to the restaurant and found Kaerrie and the girls. They noticed his approach. He eventually sat. Kaerrie spoke up. "Business?" Kahlip smiled to comfort her and spoke. "Big business." Kahlip took a look around before he sat. He noticed Doug in the corner. He threw him a solemn look. As planned, Doug acted, as though he didn't notice.

Everyone but Kaerrie seemed distracted with a menu. Kahlip looked at her and spoke. "Already know what you want?" Kaerrie spoke thoughtfully. "Yes...I think I am going turf tonight." Suddenly, Kahlip's phone rang again. He looked around and answered it. He spoke. "Hello..." He listened. Karen spoke up. "You are busy tonight on that phone." Her father smiled at her when she said that. Kaerrie looked around at all of them at the table. She felt like the odd one out. She felt boldly out of place, but she knew, with good reason. Kahlip seemed to finish up on the phone. He looked around the table and gave it another minute before he spoke. "Hey, I got an idea." Everyone eyed him when he spoke. "Why don't we skip the restaurant and go home for some take out from the Chinese deli? His daughters eyed him. Kaerrie looked at him with disappointment. She spoke up. "We can't make it another moment here at the restaurant?" Kahlip thought about what she said. Why would they make it another moment there? That didn't make sense. Kahlip spoke up, as he also considered the last phone call. "It was just an idea I had...what do you think?" Karen spoke up first. "It doesn't really matter to me." Frances and Lorande agreed. Kaerrie seemed the only one opposed to the idea. In the end though, Kahlip's new idea won out. They all left the restaurant. Kahlip took their orders and told his daughters he would pick it up and meet them at his house.

By now, Frances had a key to the house. So, when they arrived, Frances let everyone inside. Karen and Lorande questioned how she got a key. Frances then went on to explain that she was getting kicked out of her house, and that their dad was letting her move in. Lorande thought about what she said, and at first took what she, as true. But deep down, she questioned it. It didn't make sense. This was sudden. Frances and Lorande were too close for Frances not to tell Lorande that she was being kicked out. Lorande let that go for the moment. Then, Frances, as they went into the living room to await their dad and Kaerrie, thought about something. She looked at her sisters, as they were sitting comfortably in the living room. She spoke up. "Remember what dad said about the dinosaurs?" Karen and Lorande looked at Frances thoughtfully, as she spoke. Karen spoke up, she was feeling a bit tired at that moment. She tilted her head back and closed her eyes. "Yeah… what about it?" Frances looked at her sisters. "Well…how much sense does that make?" Lorande thought about what she said. Karen still had her eyes closed, as she listened. Lorande spoke up. "It explains why they were here. I mean…look at it. How could we have gotten here from just nothing after the dinosaurs just seemingly died off? Granted the meteor thing sounds feasible, but not much else in contrast to everything else." Karen raised her head thoughtfully. She spoke up. "The dinosaur thing makes too much sense the way he explained it. Besides, that was dad saying it. I have come to understand something about him." Karen stopped speaking, as she looked at her sisters. Frances spoke up. "What's that?" Karen looked at Frances for saying that. "Dad doesn't screw around when he speaks. He seems to mean what he says. So, he actually believes what he's saying. Besides that, we don't know everything for our individual lives we need. There are those who come into our lives to share some knowledge of things we haven't figured out. To me…everything about dad makes sense. I think he's right." Lorande sat thoughtfully, as Karen said that. She looked at Karen, then at Frances and spoke. "And if he's right about that, then there is a lot more that he's valuable for." Karen thought about something, as Lorande spoke. She spoke. "Besides all that, look at what he's done in looking out for us, as we grew up. I don't know about you two, but I won't doubt him. He's been more a father than most have when their fathers are supposedly around." Lorande and Frances spoke up at the same time. "You're right about that." Lorande thoughtfully spoke up again, after another brief moment of silence. "It seems as though he seems to know something important too…I don't know…it's odd what he knows." Karen spoke up quickly, eyeing her sisters. "Have either of you deeply considered that the moon craters are actually dead volcanoes?" Frances thought about what Karen brought up. Lorande did, as well. They each looked at one another. Lorande spoke up. "It never crossed my mind before dad said it." Karen thoughtfully looked at Frances and Lorande. "That is exactly what I am talking about. Why hadn't we considered it before he said it?" Lorande thought about what she said. She also thought about something else he said. She spoke up. "Remember what he said about harvesting?" Frances chimed in. "Yeah…consciousness weak is harvested." Karen looked at them both. "That was his point. A weak consciousness has little within it. In other words, where vegetables get big to be harvested, consciousness to be harvested has to be emptied." Frances thought about what she said, and spoke. "It's like dad is trying to fill us with things to know." Karen thought about something, as she said that. "That's it. You said it. And, think about something else. The age of the Universe we're in can be better understood if we take the amount of time; it took for the moon to die, as a planet. Now, picture more planets in this Universe. Space rock floating in space is the remnants of old planets, which had to be destroyed for some reason. Planets have been dying for myriads of years. Dad is only saying that at one point, we knew it and knew why. Now, he has indicated the reason why sentient beings don't know that much or are not, as consciousness as they were once." Frances and Lorande eyed Karen for saying that. They each sat thoughtfully. Frances spoke up. "I think the school idea was a good one."

Kaerrie and their father returned with dinner. They sat at the kitchen table to eat, chatting casually through the meal. Kaerrie tried not to say too much by keeping her mouth full the whole time. And, they finished the next couple hours after the meal, in the living room just casually chatting. Kaerrie wouldn't join them. She claimed she was tired and went to the bedroom. Kahlip kept his feelings about her ulterior motives to himself, but Frances was only reminded of what she felt about her. Her seemingly antisocial behavior was astounding evidence. Frances still wasn't sure what her intentions were just yet.

The Chapter for Solution III

It was the next day. Kahlip awoke and Kaerrie was gone... again. Actually, sadly everyone was gone. Frances must have gone to work. And, Lorande and Karen did spend the night, but must have left earlier, as well. Kahlip was left alone. However, he would find that it might be a good thing. Kahlip went to the coffee maker first thing. He found a note saying that all he had to do to make coffee was turn it on. He instantly thought of Frances. He didn't know why, but he did. He spoke up almost silently. "I could get used to this." He turned it on and it began making those wonderful coffee-making sounds, then there was that Arabica aroma, which made for a good morning. From there and until the coffee was made, he went around the house straightening up a bit. The house wasn't in too much disarray. And, of course, at some point he would have to tend to the yard that day. From tidying up the house, he went to throw on some clothes from his night shorts he slept in. As soon, as he was dressed in another pair of shorts and an undershirt, someone came knocking, and he went to the door. He opened it, and noticed that it was Doug. He greeted him, and offered him to enter. Doug walked in and Kahlip shut the door. He thought about something and spoke up. "So...to what do I owe this pleasure?" Doug looked at him plainly. He didn't seem happy in that moment. Kahlip noticed. In the place of Doug's usual cheery banter, lies a morose sense of despondency. Doug solemnly walked into the living room, ignoring Kahlip's cheer and question. Kahlip noticed his ignorance to him, and that wasn't usual either. Instantly, Kahlip thought about a cup of coffee and then he could face Doug in the living room. He called to Doug. "Coffee?" Doug spoke up quickly. "Heavy, dark and sweet." The only thing usual about Doug was his thick, heavy voice when he spoke.

Kahlip made two cups of coffee and went to the living room, anticipating Doug's mood, which wasn't easy. He couldn't figure out what went wrong from last night to that moment. Once in the living room, Kahlip played coffee delivery. Doug took his cup easily, as Kahlip then sat on the sofa. He looked at Doug who stole two, quick sips from the cup, and then proceeded to talk and hold his cup. He rambled on at first in his heavy voice, then, stopped speaking. He looked squarely at Kahlip, seemingly attempting to regain his sensibility. Kahlip waited for that. Doug spoke again. "Sorry for that…Dad…Joe's dead." Kahlip looked at Doug at first, then, the words really hit him. He stood, as Doug watched him leave the sofa. Kahlip walked with a heavy step, as he thought about Joe. He spoke. "Doug… how?" He stood looking at Doug waiting for an answer, but Doug was lost for words. Kahlip spoke again. "Was he reaped Doug?" Doug sat thoughtfully. "Dad…you know that is…is hard to tell." Kahlip spun away from Doug thoughtfully. He thought about Joe, considering his possibilities for death. He spoke up with frustration in his tone. "Doug…he was too young. My goodness…this is Joe we're talking about!" Doug spoke up. "I know, dad. I know…see why my cheer is gone?" Kahlip quickly spoke up. "Yes…Doug…of course!" Kahlip thought about something instantly. "He wasn't Plaenellian, Doug…do you know?" Doug sipped from his cup thoughtfully. He spoke up. "I had my suspicions." He stopped speaking thoughtfully with Joe in mind. "Dad…he…you know death is so random now. It's hard to tell when the reaper gets another one. Joe was sick…you know." Kahlip turned to Doug when he said that. He spoke quickly. "Doug…it wasn't always this way. You know that. It only got this bad a few hundred years ago. And, that is why it is important to find the solution. And, yeah…I know…Joe was sick, but you know what that means." Doug thought about what he said. He didn't speak before Kahlip spoke again. "Doug… this is the knowledge to power thing. What did Joe know? How well was he at implementing what he knew? It's those kinds of things that define one's future, not the random sense of life and death. I've always taught you that the more you know and use, the further you can go. Haven't I?" Doug thought about what he said. "Yes...dad...of course." He tried looking in Kahlip's direction. Kahlip was almost directly behind him. Kahlip spoke again. "Sickness is a way to understand what one doesn't know or information one isn't using. It's that simple." Doug thought about something in that moment, and to what Kahlip said. Doug spoke up. "Yes...dad, but remember, I am like you, even though you found me and adopted me. Joe isn't like us. He's not under the protection of the Plaenellian heritage." Kahlip thought about what he said. He spoke with frustration. "I knew that about Joe, but it didn't matter. I tried to get him to see higher concepts. It's why I adopted him too, but we never got that close...not as the two of you." Kahlip stopped speaking thoughtfully. He turned to the sliding glass doors. "That's what I was hoping you were able to do for him." Doug thought about something in that moment. He spoke up. "Dad...it's like you always told me. The harvest cannot be enlightened...the field or the crop has to be moved. Remember that?" Kahlip smiled when Doug said that. He spoke up. "Well...it's nice to see that you kept something I said." Doug smiled and spoke. "Yes...dad...I did. You helped me, but again, I am like you. It was easy. You know as well, as I that the average alien consciousness on any planet is at risk because of what they lose in consciousness. Remember the moon, dad, you liked to use that one on me all the time. But you try getting the average alien consciousness thinking itself, human to understand the moon as a planet once, and you will fight forever to get them to forget it, as a satellite." Doug stopped speaking thoughtfully. He considered something and spoke again. "You once told me that consciousness is at a loss, and that supposed human understanding is only going so far." Doug stopped speaking and thought about something, as he sipped from his cup. Kahlip heard him and spoke. "I did...and then I implied there was a solution to that." Doug listened thoughtfully. He spoke up. "That is why I came to you directly with news of Joe...outside of the obvious." Kahlip quickly spoke up. "Oh, come on Doug. You know Joe and I weren't that close. It has been a year since either of us talked. He just couldn't understand what I tried to be to him. I didn't know he was that sick. Well, I knew in one way, but not that what he didn't know was actually killing him." Doug thought about something. He spoke up. "You knew his parents, right?" Kahlip thought about what Doug said. He did know Joe's parents, but that was a hard reminder of what Mickey was capable of. Kahlip thought about Ginnette and Paul, and then Mickey. He wasn't directly responsible for their death, but close to it. Kahlip quickly thought about that. Kahlip turned to Doug. "I loved Joe, as if he were my son. And, I regret his parent's death, as if I was responsible. In some ways maybe I was." Doug quickly spoke up. "Don't say that, dad…you couldn't have known." Kahlip thought about a lot of the things Mickey had done to his fellow Seyions that he himself really couldn't have done anything in counteracting it. He guessed that was why he got away with doing them. Kahlip then thought of how only too late was he capable of stopping Mickey from doing anything more, but Mickey was old at that point. Doug thought about something in that moment. He spoke up, as he felt his dad through his regret. "Dad…it's like you always told me, this is why the solution is so important. We need to try harder to find it." Kahlip then turned to Doug. He eyed him thoughtfully and returned to the sofa. He sat after grabbing his cup from the side table. He sipped and looked at Doug. He thoughtfully spoke up. "You know, Doug, we're probably years away still from any kind of a solution." Doug eyed Kahlip when he said that. He only hoped he was wrong. Kahlip thought about something else, after he stopped speaking and Doug had looked at him. He spoke up. "Probably the hardest thing to accept is that when you know something, and tell it to someone, but they look at you like you are crazy." He looked at Doug, and stopped speaking. He looked thoughtfully at him. "Doug…I am so glad you at least had the nerve to listen to me." Doug smiled when Kahlip said that. "Dad…how could I not listen to you, when you were there when I needed an ear? Besides, you made a lot of sense to me." Doug stopped speaking thoughtfully, as he looked at the man that was more the dad than he should have been. "You know…

one thing I think I learned is that there is a higher point of view. And, for those who can attain it, they will benefit. It's those that are not willing to listen that will be harvested." Kahlip thought solemnly about what Doug said. He looked squarely at Doug and spoke. "But it is that, which we are trying to stop." Doug looked at Kahlip and spoke. "Off subject, dad, but when am I going to meet my sisters?" Kahlip smiled. "Right now…your presence in secret is what they need. If we go and begin showing you off, then they will lose their protector. You see, for them, growing up I was almost the same as you to them. I would have loved to be more in their lives, but I couldn't be. So, I then chose to be in their lives when they didn't even know it." Kahlip thought about something, after he spoke. He thought about the solution. "Doug, you do realize that we tried throughout the years to awaken the various alien consciousnesses. And, my frustration comes down to the fact that we cannot give them anything more than what we've done. Their schools, their interacting, and way of life in contrast to the planet was all things we tried to use to wake them up to what they lost in knowledge of their respective home planets. That's why the solution is at hand. It is why it is important and why we cannot try to point blank throw it in their faces. We have to find the solution whether or not they care to know."

Doug looked at Kahlip when he said that. Kahlip had told him a lot of things growing up, but never before did he see Kahlip's heart in contrast to the collection of alien consciousnesses before that moment. Kahlip had a tear in his left eye that brimmed falling down his cheek. Doug never before saw any greater love in any one individual before his dad, that man that had been Lehmich, and Steve, and Kahlip, but he realized they were all the same person with an overabundance of love. Suddenly, Kahlip thought about something. He eyed Doug upon a notion.

In that moment, Kahlip was distracted by a phone call. It was Kahnelle. He answered it easily, and full of hope. As he answered it, he thought about what Kaerrie said, but in his heart, Kahnelle wasn't betraying him, and he knew it. If anything, Kahnelle was helping his granddaughter. And for that measure, Kahlip had trust. He motioned to Doug that he had to answer the phone. He exited the house for the back porch.

Kahlip stared into the ground, as he and Kahnelle conversed. Kahlip was still sitting on that comfortable lawn chair. He spoke up with finality. "Karen, then…is all right? Because you know…Kaerrie, seems to be convinced that you are working for Osodon. I had hoped that my oldest friend hadn't saw fit to charm the devil." Kahnelle laughed through the phone. "Yes Kahlip, your granddaughter is all right, but I tell you, Julius is some piece of work. Osodon has done him so wrong. Karen is a tough nut to crack, but I will get her from him. And, we shall be home." Kahlip looked up at the sky with a sigh of relief. He spoke up thoughtfully. "I am anticipating a dear reunion when you arrive." Kahnelle spoke in return. "I too, my dear brother. I too…" They each hung up. Kahlip put his phone away. He turned to look east again with hope, and the promise of a mother and daughter that should have never been separated. At that moment, Kaerrie popped her head out, and looked at Kahlip. She spoke up. "Enjoying yourself?" Suddenly, he thought about what she had said about Kahnelle, as she had her head just through the opening of the glass door. "Yeah….and I just found out that my granddaughter might be coming home soon." Kaerrie appeared confused. "Who's that?" But, as she spoke, she knew the answer. It was Karen. Kahlip looked at her and smiled. He eventually spoke. "It's Karen." Kaerrie's eyes got wide, as she appeared to be thinking about what he said. She spoke. "Oh!" As soon, as she said that, she popped her head back inside. She shut the door and mumbled. "I wonder how that's possible." Just as soon as she said that, Lorande came walking from the foyer, and heard her. "How what's possible?" Kaerrie gave Lorande a shrewd eye of ignorance. Lorande felt it, and felt uncomfortable. Kaerrie spoke as she walked passed Lorande. "Nothing…none of your business." Lorande stopped in her tracks and turned to look at

Kaerrie, as she walked away. She couldn't believe what she just heard. Lorande just passed it off, as someone having a bad day. She went to the rear porch, as she saw the man she came to see.

Kahlip eyed Lorande with a heavy heart, as she entered the rear porch. He spoke, "Hey Kiddo." Lorande smiled and spoke. "Hey, dad. Why the long face?" Kahlip looked at her when she said that. Eventually he spoke. "Kiddo, sit here with me. I have something I need to tell you." Lorande thought about how heavy he spoke and his words lingered in gloom. Lorande did as he suggested. He looked at her at first, thinking about Katy. He spoke. "Lor." He stopped speaking, as he had emotion in his throat. Lorande looked at him, as he said that. "Lor...I had your daughter living with me not too long ago. But one day she just seemingly vanished." Lorande teared up when he said that. She spoke. "You had...little...Lorande here?" Kahlip let a tear fall, as he said that, then another for her expression. He spoke up. "Yes." She looked at her father with a sense of hope in seeing her daughter again. Lorande spoke again. "You have no idea where she went?" Kahlip looked at his daughter lovingly. Kahlip spoke. "I have no idea, but her disappearance was questionable. The night before I found her gone, it was I, her and Penny in the house. Katy and I went to sleep, and Penny stayed up saying that she was going to get some fresh air. I woke up the next day, and she was gone. I don't know what happened." Lorande thought instantly about Kaerrie. Lorande spoke up. "That woman in your house knows where she is, dad...I know it. If that night went down, as you described. She knows something!" Kahlip thought about what Lorande said. He spoke. "I know, that is why she is still in my house. I keep hoping one day she will slip up, and say something that will lead me to her, but it seems like it has been so long now." Lorande thought what he said. "Dad, we got to find her. We have to get Karen and Frances in on it. Together, we can do it." Lorande thought about something in that moment, as her father looked at her. He spoke. "Lorande, Katy is special. I don't just mean because she is my granddaughter and your daughter. I mean she is something more than that. I glimpsed it a while back. See, for whom her father was, I don't think he knew what he let in here on this planet in her. We need to find her because she is that important. I have had investigators in on the search, but we keep looking." Lorande thoughtfully stood. "Okay, but now we'll get all the family in on it. We'll see how much they can keep her from all of us. See, dad, I did what I did for her, which was to protect her. I don't know if she understands that, but I have wanted to tell her for a long time now. I think it's time to get on the hunt. Are you up for it?" Kahlip smiled. He spoke. "I have had your fire since she went missing. Penny could never have it. It's nice to see it in her mother." Lorande smiled, as he said that. "Damn right, dad. Let's go find our girl!"

† Epilogue

Penelope packed for the move. Her mother was against it, but Penelope had to go. She found herself on a book journey that inspired her to live abroad. She didn't really understand where this journey was taking her, but she was going. It revolved around winding up in St. Augustine at the mouth of the Matanzas River. She read briefly about the Matanzas River and what transpired between the Spanish and French in the fifteen hundreds. There was something more to it though. That was what was hard about keeping her writing life a secret from her mother. Her mother really didn't understand why she was leaving for Florida, that she would want to stay in Florida to live. She didn't have family there. It was hard to leave for Penelope on that argument from her mother, but she felt the strong urge to go. She didn't understand it either, but she soon would. She would eventually come to know what was drawing her there that was so powerful about St. Augustine. It was something deep in her heritage that she didn't fully comprehend yet, but she soon would.

All the while, Kahlip and his daughters sought after their beloved Katy to no avail, but they never gave up or gave in to the feelings like the search was hopeless. They didn't stop and they didn't lose hope because she was that important. Penny had joined in the search for her reasons, as dishonest, as they were, but it kept Kahlip and the girls from thinking her suspect to the situation.

Too, there was the mounting plot against Kahlip and his family. And, it seemed as though the plot by Lily and John Horn would finally come to fruition. But that was with a missing element to the scenario they would have a chance at success. They didn't realize that there was a growing surge of awareness in Plaenellian consciousness that something was going down in

St. Augustine. So, this meant that St. Augustine was about to get a surge of visitors from across the nation. It was about to become a very popular place. And, unbeknownst to the Horn sisters, they were about to be held accountable for their actions, as Lily Horn was about to finally be confronted, after escaping responsibility for things she'd done. As Osodon had been or held, so would Oosiah find consequence for her crimes against the Universes. However, that would come finally from a great Plaenellian effort which the infamous Oosiah never saw coming. Oosiah thought herself above reproach, but she would learn too, that even she, as Osodon had learned, was less than what she thought of herself.

However, that was the continued battle of the Plaenellians to right the Universes once again. And, that was Kahlip's aim, even though Oosiah may find consequence, would all the Universes because the Plaenellians may be capable of restricting Oosiah from coming back to Ayeraal, would they be able, in time, to stop Ayeraal's destruction? The battle with Osodon and Oosiah was only half of the problem. Kahlip and his fellow Plaenellians had to find the solution to the Universal problems, which just might have been Osodon and Oosiah's point behind their attacks…to distract their children enough that they would lose sight of the solution.

As Kahlip and Lorande finally got together over her daughter, Karen showed up, then, it was Frances. Lorande and their father explained the situation regarding Katy. Still, it hadn't been mentioned who Katy truly was in the bigger scheme of things. Just when their father thought to enlighten them, there was a sullen knock at his door. Everyone in the house looked at each other for the knock. All the while Penny was in the bedroom; suddenly, the door opens and everyone looks to the entry of the living room. With eyes staring at who it was that just so eloquently walked in, Little Karen stood there in all of their eyes. Kahlip teared up, as did Little Karen's mother. Karen went to her, and after all these years, mother and daughter were finally reunited. Then, behind Karen, stood Kahnelle. Kahlip noticed him for all the emotion. Frances and Lorande were there greeting their niece. Kahlip went to Kahnelle. Kahnelle spoke up in that moment. "Hey, I knocked, but she just went ahead and walked in, citing she was family and didn't have to." Kahlip smiled at Kahnelle, as he said that. Kahlip spoke up quickly. "Well, you could have walked in too, dear friend…brother in arms!" They shared a manly hug and then Kahnelle went on to describe the job over in France, and just when he was about to explain what went down with Julius, Penny appeared in the doorway. She heard the commotion and wanted to see what was going on. She stood in fright, as she noticed Kahnelle, then little Karen. She turned right around and went back into the bedroom, withdrawing her cell phone. She dialed some numbers in a panic, then, held it to her ear. She entered the bedroom and shut the door.

Everyone else began the reunion that would begin the search for Katy Isaacs, or as Kahlip knew of her…Olivia Skye.

The final conclusion to the Secrets of the Keepers…?

✝

Red

Thru

Black

✝

Secrets Of

The Keepers II

The Rise of Olivia Skye

✝

The quick story behind, my mother, Monica Wentzel...

To tell a quick tale of the courage in my mother that no one really got to understand was her courage under fire. And, her guilt for something she did, for which she had the courage to endure self-thought consequence.

Sadly, this tale starts out by saying that my mother wanted me stillborn…but only because of the guilt for the affair, she had with the man who was my father, and not her husband.

Mom - I have a family now…I knew God would forgive you because I was sure thankful to be born alive…and stay alive after I was born. See, Mom, we're not always born in the most planned ways or according to God's plan, but we show the value of love when we help others to be born in situations that do not necessarily go with "the plan". Your courage to get over your guilt helped me to seek the courage deep in myself. You changed your stars for deep in your religious convictions, illegitimacy and cheating upon your husband is unlawful, but you found a way to forgive yourself and prove to be the most important person to me on this planet. That was what was so hard about losing you when I was six. As I said before, Mom, I love you… always. And, that is, in part, my life, an honor to you; for you showed me the true value of a mother. Had you been any less in your convictions I wouldn't be here today because along with your guilt and the feelings of wanting me stillborn, you could have killed me when we were alone. On that note, how can I be any less with you as my example? On a side note, Mom, I am sorry, but that one secret you kept, I couldn't because there are those that needed to understand you. There were those that claimed to love you, but didn't understand you. I do, and love you...well; I guess that goes without saying. My love for you gave me so much understanding.

> ...Always your Son
> GD Thompson, Sr.

Printed in the United States
By Bookmasters